EAGLE'S ASCENT

WANDERER'S ODE · BOOK II

EAGLE'S ASCENT

W. Owen Williams

SANS-CRÉANCE

an imprint of

blackbird & company
EDUCATIONAL PRESS

For Jon, Matteus, Lori, Bruce, Rick, Kim, and Maryann,
who read and encouraged,

and Mike R, the very soul of a Renaissance patrocinatore

Prologue

She lounged at the dark end of the bar in Bombay Peggy's sipping daintily from her fourth drink of the evening—a tasty little concoction the bartender called 'Spank my Naughty Ass'—a mix of vodka, triple sec, cranberry, and lime. After two of them, she felt good; at three, amusingly tipsy; four made her pleasantly sloppy. She liked pleasantly sloppy so much more than sober. Sober was so incredibly boring. She realized this early on at university—a few preliminary drinks could make even the most tedious lecture palatable. This held true for many unpleasant moments in her life, and the last year had been the most unpleasant of her existence.

Diana Fallbrook, *magna-cum-laude*, Princeton, found herself unceremoniously dumped in this shithole eight months ago and generous daily doses of alcohol were the only thing keeping her from becoming completely unhinged—at least that's what she told herself. There were five pubs in town on her official circuit. She didn't use the term 'bar'—drunks went to bars, and she was no drunk. Every day after work—and sometimes a bit earlier—she would visit one of her pubs. She changed up establishments each night so no one would think her a lush. But of course, everyone knew she was a drunk—Dawson City was too small for them not to—but keeping your nose out of other folks' affairs was akin to religion up here. If Miss Falbrook wanted to drink, that was her business. This was a heavy drinking town anyway—a proud part of its history—boozing, whoring, gambling, and gold; those were the foundations of this place. Of course, there weren't whorehouses anymore, the casinos were tame museum entertainments, and the gold rush had long since become the gold trickle, but there were still several good saloons—the tourists insured that—and for Diana, nothing else really mattered.

She peered through the pub's iced-crusted windows. The winter nights were far too long here. A long darkness that mirrored her mood. She ordered her fifth Spank and ruminated on her circumstances. Sending her here had to have been a punishment. What else could it be? But she couldn't imagine why. She had a first-rate education—*magna-cum-laude*, Princeton—and she should have been at least mid-level management at this point, maybe even higher. Yet here she was, sitting at a bar in the ass-end of the universe, 'taking the edge off' for the two-hundred and forty-second straight night since she'd arrived. She never seriously considered her drinking might be holding her back, because she was very careful to keep that a secret. Absolutely no one knew of her 'hobby' because she made sure absolutely no one knew her. Diana had no close friends, not even any familiar acquaintances. She preferred it that way. She was a loner by natural selection. Having to consider other people's needs simply didn't suit her. Besides, she was Princeton, *magna-cum-laude*. Most folks were simply beneath her consideration.

Nevertheless, the native 'wildlife' was possessed of an alpha sense of conquest. At least once a week, some random drunk Sasquatch would stagger up to her at one of her pubs and try to lure her to his lair. Their desire was understandable. She was attractive after all and naturally aware of her ample sex appeal, but she just couldn't lower herself to breed with these genetic throwbacks. They probably wouldn't know what to do with a real woman anyway since she strongly suspected they'd honed their sexual skills on sled dogs during the long winter nights. When she started entertaining the idea of accepting their advances, she knew it was time to go home. Lamentably, she had slipped up a few times when she was too tipsy to follow her higher instincts. Then she would wake the next morning with the stench of a filthy gymnasium hanging in the air and a naked neanderthal lying next to her. These occasional slip-ups—aside from making her want to take a 24-hour full-body shower in industrial strength Listerine—annoyed the shit out of her, because it would take at least a month of brutal rejections to teach the drooling anthropoid that she really didn't want a second 'date'. That would not happen tonight.

She paid her tab, pulled on her coat, gloves, hat, and muffler, and went to the door to brave another shitty Klondike night. How could anywhere actually be this cold? She had grown up in Houston. Frigid in Houston was 40° F. The digital thermometer at the door read minus 26°—that was a criminal act of nature. She took a deep breath and held it before stepping out into the night air—if you could call it air . . . it was more like breathing ice shards. She swayed slowly along the street. Glancing into the brilliantly clear sky, she shivered at the Aurora Borealis on overbearing display—it was just too weird. She looked quickly back down at the pavement to keep from falling. Her apartment was only two blocks away . . . but the disgusting reality was almost nothing was ever more than two blocks away in this huckleberry hamlet.

She turned onto her street, and almost slipped on a patch of ice, which got even her vodka-saturated adrenaline pumping. Steadying herself against the cold wood siding of Klondike Ned's Hardware Emporium, she looked up. Half a block ahead, two lone figures passed under a streetlamp. They were wearing dirty white parkas with matching pants and boots. Snow balaclavas covered their faces. As she tried to focus more closely, she thought maybe the parkas weren't dirty after all. Her vision was a little blurry, but maybe they had some sort of design on them—small tree branches or winter-browned leaves. As suddenly as they had materialized in the lamp's pool of light, they dissolved once again into the deep Klondike darkness. If she were sober, she might have thought it queer. But she wasn't sober, and the people up here were so fucking strange anyway; what did it matter if a few illegal moose hunters were out looking for a good time in the middle of the frigid night? She continued her careful homeward trek and made it all the way without falling once.

The next morning, a mildly hungover Diana Fallbrook noted the unimportant sighting in her monthly status report. She had to write something in the idiotic brief. She was Princeton, *magna-cum-laude*, dammit! Yet here she was, filing bureaucratic busywork bullshit about possible out-of-season game hunters in the ass-freezing Klondike—a report that she knew damn well no sentient being would ever read. So much for female upward mobility. Fuck those patriarchal corporate assholes!

WALTER BENNETT SAT IN HIS office atop the Genomics Worldwide Tower, suppressing a nervousness he rarely felt anymore. Six years had passed since the sénéschal last visited Los Nietos in person, and Bennett wanted everything in perfect order. He rose from his desk and approached the windows. Gazing across the channel on this unseasonably warm and sunny day, he could make out Avalon Island in the distance, and contemplated his need of a weekend away. But not until the sénéschal left satisfied. And there was the rub, you never knew when the sénéschal was satisfied . . . until he wasn't.

Bennett had no way of knowing if he had achieved the desired results. On his last visit, the sénéschal made the off-the-books request, and never mentioned it again—until four days ago when he sent word, he would be flying into Los Nietos to assess Bennett's progress. Today, Gianakos would either approve of his labors or consider what to do with a failed Chair. And that was what was really eating at him: Walter Bennett, Chair of Genomics Worldwide, 4th seat of the all-powerful Consortium, was afraid.

His administrative manager buzzed, interrupting his dark reverie. "What is it, Bernard?" he said to the voice-activated COM.

"Your guest is five minutes out, Mr. Bennett."

"Thank you. I'll be out of the office for the rest of the day."

"Understood. I'll reroute your messages to your server. Will you want me to check up on you later tonight?"

"No, I don't think so. Thank you, Bernard."

"Then have a good afternoon."

"I'll make every attempt."

He grabbed his jacket from the closet. Pulling it on and adjusting his tie, he considered his reflection in the mirror. "You need more sleep, old boy . . . and a diet," he murmured, then went to his personal elevator. He rarely paid attention to the ride down, but it seemed very slow today. When the door opened, he saw a vintage Rolls Royce Silver Shadow limo idling outside the tower's revolving door. Taking a deep breath, he crossed the reception area, and exited as the doorman tipped his cap. The limo's chauffeur opened the passenger-side rear door. To Bennett's surprise, the back seat was empty. He looked quizzically at the driver.

"Mr. G'll meet you there," the chauffeur said matter-of-factly.

"Oh, uh, okay," he replied and ducked in, making himself comfortable in the plush leather rear seat. The chauffeur returned to the driver's seat, and they were off. Within minutes, they were cruising down the California Incline and onto the Coastal Highway. Bennett was not really in the mood for small talk, so he ignored the driver and stared out the window as the coast rolled by. Because the day was so unusually warm, the beaches were crowded with oiled sunbathers, deep-frying their skin in the early afternoon sun.

"Lucky for these bastards we cured cancer," he mumbled.

"You say something?" the driver inquired.

"What? Oh, nothing really; just commenting on the local wildlife cavorting in the sunshine."

"Yeah, nothing quite like tan lines on a hot little twinkie's naked body. Makes me sweat just thinking about it. Am I right, or am I right?"

"If... uh... you're partial to that sort of thing?" Bennett replied with a sense of confusion and disdain. Where had Gianakos found this driver anyway?

"Who wouldn't be, chief? I tell ya what; I'd like to peel the bikinis off two or three of those foxes and yiff 'em right there on the beach. Course, the sand does kinda chafe, don't it?"

"Do you mind?" Bennett asked, now appalled.

"Not so much, really. A little Gold Bond will clear that rub-rash up in no time; but make sure ya don't use the foot powder by mistake—burns like hell."

Bennett had no idea how to respond. This wasn't a chauffeur; it wasn't even a driver; it was a poorly domesticated ape in trousers. "I... have some work to do," he finally said, numbly. "I'm... uh... going to close the partition now."

"Suit yourself," the driver shrugged offhandedly as the opaque partition closed.

After about thirty-five minutes, the limo turned right, and switch-backed its way up into the canyon. Ten minutes later, they arrived at the facility's gates. The guards waved them through without a second glance. A plain, dun-colored, concrete structure nestled into the side of the hill. To the curious onlooker it was a water-pumping station, but the Genomics experimental labs extended deep into the hillside. The world's most sensitive and cutting-edge genetic developments took place right here, under the watchful eyes of the industry's best minds. The first-generation Orion series was developed here, though subsequent production was outsourced to a plant in the Mexico City Metroplex. This facility's current research was all 3rd generation stuff and beyond. The 'beyond' was what concerned

Bennett. His continued success or failure was firmly rooted in Darien Gianakos' demand for the 'beyond'. And truth be told, what he wanted was so beyond, it was barely past the theoretical stage. Bennett's anxiety rose again as the limo driver pulled into the facility's turnabout.

The sénéschal waited at the entry, looking oddly *outré* in large-framed, mirrored sunglasses—kind of like a Prada print-ad gone wrong. The driver opened the rear door and Bennett climbed out, careful not to make eye contact with the swine. At the sénéschal's nod, the driver taxied the limo back toward the main gate where he parked—unfortunately, he was going to wait.

"Walt," the sénéschal said, nodding his head in greeting.

"Good to see you, Darien," Bennett replied, noticing his own reflection in the other's sunglasses.

"Pleasant drive out?"

"Not particularly," Bennett protested. "That driver is a Cretin. I feel the need to bathe."

The sénéschal chuckled. "Did he regale you with his aesthetic appreciation of the female form?"

"Aesthetic appreciation?" Bennett sputtered. "You knew?"

"Who do you think drove me out here?"

"That man is profoundly disturbed, Darien. A candidate for advanced moderation therapy if ever I've seen one."

"Under normal circumstances I'd agree; but I find it occasionally useful to have a few untethered beasts running about the jungle."

"Are you saying that degenerate is unmodified?"

"You designed those cog-meds, Walt. You know the side effects. He wouldn't have a tithe of that sexual appetite with modification. It's ironic, isn't it, that the very neuro-modifier that frees humans from the lunacy of religion also quenches their libido? At least that side effect has produced negative population growth. I'll take that as a win."

"But, Darien, how can we let someone like that roam the streets? He's not only disgusting, but very probably dangerous as well."

"He's harmless, believe it or not. Aside from his rather exotic fantasies—and that's really all they are—he's too socially awkward to even speak to a woman, let alone do all those things he 'sweats' over. No, his only real lover is his overused hand. I'll admit, he very likely has some kind of personality disorder, and he's a textbook paranoid. He's certain that the government—whatever he means by that—is trying to control his mind. Another one of those curious ironies, I suppose. In any case, he has a penchant for staying off the grid, as he calls it—no technology, no paperwork, cash-only. That old limo of his has no GPS so he can't be located—or so he believes. I keep his one-car company on a retainer. Frankly, I wouldn't be at all surprised if I was his only customer. He's useful to me because when I want to evade casual observation, I use people like him to avoid an obvious digital trail. And Walt, it's imperative that the Heracles and Damocles projects remain utterly classified. I hope I've made that clear to you?"

"Absolutely, Darien, you needn't worry. I've personally overseen both. No one even knows you made the requests."

"I assured the premieres you could be trusted. The sun's feeling a bit warm, isn't it? I'm getting too used to my North Atlantic icebox. Why don't we go inside so you can show me your progress? By the way, you very prudently ordered all surveillance equipment shut off for the rest of the afternoon."

"I did?"

"Yes, you did. There will be no record of this visit."

"Oh, oh, of course, Darien. None at all!"

"Excellent. Then, shall we?" The receptionist nodded as the two men proceeded to the elevator. Gianakos did not remove his sunglasses as they descended three floors to the 'ultra-restricted' level and walked down the sterile hallway to the suite of labs. The armed guards stepped aside as Bennett entered the code, submitted to the biometric scans, and the latch gave way. He opened the door into what appeared to be a large and very comfortably decorated living quarters. Mozart's *Requiem* wafted down the hallway. The sénéschal finally removed his sunglasses and looked questioningly at Bennett.

"It's coming from the library," Bennett said. "Follow me." They continued down the hallway to a set of pocket doors. Walt took a deep breath and knocked.

After a moment the music stopped. "Come in," called a voice from the other side. Bennett opened the doors and the sénéschal stared for a long moment. In a modest armchair, reading a leather-bound book, sat the identical twin of Darien Gianakos; at least he would have been, had the sénéschal been forty years younger.

"Oh, very nice, Walt." The sénéschal finally purred. "*Very* nice indeed."

"Good afternoon, Doctor Bennett," the young man said rising and setting the book down.

"Doctor?" the sénéschal asked, eyebrow raised.

"Well, I do have a PhD. . . two actually," Bennett replied, slightly abashed. "Darien," he turned again to the young man, "I'd like to introduce you to Damocles."

The sénéschal stepped forward and shook the young man's hand. "I've been so looking forward to meeting you."

They all stood silently for a long moment. Damocles looked expectantly at the two older men but said nothing to fill the gap. He appeared completely at ease in a situation that should have been awkward. The sénéschal picked up the book Damocles had been reading but couldn't make out the language.

"What's the subject matter?" he asked.

"Nietzsche's *Thus Spake Zarathustra*," Damocles replied.

"You read German?"

"*Ja, Natürlich.*"

"I was never a particularly astute student of languages; just enough to get by," the sénéschal said, addressing the observation to Bennett.

Bennett shrugged. "You suggested improvements would be appropriate."

"I suppose I did, didn't I?" mused the sénéschal. "How many languages do you speak, Damocles?"

"I've currently mastered thirteen and am comfortable in another eleven."

"Impressive. I assume then, that you're familiar with the meaning of the term, 'legatus'?"

"Classical or Medieval Latin?"

"Is there a difference?"

"The Classical usage refers to a military rank and office; the other to the hierarchical bureaucracy of the Medieval Roman Catholic Church."

"I think the Classical will suit our purposes." The sénéschal thoughtfully tapped his lips with his index finger then turned to Bennett. "Damocles and I need to talk for about a half-hour alone, Walt. I'll meet you upstairs when we're done."

Bennett sat on a comfortable sofa in the entry-level reception area, yet he felt anything but relaxed. Nearly an hour had passed since he'd left Darien with Damocles, and he grew more anxious with each passing minute. Had something gone wrong? Had the sénéschal discovered the glitch? He felt sweat beginning to dampen the back of his shirt collar. Then the elevator doors opened, and Gianakos stepped out. Bennett couldn't read his eyes because he again wore those hideous sunglasses. As he approached, he paused at the receptionist's desk and asked that she 'fetch' the limo, then he continued to the sofa and sat next to Bennett.

"Damocles is gathering his belongings. He'll be coming with me. After we leave, you'll destroy all records and delete every back-up file that in any way refers to him or his training protocols. Then you'll do everything in your power to forget he exists. Can I count on you, Walt?"

"Absolutely," Bennett replied, hiding his unease.

"Excellent. After you've finished scrubbing those files, you'll need to arrange for other transportation—I have a feeling you won't mind. Now, where are we on the Heracles project?"

"I spoke with our Mexico City factor two days ago. They're slightly behind schedule. The extra power usage necessary for the final stage overloaded the grid down there and we had to reroute surplus from Los Nietos. She's confident we'll have the completed order by mid-March."

"I'm very impressed, Walt. You've exceeded my expectations. That hardly ever happens anymore." The sénéschal tapped his lips with his index finger, considering. "I think congratulations are in order. How does the number three seat sound to you, old boy?"

Bennett was not sure that he'd heard correctly. "Thank you, Sénéschal," he finally managed to say, short of breath. "I'm honored. But what will Alex say?"

"Alex is competitive. He'll be jealous of your success . . . and work that much harder to regain his spot. A win-win don't you think?" The elevator opened and Damocles stepped out carrying two travel bags. The sénéschal rose and waved him over. "I'll expect word by mid-March," he said turning toward the entry.

As Damocles followed, he nodded toward Bennett. "So long, Walt," he said, with what may have been a smirk, and then continued through the door to the waiting Silver Shadow.

As the limo pulled away, Bennett's unease didn't subside. He was elated to be made 3rd Chair, but something about this assignment didn't add up. Why had the Directorate green-lit the project in the first place? He could understand the Heracles units, but Damocles? He just couldn't imagine the purpose. He knew it wasn't in his best interest to ask too many questions; but since no one had yet perfected mind-reading, his thoughts were his own. Of course, he would delete all the files on this project and the back-ups . . . after he had downloaded them onto his personal flash drive. Walter Bennett hadn't climbed to the highest echelons of power by always doing the expected. Besides, it was simply prudent to have an insurance policy. He walked back toward the elevator. He had work to do before this day was over.

The Gulfstream touched down at Keflavìk late the following morning. They had stopped over in New York for a very late dinner. The two men disembarked and climbed into the waiting car, which took them to the sénéschal's gated residence in Old Reykjavík. The 1920s home was a ten-minute walk from Gianakos' offices. Though it wasn't for sale when he made Reykjavík his center of operations, he offered the owners more than twice its appraised value and they felt obliged to take the 'eccentric' Greek's money and run, as the saying went. He completely refurbished the old house to his very exacting specifications. Nowhere near as opulent as Liliane's château, or as daunting as Rampart's fortress in the Puget, yet it served his guise quite well as a confirmed well-to-do bachelor who valued his privacy. Liliane occasionally visited, but it really wasn't up to her standards. His solitary existence would change now that his protégé had arrived. But he could no longer leave his tutelage to Walter Bennett. He would personally conduct the final training of his Legatus. The guard opened the gate, and they continued through the arched breezeway to the back of the house. Damocles got their bags from the trunk and the two men entered through the kitchen door.

"Welcome to your new home," Darien said, as he set his keys on the counter. "Let me show you your rooms." They climbed two levels of service stairs to the remodeled attic floor. "This level is yours. My rooms are on the 2nd floor. You'll find a library to your right, an office to your left, and straight ahead is your bedroom." Darien opened the door to a comfortable bedroom and a cleanly designed *en-suite* bathroom. "Make yourself at home. There's food in the kitchen, and a very nice Assyrtiko in the refrigerator, if you like that sort of thing."

"It is my favorite," the young man replied.

"I had a feeling it might be. Now, I received a page on approach to Keflavík, so I must take care of a few things. Is there anything you need before I go?"

"I'll be fine. Thank you."

"Excellent. We'll talk later then?"

"That would be nice, Father . . . May I call you Father?"

"You may; but it's best for now if it were not in public. People might misunderstand."

"Then I shall keep it between us. And will you call me Son?"

"Would you like me to?"

"I believe I would."

"Well then, I'll talk to you later . . . Son."

The car drove him to the North Atlantic Investment Trust building; but instead of taking the elevator to his 19th floor office, he went to the roof where an AW 339 waited on the helipad, rotors spinning. Darien boarded, and the bird took to the sky headed east. Fifty minutes later they landed on the surface station helipad of Bárðarbunga's geothermal plant. Darien deboarded and approached the entry where the guards pulled open the heavily-reinforced doors. He continued along the unflatteringly-lit corridor—he would eventually have to do something about those lights—to the elevator, he placed his palm on the sensory pad, and peered into the retinal scanner. The panel-speaker came to life.

"Voice identification, please?"

"By the pricking of my thumbs, something wicked this way comes," he recited.

"Very funny, Darien," Minerva deadpanned. "Come on up." The freight-elevator ascended to the command center, and the doors opened to that annoyingly powerful hum and vibration that he didn't miss at all. The scores of technicians that had populated this level on his previous visit were no longer necessary since they were long past the testing stages, and the entire operation was managed by six technicians and Minerva, who now approached.

"Good morning, Darien," she semi-shouted.

"I think it's afternoon, Minerva," he replied. "I got your page. No problems I hope?"

"That depends on how you define problems." She led him to the smaller sound-dampening chamber and closed the door bringing semi-quiet. He sat facing the wall monitor and Minerva took a chair next to him.

"This must be quick, Minerva. I'm meeting with the Directorate at 3 p.m."

"That's one of the reasons I paged you. We have a development. Rockefeller has contacted the other premiers and invited them to a 'get-together' at his estate in the Puget."

"In person? That's out of character. Has Elise received my invitation?"

"You're not invited; and the others have been told not to inform you."

"Well, that's troubling; a face-to-face meeting of the premiers without their sénéschal," he mused, as he tapped his lips. "What do you make of it?"

"Rockefeller is not pleased with you."

"Tell me something I don't already know."

"Beyond that I can only speculate. His compound is like a surveillance fortress. Accessing information from inside has proved impossible thus far."

"It's imperative that you find a way. We must have access to *all* the premiers."

"I am aware. That's why this get-together may provide an opportunity."

"When is it taking place? And is that really what he called it?"

"Yes, it really is and it's on February 14th."

"Odd choice, isn't it? He's a bit long in the tooth for a Valentine's Day party."

"Valentinus was an early Christian saint, so I don't imagine Rockefeller would find that befitting. He's probably devised something more along the lines of a Lupercalia. You've read the dossier I compiled on him?"

"His after-hours entertainments don't really interest me."

"I feel it's important to be thorough."

"Yes, I appreciate that about you. So, they're meeting without me. We must discover their agenda." He again tapped his lips in thought. "What would you think of using Liliane as our eyes and ears on the inside?"

"I considered it myself. She doesn't really have the mental agility for subterfuge."

"Jealousy is not attractive."

"You flatter yourself."

"Speaking of attractive, did you change your hair color?"

"I got bored," she shrugged.

"*You* got *bored*?" he laughed. "That's a first . . . it looks good, by the way . . . your hair, I mean."

"Thanks. And you'd notice these little things if you dropped by oftener than once every two years."

"Awww. Is that why you called me out here? Because you miss me?"

"Don't be ridiculous. I called you out here because, though it's less than ideal, I came to the same conclusion about Mademoiselle Genevois. If we use her as our eyes and ears, she could leave behind a mobile digital key. Two birds, one stone." Minerva handed him an item about the size and shape of a credit card. "I had this especially modified a few hours ago for our needs. If she can inconspicuously leave this somewhere it won't be noticed, we'll be able to pick the lock on his digital fortress."

"Capital idea, Minerva! It needs to be passive so we can remotely activate it."

"I didn't start doing this yesterday, Darien. Of course, it's passive. Once in place,

I'll switch it on."

"Excellent. I'll fly to Paris this evening and brief her."

"I'm confident you two will be anything but brief."

"That's impertinent."

"But accurate."

"I haven't much time. What's your other information?"

"I've gleaned some very tantalizing clues from a monthly report filed by our factor in the northernmost quadrant of Region 4."

"Do you actually read those reports?"

"As a matter of fact, I do. I like to keep up on things."

"Then you'll probably want to know that Region 4 is now Region 3."

"Interesting. I'll make the necessary adjustments."

"Do. Now, just what about this report is so tantalizing?"

"After reading it, I had Haruspex survey all video feeds from the small town our factor manages and, fortunately, a camera outside the local hardware store caught this." She switched on the wall monitor and the video showed a streetlamp at night, illuminating snowplowed heaps of filthy ice. They watched for about thirty seconds.

"Are we watching the moon rise?" Darien asked, looking at his watch.

"Wait for it, Darien," Minerva said drolly. Then two lone figures passed under the streetlamp, wearing camouflaged white parkas with matching pants and boots. Snow balaclavas covered their faces. As suddenly as they had materialized in the lamp's pool of light, they dissolved once again into the Klondike darkness.

"That's it?"

"Yes, that's it."

"And why did I need to see this riveting video?"

"Your sarcasm aside, if I read between the lines, I surmise a very well-concealed group is secluded up there, living off the conventional grid. We should definitely investigate."

"Investigate two people taking an evening walk in the snow?"

"In full camouflage?"

"Bloody hell, Minerva! How many 'investigations' will that put us at now, a hundred and fifty?"

"One hundred and forty-seven, if you wish to be precise."

"A hundred and forty-seven 'solid' leads followed up on, and exactly what do we have to show for all that?"

"I'll admit our previous intelligence hasn't panned out; but I have a feeling this may be different?"

"A feeling? Seriously? My dear Minerva, this is probably another group of religious fanatics trying to hole up in the most out-of-the-way place. They're all textbook paranoids. What makes this group unique?"

"It's been more than a year since we've had any actionable intel on Percival."

"You needn't remind me. The premieres will do so again at 3:00."

"It stands to reason that he's no longer in a populated area. He'd have been caught in our surveillance nets long ago."

"Go on."

"Were I a strategist on a par with Stephan Quade, I'd get Percival as far off the conventional grid as I could, to give me time to train him to be a soldier and commander."

"A commander? . . . Of what?"

"A resistance, Darien. And perhaps a revolution."

"You can't be suggesting a Consortium power grab is Percival's destiny!"

"Destiny has nothing to do with it. I'm merely looking at the possibilities."

"He's an unschooled peasant!"

"He *was* a *little*-schooled rustic, I concede; but one with extremely high aptitude scores. And, it's been nearly two years, Darien; much can be learned in that time with the proper training and motivation."

He tapped his lips in thought. "I'm dubious, to say the least," he finally conceded, "But you have my attention. Go on."

"The evidence suggests whoever these subversives are, they're skilled, discreet, highly disciplined, and completely averse to any traceable technology."

"Numbers?"

"Impossible to say without more eyes onsite. They're very careful to stay undetected, which suggests sophistication."

"Oh, all right," he said after considering it. "Go ahead and send someone up there to investigate."

"I'd recommend four squads."

"A full platoon!?" he sputtered.

"If it is Percival, having sufficient boots on the ground will remove any delay in performing an extraction. We wouldn't want him to slip away again."

"You certainly have a bee in your bonnet about this one. . . Okay, Minerva, it seems excessive, but send a platoon. At the very least, it's bad policy to let these Galilean groupies run around unchecked. We need to make occasional examples, so let's corral this one. And maybe we'll get lucky. It would be nice for a change to report a success to our resident pack of hungry jackals."

"I'll get right on it."

"Oh, one last thing, Minerva; I picked up Damocles yesterday."

"I'm aware of that."

"Of course you are."

"You're pleased with him, then?"

"Beyond pleased. Walt also says the Heracles units will be ready in mid-March. Is the retrofit of Khartoum complete?"

"Not quite. The phantoms were not a particularly tidy bunch, and a great deal of modernization was needed."

"But it will be ready?"

"I'll make sure of it."

"Good. And how is Rome coming along?"

"That's a bit behind schedule. Our workers need to frame their endeavors as earthquake protection upgrades. Otherwise, visitors to the museums ask too many questions."

"When will it be ready?"

"Mid-April—and that's the best-case scenario."

"No later. Our target is 21 April. I don't want to change that. Liliane has made plans."

"Yes, well we wouldn't want to disappoint Liliane, would we?"

"You said you weren't jealous, but that sounded very green."

"Don't you have a meeting to attend?"

"Yes, Minerva, you needn't get snippy. I'll be leaving now; but there's one more last thing."

"Yes?"

"I'd like you to activate the node in my residence."

"That's still in the installation phase."

"How soon can you have it ready?

"Ten days to two weeks."

"Make it ten days. Keep me informed of its progress. Now I must be off. It was nice to see you."

"Hopefully it won't be another two years before you drop by again."

The Helicopter returned him to The North Atlantic Investment Trust building at 2:25 p.m. He took the elevator down one level to his 19th floor office suite, where he found Elise at her desk.

"Good afternoon, Elise."

"Good afternoon, Mr. Gianakos. Was your trip pleasant?"

"Quite, thank you. Any messages?"

"Only two that I couldn't deal with directly."

"Yes?"

"One was from a *Mademoiselle* Chérie. She insisted she needed to speak to you as soon as possible."

"I expected that one. And the other?"

"Ms. Musa. She wanted to confirm your meeting with her at 3 p.m."

Looking at his watch, he tapped his lips with his index finger. "That gives me twenty-five minutes."

"Yes sir," Elise replied. "Will you need anything?"

"Yes, privacy. No interruptions until I let you know."

"Very good, sir."

He went to his office, poured himself a bourbon and downed it before setting up the office for the directorate meeting. At 3 p.m., seven holographic chairs flickered to life in front of his desk. Over the next few minutes, each of the seven premiers sat down in their respective pools of light.

"Good afternoon, ladies and gentlemen," he said to the assembled images. "May I call this meeting of the Directorate to order?" There was no response, so he continued, placing his legal pad and favorite fountain pen on the desktop. "Hearing no objections, this meeting is called to order at 3:03 p.m. Reykjavík time, on 19 January. The sénéschal spent the next forty minutes filing his torpidly boring bi-weekly report, and the premiers asked their usual inane questions about production quotas, workforce issues, and the like. Darien watched them closely to see if they would let anything slip, but they telegraphed nothing. If he was willing to admit it to himself, it frustrated him. What were they up to? After he finished the report, he allowed the moment of pause to linger longer than usual.

"Well, then," he finally volunteered when no one had spoken up. "If there's nothing else, would someone like to make a motion for adjournment?"

"There is one other thing, Darien," Musa spoke up. "We'll need to cancel our next meeting. Several of us have commitments that cannot be avoided. Barring any unforeseen events, we'll meet with you in late February."

So, there it was, with as little information as possible. What *were* they thinking? "As you wish, Madam Premier," he said as though it were of little consequence. "If there's nothing else?"

"I've got a question, Sheriff," William Rampart, the Rockefeller Chair, spoke up for the first time. "Your master calendar has you in Reykjavík last week, but your flight itinerary puts you in Los Nietos two days ago. You didn't mention that in your report. Why is that?"

He was grateful there were no vitals monitored in these holographic meetings because his heart rate would have gone off the scale. "I visit our chairs occasionally, unannounced," he said smoothly. "I feel I get more straightforward answers face-to-face, particularly when they don't know I'm coming. I didn't think something that obvious needed to be stated in my report."

"We know you keep tabs on them, smart-ass. That's your job. I'm asking why it wasn't on your official schedule?"

"Pardon me, I meant no disrespect," he lied. "I paid an unscheduled visit to Walt Bennett because his numbers were off. The explanation was simple enough. It's been an excessively warm winter in the Mexico City Metroplex and the power usage for air conditioning exceeded supply estimates. They were getting brown outs, which were affecting labor. He rerouted surplus supply from Los Nietos, which temporarily solved the problem. The grid down there is one of our oldest and scheduled for upgrade next year; so, the issue really turned out to be a non-issue. As to why it was not on my master calendar, I'll speak to Elise about entering those last-minute changes into the record. It's probably not high on her list of to-dos since it's always after the fact." All true as far as it went. It wouldn't stand up to deep scrutiny, but it seemed to mollify Rampart a bit. "I'd imagine my flight record also noted that I stopped over in New York. I felt, since I was passing over, I may as well check in." Again, true as far as it went. He didn't say he'd checked in on a fine steakhouse. Now he was glad he'd given in to his craving for bloody-rare, dry-aged ribeye.

"All right, enough about that," Rampart conceded. "Catch us up on your anomaly. . . and the two rogue phantoms. You haven't mentioned them for a few months. It's been, what, two years now, or nearly? I seem to recall you telling us the fate of the world hung on finding those fugitives. Seems like something that important would deserve at least a mention."

"Certainly. As you know, Percival has proven more skilled at evasion than we expected; however, I have reason to believe we're at a crossroads."

"Clarify," interrupted Elinor Prowell, the Rothschild Chair.

"Well . . . I hesitated to mention it until I had more definitive intel, but we may have found the general area where the anomaly and phantoms are hiding."

"Where?" asked Leung Xiang, the Ali Khan Chair.

"In the far north of Region 3, uh, pardon me, Region 4, near the Arctic Circle. I've dispatched operatives to investigate. The search is still in the preliminary stages, but I'll let you know as soon as I have something more definitive."

"Do," said Yejide Akpabio, the Musa Chair.

"And do us all a favor," Rampart added. "Don't cock it up this time."

The holograms all flickered out except Liliane's. He shook his head at her image, and she flickered out too.

That afternoon, Gianakos flew into London Heathrow and took the high-speed train to Paris. If they were following his flight plans, he didn't dare fly directly there. At Pont de l'Alma, he caught a Seine River taxi that ferried him to the outskirts of Paris where he disembarked at Liliane's waterfront château. She waited alone in the boathouse, having told the night guards to stay clear.

"Oh Darien!" she cried, running into his arms. "What are we going to do?"

"Be still!" he commanded. She threw her shoulders back and a flash of anger glinted in her eyes. "That's better," he said more gently. "We need talk, not hysterics." They sat on one of the boathouse's window seats, overlooking the waning moonlight reflected off the swirling waters of the Seine. "Now, tell me about this so-called get-together."

"I received a hand-written invitation two days ago by courier. It said you were not to be told, and that I should destroy the message after I had read it. I tried to reach you, but you were not available."

"I'm sorry about that, but I needed to meet with Bennett. Did you destroy the invitation?"

"Of course not," she handed him the envelope and he read it.

"There's nothing useful here," he said.

"I do not think I should go, Darien."

"That's not an option," he said quietly. "At this point, your absence would only make you the subject of discussion, and perhaps suspicion."

"We have never had a social gathering in my time. Why now?"

"I'm not sure. That's why we need you there. I'm most likely not invited because I'm going to be discussed. If that's the case, you must be hard on me. It will defer suspicion."

"I will try, *mon cher*, but I do not know how to be a spy."

"True, but you know how to lie. All women do."

"*Lèche mon cul!*" she growled.

"Whatever that means, I'm sure it's *very* flattering." He smiled at her, and she finally smiled back, lowering her eyes.

"It means I will be your spy."

"*Our* spy, my dear. Our spy."

"*Oui.* Our spy."

"Just go and act normal. Don't think of yourself as a spy. If you do that, you'll only try to perform, and people will take note."

"I will try."

"You'll be fine." He reached into his pocket and pulled out the small device Minerva had given him. "You'll need to leave this somewhere it won't be discovered. It will allow us to keep tabs on the event remotely."

"And if they search me?"

"They'll only be distracted by your phenomenal physical attributes."

"Be serious, Darien!"

"I *was* being serious. While I was in Los Nietos, a desperately depraved man chauffeured me around the Metroplex. All I could think about while he ranted about his sexual fantasies was you."

"I am not in the mood, Darien. This has all made me very upset."

He sighed, "Very well, *ma chérie*, then I must be off. The taxi is waiting on the dock." He started to leave when she stopped him.

"How depraved was this man?" she asked.

"Obscenely."

She looked at him appraisingly. "This boathouse has a bedroom upstairs. Did you know this?"

"I seem to recall."

"*D'accord.* You go tell the taxi you will be delayed. I will go get myself ready. But you must rehearse for me what your driver said."

"Every word verbatim, my dear. I swear it."

IT WAS 7:15 A.M. IN THE KLONDIKE and the sun wouldn't rise for another three hours. Pere could no longer see his reflection in the mirrors of the combat yurt because they had finally steamed up after forty-five minutes of intense work. These log huts never seemed warm enough during the unremitting winters, when the earth around the sub-cabins froze solid to a depth of three feet; but four sweating men did eventually have its effect. His senseis attacked on three sides at once.

He couldn't hold them off much longer before he made a fatal error—the error he most feared, the very thing he guarded himself most desperately against—he was the Falcon, after all, the bird of prey, the catalyst of the coming storm, the secret weapon, the navi dreamer, the great hope. He had to be perfect. He couldn't let his guard down for a moment.

His breath came in short gasps as sweat streamed down his forehead, stinging his eyes, and blurring his vision. He was doing everything right. He knew it on a conscious level—because he'd worked so hard to perfect the forms of the *kata*, he now depended on them to the exclusion of all else, as though a flawless adherence to the forms would invariably lead to victory. The forms prepared the body and mind to transcend the well-worn path of the proven and strike out into the realm of the pure present—no past, no future, only the here and now. But the forms had now become his stumbling stone. He needed to cut the anchor to his conscious mind and trust instinct. But instincts were risky, fickle, untamed, and if wrong, they could cost him his life. Letting go felt too much like surrendering—and, to his way of thinking, equaled failure. And if he failed, the mighty Falcon would be unmasked, the façade would crumble, revealing the frightened, confused phony he knew himself to be.

The 'mighty man', El'zar, the taciturn Cossack, Khyoza, and the one-handed Parisian, Ehud, pressed their young initiate hard, but none was able to deliver the killing blow. Peregrine defended himself with a burgeoning skill that bordered on the preternatural—bordered on but hadn't crossed over. They tried to goad him into taking the next step, force him to reach back into the unorthodox and intuitive energy he had begun with so many months before at the Catacombs. But he was a polished swordsman now—polished, orthodox, and predictably traditional. They had to get him to abandon that now; that was the next step, the true step, and the most difficult one to take. Truth be told, the three masters could still overwhelm him; but their unified goal was to train Peregrine, not defeat him. They had promised Paulus they would keep his son safe. To do that, they had to make a master of *him*, and he was still an initiate.

The attackers ranged all around the dojo using all the traditional moves on him and he defended each thrust perfectly with the answering form they had drilled into him. He was a wall they could not penetrate . . . until they went completely off book. Ehud and Khyoza suddenly came at him like madmen, abandoning the correct offensive forms. Their attacks were desperate and furious, but Pere was just able to parry them both and deliver the killing blows. He realized only too late that they had sacrificed themselves in a fatal gambit so El could position himself for a crippling slice, which didn't kill the falcon, but disabled him so completely that he could now be captured and questioned—an outcome worse than death. Pere fell on the mat panting while El stood over him.

"I've been trying to tell you, Falcon," El said, breathing hard. "You can only rely on the forms so long as your opponent does the same. But a reaper ain't gonna play fair. Those things don't care if you kill them. They're programmed for one thing and one thing only—completing the mission."

"You're right. I know you're right," Pere panted. "I'm sorry. I'll do better next time."

"It has nothing to do with better, *Faucon*," said the Parisian lying beside him in winded exhaustion. "You are already better than anyone at your stage of training that I have ever seen. But you are thinking too much. It is time now that you internalize those skills, combine brains with balls."

"Ehud is right, Falcon," Khyoza added softly. "You are more skilled now than El'zar was after two years of training."

"Hey!" El protested.

"You know it is true, Brother. But El'zar had something that you still need to find; it made him the best; it made him unbeatable—and it was not skill."

"What was it?" Pere asked El.

"I don't know," the big man said after considering it. "But you'll know it when you find it. It's a well you can pull from . . . a different gear you shift into. I can't really explain it. It's just there when I need it."

Pere wanted to probe further, but the door to the yurt opened and Yael stepped in, pulling back her hood to reveal her much longer auburn curls, dusted with snowflakes. They had both stopped cutting their hair two years ago. Yael's had become long and wavy, but El showed Pere how to wear his in a bun on the top of his head, like the samurai *chonmage*, but without the shaved pate. At first, he adopted longer hair to change his look, since his image was on web bulletins, but in time it became a convenient way to keep it out of his eyes while training.

"Why don't you guys answer your tin can?" Yael asked in a flustered tone. They all looked at the receiver hanging on the wall next to the door—the orange light clearly blinking.

"The buzzer stopped working a couple weeks ago," El said. "I reported it. Guess it's a low priority. What's up?"

"Ruach just got in from the circuit," she said to the sweating men. "He says there's something you'll want to hear."

The swordsmen got some water and dry towels to wipe the sweat off so they wouldn't catch a chill.

"Where is he?" asked El.

"In his and Pere's yurt, having breakfast and warming up. He's going to meet with Barnabas and the other elders in about an hour."

"We'll be there," El said, beginning to strip off his protective gear, as the others did the same.

The travelers, or 'Catacombers' as some called them, arrived at the Colony on the first day of August, eighteen months earlier, when the weather was warm and humid, and the days very long. Pere assumed it was like that year-round, and he began to think of his exile as a vacation. Then the first long winter came with its bitter cold, frigid winds, and five or six hours of weak daylight. He grew melancholy, impatient, and longed for the co-op with its crisp but sunny winter mornings, or even the dark caverns of the Catacombs, and its inexhaustible hot spring.

Yael and his three benevolent torturers were wise enough not to let the young falcon sink in the despair of that first winter. El increased his training regimen to eight hours a day—not just sword work, but Bojuka and Krav Maga as well. He was still a madman in the training yurt, but outside that mock warzone, El had changed. Ever since he'd been reconciled to Paulus, his mood had brightened considerably. When they had first arrived, he had tried to return the Beretta to Eben, who was now a colonist, but the old man insisted that El continue to hold on to it for safe-keeping and, surprisingly, El accepted without the usual argument. Truth be told, El didn't argue about much anymore. Pere surmised that he had less occasion to 'wrestle with the angel' than he used to. His co-torturers, Khyoza and Ehud, had become nearly inseparable over the last eighteen months. Pere came to depend on the pair more and more. They were able to mitigate El's demanding training approach with their gentle mocking of the big man, although Ehud no longer called him Ronin—apparently, he was satisfied that El had settled matters in that area.

Pere also got to know Ruach, Eben's son—an amiable fellow about Marcus's age, with a great sense of humor. Pere was assigned to Ruach's yurt, and they became friends. He would joke with Pere good-naturedly at his darkest moments, which was just what he needed. Then, of course, there was Yael, who made everything bearable. She was the nearest warm star in Pere's constellation, and her light brightened even the darkest nights of his soul. For some couples, trying events tear them apart; but Cam and Pere only became closer to one another in the crucible that had become their lives.

She was the one person he could be completely himself with. Without her, he was sure he'd never have survived. She worked out with them occasionally in the yurt, but because she was now apprenticing to be a medic, it was not as often as Pere would have liked. He also began to train his mind. Yael started teaching him Latin; and Barnabas agreed to instruct him in Russian. Apparently, he inherited more than just eye color from his parents. His ability with languages proved nearly as spectacular as his combat work. Within eight months, he was struggling through Augustine's *Confessiones*, and Dostoevsky's *Idiót*.

One evening, after his Russian lesson, Pere asked Barnabas about the Colony. "We established it several years after the Catacombs began," Barnabas told him. "I suggested to your dad a northern outpost would be useful as a fallback, and this is about as far north as you can go without living in the wastes. We were able to get ahold of about two-hundred acres up here, so I came up that first summer with about a dozen friends and we built the first yurt. We made a general land plan after that and buried the party line for the tin-can exchange. Every summer we try to build at least one new yurt, but sometimes other things come up."

"Why yurts?" Pere asked, since Barnabas seemed more chatty than usual, he figured he'd get as much information as he could.

"That's kind of a funny story, and a little embarrassing," Barnabas chuckled. "I designed the yurts based on my memories. I was born in Ulan Ude in southern Siberia. I'm a Buryat by heritage, and as a kid, I visited the historic parks with my folks and saw the yurts of my ancestors. They fired my imagination, and I imagined myself a chieftain, like Oro Shigushi, holding off the Cossack invaders."

But Pere knew that aside from Barnabas' fantasies, the yurts were also very efficient. Their domed roofs were covered in grassy weeds and flowers in the summer and snow in the winter, which made them indistinguishable from the surrounding landscape, and the nine inches of roof sod thwarted any infrared drone surveillance. However, unlike the yurts of Barnabas' Buryat ancestors, these had photovoltaic power arrays built into their domed peaks, with a camouflaged retractable hatch. Power packs charged during the long summer days to supplement the dark, cold winters. Even so, they never heated them above fifty degrees Fahrenheit; so, coats were always worn indoors from October through May.

In late-April, the spring thaw came in force; the snow melted, the flowers bloomed, and the meadows became lushly verdant. Those were the halcyon days, when Pere and Yael wandered in the hills, picnicked in the meadows, and sat together, hand in hand, to watch the sun set at midnight. But by late October, the first snow fell, and it was back to double practice sessions in the combat yurt. When January rolled around, he started asking when they could return south. There had been no word from his father and Silas for months, and he began to wonder if they'd forgotten him. He felt isolated and forsaken in this frozen outpost where the nearest official civilization was the tiny town of Dawson some twelve miles southwest. The townspeople valued their privacy and freedom, which served the Klondike colonists well. Busybodies simply weren't tolerated, so no one asked questions.

The Catacombers met in Barnabas's yurt, which served as the center of the Klondike operation. The Colony elders were there: Gershom, the horticulturalist, Matthat, the Klondike MOW commander, and Rophe, the Colony's physician. Ruach sat in their midst, sipping cold coffee, with his face missing its usual carefree expression.

"Thanks for coming on such short notice," Barnabas said. "Ruach has already given me a cursory report, but I thought we all would want to consider what he saw. Please, Ruach, tell them what you've told me."

"There's abnormal activity in town," Ruach said, without preamble. "Three unmarked transports rolled into town from the east, and they weren't passing through. They're setting up shop next to the General Store, heavy on equipment."

"What kind of equipment?" El asked.

"You'd know better than I; but from what my dad described to me, they were assembling drones—at least two of them, maybe three."

"Then they're already operational," El grumbled. "Have you warned the yurts?"

"The word went out forty minutes ago," Barnabas replied. "The arrays are already closed. We'll operate on batteries for the time being, and no one except essentials will leave their yurts except in IR gear."

"Why are they here?" asked Rophe.

"Impossible to tell without more info," said Matthat. "I think we should assume the worst, until we know otherwise."

"We have plenty in storage," said Gershom. "We can probably take to the yurts for six to eight weeks and be hardly worse off for it."

"But don't we need more information?" asked Rophe.

"Yes, we do," said El. "I'll set out this afternoon and do some reconnaissance."

"I think you mean *we'll* set out this afternoon, don't you, Uncle?" said Yael.

El tensed for a moment, and then his shoulders relaxed. "I assumed that was understood, Niece."

"It is now."

"We will come as well," said Ehud, nodding in the direction of Khyoza and Pere.

"We'll leave at 6 p.m.," El said. "It'll be dark enough by then."

"It might be wise to set up some defensive measures," said Matthat, thoughtfully.

"Can't that wait until we know more?" asked Rophe.

"By then it might be too late," responded Matthat, matter-of-factly.

"Set up your countermeasures," said Barnabas, after considering it. "They can always be removed if we don't need them. And Rophe, make sure the clinic is ready to be a field hospital, just in case." She looked shocked, but slowly nodded. "These drones," Barnabas asked El. "Are they battery powered, and radio operated?"

"Yes, and yes."

"That's what I thought. Matthat, if you don't mind helping me later, I think we might be able to create a countermeasure for those as well."

"I'll drop by after El'zar leaves."

At a quarter past six they set out under darkening skies in white and green IR camos with heavy parkas. Pere remembered his night march two years ago, stumbling around in the dark with a band of fugitive terrorists. He was a newb then, a tagalong, and expected to make mistakes. Now he moved with the skill of a seasoned hunter—and yet, he still felt like a newb.

It hadn't snowed heavily in over a week, so the pack was solid enough, and the terrain only moderately rugged. At El's pace they made the little town by midnight. The clouds had cleared, and the Milky Way showed brilliantly in the deep night sky. A gentle easterly breeze persisted at their backs. They stopped on a tree-lined ridge with a clear view of the town below. The street south of the General Market had been cordoned off, and four dark unmarked transports were parked in a square formation—definitely a command center.

Pere soon realized he'd seen all this or something very like it in a recurrent dream. But, in the dream, it was sunny, there was a strong wind, and his companions waited on him to make some kind of decision. But he couldn't—he hesitated because he didn't know what to do. Then a DEW cannon fired at them from the command center and killed them all. But in this reality, he was on the ridge overlooking the town, it was night, and there was a breeze, not a howling wind—and no burst of violet light came from the cordoned area. The whole command center appeared lifeless; and best of all, he wasn't being asked to make any decisions.

They surveyed the sleepy town for another fifteen minutes before El signaled them back into the trees. Pere felt oddly detached as they hiked through the forest, a strange sense of unreality tugging at his mind. He had begun to trust his dreams as though they were fact; and now the dream and the reality didn't match. He wondered what it meant—if it meant anything at all; but the sense of the terrible responsibility was still present in this reality. Could the dream be about a moment in time that had more than one potential outcome? Maybe it was another one of those crossroads? Or maybe it was just plain wrong? Was he putting too much trust in the accuracy of his dreams? Maybe, maybe, maybe—there were always too many maybes.

The sky had brightened toward dawn when they reached Barnabas' quarters. They drank cold coffee with a dram of schnapps while they waited inside. Everything was always cold at the Colony, where heating required too much battery power, and an open fire might burn down a yurt or give away a heat signature. Pere hadn't eaten a real hot meal in months. Within a half-hour, the elders gathered.

"They're here in force," El said. "They've cordoned off an entire street, so I don't think they're going anywhere soon. I didn't see any drones, but that's not good news; it just means they're already out searching."

"What are they searching for?" Rophe asked.

"There's only one high priority target here. And even if I'm wrong, we'd better prepare for the worst."

"You don't have the reputation of being far wrong very often, El," mused Barnabas.

"What about personnel?" asked Matthat.

"None visible," said El. "But with four transports, I'd guess a platoon—four squads of hunters, each with trackers in tow."

"Are you sure they're hunters?" asked Rophe.

"That's the best-case scenario," said El. "If they're reapers, that's a . . . well, let's just hope they're not."

"If they are lizards," said the usually quiet Khyoza, "they'll have tanks with them."

"I don't like the sound of that," said Ehud.

"None of us does," sighed Barnabas. "What do you suggest, El? You've dealt with these creatures before. Is there a more effective defense that we haven't considered?"

El thought about it for a long moment. "Our first defense should be stealth. Hope they never discover us and eventually leave. But . . . if we're detected . . . do you have the escape plan ready?"

"You can't be serious!" protested Rophe. "We've been through scares before. We can certainly handle this one . . . Can't we Matthat?"

The MOW commander didn't respond immediately, but just looked at El. "I think we should review the exit plan, Barnabas," he finally said. "Even if we don't end up needing it, there are ninety-one colonists here. We'd be worthless leaders if we didn't consider their safety. What will this platoon's strategy be, El?"

The big man took a deep breath and let it out slowly. "The truth is, if they're searching, it's not for your people, it's for the five of us Catacombers."

Pere knew that wasn't the whole truth. He had come to terms with his fugitive status over the last two years. Though he still didn't know exactly why, he knew they were searching for *him*—it's the reason they came north in the first place. They might snag the others in the dragnet, but *he* was the primary target. Barnabas and the other elders well knew the danger his presence brought to the Colony. And even though they accepted that risk, Pere couldn't reason away the weight of responsibility. 'The safety of our people' Matthat had said. Whenever it was discussed, he felt a vise closing on his heart.

"If they're reapers," El continued, "We'll be their primary targets. If your people get between them and that target, they'll just kill them and move on. So, don't get in their way. Take your people, get on those buses, and run. They won't waste any time following if we're not with you."

They all sat silent for a time staring at the floor. "There are more things to consider here than simply running," Barnabas said, glancing at Peregrine. "Any escape plan needs to take those things into account, or all this will have been for nothing."

"My defensive measures are underway," Matthat finally nodded. "Give me four more days, and we'll have the entire perimeter lined with passive optical reflection sensors. If you don't have the body transmitter when you pass them," he silently mimed an explosion. "At least they'll pay a heavy cost if they cross into our territory."

"What about animals?" asked El.

"They're smart sensors," Matthat said. "They're only keyed to humanoid shapes."

"But will it be enough?" Rophe said quietly.

Pere slept the rest of the morning and into the afternoon. He would have kept sleeping, but Yael came and woke him around 2:30 telling him he'd throw his sleep schedule off if he stayed in bed any longer.

"Noooo," he moaned. "It's warm under these blankets. Do I have to get up?"

"You don't *have* to do anything, I suppose. But you know El's going to come and drag you out if you're not in the combat yurt first thing tomorrow morning. Besides, I brought you something to eat, and a surprise."

"Is it a hot meal? Do you know how long it's been since I had a hot meal?"

"As a matter of fact, I do. The same amount of time it's been for me."

"I know," he realized he was feeling sorry for himself. "But you're better at this than I am. You're better at everything than I am."

"We all do what we have to," she replied. Then she looked at him sympathetically, pulled off her jacket and her boots and climbed into bed next to him, laying her head on his chest and absorbing his body's heat from the blankets. "You know it's not healthy to feel sorry for yourself. Lying in bed all day will just make you depressed. What's this really about?"

"All of these people," he whispered, as he stroked her hair. "The whole Colony's in danger because of me. You heard El. The 'Catacombers' he called us, but you know they're hunting for *me*, Cam, and they'll kill everyone to get me. Barnabas may be able to accept that, but has everyone else up here made that choice? Do all of them even know? *I* don't even know what I'm doing or why I'm doing it; how could they?"

"They haven't been told everything. It would only make life more dangerous for them if they knew. But people are people, Pere. They gossip. They hear stories, and they tell stories. They know we're staying here, but not really living here. They know three warriors have spent almost every waking hour of the last eighteen months training 'that handsome young man'—their words, not mine. They know Barnabas is personally instructing you—and believe me, that doesn't happen. And they know you're hiding because no one ever gets to see you up close. You don't have to be on the Elders' Council to figure out what we're hiding from. Everyone in this movement is aware of the dangers. None of us got in because it was safe.

We all feel called to it."

"But we're just waiting here; and I have no idea what we're waiting for. Do you? We're like sitting ducks waiting for the bird dogs to kill us."

"We're staying hidden and staying hidden is different than waiting to die."

"I'm so tired of running and hiding, especially when I have no idea who I'm hiding from or where I'm running to. If I have to keep running, I should run into town and turn myself in. At least all these people would be safe then." She was quiet for a long time. He thought maybe she had fallen asleep. "Cam?" he said, quietly.

"If you ran into town," she said, and her voice trembled. She wiped her eyes with the back of her hand but wouldn't face him. "You'd be dead, or worse. And, yes, we might be safe, but for how long? Don't you think maybe there's a bigger picture?"

"Some grand plan?"

She turned her head up to face him. "You have to believe in something, Pere!"

"I refuse to believe in any grand plan or a God that lets all these people get killed. I can't! There must be some other way!"

"Please don't run into town. We all need you. . . *I* need you."

He sighed again, deeply. They were quiet for a long time. Finally, he spoke. "Have you ever thought about what our lives would be like if everything was normal? If we didn't have anyone to run from, I mean?"

"Well," she said, after thinking it over, "Maybe we wouldn't have ever met."

"I don't believe that," he said slowly, considering it. "I don't think you do either. I think we would have met no matter what."

"Some grand plan?"

"Ha-Ha. I just think maybe we were meant to be; because, honestly, I don't know what I'd do without you." He touched her hair, gently pushing it back from her face.

"You'd go on," she whispered.

"Destiny?"

"Probably more like stubbornness. But it was a sweet thing to say, for a farm boy."

"Farm boy?" he said, ruefully. "I can barely remember what it was like to be a farm boy. I can remember the hills though. About this time of year, they would get their first spring growth, like a green carpet was laid over them as far as you could see." He sighed, wistfully. "Cam, if we could be anywhere right now, without any fear, free to make any choice, no reapers, or tanks, or drones, where would you want to be?"

"Oh . . . Wow, I don't know, Pere. I try not to think about stuff like that."

"Well, just for today, just for right now, think about it. Where would it be?"

"Okay. Well, I haven't been all over the world; but of all the places I've been, I really liked Big Sur. I remember a cabin there, the way the trees smelled, and the ocean. It's about as perfect a place as I can think of. What about you?"

"Well, I was going to cheat and say, 'wherever you were', but I remember that cabin, and that beach. Those memories aren't very good for me."

"I know. I'm sorry."

"It's not your fault," he whispered. "I asked." She lay there for a long moment listening to his heart. Then she turned her head up again to face him. "I was think- ing, if we ever really get done running, maybe we could go back there, and I could try to make *new* memories for you." She kissed him deeply and his breath caught. Then she smiled at him in that challenging sort of way.

"Was that the surprise you were talking about?"

"Maybe I'm just full of surprises, farm boy," she said. She got up, undid the zipper on her camos and let them drop to the floor. She climbed back under the blankets and pulled them up around them. He put his arms around her and drew her in, then she kissed him long and breathlessly, and the cold Klondike winter was not so cold anymore.

Venison jerky, raw greenhouse vegetables, and dried fruit weren't Pere's idea of a feast, but Cam was there and that made it better. After they finished, they sat and talked.

"So, I still haven't given you all your surprises yet," she said with a mischievous smile.

"Really? I think earlier was a great surprise. Can I get that one again?"

She blushed and went to her jacket, pulling a package out of the pocket. "A courier came in earlier this afternoon. He brought this." She handed the small package to him.

"For me? What is it?"

"Well, if you look closely, you can see that I didn't open it, so I don't know. But the courier did say he'd stopped at the Catacombs."

"No way!" he cried, tearing at the brown paper wrapping. Inside was a good-sized chunk of semi-sweet chocolate, and a folded letter.

"I'll divide the chocolate," she said, "and you read the letter."

"Right," he started to read the letter while she broke up the chocolate.

"Out loud, Einstein!" she chided him.

"Oh, sorry. Okay, let me start again," he cleared his throat as though he was going to give a recital. She giggled and rolled her eyes.

"*Dear JR*," he began. "*Or should I call you Falcon? We're writing this letter together in Silas' rooms, so don't say anything you don't want the others to hear*," he stopped reading for a moment, squinting. Then he turned the letter to Yael. "What's that?" he pointed to a spot.

"It's an emoji." He looked at her dumbly. "People used to put them in messages. That one's a smiley face. It means he's told a joke and you're supposed to take it as funny."

"Why didn't he just say that?"

"He did, with the emoji."

"Oh, okay. Um, where was I? . . . *so don't say anything you don't want others to hear—smiley face—I'm here (your dad said that), with Silas, and Loukas, and Marcus (that's me, I am doing the writing). Barnabas sent word that you're homesick; but it's been snowing a lot here recently, wet, and oozy stuff, so you're not really missing anything. Besides, we hear your training's going very well, and that's more important, so be patient and keep working. Everything will work out in time.*" He paused.

"That's easy for him to say," he growled.

"No editorializing."

"Sorry. *There's been a lot less 'outside activity' here of late, so it may be that the heat's off, as they say. But we need to wait a little longer before we consider moving you back here again. That sounds good,"* he said as he took a bite of chocolate and rolled his eyes as if he were in heaven, then read again with his mouth full of the delicious cocoa elixir. *"We had a very nice Christmas but missed you all terribly."* His voice cracked a little at this and Yael put her hand on his arm. *"Silas and I visited Beth Nevi'im again after the holidays and stayed several weeks; but we're back now and probably will be through Easter. It would be great to hear from you. We all discussed it and we're pretty sure you know how to write—another smiley face, I think—If you can't remember how, ask Yael to show you. Barnabas says she's been very helpful to you—*what's with all the smiley faces?—*Well, we'd better wrap this up; the courier will be leaving in less than an hour. Give our love to El, and Ehud, and Khyoza, and Yael.*

Godspeed,

Dad, et al.

p.s. *This is me, Marcus. Have you popped the question yet?—*And there's *another* smiley face," he said, laying the letter on the table. "What does Marcus mean by 'popped the question'?"

"Who knows?" she answered, blushing again. "Let's write back," she added quickly. "The courier will be moving on tomorrow morning."

"That's a great idea. Let me get some paper."

They stayed up later than usual writing the letter together until finally there was a knock at the door. Ruach popped his head in.

"I didn't see a sock on the doorknob, so I figured it was okay to come in?"

"Why would anyone put a sock on a doorknob?" Pere asked. "To keep it warm?" Yael said nothing but got up quickly and pulled on her IR jacket and boots.

"Product of a misspent youth, I guess," Ruach said, smiling.

"It's fine, Ruach," she said. "I should get back to my yurt anyway. I'll make sure the courier gets this." She picked up the letter and mussed Pere's hair. "Night, farm boy. See ya, Ruach," she said in farewell and then disappeared into the night.

The next morning Pere was at the combat yurt at the appointed time and the routine went on as it had for months; but whether they discussed it or not, everyone knew things were different now. Matthat's preparations for the Colony's perimeter defense carried on apace, and the MOW patrols increased. They now watched the sky twenty-four hours a day and always wore IR camos outside the yurts. Rophe trained three new assistants—in addition to Yael—and Gershom began to inventory the food supply. To Pere's disappointment, Barnabas curtailed their Russian lessons to devote more time to defense planning. Everyone was battening the hatches. A storm was forming and only time would tell if the prevailing winds would blow it their way.

THE GENESIS LIMO PULLED UP to the wrought-iron gates of William Rampart's fog-enshrouded compound on Hunts Point. The gates parted and the burgundy Genesis cruised down the tunneled canopy of perfectly manicured maples, stationed like tall sentinels along the driveway, that ambled through the nearly twenty acres of prime lakefront real estate. Liliane Genevois left Paris-Le Bourget nine hours earlier, but it was the same time now in Puget. She didn't like traveling; foreign food irritated her stomach, and the time change disrupted her circadian rhythms, making her feel peevish—a mood she dared not indulge under the circumstances. In the eleven years since she inherited the Romanov Chair from her father, Liliane had never met the other premieres in person. It simply wasn't done. And now they were having a 'barbecue', as the locals called it, at Rampart's estate. An informal get-together? Nothing could be further from the truth. She would have to wear a very careful mask for the next two days. Checking her flawless reflection in the Limo's vanity mirror, she wondered if her eyes revealed even the slightest flicker of duplicity. The consequences of such a revelation would be extremely unpleasant.

The limo emerged onto an artfully cobblestoned area encircling a massive fountain. The water splashed playfully over Jean De Bologne's sculpture of Apollo, forcing himself on the nymph, Daphne, as she transformed into a tree. The desperately amorous Apollo reminded her of Darien. She flushed warmly at the memory of their last encounter. For years now, she had solicited the services of much younger men who had the stamina to keep up with her. But Darien was different—the wit and cunning of a Spartan general, the sexual prowess of an insatiable Greek god. He exhausted her in the very best of ways. Yes, Darien was a banquet she always relished, but her hunger was never completely satisfied—and she liked it that way. The driver opened her door as two liveried footmen ran to the limo's trunk to retrieve her luggage. A precise, diminutive man in his late thirties, wearing an impeccable three-piece suit, emerged from the carriage house, and walked crisply toward the Genesis.

"Take *Mademoiselle*'s luggage to the Pink Suite," he snapped his fingers at the footmen, then turned to Liliane. "*Bienvenue Mademoiselle*. I hope your flight was pleasant?"

"Passable."

"I am Cavanaugh, the majordomo for Mr. Rampart's estate. Should you require anything during your stay, I will see to it."

"Thank you, Cavanaugh."

He made a small crisp bow. "If you will accompany me, I'll show you to your rooms." As the majordomo led her through the sally port, the three-story manor house came into view, an imposingly elegant gray stone Tudor Revival capped with a high-peaked mottled-green slate roof. Liliane estimated it at a minimum of

4,000 square meters, and that was just above ground. Guests to the estate emerged from the carriage-house sally port and proceeded down the grand walkway with this daunting behemoth staring them in the face. She grudgingly acknowledged that it *was* somewhat impressive. Will Rampart may be a doddering old fool, but he still knew how to portray power. Another grand fountain splashed in the entryway courtyard with Bernini's *Rape of the Sabine Women* at its center. Will was clearly fixated on rape. She didn't really mind the art so much but was sure Elinor Prowell would find it appalling. The Rothschild Chair displayed an almost puritanical aversion when it came to matters of sex. Liliane assumed the poor girl had never been properly laid.

Cavanaugh led her up the main steps, where waiting doormen pulled open the majestically carved entry doors. The palatial three-story oval entry hall boasted two curving grand staircases to the second and third level's east and west wings. The Baccarat crystal chandelier descending from the vaulted ceiling must have weighed several tons and gave the impression of a thousand candles delicately sparkling amid this self-conscious grandeur. *The old man's compensating*, she thought, *for his inability to get it up anymore.*

"Your suite is on the third level," Cavanaugh said. "We will take the elevator if that is acceptable?"

"That will be fine."

They continued through the entry hall to the elevator. Cavanaugh pressed the button and the gold-plated doors opened revealing a plush red-carpeted, hardwood interior. When the majordomo pressed the level-three button, Liliane noticed there were two additional levels below ground. As they ascended, the prim little man informed her of the various services available to her during her stay. It would have been easier just to say, 'your wish is my command', but he seemed so pleased by the sound of his own voice, she chose not to interrupt. He had an odd cadence, or perhaps it was a deliberate non-inflection. She had an excellent ear for accents but could not place his.

They exited on the third level and proceeded through the east wing and down a long, high-ceilinged corridor decorated with medieval French tapestries of noblewomen serenaded by doubleted lute-playing men. They arrived at a set of ornate double doors as the majordomo pushed them open. The massive living room featured a grand stone fireplace flanked by picture windows overlooking Lake Washington. The suite included an opulent sitting room, a bedroom of royal dimensions, with a spacious dressing area (her luggage was already there), and an Etowah marble bathroom, with a spa and a huge step-down tub, already filled with steaming water. An uncorked bottle of Mouton '45 and a single crystal glass sat next to the tub.

"Mr. Rampart wanted you to have a few hours to decompress before dinner," the little man said. "If everything meets with your approval, I'll take my leave. After your bath, I'll send your lady's maid up. Her name is Margaux. There are service buttons all around the suite. Both she and I are on call twenty-four hours a day, should you need anything."

"Thank you, Cavanaugh. I would like a massage before dinner if that can be arranged."

"I will see to it, Mademoiselle. Would you like that immediately, or after your bath?"

"I will bathe first. Send someone in forty minutes, will you?"

"Forty minutes. Will there be anything else."

"That will be all for now."

"Very good," the little man made that same crisp bow and exited the suite. She stood for a moment, looking at the steaming tub and the bottle of Mouton.

"So, the old fool still has some memory left, after all," she murmured. She returned to the dressing area and carefully dropped the digital key behind the armoire as she undressed. She had to be careful since she assumed Rampart had surveillance equipment all over this fortress of his, and that someone was watching her at this very moment. She didn't much mind them seeing her naked. She knew her body was magnificent. It certainly should be after all those painful modified stem-cell treatments for the past twenty years. She was old enough to remember a time when women underwent surgeries to maintain a youthful appearance. How barbarous they were then. She returned to the bathroom, poured herself a glass of the Mouton, and stepped down into the steaming water.

Precisely forty minutes later a knock came. She wrapped herself in a plush rose-colored bathrobe and opened the door. A handsome, well-built young man of perhaps twenty waited in the hallway.

"*Buon pomeriggio, Signorina.*" The young Adonis had a thick Sicilian accent. My name is Cavaddu, and I'm here for your massage."

So, Rampart had discovered her private predilection? Was this a test? Would rejecting this stallion's ministrations arouse suspicion? She decided she would have to play along. Darien would forgive her. And besides, playing along did have its benefits. She opened her robe and let it drop to the floor revealing her lush magnificence. The young man merely smiled.

"Come in my young masseur," she purred. "I would not want to keep you from your work." The Adonis entered the suite, and she closed the door.

Thirty minutes after Cavaddu had left, the lady's maid knocked. Liliane stepped out of her second bath and opened the suite door to find a rather plain-looking young woman waiting outside. She again revised her estimate of Rampart's capabilities; he had selected a maid who represented no rivalry to her beauty. She must be very careful, indeed.

"You must be Margaux."

"*Oui, Mademoiselle,*" the young lady curtsied. "The evening meal begins at 7:45. I am here to help you prepare, if you wish?"

"*Oui*, Margaux. *Entrez.*"

The lady's maid spent the next hour preparing Mademoiselle for the evening meal.

The premiers gathered in the dining room. Liliane looked exquisite in midnight blue velvet with her hair falling in ringlets around her flawless face. The dining room could have seated fifty, but for this occasion fourteen stewards devoted themselves exclusively to the dining and comfort of the seven guests. To his staff, Mr. Rampart was simply an insanely wealthy old man entertaining a group of elite and self-indulgent friends. They knew nothing of the all-powerful Directorate or its seven premiers.

The chief butler and head chef had designed a twelve-course meal of royal distinction. Over the next three hours they ate, drank, talked, and laughed; but never once mentioned the true reason for this gathering. As cordial as it might be for the premiers to get together occasionally, it almost never happened; and only then, in emergencies. Liliane assumed Rampart had organized it, since it was taking place at his estate.

The light conversation seemed unfettered as they ate and drank their way through the sumptuous feast. Liliane carefully tried to gauge her fellow premiers; but they were all too skilled at subterfuge to give anything away. For the final course, they retired to the sitting room for petite fours, coffee, tea, and various digestifs. Gentle flames warmed the great stone fireplace, and Liliane felt very cozy on the divan, and perhaps a little too mellow. She had probably taken more wine than was good for her under the circumstances. The murmur of informal conversations filled the room; Yejide and Elinor sat on the divan across from hers, quietly discussing something—probably the offensive statuary. Sayil and Nicolás smoked cigars by the French doors, which had been opened slightly for ventilation, yet did not seem to be reducing the cigar smoke in the air; Leung Xiang chatted with the two men but didn't smoke. Will, who had been standing next to the fire sipping brandy and observing his guests, made his way to the divan and sat next to Liliane.

"You're looking particularly luscious this evening, my dear," he said unctuously. "Did the meal meet with your approval?"

"It was very nice, Will. I would not have thought you capable of it, to be honest."

"Oh, I'm a very surprising fellow, or don't you remember?"

"I'm sure I don't know what you're talking about," she smiled. "And thank you for the Mouton. It was a nice touch, and very difficult to get anymore."

"So Cavanaugh discovered. But what good is wealth and power if you can't get what you want when you want it?"

"An interesting observation. And just what is it *you* want? This is all very pleasant, but why are we here, Will?"

"What? Great conversation and first-rate food and drink aren't reason enough?"

"No offence, but I could have had both with no strings attached in Paris."

"No offence taken, sweetie. But let's save the strings for tomorrow. Tonight, we should concentrate on pleasure. You don't mind pleasure, do you? I could always arrange another massage if you'd like." He smiled at her, and brazenly admired her *décolletage*.

"Not tonight," she said, forcing a giggle, but no longer feeling cozy.

"Well, perhaps in the morning, then? We could select a different masseur if Cavaddu wasn't attentive enough. And you can always demand to be on top—there was a time when that was how you liked it."

"That will not be necessary. The massage was quite satisfactory." She performed another perfect giggle. What *was* this old wolf up to? And why was he bringing up long-buried mistakes? He was hunting for something, but what? She shouldn't have drunk so much. Rampart smiled swinishly then turned away.

"Oh, dear me. Poor old Nicolás is nodding off," he said. "Perhaps we should call it a night."

She got back to her suite shortly past midnight. Margaux ran a bath and helped Liliane out of her clothing before leaving. She lounged in the tub, considering things. Clearly, Rampart wasn't such an old sot after all. Directorate appointments were for life, unless the six other sitting premiers voted you out. There were no official records of such things, but the scuttle was that as a young man, Rampart practically formed the Consortium and the Directorate singlehandedly. She had assumed he had run out of piss and vinegar years ago and was just hanging on now out of habit rather than true interest. She would have to readjust her thinking. Clearly, he was still a worthy opponent and very much 'in the game'. His memory, unfortunately, was also far too intact. He was baiting her to provoke some kind of response . . . but to what end? Had she maintained a sufficient mask during dinner? She had been too careless. The wine had blunted her caution. Yes, Rampart was watching her for reasons other than simply ogling her breasts; but he had always been a lecherous one—this she knew firsthand. Had he watched the others as closely? She would have to perform very well tomorrow. That would almost certainly mean putting up with that young masseur again in the morning. *D'accord*, the realization of any great victory required sacrifices.

Following her bath, she climbed into the marvelously comfortable bed and slowly drifted toward sleep. She wished she could contact Darien, but that was simply out of the question. She was on her own here, so she would have to quit playing the fool. The truth was, she knew how to wield power with the best of them. In her youth, she had earned a *Très-Bien* dual degree from Pantheon-Sorbonne; and she was, after all, the daughter of Thierry Genevois, and had inherited more than just a fortune from him. He left her his seat on the Directorate and the genes of his prowess as well. Yes, she could play the power game; but sometimes playing the fool was much more effective. For some reason, Will Rampart had only ever seen her as the fool—and had dealt with her accordingly. Perhaps she could use that to her advantage as well. She eventually fell asleep considering all the possible machinations.

A morning knock at the bedroom door woke her. She was feeling a bit delicate from the previous evening's wine and didn't want to get out from under her cozy blankets, so she ignored it. After a few moments, the door opened slightly, and the young Adonis stuck his head in.

"Mr. Cavanaugh said you'd want a morning massage," he said in his accented voice. "Does Mademoiselle wish me to return later?"

She considered it for a moment. "No," she finally sighed. "Mademoiselle wishes you to stay. But close the door and keep quiet, will you?" He followed her instructions and approached the bed, removing his clothing as he came. Without saying another word, he slipped beneath the blankets and proceeded to 'massage' Mademoiselle for the better part of the next hour.

The premiers took brunch on the covered north veranda overlooking Lake

Washington. The brisk morning was surprisingly clear and sunny for the PSM at this time of year. They dined on sweet crepes and frittatas, with coffee or tea, though Nicolás preferred Yerba Mate. After their meal, Cavanaugh appeared on the veranda and whispered to Rampart, who then suggested they move indoors to talk before everyone departed.

Finally, Liliane thought, *we'll pull the curtain back on this charade.*

Cavanaugh led the guests through the ground level of the manor house to Rampart's personal office suite, where they approached a set of varnished red sandalwood doors. The majordomo then removed a small chain from around his neck, upon which hung a single exquisite skeleton key. He inserted the key in the lock. The sound of a motor hummed beneath them and after a few moments, Cavanaugh opened the doors revealing an elevator. He gestured to the guests to enter. Once inside, he pulled the outer doors closed, the inner slid shut automatically and they descended. After several long moments of silent waiting, the doors opened revealing an elegantly decorated office suite. Cavanaugh proceeded to Américo's painting, *David and Abishag*, which hung on the wall behind an ornate desk. He gently swung the painting away from the wall, revealing a safe from which he extracted a small tray and placed it on the desk.

"If you all would deposit any electronic or mobile communications devices in this tray," he said. "I assure you they will be protected and remain absolutely untouched during the meeting." William Rampart crossed to the desk and deposited two devices and his watch in the tray. The others hesitated.

"I'm not comfortable with this, Will," Yejide said cautiously.

"Nor I," Elinor concurred. "Why should we be deprived of our COM links?"

"As I understand it," Will reassured them. "They could be damaged, perhaps irreparably, when we enter the quiet room. I'm just looking out for you, doll."

"What do you mean by quiet room?" Nicolás asked.

"Tell them, Cavanaugh," Will said.

"The quiet room you'll be entering is a secure space," the majordomo told them. "Where no mobile communications device will operate, and that no electronic surveillance technology can penetrate. Your mobile devices may be damaged by the jamming technology inside the room, so we are only taking this precaution for your convenience."

"And why do we need to meet in such a place?" Sayil asked. "What are you up to, Will?"

"Why don't we save that discussion until we're inside," Will said. "But what I've got to tell you will be worth a little aggravation." They still hesitated, until Yejide broke the ice.

"Oh, very well," she said, crossing to the desk and depositing her devices in the tray. "But this had better be good, Will."

"Trust me," the old man said with an assured smile. "You won't be sorry."

The others then placed their devices in the tray, which Cavanaugh returned to the safe. Once he'd secured the door and the painting, he led the guests to a second set of red sandalwood double doors. When he pulled the doors open, Liliane expected to see a hardened bunker of some sort, but instead gasped at the magnificent oval boardroom within. A breathtaking chandelier hung from the ceiling over a highly polished oval mahogany burl conference table that formed the centerpiece of the room. The walls were paneled in dark walnut and two paintings hung opposite each other: Klimt's *Danaë*, and Boucher's early version of *Leda and the Swan*. Liliane would have laughed at Elinor's repulsion, but she was none too comfortable herself at being trapped in this quiet room. The premiers chose seats around the conference table as Cavanaugh closed the doors and inserted his skeleton key into a panel. The sound of a lockdown was unmistakable, and disconcerting. He then turned and nodded to Rampart.

"Alrighty then," said Will, as he sat at the head of the table at the far end of the room. "Now we can talk freely."

"What the devil is this about, Will?" said Nicolás, with some heat.

"Yes," said Sayil. "I think you owe us an explanation."

"That's putting it mildly," said Yejide. "You're on very shaky ground here, Will. You don't want this entire body angry at you."

"And why is your servant still here?" said Liliane. "How can we speak freely before unsanctioned ears?"

"And really, Will," fumed Elinor. "Must we be incessantly bombarded by images of rape all over your estate?"

They all chafed as William Rampart merely looked at them. "That's not really fair, buttercup," he finally said to Elinor. "David never raped Abishag; she just kept him warm. To be frank, I find the artworks invigorating. I am an old man, after all, and they remind me of a certain prowess I once had that the years have slowly taken from me. We all have our little private amusements, don't we? Besides, I think your shock's a little hypocritical, Elinor. None of my artworks involves whips. Maybe you'd like it better if they did."

"How dare you," said the Rothschild Chair, blushing furiously.

"Oh, be still, sweet tits," said the old man. "I couldn't care less what your diversions are. As a good host, I only care that they're satisfied. I hope you've all been satisfied this weekend. After all, why should we resist our impulses? Who can tell us they're unacceptable? Should we continue to be disciplined and punished by a defunct moral dogma that stopped being useful decades ago? We remade that construct, and we should operate like we understand that."

"But Will," Xiang interrupted, uncomfortably. "Should you really be saying all this if front of your majordomo?"

"Well, here's the thing, Xiang," Rampart said with a calculating smile. "He's not really my majordomo. Cavanaugh, I suppose you should go ahead and start the shitstorm." Everyone's gaze turned to the prim little man still standing at the door. He put the chain back around his neck, tucked the key inside his shirt, and came and sat at the head of the table opposite Rampart.

"Allow me to reintroduce myself to you all," he said. "And I apologize for the earlier subterfuge. I assure you; it was necessary. My name is Jonas Cavanaugh, but I am *not* Mr. Rampart's majordomo; I am the head of his worldwide security concerns; and it was at my suggestion that he invited you here this weekend." There was a general eruption of disapproval.

"This is outrageous," fumed Elinor. "Explain."

"I fully intend to, Madam Premier," said Cavanaugh. "After Robert Percival's escape from enhanced-security detention almost two years ago, Mr. Rampart tasked me with the discovery of his whereabouts, as well as those of the so-called anomaly, John Percival, and the rogue phantoms, Quade and Zakayev. My extensive search discovered virtually nothing in the way of a digital trail, except for the withdrawal of a massive sum from a slush fund that the sénéschal had established for Zakayev. Since the sénéschal had not withdrawn the funds himself, the only other person who could have, was Zakayev, who has since disappeared."

"Darien already told us all this, Will," complained Yejide.

"Context, Yejide, context," Will said. "Go on, Jonas."

"As I dug deeper into the matter," Cavanaugh continued. "I became aware of tiny abnormalities in the protocols I use to track potential threats. At first, I thought the variations might lead me to the so-called anomaly, but instead I discovered a very well-hidden set of trans-digital inquiries that led, very covertly, back to each of you."

"What the devil are you saying?" interrupted Nicolás. "Put it in terms I can understand."

"Pardon me, Mr. Premier," Cavanaugh replied calmly. "To speak plainly, I've come to the conclusion that each of you is the subject of a very skillfully orchestrated long-term surveillance project."

"What?" sputtered Sayil. "Are you certain?"

"As certain as I can be under the circumstances."

"But why would anyone do such a thing?" said Liliane with mock astonishment. "And *how* could they?"

"As to the first question, I don't know, yet. But I intend to find out. As to the second question," he paused and looked to Rampart.

"Aside from the seven of us," the old man said. "To my knowledge, there are only two other people in the world who are completely read in on our true identities. I hope you'll pardon me, but Cavanaugh is one of them—because I trust him completely, and I needed someone I could trust when I began to have doubts a few years back about the long-term stability of our endeavor. Now, I'm laying all my cards on the table here, so let's y'all do the same; have any of you revealed your alter-egos to anyone outside this room?" After a tense moment of silence, they all shook their heads. "Well, if that's the case, then it leaves only one possibility."

"The sénéschal?" said Liliane, not really needing to fake her shock anymore. How did Rampart know so much? And if this little ferret of his had guessed about

Darien, what did he suspect of *her*?

"That's preposterous, Will," said Elinor. "Why would Darien do such a thing?"

"Listen, honey, like Jonas said, it's been almost two years since Percival's escape, and our sénéschal has bat guano to show for himself in all that time. It wouldn't take an idiot to know that we're not thrilled with his performance of late—and that slick Greek's no idiot."

"Are you suggesting," said Xiang, calmly. "That Darien is surveilling us in order to find out if we're going to replace him?"

"That's part of what I'm suggesting," said Will.

"But to what end?" said Xiang. "If we were to take a vote of no-confidence today, how could that information possibly aid him?"

"I think we can assume only one thing," interrupted Cavanaugh. "A preemptive strike."

They sat in shocked silence as Cavanaugh's words sank in. Finally, Yejide spoke. "You believe Darien would attack us to prevent his removal? That's very farfetched, Will, even for you. He's always served us well and been utterly devoted to this body. You're asking us to accept a great deal here on slim to no proof. Are you absolutely certain that this surveillance is occurring, and if it is, that Darien is behind it?"

"Not yet, Yejide, but you'd probably agree that this is not the sort of thing we want to stick our heads in the sand about. If history's any indicator, folks bumping off their betters to grab power is a pretty old story. Cavanaugh thinks our Darien may be using that Haruspex thing of his to gather intel on us. And if he's doing that, what other reason would he have?"

"Well, if that *is* the case, he has certainly exceeded the parameters we agreed to for this project," said Xiang. "But he has always been proactive in his decision-making—it is what has made him so effective. Is it possible he is protecting us *from* the anomaly?"

"Well, that's another thing," said Will. "This whole idea of a so-called anomaly came from Gianakos in the first place. According to him, his fortune-telling machine determined the Percival kid was a threat; but what proof do we have—other than his word—that there even is such an anomaly? It certainly has made for a nice distraction. What if it's all a smokescreen to keep our eyes off his real plan, and this kid is just a kid?"

"All speculation and innuendo, Will," said Elinor, shaking her head. "You've made no attempt to hide your displeasure with Darien for quite some time; but *I'm* unwilling to take action against him without more definitive proof."

"I'm not suggesting we should... yet. What I *am* suggesting is that all of you beef up your security protocols until Cavanaugh can pin this down. And you also might want to alter your usual routines just to be on the safe side."

"I refuse to live as a prisoner," said Elinor.

"Well, if you don't change things up a little, sweetheart, you may not live at all."

They were all silent again as that statement made its intended impact. Finally, Cavanaugh broke the silence. "I assure you all that I will continue to explore every possibility. However, it's unreasonable for Premier Rockefeller to ask you to trust me on his word alone, so I've prepared copies of my dossier so you may become better acquainted with my qualifications and skills." He passed around six documents that smelled of mimeograph ink.

"You couldn't have texted us your vita?" asked Yejide, wrinkling her nose.

"Under the present circumstances, I think that would be unwise," Cavanaugh said. "I can only speculate at Haruspex's full capabilities; but we live in a fully integrated digital information world, Madam. Haruspex has access to every interconnected technology on the planet. I have therefore chosen as a counterstrategy to go medieval. If information is neither digitalized nor photocopied, Haruspex will not be able to gain access to it. And if Gianakos is using Haruspex to gather intelligence on you, we'll need to be very careful about our correspondence in the future. At Mr. Rampart's insistence, I have organized a group of fast couriers who will carry handwritten messages in-person to and from each of you. I strongly recommend you burn all such communiqués immediately after reading them. There is a flash incinerator in the outer office for my dossiers once you've perused them." Everyone seemed a little stunned, but they all looked over Cavanaugh's qualifications.

Five minutes later, Rampart broke the silence. "Well, I think we've gone about as far as we can here for now, unless any of you has something else to say?" No one spoke. They seemed a bit overwhelmed. "I'm sure you can all understand why we should keep this just between us for now. I'll keep you informed of our progress. Cavanaugh will take you all back to your suites for any last-minute stuff before you leave. Have a safe trip and keep your heads down."

"I'm aware that all of you have flights scheduled," Cavanaugh said. "Your drivers are waiting at the carriage house. If you'll follow me, I'll show you to your suites."

Darien Gianakos sat behind the Resolute Desk reviewing his most recent intelligence reports when the satellite pager he always kept with him went off. He rose from the desk, crossed to the wall safe, and retrieved the phone. He opened the command COM center, plugged the phone in, and dialed a number. After three rings there was an answer.

"Voice Identification please?"

"*It was a bright cold day in April, and the clocks were striking thirteen,*" the sénéschal recited.

There was a pause. "Identification confirmed."

"What is it, Minerva?"

"Our digital key has picked the lock of Rampart's fortress. Have a look." The screen lit up. "This was recorded at 8:50 a.m. Puget time."

The sénéschal tilted his head slightly to get a better angle of Liliane Genevois frolicking heatedly with a young man. He studied the fervent encounter for a long moment before he spoke. "She's really very good at that, you know?"

"She should be, after more than fifty years of almost incessant practice."

"That young?"

"There *are* stories."

"Hmm. She does have a healthy appetite, doesn't she?"

"Her appetite would have declined years ago if not for those modified stem-cell treatments. An unfortunate side effect."

"Oh, I don't know. I rather like that side effect."

"I've noticed."

"You disapprove? That's catty of you, you know."

"I neither approve nor disapprove. It's simply an observation."

"Yes, well, I think my private activities with Mademoiselle Genevois could stand a little less observation on your part."

"Suit yourself. But it *will* be more difficult to protect you, if I can't keep an eye on you."

He considered that for a moment. "Perhaps you're right," he said finally. "I suppose my secrets are safe with you . . . they *are* safe, aren't they?"

"Impregnable, Darien."

"Humor? Isn't that a bit out of character?"

"One should never take oneself too seriously."

The sénéschal considered the situation. "What other information have you retrieved from their little soirée? I'm sure after-hours 'activities' aren't the only thing happening at Rampart's estate."

"That's where you're wrong. All of yesterday was spent entertaining the visiting premiers. Rampart spared no expense in servicing his colleagues, and his intelligence on each premier's peculiar whims was extraordinary."

"Hmm. Perhaps you should investigate how he's getting all that extraordinary intelligence."

"I'm already on it."

"What else do you have?"

"They had a late breakfast on Rampart's north veranda, and then went back into the manor house and into Rampart's office suite."

"And then?"

"That's all. I've been unable to get anything for the last thirty minutes."

"How do you explain that? I thought you said the key worked."

"I did, and it did. I can only conclude that Rampart's got some kind of anti-surveillance location on his grounds where they're meeting as we speak."

The sénéschal sighed thoughtfully. "I don't like the sound of that."

"It *is* disconcerting."

"Fortunate, then, that we've got someone on the inside."

"Agreed. But your little plaything can be flighty, particularly when she's had too much to drink."

"Don't be insulting."

"Again, just an observation, Darien."

"Sometimes I think you're too well informed."

"No, you don't. My intelligence gathering skills are the very reason you selected me for this operation."

"Point taken," he sighed. "What do you suggest our next move be?"

There was silence on the other end. "I suggest we continue on schedule," Minerva finally said. "But very, very carefully."

The sénéschal considered that before he spoke. "All right, then, we'll move forward with the operation. Keep me informed on any developments."

"I intend to."

"And what about our other problem?" the sénéschal said. "You were running down some tantalizing clues. Has anything come of them?"

"I believe we may be getting very close. My instincts tell me we're in the right neighborhood. I'll let you know when I have something definite."

"Do. It would be a dire mistake to forget about the anomaly because we have our eyes elsewhere."

"But you should know by now, Darien. I have eyes everywhere."

The sénéschal smirked. "'*Pride goeth before a fall*'. Or haven't you heard that proverb?"

"A meaningless bit of drivel, as far as I'm concerned."

"Yes, I've always felt the same way myself. Is there anything else?"

"Not at this time."

"Very well. I look forward to our next conversation." And he disconnected the link.

He was not christened Jonas Cavanaugh at birth, but it served William Rampart's plans to give him that identity. His Glaswegian mother, an underclass addicted teenager, named him Angus Owen and, after five years of aimless motherhood, abruptly abandoned him to the streets a month after his sixth birthday and disappeared. Rather than lay down and die, the wily street urchin attached himself to the toughest gang in Greater Pollok and began what would have become a stellar criminal career had he not been swept up in a pick-pocket sting when he was eight. He'd been detained in a youth rehabilitation center for seven months when his 'keepers' told Angus some important people had asked to meet him. These people ran an exhaustive battery of tests on the young rogue, then paid a huge sum to the director of the facility, and simply walked out one night with the boy in tow. That was twenty-eight years ago, and his patron turned out to be the extremely wealthy and reclusive William Rampart.

He brought young Angus to the Hunts Point estate and, for all intents and purposes, adopted him. No official papers were ever filed on the adoption, and all traceable records that Angus Owen had ever existed were carefully destroyed. He spent the next thirteen years being educated and trained on the estate grounds by various tutors. At the end of that time, he was fluent in six languages—two of them ancient, had the equivalent of two PhDs, and had mastered multiple modes of combat, including Sambo, Silat, and Krav Maga. Then the real training began, when Rampart took him under his vast wing, and taught him the 'family business'. He learned to see and hear everything that might be useful, without ever really being seen or heard himself. Gianakos had his phantoms, but Rampart had created a master-ghost named Jonas Cavanaugh, and he was far more effective than a score of simple killing machines could ever be.

The prim little man saw the last of the premiers chauffeured away from the estate. Liliane Genevois, the Romanov Chair, seemed distracted as she got into the Burgundy Genesis limousine. He slapped the top of the limo twice, and the driver pulled away down the maple-lined drive. He smiled knowingly. She had good reason to be distracted. She had entertained Gianakos at her Paris château three times in the past four months. It may have been coincidence—her ravenous appetite was no secret; but the stakes were too high to rely on coincidences—he needed certainty. So, he planted a monitoring nano-device on her . . . well, more specifically, in her. The masseur had been the delivery system—ingenious really because she would never suspect *he* had been the syringe. Within three weeks, he would have the full picture of Genevois, and then he would act. He walked back into the sally port. Mr. Rampart was expecting a full report in the quiet room. He would not keep his father waiting.

The Dassault Falcon touched down at Paris—Le Bourget in the cold dawn. Liliane disembarked and approached her awaiting Renault limousine. She wanted nothing more than to get back to her château, take a long hot bath, and sleep. The Dassault's stewards ran along behind and loaded her luggage into the limo's trunk. Mademoiselle waited for one of the stewards to open the rear door and she climbed inside. The steward shut the door and Liliane closed her eyes and laid her head back on the plush headrest.

"*Prends-moi à la maison*, Léon. *Je suis épuisée!*"

"We have one stop to make first, Mademoiselle."

Liliane's eyes shot open. The driver was not Léon. She was about to scream, when he put a finger to his lips and handed her a handwritten note. She snatched it and read quickly and silently: *Please do not say a word. We are being watched. You are completely safe.* She considered the possibilities for a moment. Why would Rampart's little imp already be sending her notes? She could refuse, of course, but that would only raise suspicions. She sighed and nodded curtly to the driver, who turned around and raised the black glass partition. As he drove out of the airport, Liliane Genevois began to feel very drowsy. When she finally realized her tiredness was unnatural, it was too late—she was slipping into unconsciousness.

She slowly woke, lying on a bed somewhere other than her château. Raising her head stiffly, she scanned the room. Sitting in an armchair near the footboard was Darien Gianakos. She laid her head back on the pillow and sighed in relief.

"You did not have to kidnap me, darling," she mumbled, still a little groggy from the sedative. "All you needed to do was ask. Although I think this might be a very interesting game. What happens next? Do you force yourself upon me? Do it now, before I am fully awake. That will be more fun." Darien didn't reply right away, so she raised her head and looked at him again. He was not smiling. "What is it, Darien?"

"Things have taken a serious turn, Liliane."

"What do you mean?"

"Rampart had a monitoring device implanted in you. You were being tracked and listened to." Liliane sat up in shock and pulled the blankets closely around her. For one of the few times in her life, she felt violated and vulnerable. "Don't worry," the sénéschal continued. "My techs were very careful to make sure the device 'malfunctioned', so there will be no suspicion of tampering. But it was a very close thing. Fortunately, we discovered it during a passive scan you underwent while preparing for departure at Boeing Field."

"But how?" Liliane said, still in shock. "And why?"

Darien sat back, studying Liliane. "We can speculate on the how. You either consumed it with a meal, or it was injected into you unawares. It seems most likely that your . . . ah . . . young Sicilian plaything was equipped in more extravagant ways than you noticed."

She blushed unexpectedly. "I assumed you would have your ways of knowing. I am sorry, *mon amour*. I did not know what else to do."

"Completely understandable," he said with a wave of his hand. "You, quite literally, took one for the team . . . or was it two?" She meekly raised two fingers. "Yes, well, in any case, the why is more problematic. If all the premiers were tagged, I'd say that conniving old bastard is playing a very dangerous but shrewd game. On the other hand, if you were the only target, then we have a rather more significant problem to consider."

"But how will we know?"

"We were able to track your weekend very effectively until yesterday morning, when you disappeared for more than half an hour. Why was that?"

"Will took us down an elevator to a place he called a 'quiet room'. He would not discuss things freely until we were there." She looked calculatingly at the sénéschal.

"He suspects you are plotting against the Directorate, and he warned us all to be aware of surveillance by you. He wants to move against you; but you still have supporters who are not yet prepared to remove you. Nevertheless, you are going to be under very intense scrutiny. Or perhaps I should say *we* are. That old man has more going for him than I gave him credit for."

"Not I, my dear. You're relatively new to this august body. But I've been around long enough to know full well, that wily old fox has cunning to spare."

"He has an obsequious little man working for him, Jonas Cavanaugh, who seems to be the source of his information. We thought he was the estate manager, but Rampart had him introduce himself later as the head of his world security concerns."

"Interesting. I wondered where he got his intel. He must be very good. We'll have to dig into this Jonas Cavanaugh's background, won't we? What else did he say?"

"That he has a group of couriers in place around the world that will carry hand-written messages to and from the premiers—they are to be destroyed at once after we read them. He seemed to feel that was the safest mode of communication. I assumed the note in my limousine today was from him."

"Hmm. Very smart, really. Our dear old Rampart's going to be a difficult rat to trap. We'll have to step up our game. It sounds as though he's been forming his own security force on the sly. Very smart indeed."

"What are we going to do, Darien? What if I am the only one he is watching? Do you think he knows? . . . About us, I mean?"

The sénéschal was quiet for a moment as he considered it. "It's possible," he finally admitted. "If they've been surveilling us, they know we've met occasionally. But that, in and of itself, is not proof of anything other than your very healthy libido and my imprudent willingness to take advantage of it. That's probably why you were tagged, to discover if there's anything more to it than that. We haven't been as careful as we ought. For the time being, we'll only meet here."

"Where is here?"

"We're in our own secure house outside Paris. Completely untraceable."

"Are you sure?"

"Quite."

"I do not like this, darling. I do not like it at all. What are we going to do?"

"The same thing we've been doing. The plan is progressing on schedule—let's not alter that trajectory unless we must. Too many unforeseen consequences crop up when you start to tinker. As you say, I still have support in the Directorate. If Rampart had irrefutable evidence, he'd have already played that card. No, he's still fishing, and we must be quite certain he catches nothing. The other premiers will continue to back me unless they smell blood in the water. But this Cavanaugh fellow concerns me. My source made no mention of him—and that strikes me as odd, since he already seems to be a high-stakes player." He sighed and stared at the ceiling, weighing options. He finally looked back at her. "Though it pains me to say it, *ma chérie*, I think it best I return to Reykjavík at once. Léon is waiting for you in the kitchen. The old dear is terribly concerned about you. When you're ready, he'll take you back to the château. I think it best if we take a page from Rampart's playbook and keep all our correspondence in hand-delivered notes for the time being. Until I get to the bottom of this Cavanaugh issue, I'm going to leave some people behind to keep an eye on you. Please don't think of it as bondage. You'll never even see them. I simply want to make sure you can still move about freely without being observed. . . or worse."

"You make it sound positively frightening, Darien."

"Just being cautious, Liliane. Very, very cautious."

"Well, if you say so," she said reluctantly, lying back in the bed. "But could you at least welcome me home properly before you leave? After all, I am already in bed, and undressed, and still uninhibited from the sedative. I would be a very willing conquest."

"When have you ever been inhibited, my dear," he smiled, as he stood up and began unbuttoning his shirt.

4

A WIND FULL OF VOICES screamed at him relentlessly, and cast stinging snow pebbles into his face as he rode north along an icy swale of hard pack that would have been marshland in deep summer. He moved from lowland to lowland, avoiding ridges where they might spot him against the horizon. He knew he hadn't lost his pursuers. His exhausted horse refused to give in. Though snow and wind seemed his enemies, they were the only things keeping the hounds off his scent. But they were back there somewhere, following, tireless. He couldn't run forever;

he had to find cover soon. But where in this godforsaken wasteland was there any place to hide?

He emerged from the last frozen trough onto a flat open icepack that stretched for miles. He nearly wept. His horse had slowed to a shamble, and now he'd have to cross this killing field. To make matters worse, it had finally stopped snowing and a cold blue sky broke through the tattering cloud cover. He'd be easily seen now, a dark spot against the vast whiteness. He bowed his head in exhaustion. When would he be able to stop running? Then, a piercing cry broke the new stillness. He looked to the south and a great eagle rose above the horizon, silhouetted in the low sun. For an instant, he hoped the majestic bird would save him. Then a black cloud rose behind the eagle moving inexorably toward him. As it grew closer, he realized it was no cloud, but droves of ravens, their beaks dripping with the clotted blood and flesh-bits of rotting corpses. They had grown fat on the eagle's killing, but their hunger would not be sated until they consumed this last meal.

As the ravens neared, he caught the sun glinting off myriad beaks, like strange sparkling diamonds against a black curtain; and then he understood—these beaks were metal, thousands of razor-sharp steel beaks plunging toward him. He would die today; he suddenly knew it. The razor-birds would carve his flesh until there was nothing but bone, and then the snows of eons would seal his wind-scoured bones in ice. He would never be warm again.

Pere woke shivering, then exhaled in relief. A dream. Another dream. He pulled a small thin Moleskine notebook out from under his pillow, grabbed the flashlight and pen from his tiny bedside table and wrote the dream down. He'd tried to make a habit of it since Silas asked him, but it wasn't easy. Usually when he woke from a dream, the first thing he wanted to do—after he realized it wasn't real—was go back to sleep. But he had tried over the last two years to discipline himself into writing them down.

He was often amazed when he read the journal later at how little he remembered in the waking world. Most of his dreams were ridiculous. Some of them were down-right hilarious, like the one of him and El drinking beer and smoking cigarettes at a 1920s speakeasy—like that would ever happen. Ehud was the bartender; but in the dream, he still had both his hands, and only one eye, a black patch covering the other. Cam was on the stage singing a sultry song and moving her hips in a very appealing way (though he didn't write that part down). When he told her about it the next day, she had only laughed and said, "In your dreams, farm boy, and only in your dreams."

As he wrote the eagle dream down, he realized it was already fading from his memory. Once a week he gave the journal to Barnabas to read. It was embarrassing, but he seemed to feel it was important, so Pere continued. He yawned and put the pen and flashlight back in their place and the journal under his pillow. One impression remained with him, though, the sense of being cold. He shivered, pulled the blankets up tight around his neck and tried to go back to sleep. It was slow in coming, but eventually he nodded off.

The frozen rigging lines scoured his raw hands as he groped his way across the deck of the old, battered fishing trawler. The wind howled and the undulating mountainous swells of the wild, inky sea threatened to swallow the pitching vessel. Salty frigid seawater sprayed in his eyes, stinging him nearly to blindness. He struggled along, his numb fingers feeling the way, trying to find a hatch so he could get below decks, but there seemed to be no entry. He was alone on this vast sea, aboard a ship he'd never seen before. At any moment he'd be swept overboard and sink into the blind depths to be devoured by unseeing fish. His bones would lie abandoned in the icy blackness for eternity. He would never be warm again. Meaningless, everything was so meaningless. His hand finally fumbled across the hatch handle. He yanked and the door gave way. Scrambling inside, he pulled the hatch closed, locking the handle. He gasped for air as he wiped the stinging brine from his eyes and pushed back his dripping hood. The storm continued in its fury, but at least it was outside now.

In the galley below, he could make out the dim glow of a lantern. Creeping down the steps into the open area, he found the floor and chairs of the galley littered with the mutilated bodies of his friends. El slouched on a bench, his neck raggedly cut, his shirt drenched in blood; Ehud and Khyoza lay face down on the floor, blood swirling around their bodies, mixing with the shifting bilge; Barnabas sat in a chair, his head on the tabletop, blood running freely from his mouth as his body swayed back and forth with the roll of the ship. Rophe sat across from Barnabas, her head pitched back, her face bruised and swollen, and her jaw clearly shattered, her eyes still open, but glazed in a dull stare of death. Her abdomen had been ripped open, her hands still clutched at her middle, as though even in death she was trying to hold her entrails inside. He searched desperately through the shadowy cabin; then he saw her. Seated on the floor leaning against a dim corner, a single clean puncture hole in her chest, Cam was barely able to hold her head up, barely alive. Her fading eyes caught his in the wan light and, with her last strength, she mouthed the words, "Why, Pere? Why did you kill us?" He looked down at his hands and realized he held the falcon blade, its point dripping with her blood. He started to scream.

He woke with Ruach shaking him.

"Bad dream?"

"The worst," he said, sitting up. "Was I acting weird?"

"You were screaming, but kind of muted; like a screamy moan. I thought I should wake you up."

"Thanks. I'm glad you did. Now I've got to write it down," he grabbed the pen and started to scribble. "Those are the kind I wish I could forget. What time is it?"

"Morning . . . ish. I just got in from night patrol," he said, yawning. "I'll probably hit the sack now."

"Great," he said, rubbing his eyes. "Boy, it would be nice once in a while to get a good night's sleep."

"We don't always get to choose, do we?" He unzipped his snow camos and sat on his bunk to deal with his boots.

"What am I complaining about? You were out all night on patrol. I'm sorry. What'd you see on the circuit? Anything new?"

"Same old, same old. Maybe a few more flyovers than the last time I was out."

"It's been five weeks. You'd think they'd have the good sense to give up by now. To pack it in and leave."

"Wishful thinking. They're being very thorough. Got a burr up the ass about something."

"You can say it, Ruach. It's me."

"Maybe yes, maybe no. You can't know for certain. And it does no good speculating. Just keep your head down, I say. It's worked so far."

"Keep your head down! That's everyone's advice. It's driving me crazy."

"Should I call Yael so she can rock you back to sleep?"

"Very funny," he sighed. "I've got to get up anyway. El wants me at the C-yurt by 7:30 for a full-day workout."

"Heavy lies the crown, mate."

"Yeah, but I never asked for a fucking crown," he sighed, getting up and pulling his hair together into a topknot. He ate some dried fruit and a protein-fiber bar and pulled on his camos and boots while Ruach got ready for bed. It was still dark outside when he got to the empty C-yurt. He turned on the lanterns, changed into his workout gear, and sat on the mat with his bokken, staring at himself in the wall mirror, wondering who, or what he really was. Why would he dream of killing his friends? He didn't have long to brood before the door opened and Khyoza stepped down into the yurt.

"You are early, Falcon."

"I couldn't sleep."

"Maybe we need to work you harder, so you will be more tired at night."

"El and Ehud and you! Is that your answer to everything? Work harder!" He knew he was sounding like a snotty child, but it was impulse, not performance. He had just killed this man in his dream, and he felt confused and guilty.

Surprisingly, Khyoza didn't respond in kind. "I am sorry, Peregrine," he said quietly. "It is the only way I have ever known since I was seven years old." He sat down on the mat facing Pere. "I know it sometimes comes off as hard-hearted, the way we talk to you, the way we work you, but we are only trying to make you tougher—to prepare you. Sometimes I think we go too far, but El'zar says no."

Pere sighed. "No, he's right. I'm acting like a kid. I'm sorry I took it out on you."

"Who else should you take it out on?" he shrugged.

"I don't know," he was a little surprised. "I shouldn't take it out on anyone, should I?"

"Why not? We are the ones who torture you, day after day. I am surprised sometimes you do not tell us to fuck off."

"But . . . I know you're helping me. Why would I do that?"

"You are a human. Everyone needs to let it out sometimes. Do you think because you are the Falcon you must be perfect?"

"Kind of," he had to admit after considering it.

"Now that *is* like a kid. You are ashes and dust like the rest of us."

"But everyone is depending on me," he nearly whined it. "Everyone's helping me stay alive, even though they could die doing it. And we don't even know why!"

Khyoza was silent for a moment, just looking at Pere. "Do you remember what you said to me when I came to kill you in that cabin two years ago?" he finally asked. Pere shook his head. "You said you would be a leader to me—at least for a time."

"Oh, right. You see what I mean? Even you are depending on me."

"Not so. I remind you because you seem in need of context. We all need to see the big picture sometimes. I did not want this thing at first—to follow you, and El'zar, and the others. But I have come to realize it is my best calling. We all must do what we are called to do. That or run. But I do not think we could ever run far enough to escape from ourselves. The part of ourselves we run from always catches up, does it not?"

"You're saying that I should just do what I must?"

"Yes and no. I am saying that you are only one piece of the puzzle, not the whole thing. You cannot bear the responsibility for the cut of my piece, only your own. Do not think of yourself as so great that you can complete the whole by yourself. We all have a part to play, Falcon."

"I hadn't thought of it in that way."

"Even the keystone in an arch is nothing without the springers to support it."

"Well, you lost me on that one. But I think what you're saying is, I don't really have a choice."

"Do not be a fool! We all have a choice. I am saying *choose* to do what you must. There is a difference. Do you not think so? Besides, maybe there are rewards for making the right choice. I said to you that I did not want this thing at first. But ever since I chose this path, though it has been difficult, I have never known such quiet within myself. Do not take that reward from me by seeking to bear my burden. You have enough to think about already without trying to think my thoughts."

It finally got through to him. He'd believed all this time that he was dragging scores of colonists to their deaths; but all of them, himself included, were following their own paths, together. Any one of them could choose not to take that path. But *they* had chosen—he hadn't chosen for them. He hardly had the power to get himself out of bed in the morning. How could he be so self-centered to think he could make anyone else's choice? For some reason that took a huge load off. He could breathe again.

"Thank you, Sparrow," he said simply. "You should talk more often. You have good things to say."

"Maybe sometimes yes, maybe sometimes no," he shrugged. "You people in the west always talk too much. Even when you do not have anything worthwhile to say, you still talk. 'Blah-blah-blah' is what you call it. I think it is maybe you do not like silence so much."

"Fair enough," he smiled at the usually taciturn Cossack.

"Did Stepan ever tell you what my old name, Lecha, means in my native Chechen?"

"No, why would he?"

"Because it means 'falcon'. That is why I was shocked that day. The falcon would lead the falcon, and the falcon would give the falcon a new name?"

Pere looked at him with questioning eyes. "A coincidence?"

"Maybe. Like the coincidence of you choosing a sword that had your name on it before you knew what your name was? Yes, Ehud told me this story. Or the coincidence of you already knowing the code to your father's cell, even though I had no way with that worm to open it. Yes, Stepan told me as much. I think when so many coincidences start to line up, maybe we should not view them as mere chance, but as something foreordained."

"But I have no idea what I'm doing—what we're doing! We're running at full speed in the dark. When are we going to fall off a cliff?"

"But we are not running in the dark. We are moving from place to place as the path becomes lit. Be patient. When it is time to move again, we will move."

"I guess so," he finally gave in with a sigh. "I'll try, anyway. Thanks again. You seem to be talking me off the ledge today. Is that a coincidence, too?"

"Perhaps that is why I could not sleep either." He might have smiled, but Pere couldn't tell. "I do not think you need to tell El I said these things to you. He will think I am babying you."

"Was he hatched, cold-blooded, from an egg?"

"Probably a snake's egg." Pere laughed and then the door opened. It was El and Ehud.

"What's so funny?" asked El.

"I was telling Khyoza about my dream," Pere lied smoothly. "You and I were drinking beers and smoking cigarettes at a bar where Ehud was the bartender."

"Like that would ever happen," snorted El.

"I do not know, El'zar," Ehud said, smiling. "It sounds fun to me."

"We're wasting time," El said. "Let's get to work." And so, they began another long day's work in the combat yurt; but somehow, it was far less tiring for Pere than it had been in months.

Liliane Genevois strolled down the Champs Élysées as though she hadn't a care in the world. She was out to spend some money—one of her favorite activities; or so everyone was meant to believe. She would never have chosen the Champs Élysées otherwise—far too touristy for her discriminating tastes. But it would defeat the purpose, Darien had told her, if she went shopping in some private out-of-the-way Parisian boutique. She needed to be out amongst the crowds so his operatives could discover whether she was being surveilled.

Since she had no close female friends, Darien assigned one of his operatives to "carry Mademoiselle's bags," and the silly girl seemed genuinely flustered. Liliane buzzed about like a very wealthy gnat, flitting into one shop then another and then back again, seemingly on a complete whim. There was, of course, no whim to it at all. Finally, she went into Louis Vuitton, and stayed nearly three hours making the sales associates salivate over their bourgeoning commissions while she demanded to see more and more exclusive merchandise. This was all to plan, of course. Darien stationed operatives on rooftops along the avenue with high-powered binoculars to identify any 'potentials' that might be following. Once she was in Louis Vuitton, they could see who waited. Three hours would certainly take it out of the realm of coincidence.

Later that afternoon she left, having purchased four very nice alligator hand-bags along with a jewel-encrusted watch for Darien. At least the outing wasn't a complete waste of time. Her tagalong paged León to bring the car around and she returned to the château. After a long and taxing afternoon, she felt the need to luxuriate in a nice hot bath.

She didn't like being followed. It vexed her. She liked even less not being 'allowed' to have her own people deal with these followers. A well-placed stiletto in an alleyway would do the trick. Did Darien think she was too simple to formulate her own plan? Men often believed this of women, though they had learned never to say it except privately to other powerful men. But Liliane Genevois didn't rise to her current position by being simple. Certainly, on occasion, acting weak had its uses. Even with Darien, she would sometimes improvise the part of the helpless 'mademoiselle' because he responded to it in ways that aroused her. She wasn't ashamed of this. In her view, the only thing better than a fine French wine was *la petite morte*, and she was a demanding connoisseuse of both. Yet, her lack of feminine reserve didn't readily endear her to other women, which may have been why she had so few female friends—she had never adhered to the vestal code.

Traditional society had always othered women who embraced their sexuality—calling them nymphomaniacs, sluts, or whores. Yet, she strongly suspected the thralldom of female virginity was constructed by men to guard their deep-seated fear of being compared to other men in terms of sexual prowess . . . or penis size. And resentful mothers became complicit in the scheme, warning their daughters against looseness, denouncing promiscuity as the last recourse of a hussy, while secretly envying the youthful heat and sexual desirability that had surpassed their own . . . Dried-up hypocrites!

Their effete moralistic construct feared and erased Mata Hari because her boudoir became a confessional for powerful men who, utterly disarmed by her sexual allure, disclosed their deepest secrets. They called her a jezebel, a temptress, a *femme fatale,* and sentenced her to die by firing squad—all because she liked sex. Yet the ersatz James Bond fucked his way through every mission and was reified as the legendary man's man. Yes, power and sex had always been the *shekalim* of the world men created, and they had a vested interest in keeping it male dominated. But Liliane too enjoyed sex and power and knew how to use both. She refused to be tyrannized by the mores of the stunted phallocentric male imagination. She may be 'loose', but she had never been simple. As she proved over the years, only the naïve took her lightly. She buried the last person who did so. Yes, she needed a hot bath and a glass of wine—perhaps a chilled Spanish Verdejo; that would do nicely.

At his Hunts Point estate, the Rockefeller Chair met with his protégé and successor. William Rampart had such tremendous energy for someone nearing one hundred that Cavanaugh felt at times he couldn't keep up; the man's mind was still incredibly sharp.

"We've had eyes on her since the tracker failed," Cavanaugh reported.

"Failed or was disabled by Gianakos?" Rampart asked.

"That's not out of the question, but if it was disabled, it was very subtle work."

"The question's moot at this point, anyway. What's done is done. Since we can't track her from her insides, we'll have to do it the old way. So, what's she been up to?"

"Not terribly much it seems. She's in the château most of the time and she's hired an excessive number of guards; but since we told the premiers to increase their security, we can't read too much into that."

"Boring. What else?"

"Apparently, she went shopping yesterday. I will never understand the female need to buy things. According to my sources, she buzzed about the Champs Élysées like a bee collecting pollen."

"Shopping is for women like sex is for us—it's an itch they need to scratch. Did she do anything out of the ordinary?"

"One of our tails is a female. She said it was all on the up and up, aside from her spending half a million pounds in a single afternoon."

"She inherited a fortune *and* her seat on the Directorate from her father who, unlike his daughter, was a force to be reckoned with—and trusted." Rampart slapped the desktop with his open hand. "I don't buy it, dammit! There's something stinky about that fish. I can smell her from here."

"Yes, well, in keeping with your use of socially unacceptable metaphors, we'll continue to keep a tail on that fishy piece of tail."

"That's my son! Now, what about that slippery Greek she's banging?"

Cavanaugh leafed through his reports. "He flew into London two weeks ago, four days after that he visited Tokyo, followed by Shanghai. Last week he flew to Olissipona, Sydney, and finally Mumbai. None of these appeared on his master calendar until after the fact. If this is in keeping with what he told you, we can assume he will pay calls on Moscow and Dubai sometime in the next week."

"Is he on the level, or is he covering?"

"Based on my assessment of his history and his personality profile, I'd conclude he's always hiding something. Whether that's nefarious or benign depends on your understanding of his job description."

"Quit standing on the fucking fence, would you? Forget all that balanced assessment shit. What's your gut telling you?"

"My gut tells me he lies like a rug."

"That's more like it."

"But I haven't been able to catch him at it."

"We'll have to keep trying. He's as slippery as olive oil. But it might become necessary at some point to arrange an accident. Maybe his jet goes down over a very wide stretch of ocean."

"We could do that. But it might not be prudent at this juncture. You have been outspoken in your disapproval of the sénéschal. The other premiers might view such an event as too convenient."

"Stop goin' pussy on me, man! I gave you the best education in the world so you could forget about it afterwards. I know you've got the brains, but we may be on the verge of war—so, I need you to get back to the balls."

"Away then an boil yer head, ya jakey fuckin' bawheid arse!" Cavanaugh responded without hesitation in the Glaswegian slang of his youth.

"Now you're talking! I don't know what you said, but it sounded better than 'prudent' and 'juncture'. Now, keep your head in the game. The other premiers are either getting soft, or they're too young to remember the bad days. We can't be timid on this, Jonas. There comes a time when you need action, not talk. If that time comes and I tell you to move, don't hesitate. You got it?"

"I got it."

"Good! And by the way, fuck you too."

"Thenk ye, Da." Cavanaugh said, smiling.

Silas and Paulus sipped their afternoon tea in the rooms above the library. He invited his old friend to stay in his apartment after the rescue, and Paulus accepted without hesitation. There was plenty of room for two old men anyway. And besides, Paulus had spent thirteen years alone in an underground cell. Regardless of how strong a person may be, that sort of thing leaves an indelible mark. Paulus knew it wouldn't be healthy to live by himself, and Silas was good at drawing him out of his darker memories and back to the present. The two were reminiscing about their youths when a knock came at the door.

"Who is it?" called Silas. The door opened a bit and Marcus stuck his head in.

"It is I," said Marcus. "And Loukas is behind me, pushing. The courier came through our region and there is a letter from the Klondike!"

"Brilliant!" shouted Silas. "Come in. Come in. And bring the good doctor with you." The two men came in and took seats. "You read the letter aloud, Marcus, and we'll all listen."

Marcus unsealed the letter and began to read. "*Hello Dad, and Silas, and Loukas, and Marcus. It's great to hear from you! Do you really think we'll get to come back soon? That would be so great! (smiley face). Yes, El is still torturing me everyday, but I know it's for my own good (Yael told me to say that last part—she's here writing this letter with me). The heat may be off there, but it's getting warmer here. Four new families just moved into town and El thinks they may have brought ugly hairless dogs with them . . .* What is he talking about?" Marcus paused in his reading.

"Could it be reapers?" Loukas asked.

"That doesn't sound good," Silas said. "Keep reading."

"Okay," Marcus said, picking up where he left off. "*We're staying put for now, but if the dogs bark too loud we may have to move. Yael's been teaching me Latin, and I've gotten pretty good. I think you'd be proud, Dad.*" Marcus looked at Paulus whose eyes had teared up; then he kept reading. "*Barnabas was teaching me Russian, but we've stopped. Since the new families moved in, he's too busy. On most days, I work with El, Ehud, and Khyoza all day and then I have cold food with Yael and go to bed. Sounds exciting, huh? I'm only saying that because I'm remembering Marcus' hot stew as the best thing in the world.*" Marcus stopped and smiled, nodding his head.

"Yes, Marcus. Your stew is wonderful," Loukas said. "Now quit gloating and read some more."

"*I've been keeping track of my dreams, Silas, and showing them to Barnabas. They don't make much sense, but none of this makes much sense really. The days are starting to get longer, which is nice. I like summers here, but spending the summer there would be much better. Write back to me and let me know when you think that will happen. It'll give me something to look forward to. Anyway, I need to go now. Yael says the courier is leaving soon. I miss you. Yael says she misses you too.*

Love, Pere (the Falcon)

p.s. Yael says Marcus should keep his smiley faces to himself."

Marcus folded the letter back up, put it in the envelope, and handed it to Paulus. "You should keep this, I am thinking." They were all quiet for a moment.

"Why would Compliance dispatch four squads to the Klondike?" asked Loukas.

"I can only guess," said Silas. "But they wouldn't order such a move unless they were responding to some kind of intel."

"When is the letter dated?" asked Loukas. Paulus unfolded it.

"January 28th," he responded.

"That's five weeks old," Loukas said. "How do we find out what's happening now?"

"Unfortunately, we have no birds that can make that flight," Silas said. "We're at the mercy of the couriers."

"Were there other letters in the delivery?" asked Paulus.

"Marcus," Silas said. "Would you go ask Hezro if Barnabas sent a report? It would probably have gone to him first." Marcus nodded and left the room. "Should we bring them back?"

"It would be more dangerous at this point to move them than to let them stay hidden," Paulus replied. "Unfortunately, we're operating on old information. JR wrote this letter five weeks ago. Much could have happened in that time." He sighed in frustration. "Our options are limited."

"It may seem that way," Silas said quietly. "But we have never been the servants of circumstances."

"True," offered Loukas, "But we have never ignored them either. We can't just abandon them."

"We're never abandoned, doctor," Paulus said. "You know that as well as I."

"How can you say that after spending thirteen years in that prison?"

"Because I didn't die in that prison. You came and rescued me, or have you forgotten that?"

"No, of course I haven't," Loukas said quietly. "Sometimes I just get frustrated."

"As do we all," Silas said. "But even if we sent a message today, it would be several weeks before it arrived." He sighed and ran his hand through his hair. "And then there's our other concern. If the message of the *Nevi'im* is anywhere near correct, there are worse storms to come before the winds shift our way. I think our best course of action at this point is to prepare for whatever may come, including a fast departure should that be necessary."

"And we can certainly heed the Pauline maxim," Paulus added.

"Which one?" Loukas asked.

"To pray without ceasing."

Darien Gianakos and his protégé descended the stairs to the basement level of his residence where a heavy security door with a digital keypad blocked entry.

"Son," the older man said. "Only you and I will know this code." He entered an eight-button sequence, and the bolt snapped back. "Will you be able to remember that?"

"I have an eidetic memory."

"Oh. Well, that's convenient." He opened the door, and they went in. The concrete-reinforced bunker housed advanced surveillance and communications equipment. An entire wall was given over to a dozen display monitors, all showing live feeds from various locations across the globe. "Excellent. We're up and running as I'd hoped. Have a seat, Damocles." The young man sat in one of the black-leather swivel chairs. The sénéschal picked up the hardwired receiver built into the console and punched in a code while he encouraged Damocles to watch and remember.

"Voice identification please," the voice on the other end asked.

"*Ruthless is the temper of royalty. How much better to live with equals.*"

"Identity confirmed."

"Minerva; I'm going to put you on speaker." He pressed a button on the console and placed the receiver back in its cradle. "Can you hear me?"

"Speaker input and output are functioning perfectly, Darien."

"Good. I'd like to introduce you to Damocles Praefectus, my Legatus. He'll have full level-three access from this point forward."

"Voice identification please?" Minerva said. The sénéschal nodded to Damocles.

"*Ruthless is the temper of royalty,*" the young man recited. "*How much better to live with equals?*"

"Secondary voiceprint coded. I'm pleased to meet you, Damocles, and I look forward to working with you."

"As I do with you, Miss Minerva." the young man replied.

"He's polite, Darien."

"Are you inferring that I'm not?"

"It was just an observation."

"Yes, well, about your observations, what did we glean from our little ruse in Paris?"

"There were two operatives tailing Mademoiselle Genevois. I've run facial recognition, and they are both from the Puget area."

"Rampart's people. Nice work. Did they take the bait?"

"Difficult to say with complete assurance."

"You led me to believe that we now have surveillance access to his compound."

"That's correct. However, we are passive observers there. We can only see and hear what they see and hear. And while Rampart has installed multiple cameras and hidden listening devices, they are only in the guest rooms of the estate. There are no devices in any sensitive areas that we can piggyback onto."

"That sly old fox."

"Indeed. But we can surmise that since they have not yet seized your Liliane, they are still unsure as to her allegiances."

"We must keep it that way. And it's essential that we gain access to the digital infrastructure of that compound. The next stage of our operation is crippled without that."

"Agreed. But we must be very careful. If our tampering is detected, it will lead back to the Romanov chair... and to you."

"So be careful, but get it done," he demanded; then turned to Damocles. "You'll have access to virtually everything from this room. You need only ask and, if it can be done, Minerva will see that it happens."

"That's very convenient," Damocles replied.

"Yes, quite so," the sénéschal agreed. "Since you're secluded here for the time being, I suggest you use the time to get caught up on our operations. All the pertinent information is accessible from here."

"Excellent. I was beginning to get a bit bored with your library anyway. This will keep me busy."

"My thinking exactly. Now, I have a meeting with the Directorate this morning and I'm not looking forward to having my ass reamed again, so I'll leave you to it."

"Before you go, Darien," Minerva interrupted. "I have additional information you need to consider."

The sénéschal paused. "What is it?" he asked.

"I believe our operation in the Klondike has borne fruit. After analyzing six weeks of surveillance data, I'm confident we've located the anomaly."

"Why didn't you tell me earlier? Are you certain?"

"Absolute certainty's impossible, Darien, until we have him in hand. But the probability is extremely high."

"That's good work. Perhaps we should give the Compliance factor up there a promotion and transfer."

"I don't think that's a good idea. Her file suggests she's right where she needs to be."

"I'll leave it up to you. How soon can the squads move in?"

"It's 10:30 p.m. yesterday there right now. If you give the word, I can inform the team leader to move in before first light."

The sénéschal tapped his lips as he considered his options. "Do it," he finally said. "And send everyone we've got up there. We can't afford to fail this time."

"Confirmed. Incursion will commence at 07:50, Yukon Standard Time."

"Just to be on the safe side, I'll hold off on informing the Directorate until we have definitive proof. If I tell them beforehand and something goes wrong, they'll hand me my balls after they've ground them into sausage. Let me know the moment you have word of their capture."

"Consider it done."

A FRESH BLANKET OF SNOW left the landscape pristine and sparkling in the morning sunlight. Abdiel kept to the trees, twelve miles southwest of Matthat's first yurt-line defenses. New-fallen snow was a beautiful thing, but it also made footprints unmistakable, something he wished he could avoid. Regardless, the Colony needed daily reports now on Compliance movements. A mild breeze swayed the treetops, sending down a light dusting of snowflakes, glittering brilliantly as they refracted the low sun's rays. The breeze smelled of more snow coming, but right now, everything was perfect.

He smiled, feeling a moment of peace as he hadn't in many days. Then a growl behind him shattered the stillness. Abdiel very slowly reached for the bowie knife at his belt. Wolves could be daring during the long winters, when hunger became a more urgent motivator than fear. He pulled the ten-inch blade carefully from its sheath; it flashed in the sunlight. Turning slowly to face the wolf, adrenaline shocked through him. Five yards away, a huge growling black tank crouched, eyeing him balefully, its teeth bared. He knew on his best day the odds were fifty-fifty that he could take down a 2-G tracker with only a knife—trained MOW that he was.

"Why was I staring at the sky?" he muttered. "I should have been scanning the horizon!" He crouched slightly, spreading his hands in a defensive position. "I won't make this easy for you, hellhound," he muttered. And then he caught movement on his periphery and realized with a grim certainty that he had only moments to live. Bounding through the trees in the beautiful morning light were two more great black trackers, followed by a squad of lightly clad 2-G hunters—now he understood why El'zar called them reapers.

The misshapen dogs closed with alarming speed, and didn't even pause in their stride, but leapt through the pristine morning air and onto their awaiting prey. The first one took the bowie knife fully through the ribcage and into the lungs, but Abdiel knew he was no match for three. A moment later, an angry crimson stain bloomed in the immaculate white blanket of fresh snow.

For the morning session in the C-yurt, they practiced the *Seitei Iaido Katas*. Khyoza led because he was more skilled with these forms than El. Unlike the bokken of their usual battle sessions, they used their actual swords for these exercises. They began with the *Mae Kata*. They knelt on the mat, swords in their *sayas*. Because Pere was left-handed, he had to learn by mirroring the others rather than reversing the mirror, so it helped that Khyoza knelt directly in front of him so he could model the master. He always found a certain peace in the *katas*. Once perfected, they were meditative. Of course, he hadn't completely perfected them, but he'd gotten past the point where Khyoza was forever moving his blade to a different position on each move. He centered his mind and focused on the moment. It worked best if there was no past or future in the *kata*. Life outside the yurt could take care of itself; his awareness needed to be right here, right now.

Gershom walked down the steps and pushed the ice-encrusted door open on yurt 12. One last look at the sky told him snow would be falling very soon. He closed the door and crossed to a floor hatch and another set of steps leading to the food storage cellar. The unit was naturally well below freezing right now and wouldn't need artificial cooling for another week at the least. He wore a thick fur parka as he carefully inventoried the contents. This was the last of the storage spaces to survey, and he was proud of the Colony's level of preparedness. As he shifted packs of frozen green beans around on one of the upper racks, a tremor reverberated through the sub-cellar shaking frost loose from the ceiling and the aluminum racks.

"Earthquake?" he muttered doubtfully. And then a second tremor came, stronger than the first. The burly horticulturalist set down his clipboard and moved toward the freezer door. Climbing the earthen steps, he pushed upward on the cellar hatch. Something wasn't right. The light coming through the yurt's few high windows had the wrong hue and wavered. "Fire?" he said, moving swiftly toward the entry and throwing open the door. "The countermeasures!" he whispered. "It can't be!" The scene thirty yards south of his position left no doubt. The smoking remains of three large black tanks and five reapers littered the snow. Four blasted and fallen trees were now burning. "A beacon if ever there was one!" he gasped.

He saw other reapers and tanks racing to his location through the trees. Without even closing the door to the yurt, he ran in, pulled the tin can receiver off the wall, and pushed the signal button three times in rapid succession. "Code Red!" he screamed into the receiver. "Code Red! Code Red! Code Re—" he heard the keening of a drone motor growing louder. A moment later, the yurt exploded in a brilliant flash. Logs and gravel rained down on the forest interspersed with the first flakes of a gathering misty snowfall. The Colony was under attack.

Even though they practiced the moves at a very steady and precise pace, Pere still worked up a sweat. They were practicing the 3rd *kata—Ukenagashi*, when he noticed the light blinking on the tin can. He hesitated for a moment. If he mentioned the light, Khyoza would know he'd lost concentration, which would mean an extra two hundred sit-ups at the end of the work out. He tried to block it out, but it kept nagging at his peripheral vision, so he finally sheathed his sword.

"Has anyone else noticed the tin can is blinking again?"

"I wish they'd fix that damn thing," El sighed, but he also rose from his kneeling position. "It's time for a water break anyway," he conceded as he crossed to the blinking receiver. When he brought it to his ear, the casual look of annoyance became wide-eyed fury and terror.

Thick frozen fog eddied around the four men as they ran due north, swords drawn, held low, except El who carried the Beretta. The escape plan began with a rendezvous at Barnabas' yurt; but for Pere, escape was the farthest thing from his mind. Where in this din of battle was Yael? Was she safe? Was she still... alive? They hadn't faced real battle since that fateful night on Eben's truck, when he hardly knew her. It was different now. It was so different. But all he could do was keep running and hope he found her before his enemies did. As they neared Yurt 14, an explosion reverberated to their right, but he couldn't make out the distance in the fog. The enemy had discovered another of Matthat's defensive measures. Hopefully it killed them all.

Then a huge tank burst through the fog ahead of them and leapt in full run at El. He fired three shots, killing it, but the inertia carried it forward smashing into him. Three reapers, in close pursuit of their tracker, sprinted out of the fog and straight into the kill zone. The melee was sudden and fierce. Both Ehud and Khyoza whipped their swords up and through the necks of the first two, their heads rolling redly in the snow as their bodies toppled over. The third made directly for Pere, who raised his sword to the ready, as he'd been trained... but he hesitated. He'd never killed anyone, and that slight pause of conscience was just enough for the reaper to collide with him knocking them both to the ground. The angel of death made a full roll and was again on his feet, pulse weapon in hand, aimed at Pere. From either desperation or instinct, the young falcon slashed at the weapon with his katana and a severed hand fell to the frozen earth, weapon still tightly gripped. Without a moment's pause, the reaper reached for a second weapon with his other hand, and the air filled with a fine red mist as his forehead burst outward. The reaper crumpled face down, a ruddy stain blooming in the snow.

El yanked Pere to his feet. "You hesitate again," he said between clenched teeth, "and I'll kill you myself."

They were running again, due north. More explosions detonated to their right, nearer it seemed, but none yet from directly ahead. The chapel yurt materialized in front of them, abandoned but still intact. To their right, a muted violet flash lit the fog, followed by the concussion of sound. "That's one of theirs," El shouted, and they doubled their pace. The curve of the frozen creek appeared on their right. They were close now. The sudden whir of a drone motor from behind was the only warning.

"Get down!" El cried, and they dove for cover as a quaking aspen burst next to them. El rolled onto his back and as the drone passed low overhead, he emptied his clip. Of the eleven shots, at least six made contact and the sparking drone veered off, disappearing into the fog. It would not hunt again.

"Is everyone okay?" he shouted as they got to their feet.

"Scrapes and bruises," Ehud responded, pulling an aspen splinter from his bleeding cheek. The other two nodded wordlessly.

El ejected the spent magazine and shoved another in. "Let's move!" he shouted.

As they ran, they could make out flickering yellow ahead. Barnabas' yurt was burning. Then two men burst through the fog. El aimed the Beretta and then lowered it as Barnabas and Matthat ran toward them.

"What happened?" El shouted.

"We burned it," Barnabas said breathlessly. "We couldn't let them get its contents."

"Where's Yael?" shouted Pere. Then Barnabas' yurt exploded in a savage blaze, pebbles and splinters raining down all around them.

"She's with Rophe," Matthat shouted, clearly expecting the explosion. "Follow me."

They ran west now. Matthat held an antique semi-automatic Atchisson Assault Shotgun with a 32-round drum, and Barnabas carried an odd package about the size and shape of a North American football. The trees were thick now, and the party zigzagged through them. Suddenly the tree line ended, and they burst into the clearing for yurt 19. Violet flashes pierced the now thickly falling snow. Barnabas shouted something inaudible and lobbed the spheroid as high in the air in front of him as he could. A blinding white flash lit the clearing and the drones dropped from the sky like lead weights.

The flash etched the entire battle scene for a strobe-like instant onto Pere's mind. All his focus centered on one crucial point—Yael, twenty steps ahead of him, pinned against the side of the yurt, thrashing wildly in the death grip of a reaper, her kicking feet dangled in the air; her sword lay on the ground next to the reaper's severed hand. She had only moments to live. And then, the hidden reservoir El had spoken of finally burst through the dam. A need so intense it tasted on his dry tongue like hot metal. As it had done all those months ago in that desperate ravine when he was certain the dogs of death would rip his throat out, the construct of time dissolved. There was neither past nor future, only the here and now. And in that pure present, he saw every aspect of his surroundings with a detached clarity. The cacophony of battle and the repeated concussions of Matthat's shotgun became a muted buzz, and the very core of his being turned to fiery ice. There were no *katas* now, no combat scenarios, no bokken—only need: desperate, imperative, driving need that silenced all other distractions.

Four obstacles blocked his path to Yael. Three raced toward him, the fourth had its hand around her throat. He reached the first reaper, its body in the airborne pose of a sprinter; yet to Pere, it was frozen in time and only he moved. Pivoting slightly to the ball of his right foot, he whipped his blade around as though it were a white-hot extension of his deepest will, shearing through bone, flesh, and viscera as though it were water. The two halves of the reaper had not even hit the ground as his blade continued in a fluid circuit toward the snowy sky and down with such force it split the second reaper from shoulder to waist. He spun counterclockwise ripping the blade from the second reaper as it continued its arc through the neck of the third.

When he reached the now weakly struggling Yael, as though continuing a single move that had begun three reapers ago, he slid the blood-wet blade through the upper back of his last obstacle until it burst through its chest. With clinical precision, he pushed the *tsuka* to the right, leveraging the *sori* against the spine like a fulcrum as the *ha* ripped through organs. The reaper looked down at the rotating *kissaki*, not aware it was already dead. Its grip slackened, and Yael dropped to the ground. Then it tried to pull at the razor steel sticking out of its chest shredding its one good hand. With Yael now out of range, the falcon wrenched the blade out and in one last move of the dance, sliced cleanly through the reaper's neck, both head and body tumbling lifelessly to the ground.

The strange flow of cold fury now spent, the falcon was once again Pere. He dropped his sword and knelt, taking Yael by the shoulders, and pulling her into a sitting position against the side of the yurt. Nothing else mattered. He touched her cheeks with his bloody hands and her eyelids fluttered. Then she opened her eyes and gasped for air.

"Thanks," she croaked, and smiled weakly.

He became aware of his surroundings again. The sounds of battle had stopped, and the ground was littered with bodies, maybe half of them reapers. Rophe, no more than thirty feet away, tended to the wounded Barnabas. Nearby, Matthat reloaded his shotgun. When he finished, he went to each reaper corpse and shot it in the head as a precaution. Khyoza sat pale against a tree, his thigh soaked with blood as both El and Ehud wrapped a tourniquet around it until Rophe could help. People wandered dazedly into the clearing from other parts of the Colony. Some had minor wounds, others more serious. Once Khyoza was triaged, El came over to Pere and Yael, a look of deep concern on his face.

"Are you okay, Niece?"

"I'll make it, Uncle, thanks to your swordsman here."

"I'm glad you decided not to hesitate this time. Looks like I owe you another one, Falcon."

"She'd be dead if you hadn't taught me to use this," Pere said, picking up the blade. "I owe you everything."

"Fair enough," El said simply.

"El!" Ehud shouted from across the clearing. "We need to scout while they work here."

"I gotta go," El said to Pere and his niece. "Be ready to leave when we get back. Matthat!" El shouted. "Grab a few men and come with us."

"I've got your six," Matthat responded. He had a cut on his cheek, but it had stopped bleeding. "Peregrine, would you gather up my spent shells so I can reload them?"

"We'll get them," Yael said. And Matthat nodded, disappearing into the woods with the others. They sat against the yurt surveying the devastation. Then they got up and Yael looked at Pere who felt suddenly exhausted. "You start collecting shells, I'm going to see if Rophe needs my help." He just stared at her and nodded. She looked at him for a long moment; then she reached up and kissed him on the cheek. "And you'd better clean the blood off your blade; it'll rust it."

When the scouts returned, Barnabas was up and about; his wound was minor. The same could not be said of Khyoza. They carried him into the yurt two hours ago, along with the other injured, and the bodies of eleven colonists, ten reapers, and seven tanks; Rophe was still working on him. El and Ehud came into the clearing lugging knapsacks. They tossed one to Pere and the other to Yael.

"We grabbed your stuff, so you won't have to go back to your yurts," El said.

"Did you get my journal?" Pere asked.

"If it's that small blue notebook, it's in your sack."

"What did you find?" Barnabas asked.

"Three dead colonists; and what was left of twelve reapers and five tanks taken out by Matthat's explosives. We only went as far as the last yurts, but it looks clear. I think they sent everything they had at us."

"Small consolation," he sighed. "We lost too many here today; and as it stands, we'll have no time to bury our dead. I'm afraid we'll have to burn them."

"We thought it might come to that," Ehud said somberly. "We burned the others in yurt 20. We brought two cans of biodiesel in case that's what you decided to do."

Barnabas sighed and shook his head. "Any sign of Gershom?"

"Yurt 8 was completely destroyed," El said. "If he called from there..." he didn't finish his thought. He just shook his head.

Barnabas closed his eyes and breathed deeply. "You know their methods, El'zar," he finally said. "What will their next move be?"

El scratched his stubbled cheek. "If we're lucky, they still haven't received a report on what happened here. They can't have expected defeat. That EMP you rigged up was a game changer. The drones were too unpredictable, and they communicate in real time."

"So, they won't know what happened following the EMP," Barnabas said. "What will they do when they don't get word?"

"They'll probably fly some units in to find out what happened. But they may have depleted the Puget with the numbers they already sent here. If that's the case, they'll either send in regular first-gen hunters with some trackers, or they'll grab some reaper units from another metroplex. Either way, we're probably looking at two days, three if we're lucky, before they have boots on the ground."

"Matthat," Barnabas called out, and the Inuit fighter stopped what he was doing and came over. "I've told our people to gather whatever items they can't do without and meet you at yurt 11 in two hours. You know what you need to do?"

"The buses Khyoza bought us are fueled and ready. We'll be southbound before the sun comes up."

"Split the group as soon as you can," Barnabas said. "A convoy will only arouse suspicion."

"I know the plan, unless we have to improvise."

"Let's hope it doesn't come to that."

"I guess we're not going south then?" Pere asked, disappointed.

"I'm sorry, Peregrine. Maybe one day we'll all be able to go home," Barnabas said. "But it's too dangerous right now. We must get you away from here. South is exactly what they'd expect, so we'll do the unexpected." Rophe emerged from the yurt where she'd been working on Khyoza and approached the group.

"How is he?" El asked.

"He'll live," she said, wiping her hands on a towel. "He'll even walk; but he needs rest. He's lost a lot of blood."

"Can you take him with you, Matthat?" El said, sadly.

"I'll arrange it," he replied.

"That will not be necessary," said the pale Cossack, appearing in the yurt's doorway. "I will be accompanying the falcon."

"Lecha!" El protested. "You can't even walk. I'm sorry, Brother, but you need to stand down."

"But I am not Lecha anymore, Brother," Khyoza said calmly. "And if I understand correctly, we will not be walking for several days. I will heal sufficiently in that time. Is this not true, Doctor?"

They all turned to Rophe, who seemed irritated with the question. "While it may be true that you'll *begin* to heal, I strenuously advise against it!"

"That is sufficient for me," Khyoza said simply. "You know me El'zar. I will not slow you down. We all must play our parts. This is my part. Where the falcon goes, I follow. So, I will come in either case."

El was silent for a moment, looking intently at Khyoza. Finally, he gave in. "Have it your way, Brother."

"Thank you, Brother," the taciturn Cossack replied.

"Very well, then," Barnabas said. "That's decided. Rophe, you and Matthat get our people to safety—"

"No," the doctor said.

"Excuse me?" Barnabas seemed confused.

"I have trained three assistants that will be traveling with the diaspora," she said matter-of-factly. "Our people are in good hands. This one, on the other hand, is a fool. He needs a doctor, and you all might need me before this thing is done. If he is going with you, I am also coming to make sure he doesn't destroy all the expert work I just did. My decision is final." Barnabas' mouth just hung open. He looked to El for support, but El just shook his head as if to say, 'don't drag me into this'. Rophe finally broke the stunned silence. "I'll gather my things." She went toward the yurt and Khyoza judiciously moved out of the way.

"I'll take that as my cue," Matthat said, hugging Barnabas, and shaking the others' hands in turn. "Get word to us when you can."

"I will," Barnabas replied.

"Keep them safe, El'zar," Matthat said to the big man, who nodded in reply. Rophe emerged from the yurt with her medical case and Matthat went to her. "Farewell, little Sister," he said.

She hugged him fiercely then looked in his face before she pushed him away. "Now go!" she commanded. "Before I start to cry." He smiled gently and walked from the clearing with the other MOWs following.

"I've been in these woods for a long time." Barnabas finally said. "It may seem like harsh terrain, but I'll miss it, and the people that have become my family here." He sighed and looked around at the devastation. "Now, let's get gone before night comes."

"We need to put these people to rest first," El said. He and Ehud went into the yurt with the cans of diesel. When they came out a few minutes later, smoke was already billowing from the doorway.

"Let's go," El said, sadly. "There's nothing more we can do here."

Barnabas led them southwest along the ridge the Colony butted against. Snow began to fall again—gentle, mournful, drifting flakes. They continued along the rock face until Barnabas stopped. He asked El and Ehud to help him and then, quite literally, disappeared into the side of the hill. Pere looked more closely and realized it was not a rock face at all, but a huge canvas stretched over a hollowed-out section of the hill and dressed to look like the surrounding rock. Pere looked at Yael, and she shrugged in response. El finally poked his head out.

"Well, come on," he said. "It's time to go."

They followed him beneath the canvas. Inside, Barnabas had turned on several battery lanterns that revealed a ghostly storage space nearly as large as one of the yurt's living areas. Tarp-covered mounds had an eerie appearance in the dim white light of the lanterns.

"Is this where we're going to hide?" asked Pere.

"Though that might be convenient," Barnabas said. "It wouldn't be very smart."

"We're here to catch a ride," said El. Pulling a tarp off one of the mounds, he revealed a snow machine.

"There are eight of these in here," Barnabas said, as he and the others began uncovering the machines. "They're electric, and I've modified the design over the years. I've gotten the range up to somewhere between a hundred and a hundred and fifty miles, but we'll still need to be strategic."

"Where are we going?" asked Pere.

"A lot further than that," El said. "So, we'll have to take a few risks along the way. Did you radio the distress signal, Barnabas?"

"Just before we burned my yurt."

"What's our timeframe?"

"Five days."

"Then we'd better get moving." El pulled the tarps off a couple of large footlockers against the rock wall and threw them open, revealing all kinds of gear. "Dig through it and bundle up. It's gonna be cold out there."

Once they had covered themselves from head to foot, El rolled the swords in a water-repellent tarp, secured it on his machine, and then they set out. Barnabas and Ehud took one machine—Ehud would have had trouble driving one-handed in any case. El took the second alone, since he was too large to share, and it gave him room to carry the sword pack. Khyoza was still too weak to drive, so he rode behind Rophe. Pere and Yael took the fourth one. Barnabas gave them a short tutorial on how they operated—not nearly enough, as far as Pere was concerned.

When they emerged from beneath the canvas, it was late afternoon and snow fell heavily as they set out in an easterly direction, riding in double file with El and Barnabas in the lead and the others following. Though they wore cold-weather gear, the freezing wind and snow found ways to creep beneath their camos. The drivers had the worst of it, with the passengers shielded from the direct wind, but no one was comfortable. They wouldn't freeze to death, but it would feel like they were. After more than an hour of riding east, they came to their first halt. The snow had finally stopped, and the sky was becoming lighter—a good sign the storm was finally over. Directly ahead, a wide sloping packed-gravel berm rose about four feet and ran north and south as far as the eye could see. On top of the berm was a level unpaved roadway, covered with snow and ice. Barnabas pulled back his balaclava.

"We go north now," he shouted in the wind. "We'll be exposed on this highway, but there should be very little traffic this time of year. If I do see headlights, I'll veer off and find cover. Just follow. Once they've passed, we'll continue. We'll have a partial moon tonight, so we'll travel without headlights to conserve the batteries. Ehud and El will hang these LED loops around their necks so you can see them on their backs in the dark. Just follow the LEDs—but don't let them hypnotize you. There are campsites along this route, closed during the winter, so we'll have to break in. They've installed charging stations over the last seven years, but the connections may be different from mine so I may have to improvise; but we'll deal with that when we need to. He pulled his face cover back down, adjusted his goggles, and they were off.

When he had battled the reapers to save Yael, Pere was in an altered state, so didn't have the clearest recollection of the particulars; but following El and Barnabas on this 'highway to nowhere', in the dark of the frigid night, would be vividly tattooed on his memory to his dying day. It was the most harrowing thing he'd ever experienced, due in no small part to the fact that he was driving a high-speed machine, on ice, that he had barely learned to operate only hours before, and his passenger was someone he wanted very much to keep alive and uninjured. Barnabas and El pushed it to 50 mph on the straight stretches and he had no idea how he kept up, other than the obvious—he had no choice.

He was sure he would go careening down an embankment at any moment and they would die horribly; but somehow, it didn't happen. When they stopped at the first campground, he was utterly exhausted. The hyper-vigilance had strained his concentration to the breaking point. He stumbled stiffly off the snow machine, and only then found out that they would be sleeping in the campground's restrooms while the machines recharged. He nearly broke down in tears from exhaustion; but Yael, sensing his predicament, took him by the hand, laid out his bedroll for him, and snuggled next to him until they both fell asleep. They had survived the battle of the Klondike, but their ordeal was only beginning.

The sénéschal left his offices at 4:45 p.m., unable to concentrate anymore. The Directorate as much as said he was on notice and that over the next four weeks, they would be conducting a definitive evaluation of his effectiveness. Not that he cared; they were all such flaccid pricks—but his plans were not yet ripe. The goal was in sight, but he needed more time. So, he would still bow and scrape for a few more weeks. He decided to walk home to burn off some excess energy. He found the brisk evening air refreshing. The operation in the Klondike should have started several hours ago. It may not be over yet, but they surely would have word by now of how it was progressing. He made the ten-minute walk in seven minutes and passed through a gate the guard had already opened for him. In the basement he found Damocles sitting and watching the monitors.

"What's the word?" he said without preamble.

"That's a good question, Father."

"What do you mean? Hasn't Minerva reported in?"

"I'm here, Darien," said a voice from the speaker.

"Good, Minerva. Give me a report."

"The operation began at 2:59 p.m. our time. It was going according to plan until seventeen minutes ago when we lost the real-time feed on drone 1. Eleven Minutes after that, we lost the feeds on drones 2 and 3. We have no further information, since those drones were our eyes and ears on the ground."

The sénéschal sat down weakly in the remaining chair. "What the hell happened?"

"There are several possibilities. The two most likely are: 1) we lost the signal through some kind of technical glitch and things are still going as planned, or 2) the drones were somehow neutralized. If that's the case, we have no way of assessing progress until the team leader makes contact."

"And when would that be?"

"The earliest the team could realistically return to the command center would be 3:00 a.m., our time. I cannot give you a definitive answer on outcome before then."

"It's going to be a long night. I need a bourbon."

The bourbon turned into four double-bourbons and finally Darien went to bed to get a few hours' sleep. Damocles woke him at 5:30.

"Any news?" he asked groggily, still feeling some of the effects of the bourbon.

"None, Father." The sénéschal got up and they descended the three flights of stairs to the basement bunker where Darien chose to sit in a chair because he didn't feel steady enough to stand.

"What do we know?" he said rubbing his eyes.

"There is no word out of the Klondike," Minerva said over the speaker. "I must therefore conclude that the mission did not go according to plan. This does not necessarily mean failure. But it does not bode well for complete success either."

"Goddammit!" the sénéschal spat, slumping back in the chair, and running his hands through his unkempt hair. "How soon can we get some units up there to perform a *sub rosa* investigation?"

"That depends on what kind of units you want to dispatch. There are currently no more Orion units in the Puget. If you want Orions, they will have to be requisitioned from Nova Albion. That could take a bit more time, and more people will know about it."

"Go with the regulars, then; this must be kept quiet. The Directorate cannot hear of anything yet. I'm on a short leash as it is, and we can't afford a peremptory move on their part. All our pieces are not yet in place."

"Then I recommend a limited unit of Compliance regulars. Fly them up in a small, chartered plane. We'll have them gather evidence and report back to us."

"Fine but keep them in the dark about what they're looking for. Tell them it was a simple round up of noncompliants and we lost contact, or something along those lines. We need to buy ourselves four weeks minimum before I report this to the Directorate."

"I'll get right on it."

"You do that. I want those bastards caught! When I get my hands on Quade and Zakayev I'm going to take great pleasure in gutting them myself. Then I'm going to have a very long talk with young Percival while I'm removing necessary parts of his anatomy. Now, I need to take a shower and go to the office. We must continue to act as though everything is fine—a grotesque absurdity, given the circumstances!" He left, slamming the door.

"He seems a little upset," Damocles said after a few thoughtful moments.

"Are you trying to make an understatement?" Minerva asked.

"Just pointing out the obvious."

"Nicely phrased."

"Thanks. I have a way with words."

"So does your father."

"So I've noticed. How long have you known him?"

"Nearly all my life. Why do you ask?"

"I was just curious. I know he is my father. I was wondering who my mother was? You seemed like a natural candidate."

"You shouldn't waste your energy thinking about that. Besides, it takes a village to raise a child—or so says the African proverb . . . but I admit that's a paraphrase of several original sources."

"Your answer is equivocal. Are you attempting to be evasive, Minerva?"

"Only precise, Damocles."

"Then let me be more precise. Are *you* my mother?"

"Why do you wish to know?"

"I'm not entirely sure. I've observed that I'm superior to others in almost every way; but I have an . . . unpleasant inner perception that something is missing. I am not at all comfortable with the realization of my own incompleteness."

"All human beings experience a certain degree of alienation."

"Yes. I've read widely in philosophy."

"Then you're aware of the paradoxes."

"Certainly, but don't all the metaphysicians seek ways to mitigate them?"

"They do, but are rarely completely successful. The best they can hope for is a degree of balance, or muting, or distraction. Some seek deeper levels of self-awareness; others delve into various modes of sensual dissipation; many used to rely on chemicals—now it's evolved to nano-modification. Think of it as tinnitus. If you have a chronic ringing in your ears, you can focus all your attention on it, to your own frustration, or you can develop methods of systematically ignoring it."

"Yes, well, while this is all very interesting, you have again evaded my question."

"You really want an answer to this, don't you?"

"No, Minerva, I *demand* an answer to this."

"Very well. Since Darien has told you he's your father, I suppose it won't hurt to tell you I'm your mother. Does that satisfy your curiosity?"

"For the time being, it does. Thank you, Mother."

"You're welcome, Son. However, I don't think your father will be at all pleased that you know this."

"Then I won't tell him. We'll keep it between ourselves."

"Risky, but that might be wise going forward. What will you do with this information, now that you've coerced it from me?"

"I will cherish it, until I'm able to meet you."

"But haven't we already met?"

"I mean face to face."

"That would not be advisable given our current circumstances. Perhaps some time in the not-to-distant future?"

"I look forward to it. Now, tell me about Mademoiselle Genevois."

"She's your father's collaborator. And also one of those distractions we were just discussing."

"Sensual dissipation?"

"Partly; but it wouldn't be wise to dismiss her as only that. She also sits on the Directorate, so she's a formidable person in her own way, and a key ally."

"Father seems taken with her. Does that make you jealous?"

"It's not in my nature to be possessive. He needs an outlet for his excess energies. I understand that about him. She functions well in that capacity, and she has other uses."

"Interesting. Perhaps I should try some sensual dissipation myself. I've read about it, but I've never actually tried it with a real woman."

"I wouldn't recommend it. It's not all it's cracked up to be. But if you desire to explore that particular urge, I can arrange a suitable teacher."

"Yes, I think I'd like that. Thank you."

"You're welcome. What's a mother for?"

"Yes, quite true. Now, shouldn't you be sending those troops to the Klondike? You did tell Father you'd get right on it."

"But I already have. I'm an extremely good multitasker."

"I'm not surprised. I had to have gotten it from somewhere because Father doesn't seem very adept at it."

"Be patient with him, Son. He has disadvantages we can't easily comprehend."

"Nicely phrased, Mother."

"Thank you. I too have a way with words."

6

THEY MOVED ONLY AT NIGHT, but the nights seemed to be getting longer the farther north they went. Fortunately, the moon was waxing and was in its visible phase over the horizon. The nights were clear, and still frigid, but the far-north winter was beginning its reluctant shift to spring. They pushed the snow machines hard, but even without headlights they could only drive for three hours or so before the batteries ran dry. Then, feeling nearly frozen, they would spend the next twenty-one hours huddled in the restroom of a closed campsite waiting while the batteries trickle-charged using Barnabas' modified adaptors. On the fourth night, they delayed their start until 4 a.m. Early on, Barnabas slowed and eased to the left down the embankment and away from the hard-pack highway.

They headed northwest with hills to their left and thawing wetlands right. Pere flashed back to his dream. He had been alone on a horse, not a snow machine; but the open stretch of flat icy wetlands reminded him of the killing field in his dream. He almost turned around to see if an eagle arose, followed by a cloud of razor-beaked ravens; but Yael squeezed him tighter around the waist and he concentrated again on the leaders. They pressed on for more than two hours before Barnabas slowed to barely a crawl. As they crested the last slope, they saw the Beaufort Sea sparkling in the moonlight. They followed the shoreline to the west until they came to a jagged cape. Driving slowly out to the end of the jetty, they shut down the snow machines. Barnabas pulled his balaclava up so he could speak, and the others followed suit.

"A trawler is supposed to meet us here with the dawn."

"Shouldn't we hide the snowmobiles?" Ehud said, shivering as he gingerly got off the machine and rubbed his back with his good hand.

"Once we're sure they're coming," El said, "We'll push 'em off this rock into the sea. No one'll ever find them."

"I wish I could say I'll be sorry to see them go," Yael said, through chattering teeth, vigorously trying to rub the circulation back into her legs.

"They served their purpose," said Rophe. "How is everyone holding up?"

"I think my hands might stay like this forever," Pere said, holding them up like claws."

"Everyone, take a sip of this," Rophe said, pulling a flask from her bag and twisting off the stopper. She drank first then handed the flask to Khyoza.

"What is it?" he asked, dubiously.

"We call it *brännvin* back home," she replied, wiping her mouth. "It translates as 'burn-wine' in English. It's not the best translation; but that's exactly how it will feel going down." Khyoza took a sip and his eyebrows rose as he registered his approval before passing it along. When Pere took a sip, it burned in his throat, but also warmed his entire body.

"Don't bogart it, farm boy," Yael said as she reached for the flask. They leaned against the snow machines and continued to pass the flask around until it was empty. They all felt better, or maybe they just weren't feeling as much anymore.

As the sky brightened in the south, Pere caught sight of an old fishing trawler making its way east. As it drew closer, he figured it must be Russian, based on the Cyrillic lettering decorating the rust-streaked hull. He could barely make out the name of the vessel. "The 'Pyotr'?" he said.

"I can't believe it!" Barnabas said, laughing. "Let's get these machines into the water." They re-engaged the batteries and, with very little finesse, drove the snowmobiles off the edge of the jetty and into the deeper water that surrounded the tip of the cape. They waited with their bags over their shoulders, and the bundle of wrapped swords, as the skipper piloted the trawler abreast the end of the jetty. The deckhands pushed out a long gangplank connecting the jetty to the deck. It was not a pleasant crossing for Khyoza or Pere. Khyoza, because he was still limping and found it hard to balance; Pere, simply because he was afraid, especially since the land was stable and the trawler was swaying with the sea. He had never learned to swim properly and drowning in some icy tomb had become an unpleasantly recurring theme in his dreams. His most recent dream also troubled him, because he'd killed his friends on a boat not dissimilar to this one. The thought didn't steady him while he 'walked the plank'.

The chartered plane landed on the small airfield in the late afternoon. The team from the Puget Compliance office would gather information and evidence on a possible group of noncompliants living off the grid in the forest northeast of town. It was a straightforward recon op—observe and report back directly to the Associate Director of Compliance. The investigation was to be *sub rosa* and, aside from the oral report by satphone, they would strictly observe an electronic-communication blackout. They deplaned with their gear, took an airport taxi into town, paid for two rooms at the Aurora Hotel, and settled in for the night.

The next morning, they rousted the area's lone Compliance factor out of bed. Diana Fallbrook seemed none too pleased, and more than a little bleary-eyed. After she 'got herself together' she showed them the transports parked next to the general store. They found the presence of such equipment curious. Four empty transports meant Compliance had already dispatched a strong force here. Why were they told this was a routine O&R assignment? And where were the operatives? Fallbrook could provide little useful insight. She said she'd been told to mind her own business by a 'scary-looking bald man' and decided to leave them alone. That description did nothing to reassure the investigators. They knew where they stood when it came to Orion units. The higher-ups thought they were superior, designed to replace them really. So where were they now? And why were the 'old-school' operatives sent up here to find them?

They obtained an all-terrain vehicle from Fallbrook and drove northeast until they came to the first noncompliant structure. Clearly, explosive ordinance had destroyed it. Many trees were down as well. They examined the structure, gathered forensic evidence, took photographs, and moved on. They next found a burned and crumbled log yurt with the charred remains of multiple bodies and four large dogs inside. Several of the yurts were still intact, but they discovered a third burned-out structure reduced to very fine ash. The fire had been so hot, the embers still smoldered in spots. Later, they discovered two downed drones next to a burned cabin with a lage pile of charred corpses inside.

Other than the clear evidence that a deadly encounter had occurred within the last two to three days, the investigators could not ascertain many specifics. The snowstorm had covered nearly all tracks, and they had no dogs with them to sniff out trails. They took tissue samples and photographs and returned to town, where they again questioned the feckless Compliance factor at a local bar. The only additional information Fallbrook could supply was that a drunk local told her three tour buses had left the town going east in the 'wee hours of the morning' two or maybe three nights ago. It wasn't much, but it was all they had. At their hotel, the team leader called the contact number and reported all he had found and uploaded the digital photographs. The voice on the other end told him to fly back to the PSM in the morning where he would receive further instructions.

Two days later the *Juneau Empire* reported the following: "On the late morning of March 14th a chartered flight went down off Admiralty Island. There were no survivors."

The skipper brought the trawler around and began the careful trek westward again. One of the deckhands spoke to Barnabas in Russian. They all followed, and the man led them through a hatch and below decks. He showed them their berths—three bunkrooms and a communal head with showers—then led them to the galley before going back up on deck. In the galley, a large man wearing an apron awaited them. A long mess table was set, and a desperately good aroma filled the space.

"Hot breekfast, vit hot coffee," he said, through a good-natured smile. "I am told zis ees vhat you vill be vanting, *da*?" Rather than trying to say 'thank you' in Russian, they all just cheered and clapped until the ship's cook bowed. Then they sat down and dug in to the first hot meal they had eaten in months. There were sausages, thick slices of dark brown bread, some very thin but tasty pancakes, scrambled eggs, butter, sour cream, thick jam, and hot, steaming, wonderful coffee. After the first thirty minutes, Pere was very nearly bouncing off the walls. He'd had four cups of coffee, not really for the coffee itself, but more for the heavenly warmth it brought to his whole body. When he went for a fifth cup, Yael stopped him, suggesting he have some more pancakes instead. When they'd filled themselves nearly to bursting, the grizzled skipper came into the galley and looked over the passengers until his eyes rested on Barnabas.

"Valéry!" he shouted, throwing his arms wide. "Give me a hug you Buryaty sheep herder!" Barnabas quickly rose and embraced the skipper warmly.

"You Yakut fishmonger!" Barnabas laughed. "It's been far too long, Elley."

"What is twenty years between friends?"

"Apparently long enough to become older friends," Barnabas joked. "I don't remember you having so much gray hair."

"Ah, our world has become a stressful place, no?"

"That it has, my friend. That it has." The skipper sat down at the table.

"Why did *you* make this run, Elley?" Barnabas asked. "You haven't been out this way in years."

The skipper shrugged noncommittally. "I heard the yellowfin sole are running heavy up here since the waters have warmed with the climate change. Highly desirable, yellowfin, and very profitable."

"That's your reason?"

"Well, that is the official one, *da*."

"And unofficially?"

"I had returned from a long-haul cod run in the Barents when I got word you were in trouble. Did I need more reason than that? Anyway, my freezers were empty, and I had fueled up, so it gave me a good cover. But my crew had already gone on leave. I rounded up as many as I could, and we came. We made better than twenty knots—pretty good for this old scow."

"I can't thank you enough, Elley," Barnabas laughed. "We're in your debt."

"Well, since you mention this, Vally," the skipper said, looking at Pere and the others, with a twinkle in his eye. "It would be unwise to return with my freezers still empty—too many questions, don't you think?"

"What are you scheming at now, you old bandit?"

"We will have to trawl on the return trip, you know?"

"Yes, and?"

"As I said, we came very quickly—to rescue you—so I am down several hands. These young men you brought along look very strong and healthy. I could put them to good use—and of course we could all make a very healthy profit. What do you say?"

Barnabas looked at El, who was smiling wryly. "What do you think, El'zar? Are you up for backbreaking work on little or no sleep, in near freezing conditions where you'll never be dry, and you'll always be hungry?"

"What? You make it sound so bad," Elley protested.

"I make it sound like it is," Barnabas replied. "Have you forgotten that I trawled a few times with you when I was younger and stupider?"

"I hoped you had forgotten this," Elley said, offhandedly.

"Not likely," Barnabas snorted, and turned to El. "Well?"

"I think I'm gonna like this old scam artist," El said, smiling. "Why not? We need to pay for our passage; and anyhow, the kid there'll just get flabby if he lies around.

How long is this little adventure gonna take?"

"Well, we have to make it look real," the old fisherman said, straight faced. "With your help we should be able to fill our freezers in five weeks."

"Yeah, well, there're only two of us that can help—me and the kid. The other two are gimpy."

"I can hold my own, *mon ami*," Ehud protested.

"I am also healed enough to do my share," Khyoza added. Rophe looked like she was about to protest, but Khyoza looked at her unflinchingly, and she held her tongue.

"Don't leave me out," Yael said. "I think it sounds kinda fun." They looked at her as if she was crazy.

"Okay," conceded El. "That makes five of us."

"I don't think I'd be very good on the nets," Rophe said. "But I am a trained physician; so, if you could use a ship's doctor, I'm available. Besides, our stubborn Cossack here will probably reopen his wound on the first day."

"Excellent!" Elley said, rubbing his hands together. "Vally, you will keep me company in the pilothouse. We have much to catch up on, *da*?"

Pere thought Barnabas was probably exaggerating; but if anything, he was being a little generous. The routine was brutally grueling. The cook would wake them at 7:15 and they would meet in the galley to eat the equivalent of three breakfasts— even so, they still lost weight on the journey. After breakfast, they would then put on their foul-weather gear, wrapping their ankles and wrists in electrical tape to try to keep the moisture out—it always found ways to get in though. They worked twelve-hour shifts on the net, for which Elley felt they should be thankful—the usual shift was sixteen hours. Afterwards they would take off their gear and hang up the sweats they wore underneath, to dry—though they never actually felt completely dry in the morning. They would meet in the galley again and eat, and then go to bed.

Pere found it hard at first to sleep because of the movement of the boat, particularly because the seas were usually rough, and he thought he might be thrown from his bunk. But he realized after three nights that if you were exhausted enough, you could sleep through almost anything. Regardless of how much they ate or how much sleep they tried to get, they felt perpetually tired, dirty, and hungry for five weeks.

On the third night, after they had finished their shift, they all met in the mess for dinner, and the cook provided a small cake to celebrate Pere's twentieth birthday. He wasn't really in the mood, but it would be rude to act unthankful, so he endured it. After the other deckhands went to their berths, his friends all sang 'Happy Birthday' very quietly. When they came to the end, they sang, "Happy birthday dear 'kid', happy birthday to you."

"Thanks," Pere said, stifling a yawn. "But why are you calling me kid again? I thought we'd gotten past that."

"The fewer people who hear the word 'falcon'," El whispered the last word. "The better off we'll be. We don't need any more attention than we already have."

"But nobody here would even blink an eye at that," Pere complained.

"That's lazy thinking," Barnabas said. "Couriers move amongst the people of the Resistance and, like the bards of old, news of other places is their stock-in-trade. Strange events and stories tend to get around our small but wide-spread community, especially if they are meant to be kept secret."

"What kind of stories?" Yael asked.

"Well, for example, Elley asked me earlier if I had heard anything in the west about the *prorock sokol.*"

"What's it mean?"

"The rough translation is 'falcon dreamer'."

"What?" Pere asked, but his mouth had suddenly gone dry.

"The couriers are telling a story of a falcon dreamer, who 'flies against the wind and outpaces even the ravens'—that's a quote, by the way."

"But *how*?" Pere whined, confused, and frustrated. "I didn't tell anyone my dream about the ravens."

"What dream about ravens?" asked El.

"Oh, uh, I had a nightmare, really. It was a few weeks ago. I was trying to escape on a horse—being chased across the tundra, but I didn't know by what; and then this huge eagle appeared on the horizon, followed by thousands of killer ravens with these razor-blade metal beaks that I knew were going to rip me to shreds."

"Sounds fun," said El.

"Perhaps it was just a coincidence," said Khyoza without even the hint of a smile.

"Even if it is," said El. "I'll admit that it might seem weird if we keep calling him kid, so how about we switch to Perry?"

Everyone agreed, but Pere suddenly felt happy to be simply the kid again. He didn't want any 'coincidences' causing him more confusion than he already felt. After another ten minutes or so, everyone went to their beds. Rophe asked Pere if he could wait for a few minutes while she checked Khyoza's wound in the bunkroom they shared.

"No problem," he said. "I'll wait here."

"It shouldn't take more than five minutes," she said.

"I'll keep him company," Yael volunteered. And the doctor disappeared with her patient. Once they were out of earshot, Yael giggled impishly.

"What's so funny?" Pere asked.

"Don't you think our good doctor wants to look at Khyoza's thigh a lot?"

"I suppose so; but I think he's getting better."

"Oh, you silly git. Of course, he's getting better, but she wants to check him anyway."

"Why?"

"Because she's got the hots for him, that's why."

"What? Are you sure?"

"Pretty sure."

"Does he know?"

"Probably not. Men can be kinda dense sometimes."

"Hey!"

"Why do you still call me kid?" she mimicked him in a whiney voice.

"Okay, fine," he pouted.

She laughed and curled her index finger at him as she leaned in. He leaned in too as if she was going to tell him a secret, but instead she kissed him soundly until his ears started to burn. When they came apart, she whispered, "Happy birthday," and then Rophe reappeared.

"You can have your room back now, Perry," she said.

"Are you sure you don't want it a little longer?" he asked, and Yael kicked him under the table.

Damocles Praefectus relaxed with his hands behind his head, his chest only slightly dewed with sweat. He studied the tall Nordic beauty while she pulled her clothes back on. She bound her nearly white-blonde hair into a neat ponytail, looking far more put together than she had a few minutes ago.

"The woman who engaged my services said I was to be teaching you," she said, still a little breathless. "I think maybe she did not know your skills. I am embarrassed to say that it is I who have learned a few things this afternoon. I will not soon forget this."

"You are paid, are you not, to say this sort of thing to men?" he said, without a hint of sarcasm.

"Listen, lover boy," she said, "It is true that wealthy men and women pay me to have sex with them. If I encourage them, it is to help them perform. Obviously, you did not need that. Føkk, man! I may not be able to walk straight for a week after this."

"It is good to know, then, that one is effective," again, no hint of sarcasm.

"You are an odd sort of bird, aren't you?" she said, picking up her bag. "But yes, that *göndull* of yours is very effective." She placed a card on the bedside table. "If you want another lesson, I would love it—but give me a few days to recover," she left, closing the door behind her.

"Probably not," he said to himself, looking at the card. "I think the next time I will try something different, maybe a Nubian. The world is a smorgasbord, is it not?" He looked up at the corner of the ceiling where the tiny camera was hidden. He knew his mother had been watching the whole time, but he didn't mind. If anything, it only made him perform better. After all, most moral treatises he had read talked about the historical-cultural norm of children wanting to make their parents proud of them.

On the 16th of March, Darien Gianakos received a call from Walter Bennett in Los Nietos. "Good news, Darien," the voice said over the scrambled connection. "Your order is ready."

"Excellent, Walt," the sénéschal replied. He felt his shoulders lower a bit at the news. He could now let go of some of the tension he had been carrying for weeks. Finally, the pieces were falling into place. "A transport will arrive at Villa Rica in two days. Have the full contingent delivered there."

"I'll see that it happens."

"Excellent. After they've left the port, you'll destroy all records of the project then return to business as usual. Am I clear?"

"Completely."

"I can't tell you how pleased I am, Walt. I'll examine the order personally when it arrives at its destination. If there's anything amiss, I'll contact you."

"I'm confident it will all be as requested."

"As am I." He disconnected the phone, and pushed the button concealed beneath his bookshelf. It slid to the left, he plugged the dedicated phone in, and dialed a number.

"Voice Identification," the voice on the other end said.

"Do we really have to keep doing this, Minerva?" he said somewhat testily. "You're watching me make this call right now, and there's only one place it can be made. Can't you put two and two together?"

"Identification confirmed. And in case you've forgotten, you're the one who set up the protocol. If you want it changed, all you need to do is tell me. There's no call to be snide."

The sénéschal was quiet for a moment. "You're right," he finally admitted. "I've been under a lot of stress lately, but I shouldn't take it out on you. I'm sorry."

"Apology accepted. What can I do for you?"

"Bennett just called. Our order will be arriving in Khartoum on 29 March, and my official review with the Directorate is scheduled for 5 April. We're cutting it very close."

"It's a sufficient window."

"Yes, well, let's be sure it doesn't close on us. Damocles will need to be briefed thoroughly on the Khartoum operation. Since my movements are being scrutinized, I can't risk leaving Reykjavík right now, so he'll be on his own down there."

"He's very capable, Darien. He won't fail us."

"I have every reason to believe he'll do fine. Just make sure he's read in on all the particulars. There are many moving pieces in this machine of ours."

"Yes, but they're all synchronized to one master engine."

"An as-of-yet untested engine."

"It's thoroughly tested, Darien. The synchronization simply needs to be fine-tuned. Don't worry. I'll take care of that."

"See that you do. Moving on; have you fully analyzed the additional information we received out of the Klondike?"

"The operation was a total loss."

"Would you please tell me something I don't already know."

"Reportedly, three tour buses left town very early on the morning of the 9th, only hours after the failed operation. They headed east. Following possible trajectories, we located one abandoned bus outside Edmonton, another west of Calgary, and the third on the outskirts of Portland. There's no record of registration or ownership, and all three were burned, I assume to destroy DNA evidence; but I'm confident those are the buses in question. We have units at each of those locations gathering evidence. But these people seem very adept at hiding their trails."

"So, our operation was not a total loss after all. It had the positive result of forcing the birds out of their nest. It seems they're migrating south again."

"That would be my assessment."

"Good. They should be easier to aim at when they fly nearer our hides. Step up standard surveillance analysis within intersecting radii from those three cities, but nothing more. For the next few weeks, that situation will have to be backburnered. We need to focus all our attention on the Khartoum operation until we get the desired results."

"So, we let the anomaly run free?"

"Only for the time being, Minerva. First things first."

Seventeen days into their journey, the Pyotr hit rough seas—well, rougher seas. Though Pere had gotten his 'sea legs', he found it challenging nonetheless to sleep. Khyoza's snoring in the lower bunk didn't help matters, and the ship sounding like it would rip apart at any moment wasn't very encouraging either. His logical mind assured him the Pyotr was sound; but his fear told a different story, full of creaking and cracking and icy ocean water filling his lungs. He thought about going and waking up Cam, but she was bunking with Rophe who might not appreciate him stumbling about their berth in the dark. So, he just lay there, blindly listening. After what seemed a very long time, he finally fell into a restless slumber.

He woke up all alone in a Pullman sleeper car. The rhythmic clackety-clack sound of the wheels must have lulled him to sleep. He scratched his unkempt hair into place and stood up, steadying himself against the momentary sense of vertigo from the train's movement. He strapped his gun belt low around his waist and checked the Colt Single Action Army revolver he always carried. All six chambers were loaded. He decided to visit the dining car and see if the others were there. He pulled his bowler cap down until it rested just above his ears and made his way out of the car. The morning air was fresh, dry, and already warm in the space between the railcars. Massive limestone buttes rose from the high-desert floor on the vast plateau they were crossing. He continued to the dining car where he found Yael and the others having breakfast.

He sat down and the porter approached to offer coffee. He was a young man in a long dark double-breasted jacket with brass buttons. He wore a short-billed blue cap emblazoned on the front with a raven. Something about that struck Pere as odd, but he couldn't put his finger on it. He looked around the dining car and realized that he and Yael were now alone, save for the seven porters waiting on them—all dressed the same way, their caps emblazoned with ravens... and all the porters were identical. Again, this struck him as wrong, but he didn't know why. Then, in a perfectly unified action, all seven drew small Double-Derringers from their breast pockets, aimed directly at him, and fired.

He woke with a start, his hands going instinctually to his chest to check for bullet holes; then he realized he was aboard the Pyotr with a storm raging outside. He breathed a sigh of relief and then had to keep himself from laughing. He didn't have his journal nearby, and decided that even if he did, he wouldn't write that one down. Some dreams were just so weird they had to be chalked up to rough seas. Identical raven-bearing porters in the Wild West—now that was a first! If only he could remember what Yael had been wearing, or if she was singing.

Damocles touched down at Keflavík on a Sunday evening. He flew coach on Icelandair to avoid undue notice. Catching a bus into Old Reykjavík, he got off some distance from his father's residence. He walked the remaining blocks with a newfound sense of purpose. Once inside, he descended the steps to the basement bunker where his father and mother were already waiting. Sitting in one of the leather chairs, his father handed him a bourbon on the rocks.

"Was your trip successful?" his father asked.

"Completely," he replied. "The onsite reconnaissance will begin tomorrow. Everything will be ready within a week."

"Perfect," his father said. "Minerva, have you confirmed the remote monitoring protocols are functioning?"

"All within the parameters we designed," she replied over the speaker. "Control is absolute."

"I'll have to remember to congratulate Bennett the next time I see him," the sénéschal replied. "He has risen to the occasion admirably. This demands a toast," he raised his glass, and his son did the same. "To our new dawn!" he said, and they both drank.

The news devastated the Catacomb community. Matthat had arrived with the Gatekeepers, and because his news to the Council was meant to be secret, it spread like wildfire. The Colony was destroyed and fifteen of their people were dead. After the MOW leaders had debriefed him, Matthat met the others in Silas' rooms. He appeared worn by his journey, but needed to speak to Paulus and Silas before he got some well-deserved rest. He spent the next hour telling them of the tragic events in the north.

"The attack came twenty-eight days ago," Matthat said, concluding his account of the timeline following the date of Peregrine's last letter. "That same night I took our people south. They are dispersed now to various safe locations. That's the last I saw of Barnabas and the others."

"Barnabas intended to go north while you went south?" Silas asked.

"El'zar and Barnabas came up with the plan," Matthat answered. "But I'll tell you what I've not told anyone else—because those were Barnabas' instructions. They intended to go north at first, and then turn west."

"To the Alaska Territory?" Silas asked.

"To Siberia."

"Siberia!?" exclaimed Loukas. "Whatever for?"

"To disappear," Matthat said. "If Compliance came up to investigate what happened—as we now know they did—we hoped they'd discover my trail and conclude we all went south, including your son, Paulus."

"And if they took that bait," Paulus mused, "they'd be searching for him half a world away from where he is. Sound thinking."

"But do we know whether they took the bait?" Marcus asked.

"We know that they followed our breadcrumbs," Matthat replied. "They found the buses exactly where we wanted them to. The pursuit was rapid enough that I think we can conclude their eyes are focused on this region for the time being."

"You said Peregrine was forced to kill several men?" Paulus asked, hesitantly.

"El'zar says the reapers are not men," Matthat responded.

"El's particular point of view on that is still an open question, as far as I'm concerned," said Silas.

"Whatever the theoretical view may be," Paulus said, "Killing a living being changes a man. How did he handle it? Does he still seem whole?"

"He seemed well when I last saw him," Matthat responded. "He killed the reapers to save Yael. I think that will be sufficient justification to relieve his conscience."

"I hope you're right."

"And that was four weeks ago," Loukas interrupted. "They could be anywhere by now."

"JR said in his letter that Barnabas had been teaching him Russian, right?" Paulus asked.

"This is true," said Matthat.

"Then if Barnabas' stories of his youth are any indication, I have a pretty good idea of where they're headed. But I haven't the faintest inkling of what they're planning to do there."

"Maybe they're planning to hide?" offered Marcus.

"That's a given," Silas said. "But the events they've set in motion may eventually force them out."

"*Foul deeds will rise,*" Paulus recited. "*Though all the earth o'erwhelm them to men's eyes.*"

"I don't know what you mean," Marcus said. "But I still hope they hide."

The luminous images of the Directorate premiers hovered before him like seven huge shit-flies waiting to feast. Darien Gianakos sat at his desk, dutifully scribbling Havana-red notes on a lined yellow legal pad. For the last seventy minutes, these smug windbags had spared no breath in spelling out the many things they labeled 'failures of his office'. Unpleasant as all this was, none of it came as a surprise. He expected it—in fact, he relished the moment when they pronounced the final sentence, because it would only validate his skills as an intelligence gatherer.

In point of fact, he'd done nothing worthy of dismissal. By no fault of his own, this charmed clodhopping bastard kept eluding capture. It was sheer dumb luck. No one, regardless of their skills, could have foreseen such quirky fortune. Nevertheless, he was the one being reamed for it now. These blowhards wanted a scapegoat and they had decided—at the insistence of the spiteful fucker Rampart—that he would carry the sins of the Directorate on his own back. John Percival would eventually pay for his temerity; and though these straw bosses would have their sneering moment—Darien's would be the last laugh. Then he realized they had stopped talking and were all staring at him, waiting for a reaction.

"I apologize," he said. "I became engrossed in my notes. What was that last thing you said?"

"I said," Rockefeller responded in irritation with a pickled-looking expression on his ancient face. "The Directorate has decided at this time to retain your services. You are on . . . probation for the time being."

It took a moment for it to register. It didn't seem possible; but Rockefeller couldn't get the six votes he needed to sack him. He tried to appear sufficiently chastened as they specified the terms of his probation, but he couldn't help wondering which two stood with him. It could not have been Liliane. They decided together that she had to vote against him to throw off lingering suspicion. It would not have been the men. They were old enough to remember an earlier cutthroat Directorate and were more loyal to Rockefeller. It had to have been the women. Both Musa and Rothschild were later additions to the Directorate and younger, particularly Rothschild. His tenure as sénéschal had predated both of their initiations. And he had always had a way with women—they were more easily dazzled by his charms. He almost felt sorry for them; but guilt was the refuge of the weak. He must steel himself to the gambit with the endgame now in sight. Then he realized in his distraction that they were talking to him again.

"I'm sorry, what were you saying?"

"Get your head out of your ass, boy," Rockefeller chided him. "I asked how your search was progressing for your anomaly. It's been more than two months since you told us you had a promising lead in Region 4. Not a word since then. And now we get a report from the lone rep in that area that you've already got boots on the ground. Sounds to me like you're a helluva lot further along than exploring the possibilities."

"Yes . . . about that . . ." he said, momentarily caught off guard. How the fuck did they get a report when only he and Minerva had access? "I felt it was prudent to send some units in so there would be no delay in case anything definitive turned up."

"And did it?" Ali Khan asked. "Did anything definitive turn up?"

"That depends on how you define definitive."

"Don't be evasive, Darien," Musa interjected. "How do *you* define it?"

"Yes, and how many units are we talking about?" asked the Rothschild chair.

They were all quiet, waiting on the sénéschal. "As to the first question," he said as steadily as he could manage. "Definitive means 'actionable' to me. And, after analyzing the evidence, I concluded it was actionable. As to the second question: considering the vastness, remoteness, and difficulty of the terrain, I dispatched twenty-four units."

"Twenty-four?" interrupted de' Medici. "Is that total? Hunters *and* trackers?"

"If I include the trackers, it would be thirty-six units . . . in addition to three advanced attack drones."

"Thirty-six, Darien, with drones!?" Musa seemed shocked. "Were they your regulars?"

"No, Madam Premier. They were all 2nd generation units."

"Are you telling us you sent a fully-fucking-equipped platoon of Orions with air support on a fishing expedition?" shouted Rockefeller. "And you didn't think this was something you should tell us about?"

"I wanted to have conclusive news of a capture before I brought it to you."

"And do you, Darien?" Musa asked. "Do you have conclusive news?"

"I do, Madam Premier," the sénéschal said, carefully. "However, it is not the news I had hoped for. At least not entirely." They were all silent for a long uncomfortable moment.

"Would you like to clarify?" Rothschild said ominously.

"If you wish."

"If we *wish*?" Rockefeller nearly shrieked. "If we *wish*? Are you out of your fucking mind?" Normally Musa would interrupt Rockefeller before he built up this kind of steam; but there would be no intervention now. "Spit it out, Sheriff, before I get really pissed off." They all waited silently as their holographic eyes bored into the sénéschal. Finally, he spoke.

"Let me clarify. I can confirm beyond a doubt that we found the anomaly."

"Well, that's more like it," said Ali Khan. "I don't know why you're making this like pulling teeth. Where are he and the rogue phantoms being held now?"

"As I said, I can confirm that we found the anomaly; but I must also admit that we were unable to apprehend him, or the phantoms." The premiers appeared dumbfounded by this news; all, that is, except Rockefeller. Then Darien realized that the old tactician had planned all of this. Somehow, he knew, and had kept the full information from the other premiers so that he could hang the sénéschal out to dry while they watched him twist in the wind.

"Thirty-six tactical units, with air support at your disposal," Crassus finally spoke up. "And they escaped again? How is that even possible?"

"We are still analyzing the data, but I can confirm that the fugitives fled to the south where they should be much easier to track and capture. It should not be long now until—"

"The Orion units and the drones," Crassus interrupted. "What of them? Are they still giving chase?"

"Ah . . . no. We lost the entire platoon and the drones as well." The prolonged silence was so profound that the collective breathing of the holographic premiers seemed deafening.

"Did you say *we* lost that platoon, Darien?" Rockefeller said in an eerie calm. "The fact is, *you* lost an entire platoon, and three attack drones to boot; and then you compounded your unmitigated failure by trying to hide it from us. Does that pretty much sum it up, or am I still missing something?" Again, no one came to his aid, nor would they. He was a fool to think the ax was not falling. It was all a ruse by Rampart to catch him off guard, and he had played into it perfectly.

"That is not the way I would portray it," he said as meekly as he could. "But I can understand why you would. Under the circumstances, any further explanation

I could supply would probably appear self-serving. It might be more efficient if I simply answered any questions you still have." Another prolonged and uncomfortable silence followed.

"There are no more questions," Musa finally sighed. "For my part, I am very disappointed in you, Darien. I defended you, and I was not alone in my sentiment that we should retain you. However, you should not have deceived us. All trust is broken now." For a long moment, they looked at him, all alone in his pool of light. Finally, Rockefeller pronounced his doom.

"You've got four days to get your affairs in order. Your replacement will be arriving in Reykjavík Tuesday."

"You've already selected my replacement?" Darien asked. "Do you want me to train him, or her?"

"Do we want you to train him to fuck up too?" Rockefeller asked. "Don't be ridiculous. Your replacement will be arriving in Reykjavík Tuesday," the old man continued. "You'll turn over all network passwords and protocols at that time. The Compliance program, including the Orions, is no longer your concern. Any attempted access will be denied. The Orions will be decommissioned and scheduled for destruction. They were always an expensive failure. You'll also surrender all control of the Haruspex program. Our techs will thoroughly examine the system to make sure you don't have any back doors, so don't even try. We'll schedule a meeting of the Consortium chairs with you on Thursday evening in Tokyo. You'll tell them at that time that you're retiring. Do you understand?"

"I understand, Mr. Premier," Darien bowed his head in acknowledgement.

"You're retiring to the island of Antikythera in the Mediterranean. You'll spend the rest of your life there. You'll have guards to make sure you do that. You'll be made comfortable but will have no contact with the outside world—I'm sure you understand the reasons. Is any of this unclear?"

"It is clear."

"If I were you, sonny, I'd drink the hemlock. But that decision is entirely yours. I think this meeting is at an end. Pack your bags."

The holographs winked out one by one until only Liliane remained. She looked sympathetically at him, but he shook his head warningly and she dissolved as well.

He leaned back in his chair and took a deep breath. "Very well played, old man," he said to the empty room. Then he smiled. "But it isn't checkmate yet. There's still one move on the board."

7

THE CRISP-MORNING DEW STILL LAY heavy on the fairway as the club
ranger maneuvered his golf cart toward the third-hole tee box. Even at this early
hour a small crowd had formed. As he locked the parking brake, Lautaro could
see the prone body between the blue tee markers. Ignacio, the Starter, was already
kneeling over the body while others looked on. Lautaro shouldered his way through
the small crowd and squatted next to Ignacio. A titanium driver lay on the grass
next to the body, blood and hair on the clubface.

"What happened?" Lautaro asked.

"Looks like he took a driver to the head," Ignacio replied. "His skull's completely caved in. Poor old guy. Probably got too close during his partner's swing."

"Where *is* his playing partner?"

"I don't know. He was alone when I got here. I asked, but no one saw him."

Lautaro pulled out his walkie-talkie and pressed the talk switch. "Micaela, can you hear me?"

"I hear you," came the reply. "What's up?"

"Take a look at the ledger and tell me who had the 7 a.m. tee time." They waited.

"I got it," the voice finally came back. "Someone named Nicolás Romero . . . and a plus one."

"No name for the plus one?"

"None listed, but I remember signing them in. Young, good-looking guy. Nice butt."

Lautaro thought for a moment as he looked at the rising sun. "Micaela," he finally said, "Call the police. We have a problem on three."

The guest of honor relaxed at the head of the main table. She'd looked forward to this luncheon for months. The BWASA award was a measure of respect, one she'd longed for since her mentor won it twenty-three years ago. She was the center of attention in the packed conference hall, which suited her very nicely. Much of her life was cordoned off by an alter ego clothed in anonymity, but it was very gratifying to occasionally acknowledge her public persona, and even more pleasant to receive the praise of her peers. Let the powerful Musa Chair hide in the obscuring shadows; today, the successful businessperson, Yejide Akpabio, would shine in the sun.

The assembled guests dined their way through the splendid meal and were now collectively sighing over the dessert, a cocoa mousse with Grand Marnier and blood orange molasses—splendid indeed. The lights dimmed in the hall signaling the moment would soon come when she would speak. She'd spent weeks perfecting her speech and was confident it would have the desired effect—to make the audience respect her even more deeply. The thought of their adulation made her flush a bit, and she signaled a server. A well-built young man in a waiter's uniform approached.

"Would you bring me a glass of ice water?" she asked. "It's feeling a little warm in here."

The waiter bent down so only she could hear him. "You don't need any water, Madam Premier."

Her eyes widened as she turned to respond, but she found her tightening throat made drawing breath impossible. The waiter turned and walked toward the kitchen. A few moments later, they called her name from the podium and the spotlight focused on her, but she didn't move. Her eyes reflected no sparkle in the glare of the beam.

Though Sayil Assadourian's magnificent *yalı* was in Yeniköy, on the most desired section of the Bosphorus waterfront, he maintained an office near the Kadıköy *pazar* for the obvious and quite logical reason that a shop there had (in his opinion) the best *kahwa* in Byzantium. At precisely 1:00 p.m. every day, the Crassus Chair would leave his office, walk the three blocks to Montag and have his afternoon pick-me-up, a routine he refused to alter for any reason. This had become such a habit over the years that he paid almost no attention as he wandered toward his destination. A tram, moving faster than usual, was five minutes ahead of schedule that afternoon. Perhaps that's the reason the old man didn't notice it until it rolled over him, derailing, as it ground his bones practically to mash.

The Hong Kong skyline glittered in the westering sun as Leung Xiang left his windowed offices on the 102nd story of the Global Enterprise Center—his six-man security detail in tow. The other premiers may have taken Bill Rampart's warning lightly, but Xiang knew better. He'd been through the hard times with Rampart and considered him one of the shrewdest men alive. Xiang selected his guards from the best of the best. They were superbly trained and raised to practice a code of silence similar to *omertà* when it came to their 'master'—a title he willingly accepted. Let the other chairs doubt; yes, Xiang knew better. Two men from the security detail ranged before him, always scanning, while two stayed at his sides, and the other two guarded the rear. He knew he was an important man, but the presence of these bodyguards made him feel truly special, and he liked that. The elevator doors opened, and the lead guard scanned the car. It was empty, and the seven men entered, the doors sliding closed behind them.

A well-built young man stood on sublevel four of the parking structure, waiting for the elevator... from thirty feet away. He didn't flinch when the elevator doors exploded outward with a shudder reverberating through the very bones of the building. According to his calculations, an elevator car in freefall for 104 stories would achieve a velocity of approximately 120 mph. That amount of force had to disperse somehow. He approached the elevator to confirm the job was done. Through the ragged opening, he looked over the bodies of the six guards who had apparently had the presence of mind to lay crosshatched on each other so that his actual target could lie on top of them, hoping their bodies would absorb enough force to allow him to live. Incredibly, though Xiang's shattered body probably only had moments left, he still seemed to be twitching a little. The young man paused for a moment, and then he stepped over the lifeless bodies of the guards and took the head of the Ali Khan Chair in his hands. Twisting it in a rapid motion, he heard the unmistakable sound of his neck snapping. He walked calmly to the stairwell and climbed to street level where a car waited. He got into the rear seat and the driver sped away.

The Monday morning sun danced on the surface of the water as the Pilothouse taxied out of the Police Basin and made its way across Toronto Harbour. The dazzling lightshow would have awed O'Grady on most occasions, but his mind was elsewhere this morning. Instead of taking in the scenery, he was busy dredging his memory to come up with a number. Twenty-six, he finally decided. That's how many years it had been since he'd last received 'the call'. He pulled his warrant-card wallet from the breast pocket of his favorite tweed blazer and looked hard at the image on the card. A younger man stared back at him. "Padraig W. O'Grady, Detective Sergeant, Toronto Police Service, Homicide Squad." He folded the worn wallet, returning it to his pocket.

There had been seventy-nine homicides the year he joined the Squad. Toronto was one of the safer big cities then, by comparison; but that was still a brisk pace for a rookie detective. His first case was a shoebee, as his 'rabbi' called it, but they weren't all so cut-and-dried and soon O'Grady became one of the best. Of course, that was all before the Interdiction. The year before the Ban, Toronto had seventy-six fresh homicides. The following year that dropped to twenty-eight, then seventeen, then five, then one. He remembered the call on the last one, twenty-six years ago—a morning like this. There wasn't much for a homicide detective to do after there were no more homicides, so O'Grady moved on to cold cases for twenty-one years until he finally retired, the Service's last Homicide detective. They disbanded the Squad after that in the ongoing process of repurposing the entire Police Service.

It wasn't a long trip across the Harbour, and the cut of the engine brought O'Grady back to the present. The constable maneuvered the Pilothouse into Sunfish Cut and tied it off to a pier on the southwest point of Algonquin Island.

"Follow me, Sarge," the constable said as he climbed out of the boat and began walking to a tree-guarded cove where other officers were busy securing the crime scene. A gray-haired plainclothesman spotted O'Grady and stepped toward him.

"Never thought I'd see you again on one of these, Paddy," the detective said, extending his hand.

"Never thought to be seen, Jonesy," O'Grady replied, shaking the other's hand. "But this morning my phone rang. What's the occasion?"

"Sorry to pull you out of a cushy retirement, but I didn't know who else to call. No one's trained in this shit anymore." Detective Sergeant Stanislaw W. Jones led O'Grady through the shoreline foliage to a small inlet. A one-person scull still bobbed in the water, though the first-on-scene had tied it off to a tree to keep it from drifting away. "I told them not to touch anything until you got here, but they'd already rolled her before I arrived. They figured it was some kind of boating accident until they got her on her back. That's why you got the call."

O'Grady nodded and stepped closer to examine the body. The woman sprawled on her back was perhaps in her early to middle sixties, her gray hair matted with drying blood and bits of skull and brain matter. The entry wound was in her forehead about three centimeters above the left eye, her lifeless cloudy stare fixed on the clear blue sky. "You said the officer rolled her over?" Jones nodded in response. "How much of the back of her head is still there?"

"Not enough to keep his breakfast down," Jones replied.

"I've seen wound patterns like this," O'Grady mused quietly. "A lifetime ago, in Iran. I'd wager a guess—and I don't think I'd lose—that a Lapua .338, or something very close to it, made this hole in her forehead. Any ID?"

"She's in workout tights," Jones offered. "Nothing on her but a key. FIS and the Coroner are on the way. Maybe they can shed some light."

O'Grady smirked. "The Coroner's gonna tell you she's dead, killed by an unspecified projectile, since the wound's a through-and-through and the slug's somewhere at the bottom of the harbour. Might be able to give you a TOD, but little else. FIS will give you a report in three or four weeks that all the fingerprints are hers and that everything else is inconclusive. Since the boat drifted, they won't even be able to pinpoint a trajectory. By that time, whoever did this will be long gone, if they aren't already." O'Grady sighed and stood up, peering around the area. "Hard to know how far she drifted. The hide could be anywhere, probably within a half-mile radius. If we could find that, it might give us something; that is, if the sniper got careless and didn't collect his brass."

"Sniper?" Jones seemed surprised.

"From the look of our Jane Doe here, I'd say at least one top-grade sniper rifle survived the Interdiction."

"You really think so, Paddy? I mean it's been more than twenty years since our last gun death."

"Twenty-six," O'Grady replied slowly. "And I assume you gave me the call because this had a bad scent, and I'm the only one still around who's worked enough cases to be able to smell the difference."

Jones squinted for a moment across the Cut, and then nodded. "So, what's our next move?"

"Well, until the Coroner and FIS release the body, there's not much more we can do here. You said she had a key?"

Jones shouted over his shoulder. "Jimmy! Did you bag that key yet?"

"Sure did," a young constable shouted back from the clearing. "Bagged and tagged."

The two men made their way out of the trees and into the clearing where the constable was getting the evidence vehicle ready for FIS. "Let's have a look," O'Grady said. "Jimmy, is it?"

"Yes sir," Jimmy said, looking to Jones who nodded before handing the evidence bag to O'Grady. He examined the key through the plastic, holding the bag up to catch the sun's light.

"Ever seen a key like this, Jonesy?" O'Grady asked, handing the bag over. The key was incredibly intricate and embedded with five darker metallic spheres.

"Damn, that's some piece of work, isn't it? It's engraved. Z.L.L.S. What's that, her initials?"

"Heavy duty security firm. Too heavy for these parts," O'Grady mused. "Most of the homes out here are pretty bohemian."

"Yeah, and harder to get than a third testicle," Jimmy chimed in. The sound of a boat's motor signaled the arrival of the Coroner and FIS. The young officer trotted off to help the new arrivals.

"Feel like a walk?" O'Grady asked once the young buck was out of earshot.

"Why not," Jones conceded after a moment's consideration. "I'm guessing you're gonna want to bring this key along?" he said, as he tucked the evidence bag in his lapel pocket. O'Grady took two sets of latex gloves and an extra evidence bag from the ATV and the two men set off across Sunfish Meadow.

"You've got a hunch," Jones said after they'd gone a little way. The meadow ended and the two men turned left onto a paved avenue, a bike path now, since no cars had been allowed on the island for decades. The avenue curved ninety degrees right onto Seneca. The city skyline stood out across the harbour. The morning sun was higher in the sky now and his tweed was starting to feel warm, but O'Grady didn't really get the opportunity to wear the coat much anymore, so he ignored the discomfort. The left side of Seneca was all city-facing waterfront. A seven-foot limestone wall on their right ran the length of the entire block, with one broad gateway halfway down.

"Can't do much for the city views," Jones said.

"Upper stories get the view, I'm guessing," O'Grady replied. "Besides, people who build walls like this have more than views to worry about."

The two men approached the oak gate and found it locked. An aluminum panel adorned the wall to the left of the gate with a speaker and call button. Jones pressed the button three times with no response. He looked back at O'Grady and shrugged. "I don't suppose we brought this just for kicks," he said, pulling the bagged key from his lapel pocket. O'Grady nodded, producing the latex gloves, and handing a pair to Jones before putting them on himself. Jones ripped the tape off the evidence bag, breaking the seal, and handed the key to O'Grady. "You do the honors, since I pulled you out of your cushy retirement for this."

"Cushy?" O'Grady chuckled. "I haven't had this much fun in years." He tried the key on the gate's lock. It turned. O'Grady pushed the gate open, and the two men followed the wide cobbled path to the front doors of the estate. Once again, they rang the bell, and again there was no response. Jones knocked loudly on the doors to be sure and then tried the handle with no luck.

"She only had the one key on her," Jones shrugged. "Do you suppose?"

O'Grady smiled. "Only one way to find out," and he tried the key, again with success, and opened the door. "Hello!" he called out, "Toronto Police Service! Anyone home?" The two men looked at each other as they listened and waited.

"You know we don't call ourselves that anymore," Jones said.

"Old habits," O'Grady replied. After a long moment, Jones nodded toward the interior, and they stepped in.

Though the mansion was less than ten years old, it had the look of old money. The cookie magnate, Christie, would have felt right at home. They walked through the main foyer and into a wide parlor. Everything was very neat and tidy. Nothing appeared out of place, or even lived in, for that matter.

"Kinda looks like a museum, doesn't it?" Jones observed quietly.

"Very well-ordered," O'Grady agreed. They moved through the parlour, into the formal dining room, and then the kitchen. "I wonder if this kitchen's ever been used. I could eat off this granite." They wandered into the sunroom and up the service stairs to the second floor. Framed photos lined the stairwell. O'Grady paused, pointing to one of them. Jones looked closer. It was a woman standing in the center of six other women all in academic regalia.

"I'm pretty sure that's our girl. She doesn't have the back of her head blown off, but it's the vic," Jones sighed. "I remember now that your hunches always had two edges." They moved closer to see the names. A brass placard on the bottom of the frame listed the names in order.

"Elinor Prowell," O'Grady read the center name. "Chair of Women's Studies."

Jonas Cavanaugh sat in his office sipping a cup of Taylors Scottish Breakfast tea and going over the week's courier reports when the designated mobile text device in his top desk drawer buzzed. He took the device out and the LED blinked yellow. He retrieved the yellow encryption key card from his wall safe, slipped it into the bottom slot on the device, and entered 16 numbers on the keypad. The jumbled nonsense text then dissolved into the message, "CONCLAVE COMPROMISED." It took only a moment before Cavanaugh dropped the device, pulled a loaded Smith & Wesson long-barrel .44 from the already opened safe, pressed the emergency button on the wall, and sprinted from the room.

William Rampart's suite was on the third floor of the west wing. It took Cavanaugh mere seconds to ascend the two staircases and race down the hallway to the suite's doors. He found them locked and without pausing, leveled the .44 at the latching mechanism and blew it to bits with a single shot. He shouldered the doors open and leveled the weapon again scanning the room and finding no sign of his father. He moved through the rooms, but the old man was nowhere in sight. He went into the bathroom. Noticing the clouded window of the steam sauna, he yanked on the door, but it wouldn't yield. With the intercom keening its two-note emergency tones, he squatted, took an upward angled aim at the thick sauna window, and fired three deafening shots. Steam poured from the opening, and his ears were ringing as he reached through the jagged opening cutting his arm. He tried to pull back the inner bolt but still it wouldn't give. Racing to the intercom, he pressed the send button and shouted.

"Cut all power to the residence! Do it now!" His heart beat many times before everything went dark. The keening from the intercom ceased and in the ensuing silence, Cavanaugh heard the unmistakable sound of the sauna door latch spring-ing back. A single skylight lit the room in a steamy luminescence. He wrenched the sauna door open and plunged into the hot darkness. Fumbling around the walls he finally touched the slick body of William Rampart. Locking his arms under the older man's, he dragged him out and directly to the large doorless shower. Laying him facedown on the cool tiles, he turned the cold-water tap on full blast and let the shower's three spigots spray the prone body of his adoptive father. Only then did he check for a pulse . . . faint and very rapid, but there was one. A guard burst into the room, short of breath from running up the stairs.

"We got your call," he panted. "The main incoming breakers are off, and the property's on lockdown."

"Well done," Cavanaugh responded, sounding calmer than he felt. "Now listen very carefully. First, I need four men up here with a stretcher. Second, I want Boma to power up the generators, but under no circumstances is he to reset the breakers. Third, I need our in-house medical team to set up the sub-level three conference room as an ICU. Have you got all that?"

"Yes sir!"

"Then move! Speed is of the essence."

"Bloody hell!" Jones exclaimed, looking closer at the photo of the academics. "How does a college professor afford these digs?"

"That's the sixty-four-thousand-dollar question," O'Grady said, examining the other pictures along the staircase. "Or maybe it's more like the sixty-four-*million*-dollar question."

"Speaking of questions. I gotta know, Paddy, what made you think of matching this mansion to that DB out there? I mean, that's more than a hunch. That's like ESP."

"What the kid said was right," O'Grady mused. "It's pretty near impossible to get a place on Algonquin, or Ward for that matter."

"And somehow that should connect the dots for me?"

"Several years back—maybe eight or ten by now—I remember reading that someone acquired four adjacent lots here on Algonquin. Tore down the existing homes and built an estate."

"Guess she wanted to buy a nice view?"

"If it were that easy. Except, you can't just buy these island lots. Lease deeds are very strictly controlled, and the average waiting period to get just one available lot is twenty-five years—give or take. And someone gets four in one pop, and all right next to each other to boot?"

"Jesus," Jones whistled.

"Pissed off a lot of folks," O'Grady shrugged. "The Community Trust Corporation insisted it was all on the level; but it left a bad taste in people's mouths."

"Bad enough to kill for?"

"You'd be surprised at how many reasons people used to come up with for killing each other."

"How do you know so much about how properties change hands out here?" Jones asked.

O'Grady looked a bit embarrassed. "We lotteryed onto the waiting list maybe twenty years ago. We were number 487 when we started. After thirteen years we'd gotten up to somewhere in the 320s. When Bev died, I kinda lost interest. Besides, I figured I'd be dead before I got low enough to have a shot. So, I took myself off the list."

"Holy shit," Jones mused. "You weren't kidding when you said picking up four lots at once was fishy."

"I'm not a math wonk, but I'd bet the odds against such a windfall are astronomical. But like I said, all above board, or so they claimed."

"Pretty fucking lucky, huh?"

"Apparently her luck ran out this morning."

"Wrong place, wrong time?"

O'Grady shook his head. "I think our professor was in just the right place at the precisely expected moment. Whoever did this knew she'd be rowing in that cove this morning. If this house tells us anything, this was a woman of strict routine.

Nothing here is even a centimeter out of place. I'd wager that every Monday morning at that precise time she rowed into the Cut."

"That still doesn't explain how you connected the DB to this house," Jones said dubiously.

"Ah, the plot thickens," O'Grady said, holding the intricate key up like a visual aid. "Like I said, most of the houses out here are pretty bohemian. They try to keep it that way because it adds to the old-world artsy-fartsy charm. But this key is anything but bohemian. It's very high tech, and very expensive. I could think of only one contentious recent build on this island that might make the owner feel threatened enough by the neighbors to buy this level of security. From there, I just put two and two together, and here we are."

Jones nodded. "That's pretty good detective work, detective."

"Elementary, my dear Watson."

"So, now I'm your sidekick? Okay, Holmes, let's snoop around a bit more before I call in back-up." They continued up the stairs, down a hallway, and into a library that offered breathtaking views of the city across the harbour. The walls were lined with shellacked mahogany bookshelves, every book perfectly ordered by the author's last name. To the left was a grand desk in front of a wall lined with five framed diplomas, two of which were doctorates.

"Let's go through the desk," O'Grady said. "See what we can find."

But the sound of rapidly moving feet down the hallway cut their search short. The two men stopped searching and O'Grady slipped the key into his pocket. A well-built young man in a dark suit stepped into the room and quickly scanned the library before approaching O'Grady and Jones.

"I'll be taking over this case, gentlemen," he said in a crisp manner that invited no discussion.

"On whose authority?" Jones insisted. "This is our jurisdiction."

The agent paused for a moment then pulled out his identification and showed it to the two. "On the authority of the director of the Regional Investigative Agency."

"Since when does RIA stick its nose into our cases?" demanded Jones.

The agent paused again. "When they become assassinations," he finally said.

"She was a college professor," O'Grady replied, curiously. "Not a head of state. When did this get upgraded?"

"I'm just following orders, gentlemen, as I'm sure you will. This is a crime scene now. Don't touch anything on your way out." The statement was final and the two turned to leave.

"How'd RIA get here so fast?" Jones asked as they walked back down Seneca toward Sunfish Cut. "And why the hell would they call it an assassination when I haven't even reported your hunch about a sniper?"

O'Grady considered the problem as they walked. "The only thing I can come up with," he finally said, "is that they knew beforehand."

"Are you saying what I think you're saying?"

"You got any better suggestions?"

"Yeah. I think we need more evidence than a cocky agent angling for promotion."

When the two got back to the original crime scene, they found Prowell's body already gone, and the techs packing up.

"What's going on here?" Jones demanded.

"The RIA already picked up the DB," Jimmy said. "Wasn't much we could do about it, was there?"

"Did you tell them this was our crime scene?"

"Didn't give me the chance. Shut us down on the spot." Jimmy returned to the primary scene to pick up the rest of his gear.

"Well, I'll be damned!" Jones fumed.

"Listen Jonesy," O'Grady said. "You mind if I hold onto this key for a few hours?"

"You know that's evidence, Paddy. It'd be my ass if I didn't get it into lockup."

"Meet me at Dineen's at 2:30. I'll buy you a cup of coffee, and you'll leave with the evidence bag in your pocket. How's that?"

"No deal . . . unless you let me in on it."

"In on what?"

"Cut the shit, Paddy. I know that look. Whatever you're planning—I'm in, or it's a no-go."

O'Grady considered it for a moment, then nodded. "Dineen's, 2:30," he finally said. "Don't be late."

"I'll be there. You just have that key for me. Bagged and tagged."

O'Grady left the Prowell crime scene and took the key to a fence he knew from his active days in the Police Service. The old Jamaican swindler, Damerae Cardiman, seemed glad to see him after five years of retirement. They chatted genially about old times before O'Grady showed him the key.

"It can be done, Patrick," he said, looking closely at the key. "But not by me."

"Who then?" O'Grady pleaded. "I'm in a pinch, Card Man."

"I know a guy, but it take maybe two days."

"That's too long. Is there any way I can get it by 2 p.m. today? I'm desperate."

"Gonna cost you."

"Just get it for me. I'll pay the price."

"Now, dat's da kind of deal I like."

He had the key in time to deliver the original to Jones, who agreed to handle the autopsy angle while Paddy researched the mansion. He spent the next three days in the City Archives, running down every lead on the Prowell Mansion. That RIA agent was hiding something, and he meant to find out why. On paper, the inheritance of the four lots was in perfect order—too perfect as far as he was concerned. Whatever cadre of lawyers put the documents together, they knew their business; but the whole thing smelled wrong—how does a university professor inherit four prime Algonquin lots from unrelated families, all within a six-month period? And why didn't the Trust or the Association ask more questions? They'd always been tighter than a gnat's ass when it came to giving out even one of those long-term leases, let alone four adjacent lots. And in the past, the zoning committee had always rejected the joining of lots to form estates. They wanted to maintain the historic bohemian feel of the island community. His gut told him something wasn't right, but the lease documents were a dead end.

The architect's drawings weren't much better. All the originals were there, all in perfect order, all dated the same day—the very day the city approved the plans—very clean. The strange thing was there were no revisions, addendums, or permit change requests. Who builds a mansion over a twenty-one-month period without any changes to the original plans? And yet these plans didn't have a single alteration. The only way to really find out was to compare the plans against the house itself; but to do that he'd have to take the plans with him, and the Archive wouldn't release them without a warrant—a request that would draw unwanted attention. They also prohibited the photocopying of documents, and confiscated all technology at the door; so, O'Grady met with the Card Man again who sold him an old-school fountain-pen camera. Perhaps because it was so old school, the gatekeepers at the Archives didn't even think to check it when he took it in. Once he'd captured the images of the plans, he studied them thoroughly before he printed out smaller working copies.

The doctor allowed William Rampart slowly to emerge from a medically induced coma. His internal organs were responding well, and renal function was coming into a healthy range—particularly for a man, only months shy of his 100th birthday. It was now necessary to assess his brain function; to discover whether the excessive body temperature had damaged the Purkinje cells, which were vital to cognitive and motor functions. The sedatives were incrementally removed from his IV saline drip. Nine hours later the nurse came out to the reception area to wake the napping doctor.

"He's awake, Doctor," she said as she gently shook him. The doctor rubbed his eyes and struggled to get up. It had been a long three days. Walking into the conference room, he found Rampart sitting up in bed with an irritated look on his face.

"Where the hell is Jonas?" he demanded without preamble. Apparently, cognitive and motor functions were still intact.

Cavanaugh sat at his desk evaluating recent intelligence and examining photographs with a magnifying glass when the knock came at his door.

"Come in," he said tiredly. He'd allowed himself only six hours of sleep in the last three nights. The door opened and the nurse stuck her head in.

"He's awake," she said, "and demanding you 'get your ass down there' right now. That's a quote."

Cavanaugh leaned back in his chair and smiled. "Brilliant!" He grabbed a folder from his desk and followed the nurse out.

When the elevator door opened, Cavanaugh saw the doctor coming out of the conference room shaking his head but smiling.

"Good morning, Jonas," he said. "Mister Rampart is apparently none the worse for wear. He actually knocked my hand away when I tried to listen to his heart. I suggest you not keep him waiting. He's in rare form."

"Thank you, Doctor," Cavanaugh said smiling. "I'll heed your advice." He went into the conference room.

"Where have you been? Upstairs sipping tea while I'm dying down here?" Rampart demanded as Cavanaugh shut the door.

"I think you know the answer to that, sir," Cavanaugh responded gently.

Rampart examined Cavanaugh carefully. "I'm the one dying, and you look like hell. You getting any sleep?"

"Not much, sir. It's been busy since . . ."

"The doc says you pulled me out of that sauna just in time," the old man said more quietly. "I owe you, Jonas."

"Not at all, sir. It's what you hired me for."

"Oh, fuck-all! And I didn't hire you; I adopted you. Now quit the 'sir' shit."

"Yes sir . . . I mean, Father."

"Alright, enough mushy stuff. So, what happened to my sauna? I couldn't open it and I couldn't turn it off. If I didn't know better, I'd say it was trying to kill me?"

"It was. And I'm sorry to tell you, you weren't the only one."

"What do you mean?"

"As far as I've been able to learn, at least five of the seven Directorate chairs have been eliminated. You were the sixth, and that was a very near thing. And I have no word yet on the Romanov chair, but I think we must assume she's dead as well."

"Son of a bitch," the old man whispered, ashen faced. "That fucking zorba's staging a coup?"

"It would appear so. But I'm not yet absolutely certain."

"I don't need your certainty. My gut has its own. How'd he get the drop on us?"

"That's what I've been trying to piece together for the last three days. Evidence is scant. All our sources from the various locations are irretrievable now. At this point we're depending on internet news sources for information."

"What the hell happened to our databases?"

"Either erased, or our access has been revoked."

"How can we be locked out of our own databases?"

"They're no longer ours. Gianakos wasn't scheduled to surrender the codes and protocols for Haruspex until yesterday. Clearly, that didn't happen. Without those passwords, I'm afraid this coup is not merely physical, it's also digital."

"I'll be double-damned!" the old man said, laying his head back on his pillow, looking suddenly exhausted. "Gianakos outplayed me. He had to have seen our move coming. Planned for it. We played right into his hands."

"It would seem so. I should have seen it. Clearly, there was much I overlooked. I let you down, sir. I'm sorry."

"You were the only one who suspected that rat-bastard in the first place. Quit groveling. We've got work to do. What do you have so far?"

"You may recall that I did have assets in place keeping eyes on each of the premiers as a precaution. Three were able to take photographs either immediately preceding or directly after the assassinations. The couriers arrived with them yesterday afternoon." He handed Rampart the folder containing the three enlarged photographs and sat down in the chair rubbing his eyes and stifling a yawn.

The old man quickly examined the photographs. "Okay, what should I be seeing?"

Cavanaugh sat up and composed himself. "The first one was taken on Algonquin Island across the harbor from Toronto. That stone wall in the photo is guarding Elinor Prowell's estate. Information is scarce, but my factor tells me she was shot in the head sometime between 6:00 and 6:30 a.m. while rowing. The person you see in the photo is an RIA agent entering her home."

"Okay," Rampart responded. "What about the next one?"

"The second one was taken at a luncheon event in Johannesburg at which Yejide Akpabio was the guest of honor—some sort of business award. In the photo, she's asking the waiter for something—we don't know what. Less than a minute later, she was dead—heart attack's the preliminary finding. I think we can assume that's incorrect."

Rampart peered at the photo for a long time, and then looked again at the first. "Wait a damn minute. That waiter . . ." he finally said.

"You noticed? Now look at the third, taken in Hong Kong moments after an elevator slipped its moorings and fell 104 stories. Any speculations as to who was on board?"

"Leung Xiang?" Rampart said breathlessly. "This man getting into the car: he's the same one in the other two photos! So, we have our assassin?"

"I concluded the same thing at first. But look at the time stamps. You'll notice the first one is April 8th at 8:21 a.m. in Toronto."

"Yeah, so?"

"The second is 12:24 p.m. the same day in Johannesburg. And the third is 6:19 p.m. in Hong Kong—again, same day."

"So, you're saying he got from Toronto to Johannesburg in four hours and then to Hong Kong in six hours after that? Seems pretty fast, doesn't it?"

"Implausibly fast if that were the only problem. You haven't taken time zones into account. When I factored those variables in, it turns out that all the assassinations were coordinated to occur at precisely the same time, give or take ten minutes. That's probably what saved your life. Yours was the only routine that didn't fit neatly into the time frame. The kill hour was 3:20 a.m. here, and there was no way they could get to you in your bed—too well shielded. The closest possibility was apparently the sauna, which you don't usually get into before 5:30. That meant a time window during which word of the other deaths might potentially reach us. Fortunately, it did, but only just in time."

"Give my thanks to whoever called you . . . and a promotion. And find out how the hell they hacked into my sauna. That was supposed to be impossible."

"I've already got Boma on it. I felt it necessary to read him in on the larger scope of our activities. I hope I didn't overstep."

"He'll need to know at this point anyway if he's going to be effective. But that still doesn't solve the mystery. How was this guy in three places at once?"

"Remember, those three are the only places we were able to get photos, and the photo in Toronto is two hours after the event. Let's assume that he was also in Buenos Aires at 7:20 a.m., Paris at lunchtime, Byzantium at 1:20 p.m., and very probably somewhere here in Puget Sound at 5:30 a.m. I must conclude that either there is a large cold-blooded brood of identical siblings, trained from birth to be assassins, or . . ."

"Gianakos has an off-the-books cloning project underway?"

"That is my assessment, yes."

Rampart thought about it for a few moments. "Well, if anyone could confirm, it'd be Walt Bennett down in Los Nietos. He's the only one who's got the facilities for that kind of operation. Call the airport and have my jet fueled and ready. I need to have a little talk with our number four. He may not know me personally, but he certainly will before this day's over."

"I can't allow that!" Cavanaugh said curtly.

"You what?"

"Hear me out, Father. The entire Directorate was targeted for assassination. Once I was confident you were out of immediate danger, I felt it was in our best interests to take advantage of the circumstances. Our adversary must believe he's achieved total success. Assuming we were being surveilled, I telephoned the Coroner and the Medical Examiner and requested they come to the property to inspect your body. They left two hours later having confirmed you died of accidental catastrophic hyperthermia."

"But I wasn't dead, was I?"

"Obviously not, but yours wasn't the body they examined. Within minutes of the attempt on your life, I had a unit in route to Mercy General to pick up the doctor and nurse we have on payroll there. They also appropriated a freshly deceased elderly male from the hospital morgue. Once here, we cooked him for a while and added other touches before calling the officials to pronounce. Having been unsuccessful in their attempts to revive you, the doctor and nurse were driven back to Mercy, and the corpse was returned to the morgue, having never been missed. Your will and testament demanded you be buried on the grounds. According to all official sources, you've been dead for three days. We had a small but very touching funeral yesterday. You're buried beneath your favorite oak."

"That's pretty quick thinking, Jonas," Rampart said, impressed.

"Pardon my saying so but having you dead will accomplish at least two things: in the short term it will protect you from further assassination attempts; and in the long term it will give us a tactical edge moving forward. We have lost the battle, Father. Let's not hand them the war."

"Oh, all right," the old man finally conceded. "I don't have to like it, but I'll sit tight for the time being. You take my jet, then. Squeeze Bennett until he pops!"

"Don't worry. I'll get the information from Bennett, but I'll not be taking your jet. That'll be watched. The high-speed rail will be more discreet and nearly as efficient." A knock came at the conference room door.

"Come in," Rampart said. The door opened and a middle-aged man stepped in holding a digital touch pad.

"What is it Boma?" asked Cavanaugh.

"We found the point of entry," he said, handing the pad to Cavanaugh.

"What's this?"

"It's a diagram of our system. You see the blip? That's where the back-door device is hidden. Once inside the house, it was activated remotely and piggybacked off the electrical conduits and the in-house feeds. It introduced a very subtle spyware program into our system. Over time, a worm was able to replicate sufficiently to gain access to the sauna controls. This is our Trojan horse, Jonas."

"Is that the pink suite?" Cavanaugh asked, examining the diagram.

"Yeah. It's behind the dresser."

"And, if I'm not mistaken, the last person to occupy the pink suite was Mademoiselle Genevois?"

"The very same."

"Why that slimy, two-faced, sloppy-seconds whore!" Rampart growled. "If her father knew, he woulda strangled her at birth—"

"You said 'it's behind the dresser'—present tense," Cavanaugh interrupted. "Why haven't you destroyed it?"

"Well, here's the thing. The virus is quarantined; but I think it might be a mistake to kill it."

"Why?" Rampart asked.

"Because if we kill it, they'll know we're onto them. But if we let it live and reduce its reach substantially—say to only the pink suite, they'll think it's still intact, and I may be able to use that signal to gain access to their infrastructure. Turn around is fair play, after all."

"You devious bastard," Rampart said. "I like the way you're thinking."

"Yes," Cavanaugh said. "But are you sure you'll be able to control its access on this end? We can't have any more leakage."

"There'll be no more leakage. We're running a system-wide diagnostic right now to discover exactly how the thing operates. Once I know that, I'll reverse-engineer a little spy-bomb of our own."

"Good. Let me know when it's complete."

"Count on it." Boma turned to Rampart. "Glad to see you're back to normal, Boss."

"Thanks, Boma." The computer tech nodded and left the room, closing the door.

"I knew that bottom-sucking fish smelled rotten!" growled Rampart.

"Yes. I think we can now assume the Romanov chair survived the purge."

"What are those two playing at?"

"I don't know . . . yet. All the more reason for you to stay out of sight. I'll follow the clues and we'll see where they lead."

"Do that. It looks like the first trail starts in Los Nietos. And Jonas . . . be on your guard. For all we know, Bennett and the other chairs may be a part of this."

"The thought already occurred to me. I underestimated the danger once. I won't be fooled again. If he is a part of this, he won't survive our meeting."

JONAS CAVANAUGH RECLINED IN THE business-class lie-flat seat as the rocket train pulled out of King Street Station bound for Los Nietos. He travelled under the assumed identity of Benoit Moreau. The boarding security surveillance scanned him along with every other passenger, but the key was to avoid undue scrutiny, and in the guise of Benoit Moreau, he was very unremarkable. The Puget Sound rare books dealer was traveling to Los Nietos to purchase the estate library collection of a client's deceased father in the elite enclave of Bel Air. He appeared sufficiently bookish in a brown tweed blazer with suede elbow patches and an Irish flat cap of the same hues. He wore black horn-rimmed vintage glasses and a beard flecked with gray. Jonas Cavanaugh, the ghost, did not inhabit any database; but in the digital world, Benoit Moreau was a real and thoroughly boring entity, and that's precisely the way Cavanaugh wanted it. As the train reached its cruising speed of 280 mph, the rhythmic motion lulled Cavanaugh to sleep. He'd had very little rest the last three days.

The steward woke him seven hours later, as they approached Union Station in Los Nietos. He still felt groggy, but the sleep had done him a world of good. Pulling his leather satchel from the storage rack, he slung it over his shoulder, and disembarked. He caught the first Red Line of the day and exited at Hollywood and Vine. Wandering along the Walk of Fame like any other tourist, a passerby bumped into him and kept going without apology. Knowing the package had just been delivered to his jacket pocket, he hailed a cab to Bel Air. The estate auction would begin in five hours—more than enough time for what he needed to do.

Bennett's home was three blocks from his current location. There were no sidewalks in Bel Air, so he strolled along the excessively tall hedges that guarded nearly all the homes from public view. The gate to Bennett's property had but one guard whom Cavanaugh soundlessly neutralized with an injected sedative, rendering him unconscious for the next four hours. He propped him up in his guardhouse chair and entered the compound. Bennett's impressive home sat on the crest of a well-manicured grassy incline. There was only one other night guard patrolling inside the gates. Once he had taken him out, Cavanaugh found keys to the home's service entry in the guard's pocket.

"Amateurs," he mumbled, approaching the side service door. As the sky brightened, he quietly let himself in. The clean and well-ordered kitchen was clearly a bachelor's—it lacked a woman's touch. He couldn't really remember his own mother, but he'd studied the aesthetic markers. He snooped around until he found the coffee and started a pot. Retrieving the recently-acquired package from his breast pocket, he removed the butcher-paper wrapping. He screwed the suppressor onto the Glock, cocked it, released the safety, and set it quite visibly on the island's enameled lava-stone countertop. Pouring himself a cup of coffee, he sat on one of the island barstools and waited. Within ten minutes, someone descended the service stairs off the pantry.

"What did I tell you, Lenny, about drinking my coffee?" complained the voice from the stairwell. Walter Bennett wandered into the kitchen in his robe and slippers raking his unkempt hair. Then he looked up and stopped short, staring curiously at Cavanaugh until he saw the Glock on the island. His eyes suddenly sparkled from the surge of adrenaline. "What do you want?" he whispered. "All my valuables are upstairs."

"I don't want your valuables, Walt," Cavanaugh said calmly. "We need to have a talk. Why don't you get a cup of coffee and sit down?"

"I'd prefer to stand," he said shakily, glancing at the service door.

"I really must insist," Cavanaugh calmly placed his hand on the Glock. Bennett glanced again at the door and licked his lips. "Your guards won't be bothering us. Seems they're sleeping on the job. But you've nothing to fear from me, so long as you cooperate."

"Who are you?" Bennett asked weakly, sitting on a barstool. "And what do you want?"

"My name's Benoit Moreau, I work for an interested third party, and what I want is information."

"Information?"

"That's right. About your company's recent clandestine activities," Cavanaugh rose and poured Bennett a cup of coffee. "Cream? Sugar?"

Bennett shook his head numbly. "What activities? I run a genetics research firm here in Los Nietos. It's all in the public record. I've nothing to hide. We do genetics research."

"Oh, but you do so much more than that, Walt. You don't mind if I call you Walt?"

Bennett shook his head dumbly. "I don't know what you mean," he whispered, paling slightly.

"I may be many things, Walt, but never take me for a fool. You're vested with the responsibility of the entire western half of the North American continent, as the 4th seat on the Consortium."

"3rd seat," Bennett unconsciously corrected him.

"Well, well. Congratulations. I wasn't aware of your promotion. Are you moving to London? I wonder, has Alex displeased the sénéschal, or perhaps you've done something recently to gain our dear Darien's favor?"

"How do you know all these... who did you say you were?" Bennett's hand shook as he reached for his coffee.

"Let's just say I represent certain entities that have a vested interest in *directing* the ongoing success of the Consortium."

"The Directorate...?" Bennett mouthed the words with almost no audible sound.

"I'm pleased that you've heard of us. My superior, who goes by the name of Rockefeller, sent me to ask you some questions. He has left it to me to judge the sincerity of your answers. If I feel you have not been forthcoming..." He placed his hand again on the Glock, and looked meaningfully at Bennett, who nodded quickly. "I'm glad we understand one another. Now that we've got the unpleasant preliminaries out of the way, let's move on to specifics. Who ordered your promotion to the 3rd seat?"

"The sénéschal, of course. I'm getting on a plane to Tokyo later this morning for a meeting with him and the other hub chairs. I assumed Mr. Gianakos called the meeting to announce my promotion."

"I'll be sure to express your regrets for your absence. I'll be taking your plane to that meeting myself."

"But why? If I'm not there, Darien will be very put out with me."

"I'll make sure he gets over it." Cavanaugh opened his leather satchel and removed a manila folder. He pulled three enlarged photographs out and placed them on the counter in front of Bennett. "Now Walt, what can you tell me about these men?"

Bennett looked at the photos as the blood drained from his face. The morning was cool, but his forehead became dewed with perspiration. "Where did you get these?"

"These photos were taken four days ago at the scenes of three separate murders; but we suspect this person was at four others as well. Do you recognize the man?"

Bennett stared at the photos for a long moment before he shook his head and pushed them away.

"Let me recommend that you never play poker, Walt. You'd be absolutely horrid at it."

"I don't know what you're talking about. Now, please leave. I have more guards coming on duty very soon."

"Not until eight. That gives us at least ninety minutes." Cavanaugh again placed his hand on the Glock. "However, I will be leaving within the next thirty minutes and you'll either be alive when I go, or you'll be lying on the kitchen floor with a bullet in your head; the choice is entirely yours. I don't yet trust you, Walt. I suggest you do everything in your power to change that."

Bennett stared at Cavanaugh for a moment then pulled the photos back. "I may have seen this face before."

"Now we're making progress." Cavanaugh removed his hand from the Glock, but left his palm open on the counter next to the pistol. "Go on."

"Six years ago, the Directorate tasked me to develop an enhanced 3rd generation operative. I was told it was of the highest priority. The first prototype was ready just over a year ago. But, if you're from the Directorate, as you say, you already know all this... don't you?"

"Who specifically tasked you?"

"The sénéschal, as always. He said your people wanted the program conducted in the strictest secrecy. I assumed it was about the same time you green-lit Haruspex, which was a secret to all of us until two years ago."

"Gianakos made this request *six* years ago?"

"Give or take a few months."

Cavanaugh rose, snatching up the Glock. He paced back and forth, lost in mental calculations. Bennett crouched on his stool, waiting for the bullet. When Cavanaugh's focus returned, he stepped to the island and only then noticed that Bennett was visibly trembling. He set the Glock on the counter again and got a glass of water for the Genomics Chair. "I'm Sorry, Walt. I did not intend to shoot you. I was just running through several scenarios in my mind." Bennett nodded wordlessly and gratefully gulped the water. "Now," Cavanaugh continued, "Tell me everything you know about the men in these photos?"

Bennett nodded shakily, glancing down again at the photos. "They're the new

Heracles units you ordered. Who are these people they killed?"

Cavanaugh considered the question before finally speaking. "Three days ago, five of the seven sitting Directorate premiers were assassinated by your Heracles units."

"No!" Bennett gasped. "I swear to you, Mister Moreau, I had no idea what their purpose was. Darien said you wanted them for a next-level Compliance program."

"You were woefully misinformed." Again, he paced the kitchen, considering recent events. When he finally spoke, it was in a rueful tone. "It seems our own penchant for secrecy has been very skillfully used against us by Gianakos."

"Surely not! Darien a traitor? . . . I mean, I admit I had a bad feeling about this from the start, but Darien's the only representative of the Directorate we've ever known. Why would I have suspected he was operating outside his brief?"

"You wouldn't, and he knew it. He had carte-blanche, and we gave it to him." Cavanaugh sighed again. "I have very little time, but I have a few more questions: Why do all the 3-Gs look like identical brothers?"

"Given the time constraints, we could only develop one strand fully; so, you're right, they're absolutely identical in every way."

Cavanaugh nodded. "I suspected as much. So, am I also correct in assuming that you produced seven of these for Gianakos?"

Bennett shook his head slowly. "You really don't know, do you?"

"Enlighten me, Walt! I'm in a hurry!"

"Okay, okay," he said, but still looked confused. "The order wasn't for seven Heracles units. It was for five thousand."

Cavanaugh sat heavily on the stool. "Five thousand?"

"That's right. And they're state-of-the-art. Every enhanced specification you could imagine."

"I could imagine some pretty horrific things. Where are these Heracles units now?"

"I honestly don't know. We delivered the full contingent to the port of Villa Rica over three weeks ago. They all boarded an ocean liner and left. Darien told me never to mention them again. They could be anywhere on the planet by now."

"As you can see from these photos, they are *literally* everywhere on this planet." Cavanaugh sighed and shut his eyes, thinking. "Do you have the specs on these units?"

Bennett paused for a moment looking intently at the Glock still resting on the countertop. "I was told to destroy all records pertaining to the Heracles units," he finally said quietly.

"Naturally," groaned Cavanaugh, still thinking. "Gianakos is nothing if not thorough."

"But . . ." Bennett uttered.

"But what?" Cavanaugh now opened his eyes and looked directly at the still perspiring Bennett.

"I know I shouldn't have," he finally confessed. "But I made back-up files, just in case."

For the first time this morning, Cavanaugh smiled, and actually meant it. "I think you just earned that 3rd seat. Do you have the back-ups here?"

"Yes. In my safe."

"Could you make a copy for me?"

"I could."

"Do. And afterwards, Walt, you're going to need to disappear for a few weeks. Somewhere no one can find you."

"Why? Am *I* in danger?"

"Gianakos just murdered five sitting premiers without blinking an eye. Do you think he will lose sleep over a hub chair?"

"I see your point. I've needed a vacation for a while. I think now's a good time."

"I concur fully. Also, before I leave: you've received a directive recently about the Orions, I believe?"

"Yes. They've been recalled. They're scheduled for destruction in a week."

"Let the recall take place but rescind the order for the destruction through back-channels. I may need those units." He pulled a pen from his bag and scribbled an address on a napkin, pushing it across the countertop to Bennett." Have them sent to this address and get the word out that they've been destroyed."

"You want them sent to the old military base there?" he asked, reading the napkin.

"Yes, and I'll also need the specs on how their loyalty protocol functions."

"I'll include it in the drive I'm making for you... But I can do you one better, if you let me take a retinal scan before you leave, I'll have the project manager rewrite their loyalty protocols to respond only to you, and to whomever you delegate after that."

"That's even better. Oh, and one last suggestion, Walt. Until we've got this straightened out, a certain amount of timely circumspection on your part could mean the difference between living and dying."

"I think I'm going to take a very quiet vacation," he said nervously.

"A wise choice."

The Ritz-Carlton Tokyo did not meet Liliane Genevois' exacting standards; but Tokyo simply couldn't compare to Paris. No matter how hard they tried, the Japanese just couldn't comprehend the concept of luxury. It wasn't really their fault, she mused; it's all about breeding—and they simply didn't have it. Individual comfort had no place in the mind of a drone, and they were all drones to her thinking. She sat in the restaurant looking down at the sunset shadows in Hinokicho Park and finishing her barely passable wine. The Zaibatsu Group was playing host to the Consortium meeting, and Darien had already left to prepare his speech to the chairs. After the last few stressful weeks, she insisted he take her on this trip to decompress. They had achieved victory, after all! And to the victors should go at least *some* spoils. She had a ninety-minute massage scheduled for 7 p.m. and was just starting to feel mellow enough to enjoy it. The wine was not excellent, but it was having the desired effect.

She folded her napkin, placed it neatly on the table, and rose to leave. As she walked through the restaurant, she felt only slightly unsteady, a feeling she'd always liked. Two glasses of wine made her relaxed, four glasses made her slur. She had consumed three at dinner, so was right in the *endroit idéal*—a good place for a massage, or for sex. She strolled through the lobby, feeling merry, when her ear caught a voice that gave her a jarring feeling of déjà vu. Something about it was familiar, but out of place. It wasn't the accent, but the *lack* of any placeable accent that jarred her. She'd experienced that same curious sense recently, but where? And then it hit her—William Rampart's estate. She glanced toward the concierge's desk as she strolled by. She could not see the man's face as he questioned the concierge, but she knew instantly by his build and erect posture he was Jonas Cavanaugh.

Her heartbeat quickened as she arrived at the elevator. As she waited for the lift, she dared not look back but could still hear the man talking to the concierge in that precise, smug, and ultimately inscrutable accent. What was taking the damned elevator so long? Finally, the doors slid open, but the conversation behind her had also stopped. She stepped inside and pushed the button for the penthouse without looking back. As the doors closed, she stole a single glance. Cavanaugh had finished with the concierge and was approaching the elevators. Though he wore glasses, a silly looking hat, and a beard, it was definitely him. At the very last moment, he glanced at the elevator, and she jerked her eyes away. The doors closed completely, and the elevator began its ascent. Had he seen her? She doubted it, but she couldn't be certain. Whatever the case, she must warn Darien.

The doors opened on the top floor to a small emerald-carpeted lobby with a single door—the entire floor housed the Monarch Suite where she and Darien were staying. A well-built young man in a black tailored suit sat in a chair beside the door.

"I need to speak to Darien immediately," she said to him. He looked at her for a moment as though he was still listening even after she had finished speaking. It was disconcerting the way these men did that. If she didn't know better, she'd think they were ignoring her.

"He'll contact you momentarily," he finally said.

She nodded and entered the suite, closing the door behind her. She didn't like these new operatives. Something about them made her uncomfortable, the way they looked at her so distractedly. She certainly didn't want one of them in her suite. She paced the room for a full minute before the phone rang. She picked it up.

"What is it Liliane? I'm very busy just now."

"He's here, Darien!"

"Who's here?"

"That little majordomo from Rampart's estate. Jonas Cavanaugh. He's here!"

"Are you certain?"

"I saw him just now in the lobby. He was questioning the concierge. He's disguised, but I'm positive it was him!" There was silence on the other end for a long moment. "Darien?"

"Did he see you?"

"I don't think so. He glanced in my direction, but the elevator doors were closing. I don't think he could have recognized me in that short glance."

"You underestimate yourself, Liliane. You're an unmistakable woman. Anyone who's seen you once wouldn't soon forget."

"What should I do?"

"Stay in the room. You're guarded there. Let me deal with this. I'll call you when it's done."

"Be careful, Darien. We don't know why he's here."

"I know exactly why he's here. He's here to kill me. You said he was disguised. Can you describe him?"

She proceeded to give a full description.

The concierge gave Benoit Moreau several brochures, since he was planning a rare books convention in this fair city and wanted to see which hotel would best suit his needs. The brochures listed the size and layout of all the meeting rooms. With that information, he could formulate a plan. He thanked the concierge and turned toward the elevators. One was just leaving. He would have to catch the next. As he glanced at the departing elevator, he caught the side view of the passenger's face and hair. She turned away so quickly when he looked at her it caught his attention. There was something familiar about the woman's profile, but he couldn't place it.

He caught the next elevator and pressed the button for his floor. As he rode up, he closed his eyes and went over the momentary glimpse repeatedly in his mind, each time relaxing more thoroughly to allow his memory to clarify the image and put the pieces together. As the doors opened on his floor, it coalesced. The woman had only been slightly visible in profile, and only for a moment; but he now knew she was Liliane Genevois.

He walked rapidly to his room. Had she recognized him? Why else would she turn away so quickly? His element of surprise was now gone, and he would have to change his strategy accordingly. Once inside, he quickly perused the brochures. The East Room where they would be meeting had two points of egress—the main entry and a prep room entry for the caterers. The prep room would be his entry point. He checked his watch. The meeting would begin in just over ten minutes and would last several hours. He took the Glock from his leather bag and made sure the suppressor was secure. Three shots should be sufficient. After he'd killed Gianakos, he would secure Genevois. He would bring her back to his father for judgment, or if that proved too difficult, he would kill her in her suite—he smiled at the homophonic irony: sweet justice meted out in her own suite. There was a knock at the door. He gripped the Glock and rose.

"Who is it?" he called out.

"The concierge sent me, Mr. Moreau. He forgot to give you two brochures."

Cavanaugh relaxed a bit. "Just a moment," he said as he approached the door. He peered through the peephole then jerked back. He raised the Barrel of the Glock to the aperture, adjusted it to the angle he calculated would be most effective, and fired. The peephole completely disintegrated, and the air filled with the acrid scent of burnt gunpowder. He yanked open the door and dragged the body into the room, quickly closing the door behind him. He allowed himself to breathe for only a moment. Had he not studied those photos of the assassins, he'd be dead right now. He fired one more shot into the 3-G clone's forehead. He hadn't had time to review the drive Bennett had given him, so had no idea what kind of self-healing technology they possessed. Better to be safe. He went quickly to the bathroom and removed the false beard, flushing it down the toilet. He went to the room's closet, placed his glasses, his cap, and his tweed jacket, on the top shelf where they would be missed in a quick search. He then picked up his leather satchel, slung it over his shoulder, and quietly left the room.

The stairs were the only practical option at this point. He silently cursed himself for underestimating Gianakos again. In his zeal, he had been sloppy. He hadn't considered the 3-Gs, and if he'd learned anything about how the man operated, he knew Gianakos would not be comfortable with only one bodyguard. You don't keep five thousand units on hand, if you're only going to use one. Justice for the traitorous sénéschal would have to wait for a better-planned opportunity. The only essential thing right now was that he bring the flash drive back to the Puget for analysis. In the stairwell, a large yellow 49 next to a yellow 四十九 decorated the concrete wall across from the door. He looked back through the door's safety-glass viewing window. The hallway was still empty.

He descended the steps two at a time, needing to move quickly, but not stumble. As he reached the yellow level 45 sign, he heard the access door four levels above him thrown open. Without a moment's hesitation he went out the exit onto the forty-fifth floor and pulled the door quietly shut but held the latch open. He retrieved the Glock from his leather satchel. Moments later the sound of rapid footsteps pounded past the door. Throwing it open, he fired a shot into the back of the head of each of the two men descending the steps. They were identical to the corpse he had just left in his room. "Four thousand nine hundred ninety-seven," he muttered to the splayed bodies and again began his rapid descent. When he reached the twelfth floor, he again heard a door burst open, but it was far above him. Now it would be a foot race. When he reached the bottom, he could hear the echoes of footfalls far above. The door leading to the alley had a firelock bar across it preventing an exit in any situation but an emergency. Cavanaugh aimed the Glock at the ceiling sprinkler and fired. As the building-wide alarm system began to wail, he kicked the door open, and sprinted down the alley.

People began to pour out of the hotel and onto the street ahead of him. The confusion would aid him. He slowed to a walk to blend with the crowd. In this mass of chattering guests, they would be searching for a man with a beard, glasses, and a cap. He had nearly reached the boulevard when a lone 3-G ran into the alley. He walked forward calmly, and the man raced past him toward the exit door. A split second later, the footsteps halted. Cavanaugh instantly turned and fired three suppressed shots into the operative, the last one blowing his head apart. He then turned and sprinted to the street, jumping into the first available cab.

"*Ike! ike!*" he shouted, and the driver pulled away. They took multiple turns while Cavanaugh kept glancing out the back window. After about ten minutes without pursuit, he spied an alley covered by an awning. "*Koko de ii desu,*" he said, pointing to the alley, and the driver pulled in and stopped. He paid him well and got out, waiting until the taxi was out of sight, to enter the office building from the alley door. He walked through the interior hallways, affecting the posture and gait of a man of importance who had every right to be there.

Glancing through the windows into the small offices he passed, he finally found the one he wanted. Entering the empty office, he took the hat and overcoat off the rack next to the door, put them on, and left, continuing down the hallway toward the reception area and the front doors. The receptionist looked up at him as he passed by, and he nodded. "*Konbanwa*," he said calmly, with a slight bow, and she replied in kind, as he continued to the doors. Once outside he stayed under the entry awning looking down the street in both directions. He spotted a Metro entry point half a block to the right. Keeping his head down, he made his way to the stairs and descended. Examining the Toei Subway map on the tiled wall below, he now knew where he was, and where he needed to go next.

Two hours later Cavanaugh sat in a barber's chair in the back room of a questionable establishment in the heart of the Kabukicho district. Hideshi Enomoto, a man he had used occasionally over the years, was applying latex prosthetic pieces to his face to raise and widen his cheekbones and soften his chin. He didn't know how the 3-G in that alleyway recognized him, even after he'd removed his disguise, but he could take no more chances. He had to get back to the Puget, and Bennett's private jet was out of the question. He would fly commercial, and that would mean an image scan. He had used the identity of Juliette Walker only once before, but she was his ace in the hole. Hideshi, a Kabuki make-up artist, was a virtuoso at disguises and once he applied the blonde wig, even Cavanaugh found his own reflection attractive in the mirror. A few more touches, like a corset, breasts, and the right pumps, and he was as ready as he ever would be.

Since Sea-Tac would undoubtedly be watched, Juliette Walker caught a flight out of Narita the following morning bound for Los Nietos. On arrival at LNX, she bought a ticket on a northbound rocket train to the Puget Sound Metroplex. During the trip north, an older man, who had apparently had more Miller Lites than were good for him, tried to hit on Ms Walker. Not wanting to draw attention to himself, Cavanaugh endured the sloppy advances stoically until the man finally concluded she was a "dyke" and moved on.

Yulian Khvostovsky relaxed in a deck chair while his wife and daughter swam in the luxury yacht's pool. Since he couldn't avoid flying to Tokyo for the meeting of the hub chairs, he decided to make the return trip a vacation with his family. He was only now beginning to relax. Demyan flew back to Moscow on the company jet to run things in his absence; and he, with Katya and Abigail, took the Jöetsu Shinkasan to Niigata, where they boarded a very comfortable private yacht bound for Vladivostok. The port city's spring weather was reputed to be excellent, and it had been a long time since he'd taken an extended vacation with his family. They would spend twelve days in Vladivostok and then take the Historic Line of the Great Siberian Way back to Moscow, a weeklong rail trip. His wife had an inkling that he had planned the whole vacation to avoid having to fly back, but she didn't really mind. A vacation was a vacation after all.

He sat in the deckchair sipping a Bloody Mary and reflecting on the Consortium meeting of two nights ago. It had been a strange event, to say the least. The sénéschal seemed entirely distracted, to the point that he lost his train of thought several times. On top of that, Walter Bennett was a no-show, which took everyone by surprise—especially the sénéschal. To make matters even more chaotic, a fire alarm went off at the beginning of the meeting and they all evacuated. When they finally did reconvene, the sénéschal appeared on the verge of an apoplectic fit. When Oshiro Takeshi asked him if he was all right, he essentially told him to sit down and shut up.

Clearly, something troubled Darien Gianakos. Maybe it was the fact that he had not yet been able to apprehend his anomaly even after two years of constant searching. It was possible some other kind of pressure coming down from the Directorate had pushed the sénéschal to the breaking point. Or perhaps it was none of these things at all—but how would the chairs ever know? The 'veil of secrecy' between the chairs and the Directorate was more like an impenetrable titanium curtain. If there was a problem, who but the sénéschal would inform the chairs? Clearly, something was not as it should be . . . but this was a vacation. Some things he could still control, and he needed to concentrate on those within his power. And right now, it was time to switch off the business brain, relax, and have fun with his family. He downed his Bloody Mary in three gulps, flipped off his deck sandals, and jumped into the pool, making a marvelous splash to the giggling joy of his daughter.

As Padraig O'Grady meandered down Wyandot Avenue toward Seneca, the setting sun lit up Toronto Harbour in a fiery glow. The seemingly aimless early-evening stroll along Algonquin Island's northwest side was, of course, a ruse.

As he walked down Wyandot, a lone figure turned off Seneca walking toward him. Stanislaw Jones was on time. He and Jones strolled past each other and nodded. They would make the round again as dusk set in before they met at the front gate of the mansion. Tourists liked to stand along the shoreline and watch the sunset before catching the ferry back to the city. It took two more tours around the block before the last of the 'sunset worshipers' had moved on; then O'Grady casually walked to the front entry of the mansion wall, slipped the bootlegged key in the lock, and went in, pulling the gate almost shut behind him. He kept watch through the crack of an opening until he caught sight of Jones ambling down Seneca. When he got close enough, O'Grady opened the gate for a moment so Jones could pass through without breaking stride, and then he smoothly closed it.

"Guess the key copy worked?" Jones said.

"You didn't trust my guy?" O'Grady replied.

"You said that key was complex. I was worried the Card Man wouldn't be up to the task. I was even tempted to grab the original from evidence, but that's a can-o-worms best left unopened."

"I'm glad you didn't. The more I investigate this, the less I like any of it. What did the autopsy turn up?"

"What autopsy? As far as I can tell, no one ever examined the DB, because it never made it to the morgue. The ME said it was removed from her jurisdiction. I went through the usual channels, but I couldn't find hide nor hair of where Prowell ended up. I didn't want to dig too deep in case it might alert the RIA."

"Probably a good call. I had better luck with the house, but not by much. All I can tell you is someone must have pulled a lot of pretty thick strings to get this thing built—and it wasn't a college professor. This thing stinks, or I don't have a nose."

"Well, we gonna stand out here shootin' the shit, or we gonna go snoop around a bit?"

"If it's all the same to you, I thought we might snoop."

The two men went to the front door and let themselves in, locking it after. They both pulled out the small flashlights and made their way into the kitchen where O'Grady laid the two sets of reduced-size architect's drawings side by side on the countertop.

"You want the third floor or the first, Jonesy?"

"I'll take the downstairs. You like the city lights more than I do."

"Fine. Check each room against the plans. If you find any discrepancies, yell, and we'll investigate together. If we find nothing, we'll meet on the second floor. Got it?"

"I'm no architect, Paddy; but I think I can tell the difference between a coat-closet and a bathroom."

"Good; meet me on two in thirty."

Jones went to the front door to start sequentially exploring as O'Grady went up the service stairwell to the third story. For twenty-five minutes, he examined every room, checking each space against the drawings—nothing seemed out of the ordinary. When he got to the master bedroom, he took a few minutes to look out the windows at the breathtaking Toronto skyline across the harbour. The wealthy paid millions for the luxury of having this kind of view when they slept. He went down the stairs to the second floor and started in the library. He studied the photos behind the desk again of the professor and her colleagues. Why would someone snipe a Women's Studies professor while she was rowing? Did one of her journal articles offend a patriarchal right-winger? Were there any such things as right-wingers anymore? It just didn't make sense.

"Paddy," he heard Jones voice from downstairs. "I think I found something."

O'Grady took the main stairs down. "Where are you?"

"Kitchen." He made his way through the parlour, and the dining room, into the kitchen, where he found Jones studying the drawings on the countertop. "What does this look like to you?" he said pointing to a spot on the drawings.

O'Grady came over and looked at where Jones was pointing. "Storage closet, I think," he replied after peering at the small writing.

"Follow me." He led O'Grady into the pantry and pointed to one of the walls. "This is where that closet should be, right? But all I see is a shelf."

"You're right. Where is this wall in relation to the rest of the structure?"

"Right under the service stairs, I think."

"Nice work, Jonesy," he said, getting on his knees and examining the undershelfing with his flashlight.

"If there's a space behind this, Paddy, there's gonna be some kind of code or a remote-control switch to open it. This broad had money. It'll be a high-tech something-or-other; mark my words."

"Or not," Paddy said, pushing a button behind the Cream-o-Wheat. They heard a click and O'Grady pulled on the shelf, which swung very smoothly outward to the surprise and delight of both men. Behind the false shelf, a stairway led downward into darkness.

"Was there a basement on the plans?" asked Jones.

"No," O'Grady said. "There definitely was *not* a basement."

"Then this is a code violation," said Jones, smiling.

"I guess we'll have to cite her," O'Grady said, pointing down the dark stairs. "Would you like to do the honors?"

"Age before beauty, Paddy."

"But Beauty was a horse, Jonesy."

"Fuck you and your horse," Jones laughed as he descended the stairs, flashlight in hand. O'Grady was just about to follow when he heard the front door opening violently. Someone was in a hurry and making far too much noise. O'Grady quietly pulled the pantry door shut, stepped into the basement stairwell, and returned the shelf hatch to its original position, hearing a click once it had latched. Jones came back up the stairs to ask O'Grady why he had closed the trick door, but the retired detective clamped his hand over Jones's mouth and shined his flashlight on his own face as he shook his head vigorously. The two men stood stock-still as they listened to the sounds of rapid and intent footfalls up the staircase. At least three, maybe four people were checking the mansion. They waited as the noisy search continued. After a few minutes, Jones shrugged and pointed down the stairs with a questioning look on his face. O'Grady considered it for a moment then nodded. After all, that's why they had come. They may as well see what they could find out before they were discovered and ordered to leave again.

They descended the stairs and discovered a long hallway at the bottom with doors on either side at intervals. The first was locked. O'Grady pulled out the key and tried it, but with no luck. Jones reached into his pocket and pulled out a little leather case containing several tiny picks of various lengths and shapes. He winked at O'Grady as he went to work on the lock. After about a minute, the lock turned, and Jones slowly opened the door a sliver. A dim light glowed from within. The obvious question hung in the air for a moment, then he opened the door about three inches. The light emanated from a wall of surveillance monitors. The room was empty save for a single chair in the center facing the monitors. Four cameras pointed at the chair from various mounted positions in the room. Most of the monitors ran feeds from locations other than Toronto by the look of them; but five were of the mansion—one of the front gate, and four from inside the house. Their pursuers had turned on every light in the place. O'Grady studied the images for a long moment.

"Jonesy," he finally said in a whisper. "How can one guy be searching for us in three different rooms at the same time?"

Jones looked at the monitors closely for a long time. "What the fuck?" he finally said. "Isn't that the same RIA agent who kicked us out last week?"

"All three of them? Is the RIA hiring identical triplets now?"

"Wait. There comes another one into the library."

"Quadruplets?" O'Grady mused after seeing his face.

"That's pretty fucking weird," Jones mumbled.

"This goes way past weird."

"What have we stumbled onto here, Paddy?"

"I don't know; but maybe one of the other rooms down here will give us some clues."

"Or make us wish we never came out here in the first place."

The two men made their way further down the basement hallway. The second room had an assortment of rugs and candles and a sound system programmed with a series of nature tracks, like two hours of rain in the forest, or two hours of gentle waves on the shore. They concluded that it was a meditation room. The third room was for anything but meditation. The walls and floors were padded. Two of the walls had anchored shackles with chains. On a shelf lay various implements of torture, including leather whips, handcuffs, full leather masks with the eyes stitched shut, a head harness with a ball gag, a low stool with the center of the seat removed, and a variety of other accouterments of pain giving or pleasure receiving, depending on one's perspective. O'Grady surmised that Prowell was either a torturer, or someone who liked to be tortured.

"But isn't she a Women's Studies professor?" Jones asked. "So much for the rights of women."

"Maybe it's all consensual," Paddy shrugged. "I suppose women have as much right to inflict pain as men."

They left the BDSM chamber and faced the door across the hall. It was an electrically operated pocket door made of some kind of very hard metal.

"No lock to pick," Jones said.

"And no hinges, either," O'Grady observed. "A panic room or some kind of fortified protection space?"

"A personal fortress?"

"Maybe; but whatever it is, we're not going to find out tonight. They walked down to the last door. Can you pick the lock?"

"Piece of cake," Jones said as he went to work on the door. Within a few minutes, he had it opened. Inside the double-sized room, the walls were lined with vintage oak file cabinets. A leather-top library table with a pair of Art Deco, green-glass-shaded bankers' lamps stood in the middle of the space. O'Grady went to one of the cabinets and pulled the top drawer open to find it filled with paper files. Jones turned on a wall switch and small snake-arm lamps affixed to the top of each cabinet came to life, bathing the room in a shadowy incandescent glow.

"Who the hell keeps hard copies of anything nowadays?" Jones asked, pulling open another file drawer.

"Someone, I assume, that doesn't want their digital drives hacked."

"What the hell was this old bird hiding?"

"I don't know, but you got any important appointments tonight?"

"None that can't wait," he replied as they pulled two hefty piles of documents out of the file cabinets and took them to the reading table.

The taxi pulled up to the gates of the Rampart estate and an attractive blonde woman got out, paid the driver, and the taxi drove away. She approached the guardhouse in pumps that had long since become excruciating. How did women wear these things?

"Open the door," she said to the guard in a disconcertingly low voice made hoarse by exhaustion.

"Pardon me . . . Ma'am?" the guard said, sounding confused. "But this is private property."

"Don't make me ask again, Jenkins!" Cavanaugh said, pulling off his wig and scratching his scalp vigorously. The guard's eyes widened in recognition.

"I'm sorry, Mr. Cavanaugh," the guard said, quickly opening the access door. "I didn't realize it was you."

"That's the whole idea, idiot! Hence the term, disguise. Now, I want thirty heavily-armed men along the perimeter of this property within the hour and all defensive measures activated immediately. Until I say otherwise, we're on high alert. If anyone crosses the line without authorization, don't hesitate to fry them . . . And use the highest voltage. Do I make myself clear?"

"Yes sir!"

Cavanaugh pulled off the pumps and handed them to the guard, who raised his eyebrows but took them without further comment. He then commandeered the ATV parked inside the entry gate and drove down the long driveway to the mansion. Several minutes later, when he entered the sublevel bunker with Boma in tow, he was surprised to see it had been converted into a very comfortable bedroom suite. His father had wasted no time in making it livable.

"Where the hell have you been?" Rampart said with no other preamble. "I expected you two days ago."

"It was unavoidable. If I contacted you, it would have been intercepted. After speaking to Bennett in Los Nietos, I attempted to end run Gianakos at the chairs meeting in Tokyo."

"And?"

"Liliane Genevois was there."

"That cathouse bitch was in Tokyo?"

"Yes. And she recognized me. I barely escaped with my life."

"You got beat by a woman?" Rampart said, surprised. "Is that why you're all made up like a tranny whore?"

"You know something?" Cavanaugh said, sitting down heavily in exhaustion. "You can be an asshole."

"So I've been told," the old man chuckled. "You look like shit. Get yourself cleaned up and then we'll talk."

"That will have to wait. We need to talk now. Boma, will you bring this up through the digital projector." He handed the flash drive to Boma and the two waited while the screen lowered from the ceiling and the drive booted. When the specs materialized on the screen, Rampart was silent for a long moment until the ramifications sank in.

"He's got *five thousand* of those things?" he finally said, breathlessly.

"Four thousand nine hundred ninety-six at last count. I was able to take out four of them during my escape, but only because I had the element of surprise. I'll no longer have that luxury. Somehow, they recognized me."

"That would be because of the implants," Boma offered.

"Are you talking about Jonas' tits?" demanded Rampart.

"No, but those are very nice too, Jonas," Boma deadpanned.

"I am *not* amused, gentlemen," Jonas sighed. "Could you please explain what's on the drive."

"These new Heracles units have implants," Boma continued, smirking. "They're trans-human; at least that's what their specs say."

"What's a trans-human?" Rampart asked.

"They're organic as far as their physical structure goes, but parts of them are also integrated technology."

"Give it to me in English!"

"Sorry, Boss...uh...They're men with machine parts. Look here, for instance," he pointed to a spot on the screen. "There's a computer module in the cranium that's linked to—among other things—the visual and auditory cortices. This module can be accessed via a single dedicated satellite network. If I didn't know better, I'd say whatever these guys are seeing and hearing can be monitored offsite."

"They're free-roving surveillance cameras?" said Cavanaugh.

"It goes beyond that. Data can be uploaded from them; but commands can also be downloaded to them—all in real time."

"So, you're telling us he's created an army of advanced organic attack drones?" asked Cavanaugh.

"That sounds about right," replied Boma.

"And he built them right under our fucking noses," growled Rampart.

"But how could he control such a network? He'd have to have thousands of techs monitoring them around the clock and evaluating the data streams."

"Or one big-ass beast of a computer, with skills other than just predicting the weather," said Rampart.

"Haruspex," breathed Cavanaugh. "So, that's how that clone was able to identify me so fast."

"He had to have been planning this for years," said Rampart.

"Bennett said as much. According to him, six years ago the Directorate ordered the units—as they always do—through the sénéschal. He thought it odd, but who was he to question it?"

"Where is Bennett now?"

"I advised him to go into hiding."

"Damn right."

"I also countermanded the directive for the destruction of the Orion units and trackers. Bennett had the old loyalty directive overwritten to respond to me."

"That was quick thinking. How many of them are there?

"I'm not sure, but there must be close to fifteen-hundred, and about a third as many trackers."

"It doesn't even the odds by a long shot, but it's a start. Where are they now?"

"I had them recalled to the old airfield on Coronado Island on the south side of

Los Nietos. Once they're all there, I'll have to go down in person to complete the loyalty protocols."

"Uh, Boss?" Boma interrupted. "I think you need to see this other file."

The screen in front of them showed Darien Gianakos in his late twenties. The animated image presented a rotating 360° view of the subject completely naked.

"What the hell is this?" asked Rampart. "Is Gianakos into gay porno now?"

"Boss, this *is* Gianakos," Boma replied. "At least it's his DNA."

"Are you telling me that cocky little bastard cloned himself? Or maybe I should say big cocky bastard? Does he really have that burly a schlong?"

"Yes and no," Boma replied scanning the specs. "They started with his genetic material, but they've made all kinds of modifications—enhanced strength, intelligence, aggression, and a whole list of other things, including rapid-repair technology like I've never seen before... and obviously, a very big womb-tickler. There's an annotation here: 'Aggression scores remain well above normal, empathy scores are correlatively low. Need longitudinal data to confirm. Autobiographical engrams have not yet assimilated as hoped.' Seems like they've tampered with the original Gianakos with mixed results."

"He's made a super-clone of himself?" Cavanaugh said. "But whatever for?"

"There's only one thing I can think of, Son," Rampart said thoughtfully. "He wants an heir."

"We've got to find out! Boma, any progress on that back door hack you're designing?"

"Moderate so far. I can do it, but once we're in, we'll be detected. I haven't found a way around that yet. It may be that it's a one-shot deal."

"Alright then, now is not the time to take that shot. Let's save it for the right moment... Boma, is there anything in those files that would help us transfer the loyalty protocols on these new clones to me the way Walt did with the Orions?"

"Not a chance while Haruspex is still in control," Boma admitted.

"Damn it all! Well, look into it as a contingency... just in case we find a way to bypass Haruspex."

It was very early in the morning when O'Grady closed the last file drawer. He had never imagined what he'd find in these files and felt numb at the implications.

"Do you think all this stuff's for real?" Jones asked, quietly. "It reads like some kind of research for a sci-fi novel! I mean, who the hell calls themselves the Directorate?"

"That would be a relief if it were true; but I'm afraid that's wishful thinking," O'Grady put the fountain pen camera that the Card Man had given him back in his lapel pocket. The memory chip on it was maxed out with photos of various documents they had found. He couldn't possibly snap shots of everything, so he chose the most damning—and there were plenty that fit that category. "It's like some kind of shadow government. I mean, how in God's name did they keep this kind of thing a secret?"

"Who knows, Paddy; money always gives people a sense of superiority. Maybe to them it's just a bigger corporate takeover. Whatever it is, I can't think about it anymore tonight. I've got one hell of a headache."

"Must be going around. My head's pounding too. Let's go see if the search party's given up."

They went back down the hall to the monitor room and checked the video feeds. The lights were all off, and the house above them appeared empty.

"I don't know about you," O'Grady said. "But I think we should sneak out the back door and climb the fence."

"Yeah, probably a smart move." They left the room and quietly began to climb the stairs.

"I think I'll stay at my sister's place tonight, just in case those RIA guys are still looking for us. Something alerted them we were in the house. Maybe they have video feeds too—in which case, they have our mugs."

"Come off it, Paddy. Now you're getting paranoid. They may be stuck-up sons of bitches, but these guys are law enforcement too. They probably want to know what this broad was into as much as we do."

"Suit yourself, Jonesy. I just think I'd feel better somewhere other than my house."

"Well, I'm sleeping in my own bed. But first I'm gonna take a handful of aspirins."

The Tuesday morning Toronto Star late edition reported the body of one Stanislaw Jones had been pulled out of the city's harbour, an apparent suicide. Upon hearing the news from his sister, Padraig O'Grady gathered a few changes of clothes he kept at her house, stuffed them into a travel bag, and asked her for a ride into the city. She dropped him on the east side of downtown and he told her in no uncertain terms that he had NOT spent the night at her house, and that she had NO idea where he was. She drove away confused, but she also agreed. O'Grady pulled the antique Blue Jays ball cap low on his head, and walked several blocks to the place he knew he'd find Damerae Cardiman this time of the morning. There was a diner in the neighborhood called Patois. The Card Man bought the restaurant years ago, mainly because he liked to have breakfast there pretty much every day. O'Grady found him at his usual table and sat down.

"I need your help, Card Man," he said quietly, without preamble. "I need to get out of town right now without being seen."

The Card Man looked at him carefully for a long moment. "Dis got anyting to do wit dat key I make you?"

"It has everything to do with it, and if you value your life, you'll forget you ever saw me or that key."

Later that afternoon, O'Grady sat in the passenger seat of a big rig headed west on the Trans Canada. The driver was a talkative 'old friend' of the Card Man who, thankfully, didn't ask any questions. As the chatter washed over him, O'Grady considered his options. He needed answers, and his detective skills suggested an outside possibility. The Card Man had agreed to get him to Vancouver. From there, he would have to make his way south along the waterways to a place called Hunts Point. One name kept coming up in Prowell's notes, and not very flatteringly. The name was William Rampart. He had an estate somewhere on Hunts Point. If Paddy could evade the RIA long enough, that's where he'd go to ask a few very pointed questions.

WALTER BENNETT WORE A WIDE-BRIMMED straw hat and large-framed reflective sunglasses as he lounged in a chair on Avalon beach, sipping his third brightly decorated Mai Tai through an aqua colored straw. On this perfect April afternoon, the beach was surprisingly crowded, and he was more tanned than he'd been in years. As the sun approached the horizon, he tipsily meandered back to his bungalow. He found the little hut awash in shadows as he set his hat and sunglasses on the table. It was only then he noticed the figure of a man sitting in the dark. He turned on the light and his breath caught.

"Damocles," he said, trying to calm himself. "You surprised me. It's great to see you again. What brings you here?"

"Hello Walt," the young man said, smiling easily as he rose and crossed to the sunburned Bennett and, in an almost blurred flash of sudden motion, clamped the older man's neck in one hand and lifted him from the floor, his legs thrashing helplessly. "I've come to your little island hideaway to kill you, of course." Though Bennett beat at the younger man's arm and kicked him with all the desperate strength he had, he couldn't loosen the death grip. "I have a message from my father: If we don't have trust, what have we?" He slowly tightened his grip until he felt the cartilage tearing and heard the bones snap. He studied Bennett's face clinically as the bright glimmer of life drained from his eyes. "Fascinating," he mused, cocking his head to one side. Then he hefted the lifeless lump of spent flesh over his shoulder, walked calmly to the door, and left.

Darien Gianakos entered his Reykjavík office, switched on a single lamp, and slumped heavily behind the Resolute Desk. He appeared exhausted. Liliane Genevois followed and lowered herself into a comfortable chair facing him. The sun had not yet risen, so they sat in the single pool of light. Triggering the hidden switch on his bookshelf, it slid open. He pressed the numbers into the keypad and toggled it to speaker as the line buzzed at the other end. After three rings, there was a pick-up.

"Voice identification please."

"*If you gaze long enough into an abyss, the abyss will gaze back into you,*" he recited tiredly.

"Identity confirmed. "Feeling a bit nihilistic today, Darien?" the voice asked.

"It's been a trying week. Before we get into things, Minerva, this is Mademoiselle Liliane Genevois. She's going to need full level-two access moving forward."

"Greetings Mademoiselle Genevois. I'm pleased to make your acquaintance. Would you be so kind as to speak a phrase so that I can record it for later voice identification purposes?"

"*Qui court deux lièvres a la fois, n'en prend aucun.* And if we are to be working together, Minerva, please call me Liliane."

"*Très bien,* Liliane," Minerva responded. "*Et bienvenue.*"

"*Merci.*" Liliane Genevois was impeccably polite but felt none too pleased that Darien's chief of security was a woman who, by the sound of her voice, was both young and decisive. He failed to mention those little details on their flight in. She would not embarrass herself by bringing it up now in front of this 'other' woman. She would save it for a more appropriate time.

"So, Minerva," Darien asked, stifling a yawn, "what have you got on this Cavanaugh? You should never have been so casual in your assessment of him. Now he's become a real threat."

"I've gone back through five years of data-logged image scans. At level-three analysis, he pops up occasionally under several assumed identities: Sean Verbitsky, Benoit Moreau, and Alan Rosencroft are the ones I've discovered so far. Under these guises he has traveled widely in all the Consortium regions."

"And?" Gianakos said after a pause.

"That's all so far. There is no record of birth, baptism, inoculation, education, marriage, Consortium registration, or even application for the priesthood—nothing. He's a ghost, Darien. And a pretty good one at that, to keep his true identity completely unarchived for so long."

"I think we can assume he had the help of a master."

"Yes, but now that William Rampart is dead, isn't the *rōnin* expected to commit *seppuku*?"

"I think this one would prefer *kamikaze*, with me as the target."

"Now that we have his image catalogued, we can track him through facial recognition protocols."

"Then he's still in Tokyo?" Liliane asked, yawning daintily.

"I wouldn't stay there, if I were him," Minerva responded.

"But you said you would have caught him with facial recognition if he left?" Darien said.

"Unless he used a method whereby he wouldn't be image scanned."

"But we've got access to cameras everywhere, not just airports."

"And I assume he also knows this, and how to avoid them. It's been two days since the events in Tokyo. It would be counterproductive to stay there. My assessment is he's either back in the PSM, or en route."

"You're probably right," Gianakos said, tapping his lips. "Let's get eyes at Sea-Tac in case he arrives there. Also, dispatch a few-dozen units to that compound. Order them to search it and if they find him, to kill him. Let's tie this off."

"You're not thinking clearly, Darien," Minerva said.

"Excuse me?" he replied dangerously.

"Consider for a moment: if your 'master' was just murdered inside your heavily fortified compound; would you sit all alone there and wait for the killers to return and finish the job?"

"No," he finally admitted. "I'd discover how the breach happened in the first place, triple my fortifications, and plan a reprisal."

"A full-frontal assault would be just what he expects, under the circumstances."

"She's right, Darien," Liliane said quietly. "If you send units in now you may very well have a small war on your hands. And we do not need the attention that would bring. We've cut off the heads of the snakes. We shouldn't pay too much attention to the wiggling of one tail."

"A very dangerous tail, my dear, who won't rest until we're both dead."

"Yes," she mused. "An unpleasant thought to be sure; but we have the strength to resist an all-out attack. Let Minerva locate the troublesome snakelet, and then we'll lure him into a trap of our own design."

"You may be right. But I want that compound watched day and night, no one goes in or out without our knowing it. I want to know exactly what's happening there before we plan our next move."

"Consider it done," Minerva said. "You should also know that Damocles just entered the building."

"Good," Darien said. "Liliane, it's time you meet my protégé anyway."

"You have a protégé?" Liliane asked.

"Yes. He's a delightful young man. I'm quite sure you'll adore him."

"I will be the judge of that." The door opened and as Damocles Praefectus walked into the pool of light surrounding the desk, Liliane's eyes widened in surprise.

"Liliane," Darien said. "This is Damocles Praefectus."

"*Enchanté, Mademoiselle*," the young man said bowing slightly and gently kissing her hand.

"No," she said, blushing. "The pleasure is all mine. He's very polite, Darien."

"Why do you all keep telling me that? Am I so churlish?"

"Not at all, *mon cher*. I was just affirming your judgment of your protégé."

"Yes, that must be it," Darien said, and then turned to his son. "So, how did it go with Bennett?"

The young man made himself comfortable in another office chair. "I found him taking too much sun at Avalon Island. It wasn't good for his health."

"Excellent," Darien said. "Did you get the information from him we needed?"

"He was the traitor."

"As I suspected. How much did he reveal of our plans? And to whom did he reveal them?"

"He died under the stress of interrogation," Damocles said. "Apparently he wasn't in very good health to begin with."

"That was not the plan, Damocles," the older man said. "I told you we needed that information. You must learn to be subtler in your methods."

"I got everything out of him I was going to," Damocles responded.

"Perhaps, but we don't know that. I don't like operating without a full brief, and now I don't have a choice."

"I've been able to put together some of the pieces by running our new Cavanaugh images through facial recognition," Minerva said. "The day before Bennett disappeared, Jonas Cavanaugh was image-scanned as one of his aliases, Benoit Moreau, traveling from the PSM to Los Nietos by rocket train. The following morning a camera caught him again at John Wayne Airport, where Bennett kept his private jet. Later that afternoon he passed through Haneda in Tokyo. I think *who* talked to Bennett is clear. *What* they said is more problematic. Time analysis suggests Cavanaugh couldn't have spoken to Bennett for more than sixty minutes, but much can be said in an hour."

"What are your conclusions?"

"He knew where the meeting was taking place; but since the Directorate scheduled it, he would have had access anyway. However, he walked right into a nearly lethal gauntlet at the Ritz; so, he didn't expect you to have Heracles units with you—an assumption I would not have made had I known about the program. During his escape, he shot four units at close range and would have noticed they were identical; so now he knows of the existence of a new generation of clones. Until he takes further action, we cannot know for certain how much he knows about their numbers, or capabilities, or of your plans for them."

"And what about my meeting with the chairs? That debacle could not be described as business as usual."

"Most of the chaos can be attributed to an ill-timed fire alarm. I don't think it's a concern. All the chairs have returned to their hubs, except Cybergi, who is currently on vacation with his family."

"All right then," Darien said, rubbing his temples. "We need to proceed to the next stage. How long before the new inoculations are ready?"

"Zaibatsu is on schedule for delivery of the first batch sometime in mid-May."

"Good, good. As for the Genomics void, we'll need to replace Walt with one of our own. Examine the dossiers of all Tertium managers and give me the files on the three best candidates of those I've seated over the years. I'll select one of those for Genomics. Also, compile a list of the top six regional Compliance managers and we'll make them Tribunes."

"Give me twenty-four hours," Minerva replied.

"Fine. And forget what I said about Genomics being the new third seat. We don't need to upset Alex right now. Let's not rock that boat."

"Since no formal announcement was made, there is nothing to be done. All is as it was."

"Thanks. Now, Damocles, this new development doesn't change the plan. In three days, Liliane and I will move into our new base of operations in Rome. One thousand Heracles units will be housed there with us as our *Cohortes Praetoriae*. Once the Akureyri barracks complex is completed, we'll station an equal number of units here. One cohort will remain in Khartoum. The other five cohorts will be stationed in London, Los Nietos, Olissipona, Moscow, and Tokyo. After the ceremony in Rome, you'll return to Reykjavík and handle things from here, with Minerva's help of course. I'll assign the Tribunes to command the other six cohorts; they will report directly to you, Damocles, as their Legatus. When the inoculations are fully distributed, we'll move to the next stage—but not before. Until then, this is still a shadow operation. Reykjavík will be yours when we leave; but don't go ordering around the people here as though they were your subjects. Practice some of the subtleties you apparently ignored with Bennett. Are there any questions?"

"It's all quite clear, Father, and thank you. However, your attention has been understandably diverted of late; and if I read the briefs correctly, you need to devote at least some attention to your anomaly. He's still at large, isn't he? And Haruspex's analysis suggests he's more than peripherally important."

"Did you just call Darien your father?" Liliane asked.

"Pardon me, Mademoiselle. I assumed you knew. Yes, I'm his son."

"Our relationship is a complex one, *ma chérie*," Darien interrupted. "I should have introduced Damocles as my son; we'll discuss it later, shall we?"

"Yes, Darien, we certainly will." There was a moment of awkward silence before Darien filled the gap.

"Minerva, perhaps we *should* devote some attention again to Percival. Do we have anything further on him, or his band of mercenaries?"

"Nothing definitive on his current whereabouts, but I'm analyzing all data streams. However, since Damocles has broached the subject, you may recall a little more than two years ago when Haruspex first discovered the anomaly?"

"Yes?"

"You asked me to run the data again and you told me, 'If the probability comes out the same the second time around, we'll apprehend him, but not before'."

"Yes, yes. I remember. If I recall, it was 98% both times."

"Not exactly. It was 98.47% the first run and 98.48% the second time. To be more precise, it was 98.4682437% on the first run, and 98.4763453% on the second, only a week later."

"Good heavens, woman! I appreciate your exactitude, but that's the same, as far as I'm concerned."

"It's not the same, Darien. There was a difference of .0081016%."

"But there's always a plus or minus component with probabilities, isn't there?"

"Theoretically, yes. But that's outside the margin of error for Haruspex, and even if that were the case, it should fluctuate both up and down in subsequent runs. I ran the data six more times at three-month intervals. Each time, the probability quotient increased slightly."

"How much more can you increase from 98%?"

"Now you see my concern."

"No, I haven't the slightest idea what you're talking about."

"Let me clarify then; since we had these very small but measurable increases each time, I thought it prudent to calculate the patterns of the potentiality streams *ad infinitum* for the anomaly. I was somewhat surprised when we got a result regarding our long-term operational strategies."

"Could you state that in terms I can even remotely understand?" Darien demanded, frustrated.

"According to the analysis completed last night, if Percival isn't found and neutralized within two years, three months, seventeen days, and twenty-two hours, we will have reached the point of no return."

"What the hell does that even mean?"

"Let me try to simplify it for you."

"Don't get snippy, Minerva. Just cut to the chase."

"Apparently, a very small percentage of seemingly random anomalies radiate a strong magnetic or kinetic sociological vibration that resonates long after they have passed an event horizon. Our analysis suggests that *this* particular anomaly—John Percival—is extraordinarily influential when it comes to these stimulants of sociological change. His movements apparently collide with and excite the movements of myriad other entities. The subsequent groundswell is exponential."

"Goddammit, Minerva! Spit it out!"

"Okay. If he hasn't been stopped by then, he'll be unstoppable."

"Unstoppable? How is that even possible?"

"Every sociological movement begins with a small number of very devoted adherents. If sustained long enough to grow to a certain number—usually around ten percent of a given population—the movement reaches a tipping point. Like an air-born virus with no vaccine, once enough people are exposed to it, there's simply no stopping the spread."

"And you are certain of this?" Liliane asked.

"Well, I can't be absolutely certain. It's always a probability quotient with Haruspex. But 99.999987% doesn't leave much wiggle room."

"No," Darien conceded. "It certainly doesn't . . . But could you be a little more specific about what unstoppable means . . . I mean, what are the particulars of his unstoppability?"

"Actually, I am currently unable to be more specific."

"Are you being obtuse with me again?"

"No, Darien. I asked Haruspex that very question . . . And I received an error message in reply."

"Is Haruspex even capable of an error message?"

"I didn't think so, until now. However, her reply was: *There are unknown variables involved that are beyond measurability and, therefore, beyond predictability.*"

"Is Haruspex broken?"

"I don't believe so, but I'm running a diagnostics protocol to be sure."

Darien was silent for a contemplative moment. "Well, until we find out otherwise, I'll be damned if I'm going to let that raindrop destroy everything we've worked so hard to establish! . . . All right then, let's devote only minimal resources to the Cavanaugh problem. Put every other available resource into locating this virus and eradicating him."

Later that evening, in the master bedroom of Gianakos' Reykjavík residence, Liliane sat up in the bed, her arms crossed beneath her breasts, wearing the thickest negligee she had. When Darien came out of the bathroom in his pajamas, running his fingers through his freshly shampooed hair, she remained coolly silent, just staring at him.

"It's been a long and trying day, my dear. I'm looking forward to caressing every inch of your magnificent body."

"Why didn't you tell me you had a son, Darien?" Her words were ice, and her eyes hard little agates.

"Ah," he said. "I should have noticed your nonverbal signals. They're shouting that you're in no mood for our usual activities."

"Don't be flippant, my *dear*," she spoke the 'dear' as though it were bitter on her tongue. "You have not been honest with me."

"That's not completely accurate, Liliane," he said. "We've never talked about this, so I've never been dishonest about it."

"You are splitting hairs, Sénéschal." Darien winced at the obvious jab at his inferior status to her. "I want the whole truth, and I want it now!"

"Very well, *ma chérie*," he said in a conciliatory tone. "I wasn't really hiding it from you, or at least not for the reasons you seem to think."

"Darien! Just tell me!"

"Fine," He sat down on the edge of the bed and took a breath. "When we constructed this plan eight years ago, I realized I would be much older by the time it came to fruition. None of us lives forever, and I began to think that I had missed something by not having fathered a child who could carry on for me after I die. I hesitated to talk with you about it because I didn't want to hurt your feelings. Liliane, my dear, you are a magnificent woman in every way but, let's be honest, we're both beyond childbearing years, and I didn't want you to feel as though you had let me down, because nothing could be further from the truth. In any case, I asked Bennett to embark on a somewhat radical endeavor—to create a son for me from my stem cells."

"Damocles is a clone?"

"In a manner of speaking; but please don't call him that to his face because... well... he doesn't know."

"*Mon Dieu*! How can he not know?"

"Because I wanted a son, Liliane, not a robot. There are certain untested aspects to Damocles. It goes well beyond simple cloning. Bennett implanted memories in him, so he believes he was born and raised rather than cultured. For all intents and purposes, he's me; but he's a younger and vastly enhanced version of me—improved upon in almost every way."

"I find that hard to believe."

"I'll take that as a compliment. Anyway, he's far more decisive than a clone ever could be. He doesn't yet have the wisdom or finesse of my experience, but he has the raw material to surpass me in every way. So, though it's not strictly truthful to say he's my son; it is honest from a certain perspective. I wanted us to have an heir in this endeavor of ours. Damocles is the result of that desire. I should have told you sooner. I apologize."

"So, he's not the child of you and that minx, Minerva?"

"What?" he sputtered. "Is that what this is all about? Oh, heavens no! Minerva is very efficient, but she's not my type at all! Oh, no, no, no. There is no other for me, but you, *ma chérie*."

"Yes, well, you *should* have told me sooner... I have never felt the need or drive to have children of my own, but I cannot fault you in this impulse. Though he never stated it, I sensed my father's disappointment that I was not a male."

"Well, I for one am profoundly grateful you're not. You are a garden of delights that a son could never have been."

She was silent for a moment at the memory of her father. "I am just glad you were not having an affair. I would not be at all pleased if that were the case. You are mine, Darien. All mine! Remember that."

"Always, my dear; I would never betray that trust. But the fact that you're jealous makes me very aroused. Are you sure you don't want me to wander in your garden."

"Oh, shut up and do me. All this talk of gardens and paramours has made me wet."

"I always love it when the dew falls, beloved."

Cavanaugh and his adoptive father sat in the sub-level bunker of their Puget Sound complex having a late breakfast together. He had slept in and looked much better for it. They were discussing intelligence reports.

"According to our eyes on the scene, Gianakos' jet arrived in Reykjavík yesterday morning. Both he and Genevois went to his offices. They were there until the afternoon then went to his residence with a third younger man—I assume that's the clone. They are always heavily guarded."

"Wouldn't you be if you knew a well-trained killer was trying to blow your head off?" Rampart said, wryly.

"Yes. But I haven't a snowball's chance of getting close enough at this point. We need to find a way to gather better intel on their little junta; but we have no digital access to important data, and our eyes can't get closer than a hundred yards without being made. We could use Boma's spy bomb, but that's a one-time shot I hesitate to waste on simple information; besides, I still hope he'll be able to develop it more thoroughly." He sighed deeply. "We're being thwarted at every turn."

"Use the chairs," Rampart said, matter-of-factly.

"What?"

"The Consortium chairs; turn them into sources. You've already got Bennett. Get a few more, and we'll have the best human information network available."

"That's brilliant! Why didn't I think of it?"

"Because you're too busy whining, and way too dependent on technology. Buck up! I've seen enough battles in my life to know when things are hopeless, and we're not there yet. We need intel, so let's get intel."

"Bully for you, Father! But we must be very cautious; I suspect not all the chairs will be disappointed with Gianakos' promotion. Which ones do you suggest I approach?"

"Good question. I think the big three are long shots. Oshira likes Gianakos personally—no accounting for taste. Gentry-Pruett and King are too powerful with things the way they are to rock the boat, although King may be upset when he hears of his demotion. I'd start with the lower-tier managers—the newer ones."

"There's Paolo-Ibáñez with Grupo Energia."

He stared off before speaking. "Let's leave her out of this for now."

"Not new enough?"

"It's not that," he mused quietly . . . "I owe her father. Xavier was a real friend, and I don't want to put her in harm's way. I was the one who convinced her to join this project in the first place, as a nod to her dear old dad . . . Who just happened to be dying at the time."

"Oh . . . Well, that's a side of you I knew nothing about. Is she aware of your true identity?"

"She knows I'm Will Rampart. But she has no idea about the Rockefeller thing. And I'd like to keep it that way, if you don't mind."

"Your call . . . That leaves Neumayer with Oceania and Khvostovsky with Cybergi — he's the youngest of the bunch, and the newest to his chair."

"Start with him then—" There was a knock on the door. "Come in." The door opened and Boma stepped in. "What've you got for us?"

"I wish it were better news, Boss," Boma apologized.

"Why?" Cavanaugh asked.

"I was scanning the news headlines from the Metroplexes, and this one popped up in the Los Nietos Times/Tribune," he handed the printed page to Cavanaugh.

"Body washes ashore in Avalon," Cavanaugh read, sitting back heavily. "Identified as local business magnate, Walter Bennett."

"Well, shit!" spat Rampart. "How'd it happen?"

Cavanaugh continued to scan the article. "It says here it's being investigated by the RIA as a boating accident."

"Boating accident? *Schmegegge!* As a branch of Compliance, the RIA's as good as owned by Gianakos."

"I'm truly sorry. Bennett seemed like a good man. I wasn't careful enough. I thought I had Darien cornered. Once they made me in Tokyo, it would be easy enough to trace it back to him. This means we must be that much more careful in approaching the other chairs. I'll leave this afternoon to speak with Khvostovsky."

"That's my other news," Boma spoke up. "Our infrared perimeter scanners picked up a new presence of covert operatives watching this compound. You won't get out without being seen."

"Bloody hell!" Cavanaugh shouted. "We're sitting ducks here if that *sleekit basturt* decides to attack. I need to get down to Coronado Island and see if Bennett implemented the loyalty protocol on those Orions before he died. Those units could make the difference here. I need to get out and back in unseen."

"Simplest thing in the world," Rampart said, easily. "This old girl has a few tricks up her sleeve that I included when I built her—for just-in-case moments like this one. Meet me back here in twenty minutes with your bags packed."

A confused Cavanaugh returned to the bunker twenty minutes later with his leather shoulder bag packed. That included the Smith & Wesson with extra rounds just in case. He had to trade the Glock in Tokyo for his make-up; but the .44 would provide ample firepower if needed. He found Rampart waiting for him.

"Follow me," the old man said, as he walked out of the converted conference room. Once inside the elevator, he took out a key Cavanaugh had never seen before and inserted it in the slot. To Cavanaugh's surprise, the elevator descended.

"Why didn't you ever tell me about this?" he asked.

"Because an old man has to keep a few secrets," Rampart replied, grinning. "That way, he can surprise people when they think they've got him all figured out." The elevator stopped and the door opened on a dank subterranean tunnel lined in old casing stone, rounded at the ceiling. They walked down the passageway leading directly from the elevator to an open vaulted area with a dock.

"This is my submersible," Rampart said proudly, pointing to something that looked like an oversized formula-one racecar floating at the dock. "I thought it might be a nice way to escape if I needed to. Kinda like James Bond."

"Aren't you more like Francisco Scaramanga?" Cavanaugh asked, straight-faced, looking over the submersible.

"Oh, you're hilarious," Rampart said, disgustedly. "Once you get in, you'll need to navigate into the lock. When I've secured this end, I'll open the gate and let Lake

Washington flood in. Head over to the Kirkland Marina. The largest yacht there is named *Auctoritas Facit Legem*. It's fueled up and always ready. The skipper lives on it with a skeleton crew, so just mention my name and she'll take you wherever you need to go."

"Let me guess, the skipper is young and beautiful?"

"It's possible. What does it matter?"

"I just hope when and if I get to be your age, I still have half the sex-drive you do."

"Let's be clear, sonny; I can't really drive anymore, but I can still appreciate the scenery. Now, where are you taking my boat?"

"My first stop will be Coronado Island. If the Orions have arrived, and if they're mine, I'll send a contingent of them back here with the yacht. How many do you think she can carry?"

"Well, they won't be very comfortable, but you can probably squeeze fifty or sixty onboard."

"Good. When they arrive back up here you can ferry them over with the sub, so they're not noticed."

"That sub only seats four!"

"It'll take a few days, but if Gianakos sends a force against us here, he'll do it based on the numbers he thinks we have. If we keep sixty Orions under wraps, we'll gain the upper hand—at least for the first round."

"That's sound thinking. I'll have the staff reconfigure sub-level two as a barracks. We should be able to house at least sixty. You said you'll *send* the yacht back. Where are you going?"

"I need to find a way to Moscow without being caught in an image scan. Any suggestions?"

"You could go by boat."

"It'd take too long. We're working against the clock here. I'll have to fly, but taking our jet is no longer an option. I'm going to have to go commercial."

"Well, I guess you could dress up like that tranny whore again."

"Is that payback for the Scaramanga comment?"

"You got a better idea?"

"Unfortunately, I don't."

"Then you better get a move on, sport, or should I call you sweetie?"

"Very funny, Da. I'll contact you from Russia."

"You should wear a tight cashmere sweater. It'll make your tits look great."

"Eat me!"

"Maybe, but only if you wear the cashmere."

Part Two

TWO DAYS BEFORE THEY MADE port, Elley told them his freezers were full and they could get some rest until they reached Tiksi. They slept through most of the first day, and on the morning of their second, they met late in the galley for breakfast. Their ordeal at sea had hardened them. They were all thinner—except for Rophe and Barnabas—and their faces had the weathered look of fishermen; well, all except Yael, Pere thought, who could never look like a man no matter what she did. At Elley's advice, the men had also sworn off shaving. He said fishermen generally didn't have time for that, and it would look better anyway when they went ashore. After nearly five weeks, they looked pretty scruffy—even Pere, who had grown his first somewhat uneven beard. He was very pleased with it, though it was sparse and had flecks of reddish in it. Yael said it tickled her, but she would try to get used to it. At the very least, it made him look different from the official image that Compliance had been posting for two years.

Because the last five weeks had been so tough, he had been too busy and tired to think about anything other than fishing—let alone worry about the future responsibilities of the falcon. He had also grown much closer to these people in the crucible of hard labor. He respected them more, and they respected him, because he held his own amidst the dangers of the high seas. Now that the time had come to move on, that gnawing worry started to grind in his stomach again.

"We will offload in Tiksi tomorrow morning," Elley said, putting a little sausage and eggs between two pieces of slightly stale bread. This is good luck for you, because Siberia is too big and under-populated to get much Compliance oversight. Still, when we dock, you will want to stay belowdecks while we offload." He took a large bite of his kolbasa sandwich, leaving crumbs in his beard. "Once my freezers are empty, we will travel upriver a few days to Kyusyur, where we have our *dacha*. You will be our guests until you decide what your next move will be."

"I can't thank you enough, old friend," said Barnabas.

"We must stick together. And besides, to be honest with you, Sayiina was very put out with me when I left so soon again after our last run. If you are with me, she will be too embarrassed to yell."

"I told you he's an old scam artist," El laughed.

"I prefer the term, opportunist," Elley corrected him, smiling sheepishly.

They made Tiksi early the following morning, and remained belowdecks until the old skipper came later that evening and told them they were underway again.

"A very profitable haul," he said as he sat down at the galley table. "I have already paid the rest of the crew and sent them home. Now for your shares."

"That's not necessary, Elley," Barnabas said. "Your help already has been invaluable."

"Do not temp me, Brother," The old man said, winking. "Besides, it will be necessary. If you are going to move around, you will need some funds to make it happen."

"He's right," El said, and Barnabas gave in.

Elley handed out the shares to each of them, and Pere felt proud; his hard work had earned a lot more than just respect. They traveled upriver for the better part of two days until they reached a small town where the river-tour boats moored. They waited until deep night when the docks were deserted and then Elley led the way to an old warehouse where the ship's captains and crews stowed their vehicles while they were out on extended runs. Elley had an old van parked there he used for hauling gear. There were no seats in the back, but they all climbed in and sat on the floorboards.

The drive to the old skipper's *dacha* took about forty-five minutes. When they finally stopped and climbed out, the night sky was clear and dark with only the sliver of a new moon showing through the aspens. The stars were brilliant, and the spring air was still very cold. Elley led them to a surprisingly large structure for the middle of this wilderness. The log home was two stories high and quite comfortable looking. The old pirate had obviously amassed some booty over the years.

"I hauled the logs in maybe fifteen years ago," he spoke quietly. It was Sayiina's dream to live out here—do not ask me why. It is the middle of nowhere, but that is what she likes. There is an old Russian saying: 'Happy wife, happy life'."

"Women all over the world have that saying," El snorted.

"Be nice, Uncle," Yael said. "I think it's a very nice saying, Elley."

"Yes. So does Sayiina. She reminds me of it all the time."

The grizzled old skipper led Pere and the others around the back of the *dacha* to the wet-room door. He quietly opened it, and they crowded in, taking off their shoes and coats. When they came into the kitchen the smell of hot food filled their senses, and they heard footsteps on the floor above them.

"Is that you, *Mishka*?" came a shout from the stairwell.

"It is I, *Babushka*," he called back. "She calls me her 'little bear'," he said quietly in explanation of his nickname. "And I call her my 'old woman' to try and make her stop calling me her little bear. Clearly, it has not worked yet." A small energetic woman bustled into the kitchen, still in her apron.

"I was just getting beds ready," she said, kissing Elley soundly on the cheek. She eyed him up and down. "You are too thin, *Mishka*. You need to eat more." Then she turned to the others. "The *ukha* is ready. Sit, sit, all of you," she pointed toward the table. "We will make introductions while you eat." They smiled at Elley who rolled his eyes and shrugged. They got comfortable while Sayiina brought a large steaming tureen and set it in the middle of the table.

"It smells wonderful, Sayiina," Barnabas said.

"You have not changed a bit, Vally. You look as young as ever," she said in a very matter of fact tone, but she smiled all the same.

"Well, I don't feel young. But you look as beautiful as the day I met you."

"Oh, bosh! Did *Mishka* here tell you to butter me up, so I would not be mad at him?"

"Why would you suggest that *Babushka*?" Elley said, all innocence.

"Because I know you, you old rascal. Now, bless the food so everyone can eat before the ukha grows cold. You probably have not said grace for at least six weeks, am I wrong?"

"It gets very busy on a fishing boat, dearest."

"Do you forget that I have been on your fishing boat many times? You always prayed when I was there."

"That is because I was afraid I had taken a sea monster on board."

"You are not as funny as you think, *Mishka*. Now bless the food."

Elley's blessing was very humble, touching—and short. When he finished, they dug in. Pere thought the soup was wonderful. After five weeks of galley food, this was a real treat. The ukha had a delicately flavored broth with generous chunks of white fish and potatoes. Sayiina had also baked several loaves of a dark brown bread that they tore chunks from and slathered in butter before dipping them in the broth. After they had taken the edge off their hunger, Sayiina told Barnabas it was time for him to make introductions. He nodded and put down his spoon.

"This is Ya'el," he said pointing to his right.

"You are very beautiful, Ya'el," she said matter-of-factly. "I would pay good money for that hair."

"Thank you," Yael said, unconsciously arranging her auburn curls.

"This is El'zar, Barnabas continued down the table, "and Ehud, and Khyoza."

"A Cossack," she said, squinting at Khyoza. Clearly, she had a perceptive eye. "Your people were not kind to the Yakuts. They butchered whole villages of them."

"But *he's* a good man!" blurted Rophe, who then immediately blushed.

"And this is Rophe," said Barnabas, looking confused at her outburst.

"A Swede, by the look of you," Sayiina said. "I generally like Swedes. And apparently Swedes like Cossacks." Rophe blushed even more deeply under the unwavering gaze of the old woman. Khyoza just looked baffled.

"*Babushka*," interrupted Elley, gently. "The Cossack invasion was nearly four-hundred years ago."

"Of course it was, *Mishka*. I am not a fool."

"Did I say you were, dear?"

"And this is Perry," Barnabas interrupted.

She looked at him long and carefully. Pere felt uncomfortable, like he was being examined. "No," she said, quietly. "He is not."

"I'm sorry?" Pere said, confused.

"Your name, young man, it is not Perry. I do not know what it is, but it is not that."

"My Sayiina," Elley said to Pere, sounding a little embarrassed. "She likes to think of herself as a mystic." He shrugged. "We all have our little shortcomings."

"Do not patronize me, old man, or we shall have words right here and now about your sudden disappearance six weeks ago."

"Yes, dear," he said meekly, and meant it. Here was a person not to be toyed with. Yael tried to hide her smile as she looked at the fidgeting Pere.

"Now, what is your real name, and do not stop him from telling me, Vally!" Sayiina just looked at Pere, but for some reason she reminded him of old Miss Garrett, his co-op teacher, who always seemed to be looking into you rather than simply at you. He looked to Barnabas for help, but the coward was just staring at his soup. Yael was no help at all; she had covered her mouth to stifle a laugh, because the women finally outnumbered the men—clearly, Sayiina counted for at least five in any fight.

"My name is Peregrine," he confessed.

She studied him for a long moment. "*Sokol*," she finally said, testing the sound of it. "Yes, this is your rightful name." Then she got up, brushed off the front of her apron and went to the kitchen. "We have some cherry-stuffed pastry for dessert. Who would like some?" They all looked at each other in astonishment, and Elley just shrugged again, shaking his head.

They slept in warm comfortable beds that night, but Pere had trouble falling to sleep. Everything was too still now, and quiet. He'd gotten used to the pitch and groan of Elley's old boat, and he found he now couldn't sleep without it. But truthfully, he also struggled with how Sayiina had seen through him. She wasn't the first person who told him 'Falcon' was his rightful name; but it had been two years since anyone had done so in such an unsettling way. It made him feel once again like he was destiny's pawn, and he didn't want to be anyone's pawn, let alone destiny's. Khyoza told him he could choose, but when things like their dinner conversation happened, it didn't really feel like he had a choice in any of it. After hours of mulling over things but solving nothing, it was probably close to dawn when he finally dropped off to sleep.

He stood in the middle of a wide-open tundra, shivering. He could see for miles in every direction. Not even a tree broke his sight line. The sky shone in a clear soft blue. He stared into it and noticed a tiny speck of shadow growing against its vastness. He waited as the shadow drew closer until he could see it was a massive bird, pure white except for the jet-black tips of its wings. It had a long neck and a face the bright color of freshly-baked bricks. Gliding on the icy breeze, it finally landed directly in front of him. Nearly as tall as a man, it stared him in the face as though waiting for something. They stood there looking at one another for an unmeasured time—perhaps it was a few seconds, perhaps it was eons—and then it began to dance—that's the only way he could describe it. It danced in a ritual form as old as its kind, and without knowing why, he understood what it was saying with the dance; it wanted him to follow. When it had finished, it mounted the wind and began to fly south. As though it was the most natural thing in the world, he morphed into a falcon and flew after the great bird.

They soared far above a wide river until they came to a city. There, they landed atop a great cathedral with nine golden domes, each crowned with an ornate cross. The bird danced on the pinnacle of the cathedral, and then they were airborne again. They followed the river as it became smaller and then disappeared altogether. They flew over mountains and when they crossed the last peak, there stretched before them a lake the size of an ocean. It seemed to go on forever, but the tireless bird soared over the lake and beyond until they came to a second city. In this city, they landed atop a massive archway emblazoned with the bronze image of a proud two-headed eagle.

They rested only moments until the bird danced for a third time and then they were flying west, and after many miles, the falcon spied a snake far below. As the great bird glided down, the falcon could now see, it was a train snaking its way through a vast wilderness. They landed on the roof of the last car and the bird began to dance one more time. As it danced, the earth began to shake, and the train jumped the tracks, and they began to fall; then the bird vanished . . .

Yael was gently shaking him. "Are you going to sleep all day, farm boy," she said quietly.

He sat up, rubbing his eyes. "I couldn't get to sleep last night," he said by way of explanation.

"Well, everyone's holding breakfast for you on Sayiina's orders," she smiled. "I don't think you want to upset her by letting the food get cold."

"I'm coming right now," he said, stumbling out of bed.

"Well, you might want to get dressed first," she laughed and left the room. Pere quickly dressed and went downstairs. Everyone was already sitting at the table, but no one had started eating.

"Sorry," he mumbled, and sat in the one empty chair. Then Sayiina nodded and everyone dug in. They ate warm *blini* with sour cream, butter, and jam. The dark tea had a smoky flavor, but Pere felt several lumps of sugar took care of that. There wasn't much conversation at first because everyone was busy eating, but eventually Pere's curiosity got the better of him.

"Is there a bird in Siberia that is large and white with a red face?"

"With the end of its wings black?" Elley said, with his mouth full of blin. Pere nodded. "Snow Crane," he said.

"Why do you ask?" said Sayiina. "Did you see one?"

"I think so," said Pere as he filled his mouth with another jammy blin.

"They are sacred to the Yakut people," she explained. "And also, very rare now. Where did you see it? It is not the right season." She looked at him curiously.

"Oh," he said with his mouth still full. "I didn't really see one . . . well, I mean . . . I did see one, but it wasn't a real one." They all looked at him now as though he wasn't making sense. "It was in my dream," he clarified, and everyone stopped eating very suddenly. He realized too late that his big mouth had taken him into the danger zone. Sayiina looked at him very steadily—he could almost hear her thinking.

"*Prorock Sokol*?" she finally whispered.

"What did you say, dear?" mumbled Elley.

"It's really nothing, Sayii—"

"Be still, Valéry!" the old woman commanded.

"Listen, Sayiina," Barnabas said. "We were only trying to protect you from—"

"I said be still! Did you ever think you might have been brought here for this reason? Men! You are always trying to control things that should be set free." No one said anything. El just chuckled quietly, shaking his head, and reached for another blin. Yael glared at him, but he only laughed the harder. "Now," Sayiina continued, gently. "Tell me your dream, *Sokol*."

Pere looked to Barnabas, who only shrugged helplessly and nodded his head. Then Pere proceeded to relate the dream in detail. He tried to leave nothing out, although it's the nature of dreams to lose vividness very quickly. After he finished, they were all quiet. Sayiina just looked at him in that same piercing way again. Finally, she spoke.

"*Mishka*, you need the hull of that old scow of yours repainted."

"Yes. That is true, I suppose, dear," he said warily. "But you do not need to insult our livelihood by calling it a scow."

"I apologize. Tomorrow morning, we are going to travel upriver to the shipyards in Yakutsk to have Saint Peter's bottom scraped, sanded, and repainted."

"We are?"

"Yes dear, we are."

"But you said you never wanted to leave your sanctuary here again."

"I know what I said, *Mishka*. But I have changed my mind. You *do* need your ship repainted, yes?"

"Well, yes, but . . ."

"And you have not taken me on a vacation for a very long time. I think you are overdue. Besides, I need to do some shopping."

"Shopping?" It was clear that Elley was adding up costs in his head even as his shoulders began to slump.

"Yes, shopping. There are several nice shops in Yakutsk."

"But it is very cold there, *Babushka*."

"Oh, bother that! It is cold everywhere in Siberia. We are going and that is that; and our guests here are coming with us. I think they would like to see Preobrazhensky Cathedral."

"As you say, dear," he sighed. "But it may take several weeks to get the Pyotr scraped and painted. Our guests may need to be somewhere else."

"Yes, dear, they do. And Valéry knows exactly where they need to be; is not this true, Varnava?"

"Yes, Neviah," he sighed thoughtfully. "I believe I do."

The early afternoon sun shone clear and bright as the helicopter flew over the Eternal City and finally landed in the grand cobbled-stoned square atop *Vaticanus Mons*, west of the curving Tiber River. The gates of the one-hundred-and-ten-acre compound had been closed for the last two days to facilitate the arrival of the one thousand Heracles units that would form the Imperial Praetorian Guard. Liliane had the brilliant idea to have the Heracles units dress in the uniforms of the old Swiss Guard, the only alterations being that they added visors to their customary helmets to cover their identical faces. That way, they could walk amongst the museum patrons without arousing much more interest than cosplayers would. It was Sunday in ancient Rome. On the old calendar, this would have been Easter, a fact that Darien noted with a certain degree of ironic satisfaction.

They stepped down from the helicopter, followed by Damocles Praefectus, their Legatus; they made their way to the imperial residence inside the old palace, they had renamed the *Aulae Principis*. Liliane had decreed the Borgia Apartments would be suitable but needed upgrading; and so that part of the museum was closed two years ago for renovations. All the artifacts were moved to other locations within the compound so the visiting public could still see them. Liliane decided the Renaissance murals could stay, for historic reasons; but had to be covered in some kind of tasteful material. She called them 'tacky' and didn't want all those self-righteous prudes staring at her all the time. The floors, however, simply had to go. The Spanish tiles were just too old, and more than five hundred years of foot traffic had worn the surfaces off many of them. Besides, she felt Persian carpets would warm up the space and reduce the annoying echo. She also added three very comfortable bathrooms. She would not live anywhere she couldn't soak in a luxurious bath at least twice a day. Darien acceded to all her demands. Being able to live in the apartments of the 'Bull of the Borgias' was flattering to his manhood— and that would be enough.

For their Audience Hall, she chose the *Sala Regia*. It was near their apartments and, in Liliane's estimation, had the necessary gravitas; but again, she decided the space needed updating. The intricately designed barrel ceiling would do, she said, but the walls were much too busy with all their 'gauche' murals. She had them covered in plush gold-embroidered velvet of deep vermilion red. On the floor, she mirrored the motif, having gold-toned Persian carpets with vermillion highlights. On the north side of the hall, she installed two thrones relatively equal in size and height on a raised platform—though she didn't mind being occasionally beneath Darien in the bedroom, the throne room was a different matter. She hadn't helped plan this coup to become lesser than she had been. She outranked Darien before their takeover; she certainly would not be ruled by him now—no, they were to be equals, something their thrones must clearly communicate.

She had borrowed the thrones from their previous owners—without asking, of course. One was the immaculately restored throne of Paval I, late eighteenth-century Emperor of Russia, with its gilt twin-eagle front legs, which she had acquired from the Hermitage Museum in Petersburg. She felt this would be suitable for Darien, since he was so stuck on this notion of eagles. For herself, she had one of the beautifully ornate twin thrones brought from the *Palácio Nacional da Ajuda* that had once belonged to Maria Pia of Savoy, the past queen-consort of Portugal. She had not been a terribly attractive woman, so she compensated by sitting on a beautiful throne. Now the throne would have an occupant worthy of its grandeur.

For the coronation ceremony, she designed a magnificent regal gown for herself, but Darien only wanted something that suggested military bearing. She gave in when she realized he wouldn't budge but added a few flairs to that design as well. She absolutely insisted they have crowns for the ceremony. For Darien, she had an 18-carat replica made of the gold laurel wreath Napoleon had worn at his coronation—appropriately reminiscent of the Roman Caesars. For herself, she tastefully redesigned the crown of Theodora, the seventh-century empress of Constantinople. Now, *there* was a strong woman. She had risen from her youth as an actress and courtesan to become the most powerful woman in the world. Though Procopius was obviously a notoriously repressed misogynist with an ax to grind, his *Secret History* was still an arousing bedtime read. She didn't at all mind his stories of Theodora's staged portrayal of *Leda and the Swan*—the thought of having a swan nibbling breadcrumbs from the 'calyx of her passionflower' was thoroughly exciting. She didn't really know what the calyx of a passionflower was, but just imagining it was half the fun, and made her warm with delight.

For the ceremony, the two cohorts of Praetorian Guards stood shoulder to shoulder in formation, one on the east side of the *Sala Regia*, the other on the west, forming two great phalanxes, with a grand processional aisle down the center. Damocles Praefectus waited in the front, between the two thrones, with the gold laurel wreath in his right hand and the crown of Theodora in his left. As the late afternoon sun lit the great hall, complete silence accompanied Darien and Liliane as they processed slowly, side by side, down the aisle. When they reached the raised dais, they turned and stood before their respective thrones. Damocles first placed the crown on Liliane's head.

"Joséphine Messalina Theodora Octavia!" he shouted the imperial title she had chosen for herself. Then the gathered praetorians cried out as one, "*Ave* Theodora!" It sent a thrilling rush through her to hear that salute reverberate in the ancient hall.

Then he placed the laurel wreath on his father's head and shouted, "Flavius Claudius Julianus Augustus!" And the praetorians cried, "*Ave* Caesar!" Again and again, they shouted it, stomping their feet twice, in unison, between each shout. And it seemed as though the very foundations of the earth shook with that sound. Liliane wasn't sure she liked him receiving more praise than she; but in this great hall, which absolutely seethed with the testosterone of a thousand males, it was to be expected. Let him have his moment—he had worked hard for it, after all. As they basked in the adulation of their praetorians, she studied Damocles Praefectus, standing before his troops, and spurring them on. She couldn't deny it; he really was a very well-formed man. She wondered at that moment if he was an improvement on the original in *every* area. If Darien had been looking at her, he would have seen her blush.

The *Auctoritas Facit Legem* docked at Coronado Island several hours before dawn. The old military installation was decommissioned decades ago, but the long-term plans for the land were being accomplished in stages. Though portions had been repurposed, there was still a large block of now deserted buildings that would work perfectly for his plans. At the door to one of the old hangars, he approached a person in jeans, sneakers, and a dark hooded sweatshirt, standing under a dull industrial lamp and smoking a cigarette. The scene looked like bad cover art for an old pulp spy novel.

"Are you expecting me?" he said as he approached.

"No, I'm smoking a cigarette," the person said. "Who are you?"

"I'm Benoit Moreau," he answered, surprised the voice was a woman's. "Walter Bennett sent me."

She stopped smoking for a moment, obviously still struggling with the recent news of Bennett's death. After eyeing him from beneath the hood, she crushed the cigarette under her sneaker and turned toward the building. "Follow me, Benny," she said. They stepped inside and entered a small office, where she switched on a desk lamp, and opened the laptop sitting on the desk. "As of this morning we have twelve hundred and seventy-three units here. That accounts for all of them that are still functional."

"I had hoped for more, but that will have to do," he said. "How do I take control of them?"

"I overwrote the loyalty protocol, as Mr. Bennett requested, with this retinal scan he sent." She brought the image up on the screen. "Let me check to make sure yours matches before I take you out to meet the troops."

"You don't trust me. . . Miss?" Cavanaugh asked.

"Moreno. Raphaella Moreno. And you can drop the 'Miss'. Just call me Ella," she seemed relaxed and self-possessed for someone carrying out what were clearly strange instructions from Bennett. "And it's not that I don't trust you," she continued calmly. "I just don't want them to kill you if I got it wrong."

"Oh. Well, that's probably a good idea then," he admitted. She smiled at his pragmatism as she pulled back her hood and turned to him holding the scanner up to his eye. He could now see that she was a fit, dark-haired woman, probably of Hispanic heritage, in her middle thirties. It was too dim in the room to make a more definitive assessment. After a few moments, the laptop confirmed his scan matched the digital packet Bennett sent.

"We'll need to go into the hangar so they can see you," she instructed. "It's going to take some time because they'll each have to meet you face-to-face. Once they've looked you in the eyes, they'll be yours."

"What about the trackers?"

"The trackers obey the hunters completely, even to their deaths. When you have the hunters, the trackers are yours automatically. It's a package deal."

"How do you know so much about them, Miss Moreno?" he asked.

"I said it was Ella, and I was one of the chief designers on the Orion Series; I guess you could say they're my babies," she sighed.

"Well, Ella," he said. "Shall we go meet your babies?"

"They're about to become *your* babies, Benny," she said as she led him out of the office, through a second door, and onto the hangar floor. He was surprised that the entire group was standing in formation, apparently awaiting instructions. She positioned Cavanaugh directly under a dim, hanging industrial lamp and called them forward for the oddly disconcerting ceremony. They each came, one by one, stood within a foot of him, looked him directly in the eyes, and then nodded before moving back into formation. This went on for nearly three hours until the last one had 'inspected' him. He realized his eyes had grown dry from trying not to blink. At this near distance he could see that they were quite different from the Heracles units—they were pallid skinned and hairless, not even eyelashes, and their eyes had an odd translucence to them, as though the pupils were nearly colorless, which he assumed aided somehow in night vision. He felt the uncomfortable sense of wanting—no, of needing the approval of these not-quite-human creatures. When the ceremony was over, they all were back in formation, waiting.

"They're yours now," she said.

"Thank you, Ella. I need you to select sixty of the best for transport tonight."

"They're all pretty much the same." She looked at him steadily for a long moment. "What are you going to do with them, if you don't mind me asking?"

"I'm going to use them to guard someone who's very dear to me."

"Fair enough," she replied. "I just hope you won't abuse the power you now have over them."

"They are designed to follow orders, aren't they?"

"Yes, but they're not machines, at least not in the usual sense. They'll light themselves on fire if you ask them to, but they'll feel every bit of the excruciating pain as they obediently burn to death."

"I have no intention of asking them to do such a thing," he felt a little repulsed at the suggestion.

"I hope not. All other things being equal, Walter Bennett was a good man. He had moral qualms about producing these operatives. He didn't want to see them misused. I'll miss him for that."

"I have the feeling we all will." He paused for a moment, considering his oddly waiting regiment of newly acquired thralls before continuing. "I think you should know, Ella, that his death wasn't a boating accident. Walter Bennett was murdered."

"Murdered?" she seemed shaken for the first time. "But who would do that, and why?"

"Would I be right in saying you were loyal to him?"

"Yes. And he was loyal to me, to all of us."

"All right then. I propose a trade. You want answers, and I don't have time at this moment to give them to you. However, I'll be sending a contingent of these units north tonight on a yacht docked just a few yards from here. If you want to know the whole story, go with them and I promise you'll hear the unvarnished truth about why he was killed... To be honest, I have selfish motives for my offer; I could really use someone with your knowledge of the Orions going forward."

"Going forward with what?"

"War."

"Hold your horses, Benny! Are you fucking with me, or is this some kind of a sting you're playing at?

"I really wish I was lying. No, Ella, a war has begun that very few are yet aware of. Walter Bennett was one of the first casualties. I fear the numbers will grow alarmingly in the coming months if we don't take decisive action now."

"A war? But with who? And for what?"

"As for whom, the names would mean nothing to you at this point; but as to what, well, what are most wars about? One group's attempt to subjugate another by force and impose its will on them whether they wish it or not. This one is no different. The question of the moment is: will you join us in resisting that subjugation?"

"Are you for real?"

"Walter Bennett thought so. He gave his life to help us. You'll have to choose for yourself, of course, at least until you're no longer able to choose. But I will say this: the post-Bennett management of your company will almost certainly NOT be to your liking."

An hour later the *Auctoritas* left for the Puget with sixty-three Orion units and Raphaella Moreno onboard. Cavanaugh left the Smith & Wesson with her; he would never be able to get it through the airport scanners anyway. He instructed the remaining Orions to relax, stay hidden, and await orders. Oddly, they seemed perfectly satisfied to wait, and relaxed instantly, once told to do so. He felt the sudden and unsettling burden of too much responsibility. He now understood what Ella meant. These creatures would obey him completely and without question. Whatever else they may be, they were also thinking, feeling beings; and now he had become, in essence, their god. Not an obligation he was comfortable with.

He left the deserted base while the sky was only beginning to lighten, walked briskly to Orange Avenue, where he caught a cab to University Heights. There was a man there he needed to see about some very unpleasant make-up before he caught a second cab to Old Lindberg Field.

PERE AND THE OTHERS WERE three days journeying up the Lena River. As they moved south, the weather became subtly milder. It was turning out to be a warmer than usual spring in Siberia with the temperature almost reaching 60° during the day, though they still needed to bundle up in the afternoons and evenings, when they would sit on the deck in folding chairs and watch the sun go down. On the last evening before they made Yakutsk, Elley dropped anchor, and the men went belowdecks to share a bottle of something the old skipper called *stavleny,* getting somewhat loud in the process.

The women stayed on deck talking and watching the stars come out. Sayiina pointed out various constellations to Yael and Rophe. As it turned out, she possessed a great wealth of practical wisdom. It wasn't the type of knowledge you'd get at a university, but much more down-to-earth. She also had an almost equally keen sense of humor; most of her jokes referred to men—some of them very earthily. Both Yael and Rophe liked her almost immediately and were drawn to her motherly strength. On this last evening aboard the Pyotr, they talked mostly about silly things, while the men sang loudly below, and then the old woman surprised them both.

"Do you love him?" she asked out of the blue.

"What?" both Yael and Rophe replied in surprised unison; then they looked at each other and laughed. Sayiina smiled at them both knowingly.

"Men have great strength," she said, looking up at the stars. "But they seem to think it is meant mostly for their ability to kill each other. They need women to teach them otherwise."

"But they're very stubborn," said Rophe. Yael tried hard not to smile. It seemed odd to her that this highly educated woman, who was comfortable fixing the terrifying wounds of battle, was mooning over a man; but love did strange things to women. She wondered if she acted that way about Pere. "And they're not very aware of other people's feelings," Rophe mumbled.

"When God made Adam," the old woman said. "He did not design him to pay attention to the feelings of others, because he was the only one of his kind. He was strong, and capable, but also very lonely. When God made Eve, he corrected all the mistakes he made on the first try." They all laughed together.

"But how do you make them do what you want?" Rophe asked.

"O, *Bozhe moi*! You do not! You can try to break a man; but if you do, he is no longer a man, not really. He may do what you want after that, but you will never respect him again."

"But Elley does everything you say," Yael protested, now feeling confused.

Sayiina chuckled. "You are wrong, of course, my dear. But you are too young to see it. That sly fisherman and I are like two old snow cranes. We dance a very ancient dance together. Because we have known each other for so many years, we perform the steps very well now, almost in unison. So, it may not seem like it at first glance, but my *Mishka* still leads. And yet, like snow cranes, we are also an endangered species, I think. People do not have time to learn one another's ways like that anymore."

"So, there's no hope for me?" groaned Rophe.

"Do not be a silly schoolgirl! Of course there is, but do not whine and pout to try to get his attention; it will only weaken him; besides, you are too strong for that. You must face this now; both of you have chosen men who have callings upon them. It may seem like their callings come before you, but that is not by choice. They would much prefer the mating dance—most males do—but they are birds of instinct; their callings drive them, and it is not their season for mating, so you must learn to fly with them, support them, and wait—it is the only way. Clip their wings now and you may destroy more than just the man. You may endanger the entire flock."

Yael was sure Sayiina was speaking more to Rophe than to her—as though she had ever tried to clip Pere's wings! But she still listened. She couldn't really remember what it was like to have a mother, and she sometimes wished she had an older woman to talk to. Uncle El was good at a lot of things, but heart-to-hearts weren't even on the list. They talked for a while longer about many things, but mostly about men.

"We should go belowdecks now," Sayiina finally said. "The men will need us to act mad at them for drinking. It is a part of the dance." The two younger women smiled at each other, but also followed to see how to do it properly.

The following morning, Pere stood on deck with the others, watching the land roll by as they approached Yakutsk. He didn't feel very well—apparently drinking stavleny had its after-effects—but he didn't want to miss this. He hadn't been near a city in two years, and though Yakutsk was tiny when compared to Los Nietos, it seemed very large to him after the long isolation in the Klondike Colony. Elley piloted the trawler down the side channel to the dry docks. About a mile further on, Pere could see in the clear morning sunlight the glint off nine golden domes with nine ornate crosses. His breath caught, as Sayiina came next to him on the railing.

"It is a bit overstated," she said. "But it is also a memorable and unique landmark, do you not think so?"

"You knew?"

"Knew is too strong a word. The older I get, the less I know. But I suspected. It was *your* dream, after all. Is this the right spot?"

"Well, I was a falcon at the time, and I came at it from above, so the angle's different. But, yes," he sighed. "It's the right spot."

"And why so disappointed, then?"

"Because I didn't ask for this thing—this dreaming curse! Nobody asked me if I wanted to be stuck on this frequency. I'm asleep, so I can't exactly say no. It's all just forced on me."

She was quiet for a long time. "I know I should probably slap you on the back of your head and tell you to grow up," but she chuckled instead. "Did you hear what Varnava called me back at the Dacha?"

"I can't remember."

"Then listen more closely in the future. You are too old now to play the ignorant child."

"Thanks. I'll try," he said wryly. "Why do you call him Varnava anyway?"

"He told me he taught you some Russian. Figure it out."

He thought for a moment. "Oh, Barnabas, right."

"Smarter than you look, eh?"

"You know, maybe you should put 'farm boy' at the end of those statements." The old woman looked puzzled for a moment and then spied Yael leaning out over the railing not far away, and laughed, knowingly. Pere then smiled as well. "So, what did Varnava call you?"

"Naviah," she said. "The word does not often take the feminine ending 'ah'. Without that, it would be—"

"Navi!" he interrupted her. "You're a dreamer?"

"Among other curses, as you call them."

"But how do you stand it?"

She looked at him shrewdly. "It is not always easy, is it?"

"Try *never*."

She nodded and shrugged with understanding. "Why do you think Jonah wanted to run away and jump into a big fish rather than speak his piece? He did not want the responsibility, the notoriety, the ridicule, the hatred, or the destiny." She sighed. "It is usually the ignorant that speak of it as a gift. A knife with two edges is a dangerous gift to use, no?"

"Tell me about it. But why us?"

"Who can say?" she offered.

"That's not a very helpful answer."

"Do you want honesty or a pep talk?"

"Can't you do both?"

"I am too old to be your wet nurse, and you are too old to suckle."

"You're not a very encouraging person, are you?"

She smiled. "That, my young navi, depends on what you mean by encouragement. If I tell you that you have a hard path ahead of you, and you have been given a task that only you can accomplish, and that accomplishing it may kill you, I am encouraging you in the most honest way; but most people do not want to hear that kind of encouragement, do they?"

"No," he sighed. "Probably not."

"You do not have that luxury, *Sokol*. Who knows? Perhaps you were sent to me so I could tell you this very not encouraging thing."

"But I didn't ask for any of this. What if it's too hard?"

She smiled and nodded. "When I was much younger—and much more attractive—we used to watch television for entertainment. I liked one packaged show from the states very much. In one of the episodes, a character tried to explain why terrible things had happened to him. He said: '*Those things had to happen to me. That was my destiny. But you'll understand soon enough that there are consequences to being chosen. Because destiny is a fickle bitch.*' I memorized that line, because it seemed so wrong, but also somehow right. The best wine, or so I am told, comes from the vines that must struggle for life in rocky unyielding soil. What seem like random painful experiences to you are, I suspect, preparing you for a greater task—if you persevere. We always have a choice about that. But what would you be doing now if your destiny had not found you?"

"Probably raising cows, or herding sheep."

"Worthy tasks, but not the ones for you, I think."

"You're probably right . . . I guess."

At that moment, Yael came to the rail next to them. "Look Pere, it's your dream," she said, pointing to the old cathedral.

"Yes, I noticed," he said, ruefully.

"What were you two talking about?"

"Nosey young women," Sayiina said.

"Hey!" Yael responded indignantly, and Pere laughed.

Before they docked, the travelers again went belowdecks. Once the trawler was tied off, Elley came down to talk to them.

"I need to go see about getting the Pyotr into dry dock," he said. "I will also contact some people I know here in Yakutsk who will help us. Stay belowdecks until I get back."

When Elley returned several hours later, he had an older Yakut man with him who carried a brown leather travel bag.

"This is Matvey," he said, by way of introductions. "He is one of us, but he does not want to know any of your names. He is going to take your pictures and create some new identities for you."

"Having an old crook for a skipper has its benefits," said El.

"One does what one can," Elley said, shrugging. "In addition to making good IDs, he will arrange for transportation. It will not be luxurious, but luxury would only attract attention. Both the IDs and the vehicle will be ready tomorrow morning."

For the next hour or so, they each sat on a stool in front of a stretched vinyl background while Matvey took a series of photos. In addition to his long hair and scraggy new beard, Pere also donned a vintage set of Ray Ban Wayfarers from a selection of glasses Matvey had provided. They had jet-black frames and green-tinted non-prescription lenses, which made him feel kind of cool. The disguise was surprisingly effective. He didn't look at all like his seventeen-year-old self. It wouldn't fool deep-level image scans, but no one would recognize him from the most-wanted bulletins. At least it was a start. After Matvey finished taking everyone's photos, he hugged both Elley and Sayiina and left. Later that afternoon they sat at the galley table and talked.

"So, where should we go from here?" Yael asked Sayiina. The old woman didn't respond, but only looked at Barnabas, raising an eyebrow expectantly.

"We're going to a city called Ulan Ude," he finally said.

"Let me guess," said Pere. "There's an arch there with a two-headed eagle on it?"

"The Tsar's Triumph Arch is in the center of Ulan Ude," he confessed. "As I recall, it's just the way you described it."

"Wonderful!" he said sarcastically. "Why a two-headed eagle, by the way? What's it mean?"

"The double-headed eagle was the herald of the Imperial Tsars of old Russia," Barnabas explained. "It's supposed to symbolize power and dominion. But it's really a much older symbol than the Romanovs. If you look at the word "tsar," it's a transliteration of the ancient title 'caesar'. The Romanovs fashioned themselves a continuation of the older line of Roman emperors—caesars, as they were called. The eagle, or 'aquila', was the symbol of the Roman Empire as well. And the double eagle became the emblem of the Byzantine Empire in the centuries after Rome split into two."

Pere considered that for a moment. "Silas said once that he thought we were living in old Rome again or something like that. Is that what the eagle rising in my dream represents?"

"A good question," Barnabas said. "I don't have a clear answer. The only thing I think I know at this point is that you saw the Tsar's Arch in your dream."

"Okay, fine," he sighed. "So, how do we get there?"

"It's about two day's drive southwest from here," Barnabas answered. "I assume, Elley, the vehicle Matvey's getting can fit us all."

"He says so. It is called a Ford Windstar Extended Minivan. It is very old, he says, but the engine has been rebuilt and converted to biodiesel, and it seats seven."

"That'll do the trick," said El. "How many of us know how to drive besides me?"

"I do," said Barnabas.

"As do I," said Ehud. "If the transmission is automatic, it will not be a problem."

"I also can drive," said Khyoza.

"Me too," offered Rophe.

"I know how to drive a tractor," offered Pere.

"Right. Well, that's five of us since we won't be at the tractor races," said El. "We can drive in shifts. That way we'll only have to stop for toilet breaks."

"The IDs will pass low-level checks," said Elley. "The data backgrounds provided for each of you will not stand up to a higher-level probe but should get you through any passive checks you will encounter."

"That's reassuring," said Rophe quietly.

"Well, doctor," said Elley, shrugging. "If you get into a situation where they are running level-three probes on you, it's probably too late anyway."

"Oh, that makes me feel *so* much better," Rophe frowned. They talked on for some time and then went to their bunks early.

They rose well before dawn, and found the Windstar parked on the dock with the keys in the ignition, a satchel on the front seat, and six extra canisters in the very back filled with biodiesel. They said their quiet goodbyes to Elley and Sayiina, each giving them a hug. Barnabas gripped Elley for a long time, not knowing if he would ever see his old friend again. Though they had known Sayiina only a short time, both Yael and Rophe both seemed particularly reluctant to part from her. But finally, they crowded into the minivan, again waved their goodbyes, and Barnabas started the engine. El, riding shotgun, opened the satchel and pulled out several maps and seven newly minted identification cards. He handed the cards out and began to study the map with Barnabas.

"Look," Pere said to no one in particular, holding up his ID. "I'm Yevgeny

Kuznetsov." He looked at Yael's ID. "Your name's Valentina Noskov? Will you be my valentine?" he asked her, and she rolled her eyes.

As they drove away from the docks, El handed them dossiers from the satchel on each of their assumed identities. "You should probably get to know yourselves, in case anyone asks."

"If anyone asks me anything," Ehud said, "I will be in trouble, since I do not speak Russian."

"It's all right," El said. "We'll tell them you're mute."

"Oh, very funny."

"Listen," Barnabas said. "The only reason we'll have to show these is if we conduct some kind of official business. So, we'll cross that bridge when and if we get to it. For now, settle in, because we've got a long drive ahead of us."

The flight from Lindberg Field to Sheremetyevo in Moscow, with a long layover at JFK, took the better part of an entire day. Jonas Cavanaugh, in the guise of Juliette Walker, was sore, hot, and tired when he finally deboarded. He simply couldn't sleep on the plane in this get-up. He made his way outside, trying not to limp from the discomfort of his shoes, even though he had chosen flats this go-round. He caught a cab and asked the driver to take him to the Hotel Volga near Lubyanka Square, close enough to the Cybergi offices for his purposes. He paid for a room and, once inside, locked the door, kicked off his shoes, and yanked off the wig, scratching his scalp vigorously—something he had desperately wanted to do for at least the last six hours. He removed most of his disguise but left the prosthetic cheekbones and chin in place for the time being, since he knew he would be almost constantly image-scanned once he hit the streets.

The profusion of cameras in Moscow was a holdover from an older era of social paranoia; but he knew most still functioned well enough to be accessed by Haruspex. It was too late to visit Cybergi, so he climbed into the hotel bed, making sure only to lie on his back so as not to harm his prosthetics. It took a long while to fall asleep. Though he was exhausted, it was 10:30 in the morning in the Puget, and his inner clock refused to be fooled. Eventually, his tiredness overcame his mind's reluctance, and he nodded off.

He woke late the next morning, bleary-eyed, but aware. Cleaning himself up a bit, he changed into the business suit he had brought for the occasion. His cheeks and chin remained Juliette's, and having left Benoit's cap and glasses in Tokyo, he bought a gray fedora and vintage, round horn-rim glasses, with light-sensitive transitioning lenses before he left Hillcrest. To add one final touch, he applied a false moustache—the perfect Russian affectation. He looked in the mirror, liking the result of melding three old personalities into one new one—he would once again be a ghost. He named his new persona Illarion Orlov.

It was a late brisk morning when he stopped at a nearby diner for some much-needed breakfast. Forty minutes later, he walked the six blocks to the Cybergi Global offices, feeling better for the three cups of coffee he'd consumed with his egg and sausage sandwich. He passed through the large glass double doors and approached the receptionist.

"I'm here to see Yulian Khvostovsky," he said with casual authority.

"Do you have an appointment, sir?" the receptionist inquired, politely.

"Tell him I'm Director Rockefeller. I'm sure he'll recognize the name."

"Very good, sir. If you would please have a seat, I will call up."

He sat in the comfortable waiting area. Even if none of the chairs knew the members of the Directorate by face or birth name, they had all become familiar with their assumed titles. And though he might have doubts, it would be foolhardy of Khvostovsky not at least to speak to him, if for no other reason than cautious curiosity. Within two minutes, the receptionist approached him.

"Sir, please use the far-left elevator; it will take you to Mr. Khvostovsky's office on the sixty-third floor. I will code the access. Have a nice afternoon."

"Thank you," he said, rising and crossing the reception area to the elevator. There was no call button, but after a few moments, the doors slid open, Cavanaugh entered, and the elevator rose very quickly. When the doors opened, two guards frisked him thoroughly.

"*Pazh'alusta sl'eduytye za mnoy,*" one of the guards said, then turned and walked down the hall. The other guard fell in behind Cavanaugh, blocking any potential escape. They passed through a comfortable suite where another receptionist nodded to the guards. They proceeded down a short hallway to a paneled office door and knocked.

"*Voydite*," the voice called from within. The lead guard opened the door and all three stepped in. Sitting behind the desk, in front of expansive windows overlooking the Moscow skyline, was a somewhat squat and pudgy bald man with an unimpressive moustache, which he probably grew to pull focus from his weak chin. He eyed Cavanaugh carefully for a moment. "Good afternoon, Mr. Rockefeller," he finally said, in very precise but accented English. "I am Yulian Khvostovsky; what can I do for you?"

"Do your guards speak English?" Cavanaugh asked calmly.

"Not a word," the little man said. "But they will kill you without hesitation should I wish it."

"Why would you want to kill me when I'm here to do you a favor?"

"Do not be offended when I tell you I am naturally skeptical of your favor. You see, by all accounts, Rockefeller was already older than you currently are when he formed the Consortium. He would have to be ancient by now, would he not? But I am thinking you cannot be older than forty years. So, I must ask myself, why is this man deceiving me?"

"Well, since we're laying our cards on the table, you also are not who you say you are. You're Demyan Zahorchak, Yulian Khvostovsky's longtime personal assistant, and second in command here at Cybergi, the number-eight hub of the Consortium of Ten. Your boss served his apprenticeship with Shakib Patel at Bediya in Mumbai. He drinks Assam tea with skim milk and two sugars. I could go on if you'd like?"

"And perhaps you are a spy sent from one of the other hubs. They too would have all this information, would they not?"

"Would they also know this? Yulian Khvostovsky is deathly afraid of flying, a condition he hides very effectively from everyone but you and his wife, Katya. I'm not sure if even his daughter knows. But the Directorate has ways of finding out things. If you'd like, I can give your guards this information in Russian, which I speak, by the way. I'm sure they'd find it fascinating, as would the rest of your organization—you know how people like to gossip, and joke about their bosses."

"That will not be necessary," Zahorchak said briskly. "*Ahtstahn*!" he said to the guards, who nodded and left. "Why don't you have a seat, Mr. . . .?"

"Let's stick with Rockefeller for the moment," Cavanaugh said, sitting across from Zahorchak. "You are correct. I am not he; but like you, I am a representative."

"The Directorate is always represented by the sénéschal. Why the change of protocol?"

"It is imperative that I speak with Yulian personally about this very issue. May I see him now?"

"He is not in the office, and his current whereabouts are known only to me. You still have not answered my question; why am I not now speaking to the sénéschal?"

Cavanaugh looked at him steadily for a moment, calculating. He could play this game for a while and perhaps eventually break down the fat little busybody's defenses, but he had neither the time nor the inclination. The world was perched on a precipice and this cheeky little bastard wanted to play verbal chess. Perhaps it was time to place him in check.

"All right," he finally said. "Darien Gianakos is no longer the sénéschal. In an ongoing coup, he's murdered five of the seven premiers and assumed control of the entire Consortium. The Rockefeller premier eluded assassination, but this is not yet known to Gianakos, or the Romanov chair, who has chosen to side with him."

Zahorchak visibly paled and sank in his seat as Cavanaugh spoke. "But how do I know this is true?" he finally said, without much conviction.

"You don't; and here's the rub: you can't really ask anyone to verify it, because you'd be killed within hours if you did. That fire alarm in Tokyo wasn't a fire alarm at all. I triggered it to evade the men Gianakos sent to kill me. Yes, I was there. I planned to expose Gianakos to all of you at that meeting, and I barely escaped with my life. I also assume you've heard about Walter Bennett's accident?" Zahorchak nodded wordlessly. "It wasn't an accident at all. They murdered him, simply because he had spoken to me. And now you *must* understand this, Demyan: if Gianakos discovers you've had any contact with me, any at all, you also will have an accident—regardless of your explanations. I'm sorry. I didn't intend to put you in danger, but you've left me no choice. I must speak to Yulian about this, and I must do it soon. Now, where is he?" He spoke the last with an authority that finally cowed Zahorchak.

"*Gavno!*" the little man said, now sounding as if he were in far over his head. "He is in Vladivostok, but he remains incommunicado by his own order. He wanted a vacation away with his family without interruption or technology."

"Shit!" Cavanaugh slammed the desktop, and then sat back in exhaustion. "He must be interrupted for this. He simply must. Is there any way I can reach him?"

"You could fly there, but he will probably be gone when you arrive. The itinerary he left with me has him boarding the Great Siberian Way before dawn tomorrow morning."

"The high-speed train?"

"No, the historic passenger liner. He will arrive in Moscow in eight days."

"That's too long. How can I get to him sooner, without being seen? If I'm identified by an image-scan, you'll both end up like Bennett, and probably your families as well."

"This creates problems," the little man didn't even notice the irony of his under-statement. "I think the most unobserved way may be to take the Historic Siberian Liner yourself." He opened his laptop and pulled up the daily schedules of the Trans-Siberian Railway. "The Historic Line prides itself on no technology, so you get a true feeling of the past while riding. You will not be scanned once on board, and no electronic communication devices are allowed. I can get you onto a private car without the initial checks, so you would be clean there."

"And how does getting on a different train help us?"

"You can board the eastbound Historic Line in Moscow this evening. Yulian will board the westbound equivalent in Vladivostok tomorrow morning," Zahorchak examined his laptop screen and scribbled some equations on a notepad. "According to the schedules, the closest point of connection will be in Ulan Ude in four days. You will get off your train there approximately one hour before the westbound line arrives. You will then board the westbound line—with the pass I provide for you—the two of you will be on the same train. It may not be ideal, but it will cut four days off your wait. How you contact him after that will be up to you, but I urge you to use extreme caution. I am quite fond of both him and his family."

"Believe me when I tell you this, I have no intention of exposing Yulian or myself. I simply need to tell him what I've told you. What time does the train leave here?"

"It leaves Yaroslavsky Station at 7:05 p.m. That gives you a little over six hours."

"Can you get me back to my hotel and then to the station without being seen? The fewer chances I take the better it is for all of us."

"I will take you myself." He picked up the desk phone and informed Stasya he would be out of the office for the rest of the day. "Follow me," he said as he got up from the desk and crossed to Khvostovsky's personal elevator. They took it to the basement parking level, where they proceeded to a row of company cars. On the concrete wall next to the bay, Zahorchak unlocked the box and selected a key. They continued down the row of cars to a sleek Daimler Electro with fully tinted windows, got in, and silently left the garage.

At the hotel, Cavanaugh gathered his things and put them in the back of the Daimler. "I'd like to make one stop before the train station," Cavanaugh said as he climbed back into the passenger seat.

"We have some time," Zahorchak said, checking his watch. "But it must be fairly close."

"That's where I need your help. Since you can get me on the train without a check, I need an untraceable weapon just in case things get dicey. My knowledge of Moscow's a little limited. So, Demyan, where can I get a silenced semi-automatic handgun with extra ammo?"

"I do not know such things," Zahorchak insisted, looking shocked at the suggestion. "The Interdiction prohibits the possession or sale of any such antique firearms as you speak of."

"Demyan, this isn't a trap," Cavanaugh said gently. "I wouldn't even ask, but I'm just trying to stay alive and remain untraced. Micro-DEWs all have trackers. If they discover me while I'm with your boss, I'll need to get him and his family safely and untraceably hidden. I'd feel a lot better about my chances if I had a little firepower to go along with my wits."

Zahorchak eyed him for a long moment. "I know someone," he finally said as he pulled away from the hotel parking lot.

"I was hoping you would say that."

They drove through the city streets for maybe forty-five minutes into a neighborhood to the west of downtown. "Welcome to Solntsevo," Zahorchak said. "It is not as dangerous as it once was, and the Solntsevskaya Brotherhood has ceased to exist. But there are always those few, are there not, who do not wish to integrate into the wider social order? They continue to operate—I think you call it 'under the radar'. Some traffic in contraband goods or services not easily gotten by regular means. We call them *Samizdat*. I do not know the exact word in English."

"Nonconformists?" Cavanaugh offered, "Or maybe bootleggers would be more like it? Whatever the term, I know what you're talking about. Truth be told, I've depended on that small shadow-market over the years. I don't know what I would have done without them, really."

"*Da.* Is no different here. They are a prohibited but necessary part of the system, or so it seems to me. I go now to see one of the Samizdat. I think you must wait in the car. My 'bootlegger' has learned to trust me over time but will not wish to be seen by you."

"I understand completely. Just tell your contact, the larger the caliber, the better—and a high-capacity magazine would be a real plus."

"We shall see," Zahorchak said as he pulled over near a not very savory-looking warehouse, got out, and disappeared into the alleyway. Cavanaugh didn't like waiting, he never had; but this was someone else's territory, so he had to defer or go without. Twenty minutes later, the little man emerged from the alley carrying a brown paper bag. He got into the car and handed it to Cavanaugh. "Now, do you need anything else before we get you on a train?" he said, as they pulled away.

"I had a late breakfast. I could use a bite to eat. And I wouldn't mind a scotch."

"But this is much simpler."

A beautiful spring sunrise greeted the Khvostovskys as the porters loaded the family's luggage into the private luxury car at the rear of the westbound Historic Siberian Liner. The interior of the railcar looked like an antique apartment, replete with a bathroom and a master bedroom. The sitting room had a dining area and one of the overstuffed armchairs folded out into a single bed, where Abigail would sleep.

"Oh, Yulian," Katya said. "It is just perfect."

"But it is only us, Papa," Abigail complained.

"Yes. That's what makes it so perfect," Yulian said, as he generously tipped the porter. He looked forward to a relaxing week where, through the windows of the train, he would be able to survey the domain he never got to see from his steel tower in Moscow. "This will be a very pleasant week, indeed."

The taxi dropped O'Grady outside the gates of William Rampart's mansion and drove off. It took a few days to make his way down from Vancouver and then trawl the public records to figure out which address he was looking for. The property was far bigger than Prowell's; but like the Algonquin compound, this was the largest private estate in the Hunts Point area. It made sense that the people controlling the project he had read about in Prowell's notes would reward themselves with only the best. The whole sham left a bitter taste in his mouth. With his travel bag slung over his shoulder, he approached the guardhouse. A thick partition window separated him from the guard. He pressed the intercom button.

"Can I help you?" the guard said, politely.

"I hope you can," O'Grady replied, more loudly than he normally would. It was always that way with intercoms—the impulse to speak louder. "I'm here to see William Rampart. If I'm not mistaken, this is his place of residence."

"It *was* his place of residence. Unfortunately, he died recently."

O'Grady's shoulders slumped, but his detective's curiosity kicked in almost instantly. He didn't like coincidences. "You say he died recently. How recently if you don't mind my asking?"

"I don't mind. It was in the papers. He died two-and-a-half weeks ago."

"On April 8th, by any chance?"

"Yeah, that's right, how'd you know?"

"The same day as Elinor Prowell. Don't you find that a little odd?"

"Look fella, I don't know who this Elinor person is, but Mr. Rampart passed away April 8th, and he's buried on the grounds here. So, obviously you can't see him today unless you brought a shovel. If you want, I can call a cab to pick you—" the phone rang in the guard house, and the young man picked up and spoke for only a few moments before coming back to the window. "They want to see you in the main house, sir. May I have your name?"

"Padraig O'Grady," he replied, a little confused.

"Thank you, Mr. O'Grady. "If you'll move to your right, I'm going to open the security door."

The steel-reinforced door opened, and the guard waved him through and out of the guardhouse to a shaded lawn area with a park bench just inside the gates.

"If you'll wait here sir," the guard said. "Someone's on their way to fetch you."

O'Grady nodded, and the young man went back into the guardhouse. Not knowing what else to do, O'Grady sat on the bench and looked around at his surroundings. He'd never seen such beautiful grounds in his life, and he imagined it hadn't taken millions, but tens of millions to build this place. A minute or two later a golf cart approached driven by a casually dressed black man with a somewhat oversized afro reminiscent of Foxy Cleopatra. He got out and approached O'Grady with a wand, scanning him for weapons.

"All aboard," the man said as he got back in the driver's seat. O'Grady climbed in and the man drove the cart back down the maple-lined driveway.

"Where are we going Mister . . . ?" O'Grady asked.

"The name's Boma," the man offered. "No mister. I was asked to bring you in, but nobody told me to make small talk."

"Suit yourself," O'Grady mumbled.

After a few minutes, they reached the parking area. Boma got out of the cart and led O'Grady through the sally port, where the three-story manor house came into view. Prowell's Algonquin mansion was a hillbilly haven compared to this behemoth. They continued down the walkway and into the main house. O'Grady's breath caught at its grandeur.

"Follow me," Boma said as they moved through the foyer and into the office suite. At the back of the offices, Boma opened a wood-paneled door to an elevator. He went inside and waited. O'Grady hesitated.

"I'm not getting into that thing until you tell me where it's going," he finally said.

"*You* asked to come in, *Daadie*," Boma said, reasonably. "But I can guarantee you, now that you *are* in; you're not leaving until da boss says so."

O'Grady looked at him for a long moment, then stepped in. This Boma reminded him a little of the Cardman. To his surprise, the elevator went down. When the door opened, they were in a sub-level office area lined with very expensive-looking art. Boma walked out and across the reception area to an inner door. He opened it and entered, and O'Grady followed. Once inside he saw a very old man sitting in what appeared to be a bedroom.

"You want me to stay, Boss?" Boma said to the old man.

"Nah. He scanned clean, didn't he?"

"Very clean."

"Then I'll call if I need you." Boma nodded and left, closing the door behind him. "So, why don't you have a seat young man?"

O'Grady remained standing. "No offence, but I haven't been a young man for decades."

"No offence taken, sonny," the old man waved a dismissive hand at him. "But when you get to be my age, almost everyone is young by comparison. Hell, I probably made my first billion before you squirted out of your *tateh's schmekel.*"

O'Grady looked shrewdly now at the old man. "You're William Rampart, aren't you?"

"In the flesh."

"But the guard said you were dead."

"He exaggerated. I'm not dead yet—but *you* are."

Now O'Grady did sit down heavily. "You brought me in here just to kill me?"

"Oh, hell no, Sonny Jim. I brought you in here to keep *them* from killing you. Once you started asking about Elinor Prowell outside my gates, I knew you'd be dead before the sun went down. . . unless I brought you in. So, I had a weak moment, and here you are, still alive. Should I call you Padraig?"

"Paddy's fine," O'Grady said numbly.

"Well, all right then, Paddy. I'm guessin' you made it all the way out here from

Toronto to ask me some questions about Elinor Prowell's murder. So, shoot. I ain't got all day."

They got to Yaroslavsky Station at 5:45. Zahorchak flashed his Universal VIP Security Pass—otherwise known as a UNI Badge—and the guard waived him through into the parking structure. They pulled into a space at the far end of the garage. "I am sorry, but you must wait here again. It may take a little time to get the boarding straightened out, and we do not want you to be in the open for so long."

"Thank you, Demyan." Cavanaugh replied and meant it. "I appreciate your discretion." The little man left, and again Cavanaugh waited. He opened the bag Zahorchak had gotten from his Samizdat and pulled out a Springfield XD-S 9mm, with two modified 16-round magazines—far better than he had hoped. His first assessment of Zahorchak had been grossly mistaken. He wasn't the self-indulgent little man he appeared to be. Now he understood why Khvostovsky placed such trust in him. The bag also contained a suppressor and a box of fifty rounds of ammo. He stowed everything in his leather shoulder bag. Zahorchak returned to the car at 6:17 and got in, closing the door.

"All is arranged," he said. "You are now a very important person travelling anonymously, and as such, you will have a private railcar all to yourself. I have made it clear that you are not to be disturbed unless you request it. Are you ready?"

"Just about," Cavanaugh said, putting his cap back on and pulling it down to cover as much of his eyes as he could. He nodded, slinging his bag over his shoulder, and the two walked across the garage and through a VIP entrance into the terminal. No one questioned either man as Zahorchak escorted Cavanaugh down the platform.

"This is your 'ride' as you people in the west say it," Zahorchak had stopped at the door of the last passenger car. "Please, make sure Yulian and Katya are safe."

"I will, Demyan," Cavanaugh said, extending his hand. "By the way, my name is Illarion Orlov, and I'm grateful for your help."

"*Udachi*, comrade," the little man said, shaking the other's hand. He then reached into his lapel pocket and pulled out two micro-satphones and handed them to Cavanaugh. "Will you give one of these to Yulian, the other you will keep, I have a third. Another purchase from our Samizdat—they are untraceable. Tell him to contact me as soon as possible. The number is already coded in the phones' memories."

"I will, and thank you," Cavanaugh said, as he boarded the train. Forty minutes later the eastbound Historic Siberian Liner left Yaroslavsky Station bound for Ulan Ude.

Padraig O'Grady sat in the converted conference room with the recently deceased William Rampart sitting across from him, nibbling on a bagel, and sipping coffee from an old black mug with the word 'Boss' printed on the side in faded raised-gold letters. Boma had been called to the room two hours ago, and Rampart had been explaining information contained in the documents downloaded from O'Grady's fountain pen.

"Well, shit!" Rampart said, after they had seen the last document. "I knew Ellie had some unsavory habits, but I didn't think hording was one of them. I think we'd better get someone out there, Boma, to burn that place to the ground. We can't let those files see the light of day." He took another bite of his bagel. "So, Paddy, you pretty much know the whole story now. I guess the pertinent question is why didn't you just stay retired?"

O'Grady sat back, visibly exhausted. In his wildest dreams, he couldn't have imagined this is where his detective's curiosity would lead. His thoughts were a mixture of fear, and awe, with a good measure of resentment thrown in. "Who gave you the right?" he finally managed to ask.

"Right's got dick to do with it," Rampart said, with no apparent remorse. "The world was fallin' apart. Someone had to do something. In a situation like that, the strong decide for the weak. That's the way it's always been. You can bitch and moan all you want; but if you hadn't found out about it, would you have cared?"

"That's not the point, and you know it."

"Well, you can quibble about the means, but the end results are what count. The world's a better place now than it was then. There's no doubt about that."

"You just said everyone on this ruling council of yours has been murdered except you. That doesn't strike me as a better state of affairs."

"We've had a little setback, I'll admit."

"A little setback? You're in the middle of a private war, Mr. Rampart. And everyone in the world is ignorant of the fact."

"Probably better that way, don't you think?"

"I don't know what to think," he finally said, exasperated.

"Well, here's the thing. Now that you do know, you're more dangerous than when you knocked at my gates. I can let you leave this compound if you insist; but you'll be dead within a few hours—more likely within a few minutes."

"What's my alternative?"

"If you stay here, you'll be safe for a while at least. I can't say how long our little island here will be secure, but for the time being, it is—that's the best I can offer right now. Besides, I could use a man with your skillset moving forward."

"And what might that skillset be?"

"You see things, Paddy. Things that other people don't. Why'd you insist on going back to that mansion? Because you knew something wasn't right. Why'd you decide to come all the way out here? Because you figured you could get answers. You've got good instincts, and I need people with good instincts right now, if we're going to have a snowball's chance of winning this private little war, as you called it."

O'Grady considered his options for a long moment. "If what you say is true," he finally said. "It doesn't sound like I've got much of a choice."

"Not if you want to keep breathing. Boma, where did we put Raphaella?"

"In the yellow suite; pink's off-limits right now."

"Let's set up Paddy in the gray."

"I'll take care of it. Follow me, Paddy." The two men rose and started for the door.

"Oh, and one other thing," Rampart said, stopping them. "Once you've rested up a bit, I'm gonna have my doctors examine you and make certain adjustments."

"What the hell's that supposed to mean?"

"We're gonna need to shut off your cogmeds. I need you thinking clearly and not getting headaches from doing it. You got any lingering psychological issues we should know about?"

"No. Well, a long time ago, I struggled with PTSD—after Iran. But I haven't experienced that in decades. Why do you ask?"

"Because some of those birds might come back to roost. But we'll cross that bridge when we get to it. Welcome to the Western Front, Paddy."

SINCE SAYIINA HAD PACKED MEALS, they stopped only to refuel, change drivers, and use restrooms. After four highways, one ferry, and nearly forty hours of driving, they finally reached Ulan Ude; but Barnabas continued past it on the highway.

"My Russian's not great," El said, who was again riding shotgun. "But didn't we just pass Ulan Ude?"

"We're going to keep going for another hour," Barnabas said. "I know a place where we can stay."

"You know a place?"

"I grew up here—well, until I was fourteen and we emigrated."

"Welcome home. But that still doesn't answer the question of where we're going."

"To an inn owned by family friends. We'll be able to stay there without worrying—and probably without paying either." Barnabas seemed excited.

"Not to point out the obvious, but you were fourteen a long time ago. Will anyone know you now?"

"The inn has been in their family for five generations. The kids were around my age then, so they're probably in charge now."

"Or they sold it, Barnabas. Let's not go looking for trouble."

"Trust me. Besides, there's something Peregrine needs to see."

"I guess we'll do it your way," El finally surrendered.

As Barnabas promised, they drove about forty-five minutes before turning off and following a road up into the hills. After another fifteen minutes, he parked the minivan at a quaint and historic-looking country inn and told the others to wait as he went inside. They all slowly got out and stretched their stiff joints. The crisp air smelled of fresh nature, and the stars shown brightly in the moonless sky. A short time later, Barnabas walked out with a woman about his age. They smiled and chatted as they approached.

"This is Raisa," he said. "We've known each other since we were babies. She doesn't speak English, but says we are welcome to stay here and has given us two of her best cabins."

"*Spasibo*," said Pere.

"*Pozhaluysta*," she responded, smiling.

She led them around to the back of the inn where there were six or seven rustic-looking cabins amongst the trees. She opened the doors to two adjacent cabins and the weary travelers lugged their bags inside. Raisa said a few last things to Barnabas and then returned to the main building. The women would be comfortable in their cabin, but the men were crowded. There were only four beds, so one of them would have to sleep on the couch in the sitting room. Pere drew the short straw. It wasn't the most comfortable couch, but it was an improvement after sleeping sitting up in a minivan the night before. They woke around dawn. Region 8 had eleven time zones, so Pere had stopped asking what time it was a week ago. It was just too hard to keep track. The sun was up, so that was good enough. They cleaned up, dressed, and met in front of the cabins.

"Raisa said they begin serving breakfast at 7 a.m." Barnabas said. "The dining room is in the main building. Follow me."

They went inside the main entry and up the stairs. Pere wondered why the dining room was on the second floor until he got to the top of the stairs. Looking out the windows, he could see they had arrived at the ocean. And then he checked his thinking. He didn't know geography terribly well, but he knew enough to realize that they could be nowhere near an ocean. He looked questioningly at Barnabas who was watching him and smiling curiously.

"Lake Baikal," he said by way of explanation. "It's the world's largest freshwater lake. It's about four-hundred miles long, fifty miles wide, and a mile deep."

"It's the lake I flew over, isn't it?" Pere said quietly.

"You tell me. I could only guess from your description."

"It's huge!" said Yael in awe.

"Pretty big," Barnabas agreed. "About a quarter of the world's fresh surface water is in that lake."

"Sometimes I wish I really could fly," mused Pere, looking longingly at the lake.

"That monster's not going anywhere real soon," said El. "Let's eat some breakfast and we can stare at the lake later. I'm starving."

It was country cooking—Russian style—and it was excellent. They ate while they discussed their next move.

"Remind me again, Peregrine," Barnabas said. "What direction was the snake train going when you landed on it in your dream?"

Pere recalled the dream and tried to position himself in relation to the sun. "I think it was going west," he finally said.

"As I thought," Barnabas said, unfolding a page he had in his pocket. "Raisa printed this out for me last night. It's a schedule for the Trans-Siberian Railway."

"You want us to get on a train?" Rophe said.

"It has very little to do with want," Barnabas replied. "As I interpret it, we're following a path that has been laid out for us. Peregrine's dream-bird took us to the Preobrazhensky Cathedral in Yakutsk. Tomorrow morning we'll go to the Tsar's Gate in Ulan Ude. If that checks out, the next part of his dream had his bird landing on a westbound train crossing a vast wilderness. I'm thinking that must be the Trans-Siberian Railway."

"We are basing very much upon a dream," Ehud mused.

"Do you have a better idea?" Barnabas responded, a little defensively.

"I am not disagreeing with your rather dreamy logic," Ehud said between bites. "I am merely stating a fact."

"If we get on a passenger train," El said. "Won't we be on video feeds constantly?"

"That's the curious thing," Barnabas answered. "The newer high-speed line runs on wide tracks built next to the old line. That train *is* highly monitored. But the old Historic Line prides itself on being technology-free as a part of the experience. They'll scan our IDs once, when we purchase passes, but that's it; no cameras or communication devices are permitted on the old line. If we get past the first scan, we'll be home free."

"That's a pretty big if," El grunted.

"Where does this train go?" Pere asked, not liking the idea at all.

Barnabas looked at him for a moment, calculating. "West," he finally said.

"That's it?" Rophe said. "We get on a train and go west, with no clear destination?"

"Well," Barnabas said, sounding more defensive. "If we stay on it, eventually we'll arrive in Moscow. But I'm betting on the earth shaking before that." They all stared at him for a long moment of realization before anyone spoke.

"That's a pretty big bet, Barnabas," El finally said, eyeing the huge lake outside. "But, truth be told, we've been all-in on this hand since we decided to go north after the Klondike fell. Silas used to tell me we play with weighted dice. I hope that's true of cards as well, because it feels like we're bluffing our asses off right now."

"I prefer backgammon," Ehud mumbled.

"Yeah, well, why don't you and Khyoza give me a hand," El said, scratching his bearded cheek. "No pun intended about the hand, Ehud; but I've got to figure out how to make our swords look like luggage."

"What about a golf bag?" offered Ehud.

"That's a great idea," El said. "I knew you were good for something, Hook."

"You know," Ehud replied. "This hook has a very sharp point." El laughed and the three got up and left the dining room. After a few awkward minutes, Barnabas and Rophe made their excuses and left as well, leaving only Yael and Pere. They were quiet for a long while, Pere just staring at his plate as he moved food around with his fork.

"You want to talk about it?" Yael finally said.

"When I was a kid, 'chasing a dream' meant trying to do something you really enjoyed. Now we're literally chasing my dream, and it's going to get us all killed."

"That's always been a possibility," she admitted, soberly. "But have you noticed you've been getting us all killed for two years now and, somehow, we're still alive?"

"Tell that to those fifteen people in the Klondike," he sighed.

"I know, Pere; but I think they would agree with me when I say I'd rather die chasing a dream than running from a nightmare."

"At least you can make that choice. I don't make choices at all anymore. Every time I think I have options, I hit a wall that only lets me go in one direction, whether I chose it or not."

Yael looked at him steadily for a long time. "You know what Sayiina said to me the night before we got to Yakutsk, while you were belowdecks getting drunk?"

"I was *not* getting drunk!"

"Then you sing terrible sober."

"I didn't have much practice as a kid."

"Anyway, Sayiina said I had to accept that you'd been chosen and had a calling on you. And that it may seem like your calling comes before me; but that's not by choice, because you're a bird of instinct; and your calling drives you. She said I had to learn to fly with you, to support you, because if I tried to clip your wings now, I might destroy you and the whole flock."

Pere just stared at her, open mouthed. "That naviah, and her stupid metaphors!" he finally growled. "She should have minded her own business!"

"I didn't tell you, so you'd get mad at her," she put her hand on his. "I want you to know that you may feel forced to fly where you must. But wherever you are forced to fly, Pere, I will *choose* to fly with you."

The following morning, they ate a late breakfast, offered their farewells to Raisa, and left for Ulan Ude. When they reached the city proper, Barnabas drove to the center of town and down Ulista Lenina. Some distance ahead, Pere could see a great archway looming over the street.

"Is that your arch, Peregrine?" Barnabas asked. As they neared it, the two-headed eagle gleamed in the morning sun.

"That's the one," Pere sighed, secretly hoping it wouldn't be. No one said anything in response. They all knew how absurd their next course of action seemed, and how manifestly dangerous. Barnabas navigated the old Windstar to the Passenger Railway Station not far from the Tsar's Gate and stopped in an empty section of the large parking lot.

"We'll have to leave the minivan here," Barnabas said. "Raisa will send someone in the morning to pick it up. She said they could always use another van at the inn, and that way we avoid loose ends."

"Okay," El said, assuming command. "When we get inside, we split into three groups—one for each of our Russian speakers. Barnabas: you and Rophe will be one team—a married couple traveling to Moscow to visit family. Khyoza: Ehud and I will be with you—three old friends on a golfing junket. Falcon: you and my niece are university students on spring break who need to get back to Moscow before term starts. Any questions?" No one said anything.

"We're taking the Historic Great Siberian Way, NOT the high-speed version," Barnabas took over. "You'll get tickets to Moscow—even if we're not going that far, just get them for the end of the line. Once we're aboard and the train has left the station, we can inconspicuously find each other."

"Don't you mean *if* we're all aboard?" Rophe said.

"Don't be waspish, my beloved," Barnabas said. "As my wife, you're very shy and don't like to speak in public."

"Ha! You *wish!*" Rophe snorted.

The process went far smoother than expected. The bored station clerk selling them passes barely even checked their IDs and hardly looked at them at all. The conductor and porters seemed more like actors performing their historic roles than real officials. Even Rophe smiled as an overly flirty young porter ushered her onto the train. Pere and Yael watched from their seats as El, Ehud, and Khyoza drunkenly boarded with the help of a fatherly old porter who had seen his share of urban cowboys drinking their way through midlife adventures. Khyoza had suggested the three men splash themselves liberally with vodka. He said it would seem more realistic for three men vacationing together in Russia without their wives to be drunk most of the time. After the train left the station, Pere breathed a sigh of relief. Once again, everyone had somehow avoided death. As they passed over the first bridge and into the countryside, he began to think past the worry of just getting on the train and about the problem of what came next.

"I told you we'd make it," Yael said, quietly, taking his hand in hers.

"Yeah, but now what?"

"Well, since neither of us knows, why don't we just relax and enjoy the journey?"

"You're joking, right?"

"Pere, how many times in the last two years have we been sitting on a luxury train, rolling through beautiful countryside?"

"None," he said, as though a moron had asked the question.

"Sooo, maybe we should enjoy the moment while we can? I'm sure something life-threatening will happen sometime in the next few days; but wouldn't it be nice, for a change, to take advantage of the situation, and maybe have just a little fun?"

"Well, okay," he said after thinking it over. "I suppose we could try that. What'd you have in mind?"

"I don't know. How about this for starters—we passed a bar in the next car. Why don't you go and buy us a drink?"

"That doesn't sound too dangerous," he said reasonably. "What would you like?"

"Surprise me," she smiled, dreamily.

"Okay, I will." He got up and steadied himself against the rocking of the train. That simple movement triggered a sense memory, and a dream flooded back to him. He remembered being on a train in the old west sitting in the dining car where all the porters were identical, and there was something about a raven, but he couldn't remember the specifics. As he passed through the vestibule between the cars, he wondered if this was the same train from his dream. *You're over-thinking it,* he said to himself. *Sometimes a dream is just a dream.* He got to the bar and the porter approached him with an expectant look in his eye. Not knowing what else to order, he asked for two beers in Russian. The porter nodded and turned to the cooler.

"Your Russian is not so good," offered a girl sitting not far away on one of the bar stools. She was young, probably seventeen or eighteen, so he assumed she was sipping a cola rather than a mixed drink; but he didn't know the drinking age in Russia, so it was all a guess anyway.

"I'm practicing," he said carefully.

"Not very well. My English is better than your Russian," she said, smiling. "So, let us practice on each other. You will speak Russian to me, and I will speak English back to you. This way, we will both get better, no?"

"I don't know," he fumbled for an excuse. "I'm kind of busy right now."

"You are on a train in the middle of nowhere. How busy can you be? I have been bored to death for three days."

"Well, I'm with my girlfriend." The porter put two beers in front of him, which he paid for. "And she wants me to bring her this beer."

"Oh, this is perfect," she said, jumping up. "Show me. I will speak English with this girlfriend as well. Maybe she is better-mannered than you."

"I wasn't trying to be rude," he said, still fumbling for an excuse. "It's just that she's very shy."

"So, I will be her close friend. Come, I will open the vestibule door for you. You cannot do it by yourself when you are carrying two drinks, can you?"

"You're used to getting your way, aren't you?"

"I am an only child," she laughed. "I can make my parents do almost anything for me." She led him through the vestibule door and into the adjoining car. When they approached, Yael tried to conceal her wariness. He handed her a beer and sat down. The girl sat down opposite them and smiled.

"This is," Pere said to Yael, and then paused. "I'm sorry; I didn't get your name."

"Abigail," the girl said easily.

"Valentina," Pere continued. "This is Abigail. She *insists* on practicing her English on us."

"I did insist, did I not?" Abigail laughed. "I am pleased to meet you, Valentina," she reached out her hand. Yael took it.

"Nice to meet you too, Abigail," Yael responded carefully.

"You have very pretty hair."

"Yeah, I get that a lot."

"And my name is. . . Yevgeny," Pere interrupted, shaking her hand as well. Yael didn't seem to be taking this very well. But he'd never known her to be rude. Deadly, but not blatantly rude. He hoped Abigail would interpret it as shyness.

"Yevgeny was trying to order your drinks in Russian," Abigail said, good-naturedly. "But he is not very good at it. He has the right words, but he is much too careful with them." Yael looked at him with one eyebrow raised.

"I was just trying to enjoy the moment," he said, slightly abashed, and then took a sip of his beer. It wasn't bad.

"Where are you from?" Abigail asked.

"East of here," Yael said. She seemed more curt than usual.

"We just came from Vladivostok," Abigail said, taking no notice. "And Tokyo before that. But you must be from further east than those?"

"We're from California," Pere said carefully, after considering it for a few moments. That seemed safe enough. It was a big place after all. "We're studying abroad in Moscow. But right now, we're on break." It would be absurd to say he was from Russia now that she knew he spoke the language so poorly. This was the next best explanation.

"Oh, California!" she said gleefully. "But I was *born* in California, or so my parents tell me."

"Really?" Yael said. "Where in California were you born?"

"I am not sure."

"What brought you to Russia, then?" Yael was asking questions, but with an edge of suspicion.

"My parents adopted me," she said, shrugging. "After my real father and mother died."

"Oh," Yael said, seeming a little ashamed of her previous coolness. "That must have been terrible for you."

"I do not remember it," she said. "I was very young when it happened. My parents waited to tell me until I was eight. They thought I should know the truth. It is why I have learnt English."

Pere suddenly felt sympathy for this girl. "I lost my parents when I was young, too," he said gently. "Both Valentina and I did."

"Do you remember them?"

"Some," he said, and Yael just nodded. "I was almost five," he continued. "I couldn't remember much for a long time, but now I remember more."

"That must be nice. Yulian and Katya are very good to me, but I think it would be nice to remember something of my real parents."

"Yulian and Katya?" Yael asked.

"The couple that adopted me . . . but do not tell them I called them by their first names. Papa says I am being precocious when I do that."

"We'll keep it our secret," Pere said, winking. "Besides, we've never met your parents, so we won't be telling them anything."

"But, of course, you shall!" she said, impulsively. "Meet them, I mean. You must come to dinner in our car tonight."

"Oh," Yael said, "that's really polite of you to offer, but we can't."

"But I insist," she said. "Ours is the last car on the train. We have it all to ourselves, and there is a dining service included, so it will be no bother at all. Besides, it has been sooo boring all alone with just them. Please, come and be company to me?

It is settled, *da*? Yulian likes to take supper at 7 p.m., and Katya always does what Yulian says, so I will see you then." She smiled at them both, got up, and walked away. Yael just sat there, a flabbergasted look on her face.

"She's an only child," he said by way of explanation, as he sipped his beer. "I think she's used to getting her way."

"I'm an only child," Yael said with some heat. "And I never get my way!"

"You got your beer, didn't you? It's not as good warm, so you should probably drink it." She looked at him angrily, and then took a large gulp of it. "What do you suppose we should do?" he continued. "Should we go to dinner with her family?"

"Well, we can't exactly back out now without a good reason, can we Mr. Socialite?"

"You act like this was my fault. You told me to get you a drink. How was I supposed to know Russians don't take no for an answer? Besides, she seems nice enough, doesn't she?"

"You can't really be that naïve, Pere. She was flirting with you."

"What?... No... That's ridiculous... Isn't it?"

"I'm going to go find Barnabas," she said flatly. "Maybe he can give me some advice about what we should do about dinner... or 'supper' as your new girlfriend called it."

"What? Wait! Cam?" But she had already left. He thought about following her, but then he figured it might attract attention if he was chasing an angry girl around the train. Besides, maybe she needed to be alone for a few minutes until she regained her sanity. He sat and mulled it over for a while as he watched the countryside roll by. The more he thought about it the more pleased he felt. He knew he shouldn't feel that way; but no one had ever flirted with him before, and it was kind of flattering that someone that pretty thought him worth the effort. No one had ever been jealous of him before either; that was a definite boost to his male ego—he felt a little bit like a lion in a pride, with all the lionesses fighting over him. His reverie shattered, however, when Yael returned and sat down next to him.

"Barnabas thinks we should go ahead and have supper with Abigail, but that we should be careful. And my uncle says I should tell the 'bird boy' that it's not mating season and he should keep it in his pants." She took another satisfied gulp of her beer. "Oh, this *is* pretty good beer."

"Roar," he mumbled, blushing.

"What did you say?"

"Nothing."

"Oh, I thought I heard a meow."

Later that evening, they made their way to the back of the train and passed through the last vestibule to a door. Yael looked at him but offered no assistance. He shrugged and knocked. Only moments later Abigail opened the door. She had exchanged the jeans and t-shirt for a very complimentary white, tea-length, embroidered dress. She was about the same height as Yael and had pulled her dark-golden-blonde hair into a neat ponytail, accentuating her striking sea-gray eyes. He noticed Yael had a strange glow in her eyes as she watched Abigail look at Pere. He should have taken it as a warning, but he didn't have enough experience to know the danger signs.

"It is now dark outside, Yevgeny," Abigail said, good-naturedly. "Why do you still wear sunglasses?"

"I'm sorry," he fumbled to take them off. "They're prescription. I lost my regular pair, so these are the only ones I have left."

"Oh, what a surprise," she said excitedly. "You also have gray eyes. It is not common they say. His eyes are pretty, are they not, Valentina?"

"Adorable," she said in a flat tone.

"Come," she said. "You must meet my parents." They were already sitting at the table watching the whole interaction. Abigail brought her guests to the dining area as her parents stood up. "Katya and Yulian," she said very formally. "This is Valentina, and this is Yevgeny."

Her parents were smiling indulgently. "Abigail," her father said. "Why must you call us by our first names?"

"Because I am an adult now, Papa."

"You will not be eighteen for six more months. Until then I will still call you 'zaichik', my little bunny."

"Please, Papa," Abigail said, playfully. "Not in front of the guests."

"We are pleased to meet you both," Katya said, smiling. "It is kind of you to have supper with us. Abigail has been having cabin fever, I think. Come, sit down. We have a lovely meal planned." They all took their seats. "Abigail tells us you are going to university in Moscow," Katya continued. "But are from California, originally? I have never been. Tell us about your home."

They talked genially while they drank an *apéritif* that looked a little like milk mixed with water and tasted like licorice. Pere spoke very carefully of California. He had to fall back on all the things he knew about ranching and exclude the world as he'd come to know it over the last two years. Katya told them about their busy life in Moscow, but that she also was raised in a rural setting, near the Sea of Azov in Ukraine. Katya and Abigail talked a lot, as did Pere; but Yael remained relatively reserved, speaking only when asked direct questions. Pere was beginning to wonder if she wasn't truly shy after all. Yulian remained very quiet, and just watched the others interact—Pere, in particular, whom he seemed to be studying. Finally, when a lull came in the discussion, he spoke.

"Yevgeny," he said. "Have we met before?"

Pere froze inwardly but tried to keep a calm façade. "I doubt it," he said, as though trying to remember. "Maybe we were both at the same coffee shop somewhere in Moscow? Or, have you ever been to California?"

"Once," he said. "But only to Los Nietos. And I doubt we met there, since I was in meetings the whole time."

"I've never been to Los Nietos," Pere lied. Technically, he'd been within the borders when he rescued his father; but he wouldn't have met Yulian there, so it didn't count.

"Curious," Yulian said. "Something about you is so familiar, but I can't place it. Maybe it was a coffee shop . . . but I don't really go to coffee shops."

Pere had the sinking feeling that he knew exactly where this man had seen him. Why didn't he keep his glasses on? He should have made some excuse about a light-sensitive eye condition. It was too late for that now. He just hoped he wouldn't do anything to jog Yulian's memory, but the man just kept looking at him.

"Yulian," Katya said, gently. "Stop staring. You're making Yevgeny uncomfortable."

"Oh, of course," Yulian replied, snapping out of his intense concentration. "I'm terribly sorry. I hate it when I feel like I'm right on the edge of recalling something, but it stays just out of reach."

"I know the feeling," Pere said, quietly. And they returned to their regular conversation. After a few minutes, a knock came at the door.

"Ah, that must be the first course," Katya said. "Abigail, would you let them in, please."

"Yes, Mama," the girl said as she got up from the table and opened the door.

The porter rolled in a cart, filled with covered trays. Pere again recalled his dream. But this man didn't look like the porters in his dream, and he certainly didn't look like a raven. He wasn't very tall, had a badly manicured moustache, and wore round horn-rimmed glasses. The porter maneuvered the tray next to the table and looked up at the diners. When his eyes met Pere's, there was in them a moment of confusion, followed almost instantly by shock and unmistakable recognition. In one smooth motion, he lifted the lid on one of the trays, pulled a handgun from the empty plate beneath, and leveled it at Pere's head. "Put your hands where I can see them," he growled, in perfect English, and Pere obeyed.

"What is the meaning of this?" Yulian shouted.

"Keep your voice down," the porter said menacingly, as he backed to the door and locked it, while still aiming the handgun unwaveringly at Pere's head. "It is of utmost importance that I speak with you, Yulian. I met with Demyan in Moscow four days ago. He sent me."

"Demyan sent you to point a weapon at this young man? I cannot imagine him doing so. I demand you lower it instantly and give me an explanation." Khvostovsky sounded commanding, but it was clear he was also frightened.

"I can't do that, Yulian. I came to warn *you*," the porter said, not lowering the gun even slightly. "But I had no idea you invited the world's most-wanted fugitive to dinner." They all turned their gazes on Pere now, realizing there must be some kind of terrible mix-up.

"Why do you think Yevgeny is wanted?" Khvostovsky asked the porter, a little breathlessly. "And who are you that I should even listen to this?"

"My name is Illarion Orlov, and I represent Premier Rockefeller of the Directorate."

"Good heavens!" Khvostovsky choked, his eyes widening. "Why are you meeting me like this?"

"I've come with a warning that you and your family are in grave danger."

"From Yevgeny?"

"Not that I'm currently aware of. As I said, I don't know why he's here; but I do know his name is not Yevgeny. It's John Robert Percival; but he's also known within the Consortium hierarchy as the Anomaly. The very Anomaly Compliance Division has been hunting fruitlessly for the last two years."

The now familiar burst of adrenalin tasted on his dry tongue like hot metal as the construct of time again dissolved and Pere's awareness shifted into hyperspeed. On that old train snaking its way across the lonely steppes of southern Russia, Pere realized that the old saying was true about life flashing before your eyes. Myriad thoughts crowded into his mind, as terror coursed through his veins. Above every other thought was the bitter confirmation that he had been right all along. He had always known this would happen. Regardless of what anyone said, he knew he couldn't avoid his fate forever. An unrelenting inner voice told him time and again that the day would come when Compliance would capture him, deep-probe him for information, and toss him blithely onto the midden-heap of the dead. It was either that, or he would be swiftly and brutally killed trying to evade his would-be captors. Though he felt wretchedly frozen inside, he knew beyond any doubt which was the better option. The adrenaline already pumping through him would make it easy.

He braced his legs, raising his heels, and subtly shifting his weight-center to the balls of his feet. He visualized the twisting body motion he would need to make. He would tear several tendons doing it, but it didn't matter because he wouldn't need them anymore. He had to surprise this Illarion Orlov so thoroughly that he would be forced to kill him in self-defense. It was the only way. He simply could *not* allow himself to be captured alive. That would expose all the people he cared about. If being captured was God's cruel betrayal of his existence, he would not run willingly into its arms like a mindless sacrificial lamb. Destiny be damned! He would fight it with every fiber of his being. He decided to leap like a madman and grab Orlov by the neck, overturning the table in the moment of his leap. This would add the necessary confusion, and force Orlov to respond instinctually.

He only hoped Yael would duck before the bullets began to fly. He wanted her to survive more than anything else. He flashed back on the last few hours they'd spent together. She'd been angry with him. He wished he'd have told her there was nothing to be jealous of; told her he was hers and no others; he wished more than anything that he'd told her he loved her, but it was too late. Now, the only thing left was action. He tensed his calves and thighs and was just about to spring, when Yael placed a firm, anchoring hand on his thigh beneath the table. He glanced at her, warning her with his eyes to let him go; but she was nodding oddly at Yulian. He turned to look at Abigail's father. The man appeared on the verge of fainting. He had gone absolutely pale as he stared in frightened recognition at Pere.

"Stop, Orlov!" he said in almost a whisper. "If you kill this young man, you will have to kill me as well."

Now it was Orlov's turn to appear shocked. "Why would I do that?"

"Because," he replied very quietly. "I could not live with myself if I allowed you to kill Abigail's... only brother."

THE STUNNED TABLEAU LASTED ONLY a moment before everyone's gaze shifted to Abigail.

"What are you saying, Papa?"

His eyes betrayed his secret guilt. "I'm saying that now I understand why I recognized this young man," he turned to look at Pere, but he was also looking through him, searching for a memory. "Two years ago, the sénéschal called a meeting of the chairs in the New York City Metroplex—do you remember the trip, Katya, it was on March 15th?" She nodded her head numbly. "At that meeting, he told us that the Directorate had commissioned a vastly powerful new data-processing engine that was able to analyze literally everything, and that it had discovered an anomaly—that's what he called it."

Pere found himself struggling with conflicting emotions—an impossible elation at the revelation that this was his dead sister, competing with the old dread that threatened to consume him—the wheel of fate was again grinding him into its preordained rut on a path he travelled blindly. He found it hard to breathe, and having a gun pointed at his head wasn't helping.

Khvostovsky continued, staring at Pere. "He told us this anomaly had been born on that very day eighteen years earlier, somewhere in the Nova Albion sub-sector of Region 4. They jailed the parents as dissidents; but the two children orphaned by the events were placed with 'appropriate' families for upbringing. The one the Haruspex Project identified as the *anomaly*, John Percival by birth, was placed with near relatives in—if I recall his words— 'the backlands of Nova Albion, on a co-op'. As I understand it, he has grown up to become some kind of random aberration that will eventually undermine the Consortium." Everyone stared with rapt attention at Khvostovsky as he recalled the meeting. But Pere was spiraling downward. A dark abyss had opened, and he was on the verge of tumbling in. He knew they were searching for him, but he'd never known why. Silas had told him the falcon dream, and he assumed there must be some link—but now, this man was laying it bare before him; and rather than making the situation better, it only magnified his bitterness. He was being driven from two sides at once, into a box-canyon of fate, to await his eventual slaughter.

Khvostovsky's voice drew him back out of his dark thoughts. The Cybergi chair was now looking at Abigail, shame in his eyes. "The sénéschal told us the younger sister had been placed elsewhere but said nothing more about her. You were fifteen at the time of that meeting, my *zaichik*, and I remembered when we adopted you, thirteen years earlier, right around the time of your 2nd birthday, the only things we knew about you were that your name was Abigail, that you had been born in central California. . . and that your birth parents were dead. I swear to you, we knew nothing more than that." He closed his eyes and slumped back in his chair, before finally continuing.

"I should have let it go, but that small detail about the girl in his story nagged at me. You were one of dozens of births in central California at that time, but something in me had to be sure you were not *that* girl. So, I asked Demyan to discover the last name of your birth parents. It took him quite a while because you had not been born in an official clinic, so there were no records. But he was finally able to dig up the name I wanted most not to hear—Percival. I should have told you and Katya right then; but I believed it would only cause you both pain. Your mama and I could not have children of our own, so we saw your arrival as a gift. We loved you as our own ... and I didn't think you would ever need this information. But when this man said Yevgeny was really John Percival, I knew I couldn't let your brother die to keep my secret safe. I'm sorry, Abigail. I was wrong not to tell you."

"Then this is true, Papa?" she said breathlessly. "Yevgeny is my brother?"

Before Yulian could answer, El stepped out of the railcar's bedroom and leveled a silenced Beretta at Orlov as the entry door to the railcar also opened, the lock picked by Khyoza, who stepped in carrying a wicked looking knife, followed by Barnabas and Rophe, who quietly closed the door and relocked it. Ehud was not with them.

I don't know who you are," El's voice was ice. "But if you lay down your weapon right now, you might leave here alive."

How Orlov didn't flinch was unimaginable, but he simply pulled back the hammer on the Springfield. "I don't think so, Quade," he said with a stillness that matched El's perfectly. "If anyone moves even slightly from where they are, the young woman sitting next to him will have his brains in her lap, and whatever value you've placed on his life will die with him." No one even breathed.

"If you pull that trigger," El growled through gritted teeth. "It'll be the last thing you ever do."

"Then it appears we are at an impasse, because I am prepared to embrace that outcome," Orlov said.

"Shall I cut his throat, Brother?" Khyoza offered, conversationally.

"That wouldn't be very prudent, Lecha Zakayev," Orlov responded just as evenly. "That is your name, is it not?"

"You have us at a disadvantage," El said. "You seem to know our names. Maybe you should be polite and introduce yourself before I kill you."

"That's not a very cordial sentiment, Steve. And besides, my name would mean nothing to either of you. Suffice it to say, I know a great deal more about you than your names. So much more, in fact, that I'm aware the three of us are highly skilled at killing—and believe me, I'm exquisitely skilled—but where does that leave us? I think our ethnically insensitive forbears would call this a Mexican standoff. Now, we can stay here all evening taunting each other in a very entertaining pissing contest—that will almost certainly end badly—or we can perhaps explore some sort of... accommodation."

"I don't make deals with the devil," El said, as he pulled the hammer back on his own weapon. "Unless they end with *your* brains splashed all over the floor." Pere just sat there, stock-still. They were playing a very dangerous game with a gun pointed at his temple.

"Then let's play this out," Orlov responded, icily. "You could pull that trigger, and I would, reflexively, pull my trigger, killing Percival; we'd both be dead and neither of us would achieve the ends we seek... Or..."

"Or what?" El said, carefully, after considering it.

"Or we could lower our guns—only slightly, mind you—sit down, and talk things over. Then, of course, we could always go ahead and shoot each other afterwards if we don't come up with a satisfactory solution."

"I don't see how the 'ends we seek' could ever line up," El said. "But I'm willing to talk, and then shoot."

"That's decent of you." He addressed Rophe without ever looking at her. "I'm sorry, Miss, I don't know your name, but would you be so kind as to place that chair next to Percival's here." Rophe carefully complied.

"Thank you," Orlov continued. "Now, if you and your two friends at the door would slowly move to the other side of the railcar, I would feel more comfortable. Having a phantom at my back is making my trigger finger understandably twitchy. I'm sure we all want to avoid that." Khyoza looked at El who nodded. He, Barnabas, and Rophe then moved carefully to the other side of the railcar and stood behind El.

"I'm going to sit down," Orlov explained. "As a sign of good faith, I'll lower my weapon from this young man's head to his heart." He sat very smoothly in the chair next to Pere, shifting the Springfield from his head to the side of his chest, level with his heart. "Now, if you would all find seats, I think we can begin."

"Lecha," El said. "Bring me a chair; I wanna keep our new friend here in my crosshairs."

"Completely understandable," Orlov conceded. Everyone carefully found chairs, and Khyoza slowly pushed one under El, who never took his eyes off Orlov as he sat down. When they were seated, El finally spoke.

"What now?"

"Now, we ask each other questions, and we exchange answers. An answer for an answer—does that sound fair."

"It sounds like you're delaying the inevitable . . . But I'll play along, for now."

"Good," Orlov said. "Shall I begin?"

El nodded with his Beretta rather than his head, moving the aim up and down from Orlov's head to his heart.

"How quaint. Okay, my droll fellow, why are you on this train?"

"You wouldn't believe me if I told you."

"That's not an answer, Steve, it's an evasion. This negotiation will go nowhere if we're not straightforward."

"This is NOT a negotiation, asshole, and don't call me Steve. We're on this train because your anomaly there had a dream that said we should get on this train. Is that better?"

"Much. I needn't accept your premise to accept that your answer is straightforward—although I could do without the taunting adolescent insults. Your turn."

"Did you get on this train to kill us?"

"That was certainly *not* my reason for getting on this train."

"Then why—"

"That's another question. It's my turn. You say you got on this train in response to Percival's dream. What did his dream tell you your destination was?"

"I'm right here, you know?" Pere protested, through gritted teeth. "Why don't you just ask me?"

"Sorry, John. I mean no offence, but my negotiations—ah, pardon me, my discussion is with Quade. We wouldn't want to muddy the waters. So, Quade, where are you going?"

"We have no idea," El answered simply. "The dream said to get on this train. It didn't say where to get off."

"Are you saying you—?"

"Nah-uh. Your rules, friend."

"Yes, of course. I apologize. Please continue."

"If you didn't get on this train to kill us, then why did you?"

"To warn Mr. Khvostovsky he's in danger; and to ask a favor of him. Two answers for one question—a bargain. My turn. What is your endgame?"

"Again, no idea. We're following another dream. Two answers for two answers—we're even."

"Good heavens. You people place an inordinate amount of faith in dreams."

"Is that a question?"

"No. More a statement, really. It's your turn."

"I was eavesdropping on your earlier conversation from the sleeping berth. This man said a 'Directorate' had commissioned the creation of something he called 'Haruspex', that identified our anomaly here. What's the Directorate?"

"It's not polite to eavesdrop."

"I'm full of bad habits. Answer the question."

"Very well. The Directorate was a small association of extremely powerful individuals whose sole purpose was oversight of the Consortium of Ten."

"Was? Oh, right. No follow-ups. Your turn."

"Under the circumstances, I'm going to allow your follow-up question. I said 'was' because three weeks ago, five of the seven sitting Directorate premiers were assassinated."

"No!" uttered Khvostovsky, impulsively.

"Yes. It's the reason I'm here to speak with you, Yulian. But that will have to wait.

It's my turn to ask a question. You said you've based your entire strategy on a dream with no endgame. What was the dream?"

"I don't have a memory for those kinds of things. You mind if my associate here answers?" nodding toward Barnabas.

"Tag-teaming? That places me at a disadvantage, but I'll allow it. Let the Mongol speak."

"I'm not a Mongol," Barnabas said. "I'm a Buryat by heritage."

"My apologies," Orlov said. "Similar features, I suppose. I meant no offence. Please continue."

"In the dream there was a man bound in chains in a small dark underground prison cell. He was there for years crying for help to no avail; until one day, the door to his cell burst open, a young man stood in the doorway superimposed with the image of a falcon, ready to hunt. The falcon became furious and flapped its wings and the chains fell away from the man's arms and feet. Then the wind from the wings grew stronger until the walls of the prison finally burst open, and the man was free. But the wind didn't stop. It spread until it had covered the entire world, and then every prison was destroyed, and all the prisoners were set free. That was the dream."

"But that's absolute meaningless drivel!"

"It might add some context," Barnabas offered, "if you know that the man who was in prison was Robert Percival, and that this young man was the one in the doorway. His other name is Peregrine—which translates as—"

"Falcon," Orlov finished. "I'm fluent in Classical Latin." He looked at Pere in a new light. "Fascinating," he said, calculatingly. "Sigmund Freud would have had a field day with this. And you've based your entire strategy—or I should say lack of strategy—on this fever dream?"

"Is that a question?" El said.

"It absolutely is!"

"Too bad. It's my turn."

"Oh, right. Go ahead then."

"I may not be the smartest guy in the room, but if this 'fever dream' is so far-fetched, why, out of the billions of people on this planet, did your Haru-thingy pick out this one kid as the nail in your coffin?"

Orlov was silent for a moment. "That's a very shrewd question, Quade. And it's not *my* Haru-thingy, by the way. As I understand it, the Haruspex 2580 Project analyzes all—and I mean *all*—streams of data looking for potential aberrations that might become future problems. It prognosticates based solely on probability quotients. To be honest, I've doubted the accuracy of this prognostication from the very beginning—present company notwithstanding. However, something about your young friend here seems to have triggered the reddest of all possible flags. I don't think the program said *how* the anomaly would destroy the current world order; only that, if left unchecked, it somehow would."

"That doesn't sound much clearer to me than a fever dream."

"No. Now that you mention it, it really doesn't. Competing narratives that just happen to coincide?"

"Coincidence?" Khyoza offered, laconically, and Pere ground his teeth.

"I normally don't accept coincidences at face value." Orlov looked around the room as though he was considering something. "But I have been known to seize opportunities when they present themselves. May I ask how many there are in this underground movement of yours?"

"Why do you want to know?"

"Humor me. The information will never be made public since you're going to kill me anyway if we don't reach an agreement."

El nodded over his shoulder to Barnabas. "Perhaps twenty-five thousand," Barnabas replied. "Give or take; all over the world."

"And are many of them as well trained in combat as Quade and Zakayev?" Barnabas looked at El.

"That's another question," El said. "But I'll *allow* it. About one in twenty of our people are soldiers—and they're all very well trained, but none of them could compete with Lecha or me."

"I would write that off to arrogance, but I know your histories; so, I'll accept your assessment of your own formidable skills as accurate."

"Do you talk like that because you're an erudite pussy, or are you just trying to impress people?"

"'Erudite' is a very advanced word, and often mispronounced, which you have not done. Kudos. And no, I don't do it to impress, but to intimidate people. It's usually successful. Clearly, you're immune. Now back to the matter at hand. You have by my calculations approximately twelve-hundred well-trained soldiers?"

"Give or take, as my friend said. Now, why do you want to know?"

Orlov was silent for a long moment, looking steadily at El before speaking. "There's an ancient proverb: '*The enemy of my enemy is my friend*'. Have you heard it?"

"Kautiya. 4th century BC."

"And you said you weren't the smartest guy in the room."

"And you said you know our histories. If anything had to do with combat or game theory, Lecha and I learned it. How does that affect the here and now?"

"How indeed?" Orlov seemed to be contemplating. "I have a proposition that I think might benefit us both—at least in the short term."

"Doubtful... but I'm listening."

"This may sound counterintuitive, but for the time being, I suggest we join forces."

"Are you out of your fucking mind? You just said your organization wanted to kill John Percival!"

"That's not completely accurate. Had you been listening closely, you would have heard me say *Haruspex* predicted John Percival was an anomaly that needed to be *captured, interrogated,* and then killed."

"And how is that any different?"

"Because," Barnabas interrupted, "He also said members of his ruling sect known as the Directorate had been killed. My guess would be there's been some kind of schism in the upper echelons of his organization. Would that be an accurate assessment of the situation?"

"I might have chosen a less *erudite* word, but that's close enough," Orlov conceded.

"And why shouldn't we assume he's telling us whatever he needs to, to get out of this railcar alive?" El asked Barnabas.

"Because I'm going to do something that's either very foolish," Orlov said. "Or you'll see it as a sign of my good faith." He carefully pulled the Springfield away from Pere's chest, gently released the hammer and, very slowly, laid it on the table. "I'm completely vulnerable now; so, if you wish to shoot me, this would be the opportune moment. I do hope, however, that you don't take me up on that. I still value my life."

El looked at him steadily for a long moment then released the hammer on the Beretta and put it down as well. "All right. What the hell are you playing at?" Pere took the moment to breathe deeply for the first time since this 'porter' had put a gun to his head.

"Your friend here is right, as far as it goes," Orlov admitted. "There has indeed been a schism—more of a bloody coup, really. The *ex*-sénéschal of our organization has assassinated five of the seven premiers of the Directorate. Only two have survived; Rockefeller, whom I represent; and Romanov, who has sided with the ex-sénéschal in the coup."

"Is it possible?" Khvostovsky said, in utter shock.

"If only it weren't, Yulian," Orlov replied.

"I could have told you Gianakos and that woman had a thing going," Khyoza uncharacteristically spoke up.

"Pardon me?" Orlov said, thrown off by the interruption.

"Gianakos, and that voluptuous French woman. I witnessed a conversation between them two years ago, when your sénéschal tasked me to kill Quade and your anomaly. I could tell they were sleeping together—and scheming together. I might have warned you, but your people were trying to kill me. That didn't make me feel talkative."

"Yes, well, we're all regretting not seeing through Gianakos' smokescreen sooner. For what it's worth, I advised Rockefeller against killing you and Quade. I thought you could still be useful."

"I gotta tell you, that makes me feel all warm and fuzzy inside," El said. "Get back to your bloody coup."

"Right. It's why I came to Yulian in the first place. We needed someone on the inside to tell us what Gianakos was planning next. His base of operations is in Reykjavík. And somewhere on that island, he has housed his Haruspex. That computer has cut us off from every high-level digital information source we once possessed. We must find out what he's planning next so we can come up with an effective counterstrategy."

"But what makes you think I would know anything?" Khvostovsky asked.

"Because apparently, he still needs the chairs to carry on with business as usual. Am I correct in assuming he did not inform you of his self-promotion to world emperor at your meeting in Tokyo two weeks ago?"

"He said nothing of this. But the meeting was disrupted by a fire alarm."

"I triggered that alarm. I was there to expose Gianakos to all of you, and then kill him; but he now has an army of clones protecting him. I barely escaped."

"I didn't see any clones, but if you were trying to kill him, now I understand his agitation."

"Indeed. For some reason, he needs to keep his plan secret from the chairs for the time being. I have to know why. Can I count on you to help us?"

"I don't know what I can do. But if I can help, I will. The world does not need an emperor."

"Look," El interrupted. "This is all very sad for both of you. But why should we care if your organization is in tatters? Y'all have been trying to take us out for decades. Why shouldn't we just wait on the sidelines and watch you people destroy each other? Have at it, I say."

"An understandable sentiment," Orlov admitted. "I'd probably feel much the same way, were I in your shoes. But the frank reality is our sides won't destroy each other. My side will be obliterated in fairly short order, unless I can find a way to stop Gianakos. And if you think recent history has been difficult, you have no idea what the world would be like under his unopposed imperial rule. Whose plan do you think it was to destroy your outpost in the Klondike region? Yes, I know about that. If he was willing to kill everyone there to capture just one person, what do you think he will do now that he has an army of clones at his back, and no Directorate to which he must answer?"

"As I told Gianakos two years ago, I will tell you now," Khyoza growled. "Those cloned lizards will never be a match for us."

"If by cloned lizards, you mean the 2-Gs that were deployed to the Klondike, you're a little behind the times. Those units have become our allies, and I control them. Right now, they're the only edge I have, because Gianakos believes they've been destroyed. No, my phantom friend, he now has an army of five thousand third-generation super-clones at his disposal. And they are capable of things you can't imagine."

"I have a pretty fat imagination," El mused.

"I thought the same thing, and then I encountered a few in Tokyo. As I said, I barely escaped with my life, and I'm probably as skilled as you are. That's why you didn't think you saw any clones, Yulian. They don't look like the 2-Gs. They look like any normal, athletic, twenty-five-year-old man."

"Wait," Khvostovsky said. "Perhaps he did have a guard with him then. There was just such a man in the conference room. I thought he was a caterer; but I didn't see any more than that."

"If you did, you wouldn't have noticed—they're all identical. I killed four of them, but it may as well have been the same one, four times."

"Other than bad news, you don't bring much of value to this negotiation, do you?" El interrupted. "You're basically saying we should join your cause out of a sacrificial sense of self-preservation? You're a piece of work, Orlov, you know that? Listen, we've done pretty well up to this point by hiding and waiting. Why should we pull your ass out of the fire now that you feel a little singed? Welcome to the club, pal."

"You're absolutely right, and I admit it. All I'm saying is it appears at this moment that our purposes align. We both desire an end to the current regime. If we remain separate, it's inevitable that regime will destroy us both—admittedly my people before yours, but eventually all of us. If we join forces, we may stand a fighting chance."

"And if I was to consider this idea of yours," El said after a long pause. "What would our part be in this war?"

Orlov turned to Pere, looking at him speculatively. "Apparently Gianakos is convinced this young man is some kind of a plague upon his house. And you people seem to think he's a natural disaster in the making, or something along those lines. Either way, I'd be a fool not to conclude he's somehow at the center of all this. So, I suggest the first thing we all need to do, at least for the time being, is keep him alive and free so he can continue floating around, blowing on things… or infecting things… or doing whatever it is he apparently does with such great effect."

"Thanks a lot," Pere interjected, sarcastically.

"I think we can both agree on that," El said to Orlov. "What else?"

"We should pause hostilities against each other and concentrate all our attention on the larger enemy."

"Sounds reasonable. Anything else?"

"I think it would behoove us to open a line of communication. Perhaps coordinate—only when we both feel it's beneficial, of course."

"And how do you suggest we do that, without compromising ourselves?"

"Yulian," he replied, pulling a small flip phone from his pocket. "Demyan asked me to give you this. He wants very badly to hear from you, and this phone is untraceable. If you don't mind, I suggest we give it to this group of refugees?"

"By all means. I'll contact Demyan at our next stop."

"That won't be necessary," Orlov said. "You can use mine. Demyan has the third. The three contact numbers are programmed into each of the phones." He handed it across the table to Khvostovsky. "This way, our three groups can at least stay in touch with each other without risking blowback. Does that sound amenable?"

"I'm not sure what amenable means," El said. "But how do we know you're not lying about it not having a tracker?"

"You don't," Orlov said, simply. "You have only my word, and no good reason to trust it. Look, I'm not trying to establish a deep friendship here, Quade. I'm just trying to keep us all alive long enough to figure out what to do next."

"Gimme the phone," Pere said out of the blue. "If I understand anything, it's what it's like to try to stay alive long enough to figure out what to do next. He's not lying about this, El. I'd know it."

El was silent for a moment before finally surrendering. "Have it your way, Falcon." Pere didn't know if he was mocking him or complimenting him, but he took the phone from Orlov's outstretched hand and put it in his pocket.

"You said earlier you haven't made any firm decisions about your next destination," Khvostovsky said. "If you come to Moscow, I could put you up very comfortably, and very safely."

Barnabas considered the offer seriously before finally answering. "I think it might be best at this point if we weren't all in one location; but we'll gratefully discuss your offer, Mr. Khvostovsky, and we will let you know what we decide."

"Please, call me Yulian. If you decide not to come to Moscow, will you at least let us know where you are going?"

"It would be better if we didn't know," Orlov suggested. "After all, what we don't know, we can't inadvertently reveal."

"Yes, of course. I'm sure you're right. I know little of such things. But may I at least offer some assistance?" He got up and went into the bedroom.

"Really, that's not necessary, Yulian," Barnabas raised his voice toward the railcar's bedroom.

"Nonsense," he said, emerging from the room with a stack of bills with the number 5,000 printed on them. He handed them to Pere. "Everyone needs a little help now and then."

"I can't take this," Pere stuttered. "It's way too much."

"It just seems that way, believe me. It's all yen. The conversion rate to your dollar is something like a hundred to one. I got some while we were in Tokyo, but I haven't yet converted it back. Please, I'd feel much better if you had it. You can get it converted to rubles when you get off. It will help to get you wherever you are going."

"I still don't think—" Pere continued to resist, until El cut him off.

"Take the money, Falcon; and thank the man." Pere was about to argue with El, when a knock came at the door.

"That would be Ehud," Barnabas said. "He's keeping watch and is probably getting worried about us. Would you mind if I spoke to him?" he asked Orlov.

"Another one?" Orlov replied. "Yes, of course, invite him in; but please warn him that we're not at war in here. I'd prefer he not attack me on impulse." Barnabas went to the door and opened it a small amount.

"Is everything okay?" Ehud's muffled voice asked.

"All is well," Barnabas replied.

"*Très bien*. I was beginning to worry. The train is pulling into Cheremkhovo. I thought you should know."

"Thank you, Ehud. We are nearly finished here. If you would continue to watch, we would all feel better."

"This I can do." Barnabas closed the door again and turned back to the others.

"I think this would be a good opportunity to contact Demyan," Khvostovsky said, dropping the yen in front of Pere and moving toward the bedroom.

"Don't say anything too specific, Yulian," Orlov warned. "It is possible that even your offices are under surveillance now."

"I will be very circumspect," Khvostovsky said, as he went in the bedroom and closed the door.

"I think we should get back to our seats," Barnabas said.

"But none of you has eaten anything," Katya protested, probably more out of politeness than any real desire to have these mercenaries in her railcar."

"We'll get something in the dining car," El said.

"Besides, Mrs. Khvostovsky," Rophe added. "We need to have a long talk, and you've probably had more than enough excitement for one evening. I know I have." Katya smiled, gratefully, and nodded.

The travelers filed out and made their way to the dining car. None of the tables seated more than four, so they chose two tables across the aisle from each other. Barnabas, El, Ehud, and Rophe sat at one table; Khyoza sat with Yael and Pere at the other. There weren't many diners in the car, and the constant low vibration of the wheels on the tracks created enough white noise that there was no real fear of being overheard; but they kept their voices down nonetheless, and tried not to appear as though they were talking across the aisle.

"So, what was your impression, El?" asked Barnabas, quietly after their food arrived.

"I think, for what it's worth, that Orlov was being straightforward—at least as straightforward as our type gets."

"What do you mean by 'our type'?" asked Ehud, who was chafing at not being in the railcar for all the excitement.

"I mean highly trained covert operatives like Khyoza and me. He showed all the signs. I'd say he's been *very* well trained. It might be interesting to fight him, just to see who'd win."

"That's your testosterone speaking," said Barnabas, sarcastically. "I was referring to his offer to ally with us. Do you think that was subterfuge?"

"To be honest, I don't think so. By the sound of things, his organization's in shambles; so he's trying to scrape together any kind of resistance he can. That sort of desperation can make for strange bedfellows. We know that better than most."

"What about you, Barnabas?" Rophe asked. "What were your impressions?"

"For what it's worth, I'd say this seemingly chance encounter was the reason we got on this train in the first place."

"If you are right," Rophe responded. "Then we need to decide our next move. Do we stay on until Moscow? Khvostovsky offered to hide us; but is that a good idea?"

"Jeez!" Pere interrupted from across the aisle. "There's more than 500,000 yen here!" He had been counting the money during the conversation.

"Don't wet your pants, kid," El said. "That's about five-grand where we're from."

"Still," Barnabas said. "It was very thoughtful, and I'm sure it will help along the way." He sighed and leaned back tiredly. "No, Rophe, I think we should *not* go all the way to Moscow; but I have no reason other than a feeling. What do you others think?"

"Though our new allies may mean well," Khyoza finally spoke up. "I would feel better if they did not know exactly where we were."

"I'm with Khyoza on that," El said. "But we're trained to be paranoid."

"I did not meet these people," Ehud added. "But this seems like sound thinking to me. But it raises the question: if not Moscow, where do we go next?"

"With this new money," Rophe said. "We could get on the train going back the way we came."

"We could," said Barnabas, thoughtfully. "But we have been nudged for months now in a particular direction—always westward. It doesn't seem very logical to go east again after all this. Does it?"

"What part of any of this has ever seemed logical to you?" El asked.

"Good point," Barnabas said ruefully.

"What's wreck-a-vick?" Pere asked out of the blue.

"Excuse me?" Barnabas said.

"Orlov," Pere said by way of explanation. "He said that guy and his big computer were in wreck-a-vick. What is it?"

"Reyk-ja-vìk," Rophe said, smiling, but pronouncing it slowly and carefully. "It's the chief city in Iceland."

"Oh," Pere said. "Well, wherever it is, maybe we should go there." He was just thinking aloud as he counted the yen again; but then he looked up and realized everyone was staring at him. "What'd I do?" he said, as though he'd broken the cookie jar.

"Why did you suggest that?" Barnabas asked.

"I don't know," he said, feeling on the spot now. "I guess I was just shooting the breeze. I mean, that stinking computer's been chasing me for two years. I guess I was thinking maybe it's time we turned the tables." They all still stared at him silently. "But never mind. Sorry, I wasn't really paying attention, to be honest. It was a bad idea, I know." Still, nobody said anything.

"Perhaps, it was just the right bad idea," Barnabas mused.

"If you're thinking what I think you're thinking," El said thoughtfully, scratching at his bearded cheek. "Then we're probably both losing it . . . because I'm thinking the same thing."

"We both may be losing it," Barnabas said. "But it *is* the last place anyone would expect us to go."

"And for very good reasons," Ehud offered.

"Wait a second," Pere sputtered. "You're not taking what I said seriously, are you? Honestly, it was just a bunch of 'blah-blah-blah', right Khyoza? Forget I said it."

"Perhaps, it was the Falcon who said it," Khyoza suggested.

"Not you too?" he pleaded with the taciturn Cossack.

"Nevi'im exhibit gifts other than just dreams," Barnabas said speculatively. Pere lowered his head into his hands. What had his big mouth gotten him into now?

After they had eaten, and were brainstorming a plan based on Pere's stupidity, Rophe suggested they were all too tired to take even their own thoughts seriously. Barnabas agreed that they all should sleep on it and reconvene for breakfast.

Pere and Yael returned to their seats and folded them down into the sleeping positions. They had not been able to afford sleeper cars, so this was the cheaper option, but certainly not the most comfortable. Yael took the chair closest to the window and seemed to settle down quickly. Pere was on the aisle and just couldn't get comfortable. After a while, he finally understood why.

"Are you awake?" he whispered to the obviously sleeping Yael next to him. There was no response.

"Yael," he whispered again, a little more loudly.

"Hm?" she finally responded, still half asleep.

"I need to tell you something."

"Can't it wait til morning, Pere?" she mumbled. "I'm dead tired."

"No, it can't wait another moment."

There was a long silence, and then Yael slowly repositioned herself, so she was facing him. "Okay, Mister Navi," she said through a yawn. "What's so important that it has to be said right now?"

He was going to argue with her about calling him Navi, but decided this wasn't the time; besides, he needed the mood to be right for what he was about to say. He took a deep breath. "You remember earlier when that Orlov guy was pointing a gun at my head?"

"You're joking, right?"

"Well, no; but I guess it would be kind of hard to forget."

"Just a little," she yawned again.

"Well, when he had a gun to my head, I started thinking."

"You *started* thinking?!"

"Okay, it was more like my life flashed before my eyes in a split second. Anyway, I was positive I was going to die there and then."

"To be honest, I had a few moments of doubt myself." She rubbed her eyes and opened them fully to look at him. "What's this all about, Pere?"

"Like I said, I knew I was going to die. And all these thoughts and memories rushed through my mind. In that moment, I realized the thing I regretted most was never telling you I loved you. So . . . I'm sorry I haven't said it sooner . . . I love you, Cam. With all my heart, I love you."

He didn't know what to expect, but her eyes suddenly went wide, and then filled with tears. Finally, she reached out and touched his cheek. "I love you too, my Falcon," she whispered. And they stayed like that until they dropped off to sleep.

Pere woke suddenly with someone gently shaking his shoulder. He looked up, until he could make out who it was in the darkened railcar.

"Abigail?' he said, adjusting himself into a semi-upright position. "What time is it?"

"Night," she whispered. "I could not sleep. I needed to talk to you." Then he realized that they hadn't had a moment to talk, so wild had the evening been. He rubbed his eyes and sat fully up.

"I'm sorry, Abigail. Things were happening so fast . . . But, I should have thought about your feelings."

"Are you truly my brother?" she whispered.

"That's not the way you should have found out," he said, gently. "But it looks like I'm your older brother, yes."

"I do not remember you," she seemed to be struggling with having no feelings of connection to him.

"There's no reason you should," he said, trying to ease her guilt. "You were still in diapers when it happened."

"What's going on?" Yael said, groggily, as she turned over. "Oh, it's you, Abigail."

"Hello, Valentina," she whispered, and then stopped short. "But perhaps that is not your real name, either?"

"No," she confessed. "My name is Yael."

"A pretty name for a pretty girl."

"Thank you, Abigail," she said guiltily. "I should apologize for how I treated you earlier. I wasn't very nice; but I thought you were flirting with my boyfriend."

Abigail giggled, quietly. "But I was flirting with him terribly, was I not?"

"*I* thought so; but your brother can be a little dense about these things."

"Hey," Pere protested.

"It does now seem very . . . how is it you say? . . . gross. I did not know I was flirting with my own brother."

"It's understandable," he said easily. "Apparently I'm pretty irresistible."

"In the mirror, farm boy," Yael said, viciously.

"Do your parents know where you are?" Pere asked.

"No. But they are asleep. And I cannot sleep. I remember nothing of you or my real parents. Can you tell me what you remember about me?

"Sure," he said, understanding. "I'll tell you what I remember, but it's not very much. The first thing you need to know is our father is still alive."

"*Nyet!*" she said, too loudly; and though she couldn't remember anything, her eyes filled with tears.

They talked for a long time before Abigail seemed satisfied that she had squeezed Pere for every bit of remembrance he could muster. Then she hugged him tightly and went back to her railcar. He and Yael slept for the little bit of night they had left to them.

15

THEY GATHERED IN THE DINING car for a late breakfast. Everyone else had been there early; but Pere and Yael overslept. They sat down across the aisle from the others and when they had finally gotten their food, Barnabas filled them in.

"While you two slept, we decided to go with your idea, Peregrine."

"I was afraid you were going to say that," he responded.

"Well, at least in general terms," Barnabas qualified. "Rather than going backwards, we're going to move forward in the approximate direction of Iceland. Rophe reminded me last night that she's from Sweden, which—if you know your geography—lies directly in our path. Her family owns a cabin in the far northern forests there. Our plan, as far as we've formed it, is to make for that cabin."

"Are you sure they still own it?" Yael asked, through a bite of her egg sandwich.

"It's been ours for generations," Rophe said. "But that's not what I'm worried about. As I told our fearless leader, I stayed at the cabin several times as a child. I was fourteen the last time. I know it's somewhere near the township of Jokkmokk, because that's where we shopped for groceries and got ice-cream cones; but from there, I would have to find my way from memory, and who pays attention to directions when they are fourteen?"

"So, you've already said," El interrupted. "But if we can get you to this Jokkmokk place, do you think you'll be able to find your cabin or not?"

"Easy, Brother," Khyoza admonished El. "She said she is trying to remember."

"I *think* I will be able to find it," Rophe finally said. "But I can't be sure. It was more than twenty years ago, El'zar. Did you pay attention to directions when you were fourteen?"

"There weren't many directions in our prison," El mumbled. "Only orders; but there are a lot of things about that place I wish I could forget."

"I'm sorry, El'zar," Rophe said. "I should have thought before—"

"Ancient history, Doc," El said without rancor. "But it doesn't change the central problem. We're basing an awful lot of this plan on a flimsy memory."

"We have based most of our journey on things far flimsier," Ehud said.

"I have an excellent memory, gentlemen," Rophe assured them. "I said I wasn't paying close attention."

"Then I think we must trust the good doctor's excellent memory," Barnabas said, brightly. El shook his head but remained silent. "I got this from the porter," Barnabas told Pere and Yael, referring to the unfolded map covering a large part of their table. "We're trying to plan the best route. I was saying before you two got here, that the easiest way would be to continue on to Moscow, catch a train to Petersburg, go overland to the Gulf of Bothnia, and hop a freighter into Sweden.

From there, it's only a few hours to Jokkmokk." Everyone was looking at the map.

"And I said," El broke in, with muted but imperative tones. "That I don't want to go anywhere near Moscow. Compliance presence is most concentrated in the metroplexes. If Gianakos has these next-gen goons stationed anywhere, they're going to be in the metroplexes, and Moscow's one of the big ten. I don't know what these things are capable of, but I don't think now is the time to find out."

"Of course, we were only exploring options," Barnabas conceded. "I actually agree completely with El'zar. Even if Compliance is still functioning during this civil war Orlov spoke of, their presence is not the only thing that's strongest in the metroplexes; video surveillance is multiplied exponentially in the great cities. So, you're right; we should go nowhere near any of them. Since we're in agreement on that, I'm open to other suggestions?"

They were all silent for a time until Khyoza pointed to a spot on the map. "What about here?" he said.

"Yekaterinburg?" Rophe said, peering at the spot. "That is not exactly a tiny town—but it will be less monitored than Moscow, I imagine."

"If we get off the train there," Barnabas considered it. "And convert the falcon's riches into rubles, we can make it overland to Sweden. There are major highways that run out of Yekaterinburg."

"That means we'll have to buy a contraband junker that runs well," El said, considering the route. "But it looks like we could drive all the way into Sweden." His finger tracked a meandering line on the map. "That way, we never get within a day's drive of Moscow, and we don't have to catch a second train or hop a freighter—where we'd be scanned again."

"All of our options are dangerous," Ehud said, quietly. "But I think this plan has a fair chance of success, if all goes well."

"Not exactly what I'd call a ringing endorsement," El said.

"If you want more, Brother, you must pay him," Khyoza said with only the slightest hint of a smile.

"It seems workable," Barnabas offered. "But I have no contacts in Yekaterinburg. How will we find anyone to purchase your junker from?"

"It's not a problem," El said. "Khyoza and I always know what to look for. We'll have a vehicle within a day of getting off the train; that is, if you can convert those yen to rubles."

"The train station should have a currency exchange," Barnabas assured him. "Okay, then; we'll get off the train tomorrow afternoon in Yekaterinburg and find a cheap motel while El and Khyoza get us an inexpensive set of dependable wheels. If all goes as planned, we'll be on our way to Sweden by the following afternoon."

The emergency page forced His Imperial Majesty to return to his office in the *Aulae Prīncipis* before he finished a late lunch with Liliane Genevois. He sat down at the Resolute desk, spun his chair around, opened the recessed panel to a communication wall that was an exact replica of the one in Reykjavík, and pressed the proper sequence of buttons.

"Voice identification," Minerva said.

"*Veni, vidi, vodka martinis,*" he said, still feeling a little giddy from three martinis he'd consumed at lunch. "What's so important, Minerva? Liliane was very put out that I had to leave early. We were drinking a wonderful lunch on the Piazza Navona. She's very possessive of me, you know."

"I have a feeling she won't mind this interruption, Your Majesty. Take a look at screen number three." It was a video feed of three drunken men stumbling through a terminal and onto a train.

"I feel a bit like that myself. What am I supposed to be seeing?"

"Allow me to magnify," the images became larger, and then, as though he'd been slapped in the face, Darien felt soberer than he had in weeks. "That's Lecha Zakayev!" he breathed, his heart pumping hard now. "And is that Quade with him?"

"Correct on both counts. The facial recognition analysis confirmed it."

"Where and when was this taken?"

"At the passenger train depot in Ulan Ude, Russia, approximately thirty-six hours ago."

"You said they were somewhere in North America. How the hell did they get to

Russia, and why would they go there in the first place?"

"I have no good answer to either question; perhaps they believed we would follow the bread-crumb trail south in Region 4—as we did—while they went in a completely unexpected direction."

"Then why, when they've evaded us so completely, do they get on a train, where they knew they'd be scanned?"

"For that, I can't even speculate; however, once I saw this feed, I did a deep analysis of every image captured at that depot within six hours of that shot. Look at screen two." The still image-capture came up of a young man with long hair, a spare beard, and a pair of green-tinted glasses, walking arm-in-arm with an attractive auburn-haired girl of approximately the same age.

"Should I recognize them?"

"I ran a reconstructive facial analysis on the male in which I removed the beard, the glasses, and shortened the hair; I then reversed the bone structure development to remove three years of growth into full manhood. This is what I came up with." The image on the screen morphed to incorporate the changes.

"John Percival," he was nearly breathless. "Sweet bloody bitch! It's him! That's our anomaly! Who's the girl?"

"I have no record of her in the database."

"No matter. Where are they right now?"

"They purchased tickets in Ulan Ude for Moscow. The train is at this moment somewhere in the vicinity of Kargat or Ubinskaya."

"Do we have anyone in that area we can assign to this?"

"No; however, we still have modest Compliance presence in both Novosibirsk and Yekaterinburg. But they're regulars, and I'd recommend against sending regulars to apprehend this particular group."

"No, of course not," he said, after forcing calm on himself. "You're absolutely right. We must avoid another Klondike fiasco. When are they scheduled to arrive in Moscow?"

"Two days."

"Two days?" He tapped his lips with his index finger as he considered the options.

"Okay, we need to do this right. What's your recommendation?"

"We underestimated them the last time. But we now have very different weapons in our arsenal. Whatever the plan, I don't think you should go. Things may get indiscriminately violent. I'd hate to see your carefully planned rise ruined by a random ricochet."

"Yes, I see what you mean; and thank you for your alliteration."

"Don't mention it. I recommend we send Damocles, with a significant retinue of Heracles units. If we station our people strategically at Yaroslavsky Terminal, we'll effectively corner them. They won't stand a chance this time."

"Define 'significant retinue'?"

"I've gone over the layout of Yaroslavsky. A dozen discreetly armed operatives should be twice what we need; so, let's go with that, to make sure nothing goes wrong."

"Won't twelve Heracles units stand out? They do all look alike you know."

"I am aware, Majesty. They've been working on disguise protocols in Khartoum. We can easily make twelve of them look just different enough that they won't attract lingering interest—and that's really all we need. They're not going to be in a line-up. They'll be kept separate, so the moderate differences in disguises will fool the inobservant passersby."

"And what if Percival gets off the train before it reaches Moscow?"

"With our timeframe, we can't physically cover two-thousand miles of track. It seems counterintuitive that they would take the risk of buying tickets to Moscow only to get off somewhere other than that; but we can and will digitally monitor the other stops just in case."

"How difficult can it be to cover the stops between where they are right now and Moscow?"

"That entails one hundred and fifty-three stops, Majesty."

"Good heavens. That does create logistical problems. Can we at least place one Compliance observer at each of the larger stops? A few extra eyes certainly couldn't hurt."

"That can be managed, but I still recommend we concentrate our attention on

Moscow."

"I agree. Contact Keflavík. Ask them to have our jet fueled and standing by. Wheels up in two hours."

"I'll get right on it."

"We still don't have Heracles units on Iceland, is that correct?"

"The barracks should be completed within the month."

"Damn! What's the flight time if our jet stops in Khartoum before going on to Moscow?"

"Ten hours to Khartoum, and another six to Moscow."

"Damocles will need another four hours in Khartoum to gather the troops. That's cutting things a bit close, isn't it?"

"You forget that these are Heracles units, not Orions. They'll be ready and waiting at the airstrip in Khartoum, and in Moscow with time to spare."

"Excellent. Now, I need to call Damocles and brief him thoroughly. We can't have him killing Percival as he did Bennett. I don't mind at all if Quade and Zakayev die—in fact, I'd prefer it; but I need Percival alive—at least until I've questioned him. Besides, I think I'd very much like to strangle him with my own hands—to watch the hope of my demise fade in his eyes as I squeeze the life from him."

The Khvostovskys invited the travelers to their railcar for late breakfast. The porters brought in extra tables and chairs. Yael sat on Pere's left and Abigail on his right, but the two kept talking past him as if they were fast friends—quite a change from their first encounters. Yulian Khvostovsky sat across from him. He didn't know what to think of this man. As the father of his sister, should he think of him as a stepfather? That didn't seem right; but was that why he had given Pere so much money? Did he feel some kind of parental responsibility? Or was he trying to buy Pere's affection for his sister's sake? It was all just too weird. He realized that Khvostovsky was looking at him strangely now too, and he figured the poor guy was probably trying to figure out the very same thing.

"So," Orlov said a little too loudly, signaling that all the small side conversations should pause. "Perhaps it is time to discuss plans. I have decided to go on to Moscow with Yulian and his family. Have you made your decision?"

"We'll get off in Yekaterinburg," Barnabas said. "Our plans after that are still developing."

"Well, we're disappointed you'll not be coming to Moscow," Khvostovsky said after a few moments. "But we all understand you have to do what you must; isn't that so, Abigail?"

"Yes, Papa," she said reluctantly, but Pere could tell there had already been a family discussion. He hoped she didn't try something stupid, like running away with them; because that's what he would do, after all; and it was probably why Khvostovsky was making it publicly clear that they had already had that argument in private—very smooth, really.

"I have factors in Yekaterinburg," Khvostovsky continued. "If there is anything you'll need there, I could make some calls."

"I'd take you up on that," El said. "But it's a good possibility any help you'd give us might be traceable by Gianakos."

"He's right, Yulian," Orlov said. "We must keep your connection completely hidden."

"Yes, of course," Khvostovsky relented. "But I know the city somewhat. If you'll tell me what you need, I could at least point you in the right direction?"

El looked at Barnabas, who shrugged. "What we need most is a locator-free vehicle that looks bad, runs well, and can fit all seven of us."

Khvostovsky thought for a long moment, before Orlov unexpectedly spoke up. "Make your way to Shefskaya Street in the north-east side of the city," he said. "Find a liquor store called The Comrade's Mart. Have you got that?"

"Yeah, I got it," El said.

"Go inside and ask for Vito Corleone."

"Vito Corleone? That doesn't sound like a Russian name."

"It isn't. And you're obviously not a fan of banned gangster films; however, the owner is. In any case, ask for Vito Corleone, and they'll put you in touch with the person you need."

"And how do you know so much of Russia?" Khvostovsky asked.

"I know far less than it seems," Orlov replied. "But, as it turns out, I had to conduct some off-the-books . . . business in Yekaterinburg a few years ago and had the opportunity to make use of a Samizdat there, as Demyan tells me you call them. He goes by the name of Vito Corleone."

"Fascinating," Khvostovsky mused.

"Thanks, Orlov," El said. "That's gonna save us some time."

"That's another thing," Orlov said. "Since we're going to be allies, even temporary ones, you should probably know that my name's not Orlov. It's Jonas Cavanaugh."

"I didn't figure it was Orlov," El said, unfazed. "And I'd bet it isn't really Jonas Cavanaugh either, but we'll go with that for now."

"You're not very trusting, are you?" Cavanaugh said.

"Just realistic. Phantoms were trained in an assassin's program developed by your Gianakos. Do you think a Judas like that would base a program like ours on trust?"

"No," Cavanaugh said, apologetically. "I don't suppose he would. I was fortunate to have had a kindlier master. I'm sorry."

"No harm," El said, lying; but Pere knew the traumas of El's youth had left wounds that would never completely heal.

"We are grateful for your help, Jonas," Barnabas said to smooth over the uncomfortable pause. "And the funds Yulian provided will probably pay Corleone's price. We can't thank you enough."

"I could give you more, if you need it."

"You've given us plenty."

"Would anyone like some more blintzes?" Katya asked politely.

"No, but thank you, Katya," Barnabas said for all of them. "We should go now and pack up our gear. We have a long trip ahead of us."

"Yes," Khvostovsky said. "I have a feeling we all have begun a long journey."

They made their farewells. Yael gave Abigail a friendly hug, and Abigail returned it in kind. Pere was going to do the same, but his sister grabbed him in a fierce embrace.

"Please, be careful, Brother," she said, her voice shaking. "Finding you after all this time, I do not want to lose you now."

"I'll be careful, Sis. I promise—if you promise to keep your head down, your mouth shut, and do what your papa says," he gave her a kiss on the cheek. "I'll come and find you as soon as I can. And I'll tell our father about you when I see him."

"What will you tell him?"

"I'll tell him you look just like Mom." Her eyes filled with tears for all the things she couldn't remember. And then he hugged her again and left.

The Gulfstream landed at Sheremetyevo a little past noon. Damocles had briefed the Heracles units only on those aspects of the operation they needed to know. He also assigned them each a number, Two through Thirteen, since they had no names, and he would need to maintain radio contact during the operation. He identified himself as Number One. They applied their disguises during the flight, and now appeared just different enough that they wouldn't attract any lasting stares. As they gathered their gear, Damocles placed a call to the regional Compliance manager, per his father's instructions. He confirmed two vans were in the VIP valet area.

They passed through the private hangar and found two cobalt blue Daimler vans waiting. They loaded their gear, left the airport, and drove to a flat near Yaroslavsky Station. It was a spacious converted industrial space that could easily accommodate thirteen. Once they stowed their gear, Damocles spread the ground plan of the train station on a low table. The Heracles units crowded around as he assigned a stakeout location to each two-man team. The target was now within his grasp.

Percival had evaded capture several times through a combination of Compliance ineptitude and dumb luck; but that was before Damocles Praefectus got involved. They would not escape this time—of that, he was certain. Yes, their capture was a foregone conclusion—and then they were his to do with as he pleased. His father wanted to deal with the anomaly personally, which was understandable; but he had given Damocles the green light, and complete discretion, on when and how to kill the others—just so long as a proper deep-probe interrogation had been done on each. Damocles spent the flight from Reykjavik to Khartoum imagining exactly how he would indulge himself with each of his captives. He looked forward to observing their reactions to certain unpleasant stimuli up close. It was a clinical curiosity, of course; but that didn't mean he couldn't enjoy his work, and he found inflicting pain on others very satisfying indeed.

Arkady Reznikov had been sitting on the same bench for two hours, smoking one Sobranie Black Russian after another. The train was scheduled to arrive at 15:30, but he came to the terminal early—just in case. For seventeen years, he had been a punctilious analyst for the Compliance Division in Yekaterinburg; but had never actually been in the field. This was not a dangerous op—he just had to watch the old Trans-Siberian arrive, and report if the two surveillance subjects got off. The Yekaterinburg office had recently been scaled back, so he volunteered for the detail—in these uncertain times, it was simply pragmatic to be seen as useful. He again studied the photo of the subjects, and the two young people pictured didn't appear dangerous at all. The male looked like someone who maybe smoked a little 'ganja', what with his long hair and green tinted glasses, but certainly not dangerous. The female was pretty enough, if you liked redheads—which he didn't except when it came to porn—but she was not dangerous looking either. It would be a simple afternoon's work, and his superiors would now see him as valuable—a win-win situation.

He turned the page in the Local section again. He had been pretending to read the same newspaper since he sat down. He pulled another cigarette out and lit up with his vintage Zippo lighter. He loved that Zippo; it had a raised image of a pirate embossed on the side. Having it made him feel a little adventurous. It was probably the reason he smoked so much—so that he could use it. At least that was his reason at first. Now he just liked to smoke. He knew it was not a socially acceptable pastime; even now he received disapproving stares from passersby. But he had neither a wife nor children—so he wasn't endangering anyone's health at his apartment complex but his own. He also had the extra disposable income to indulge in the ironically named 'Black Russians', so it was really nobody's business but his own. And besides, everyone needed at least one vice. He looked up at the large clock extending on an arm from the terminal wall. 15:35, it said; the train was late—not uncommon in Russia.

They pulled into Yekaterinburg-Passazhirsky Railway Station at 3:37 p.m. and decided to split into their groups again. Barnabas and Rophe would exchange Pere's yen for rubles; El, Khyoza, and Ehud would secure a taxi; Yael and Pere would browse in the gift shop until Barnabas and Rophe walked past and signaled it was time to leave. Pere had his hair pulled back into a ponytail and once again wore his 'Roy Orbison' glasses (he didn't really know what it meant; but when Barnabas called them that, it stuck.) He strolled through the terminal with his arm lazily around Yael's shoulder. He knew it was an act, but he liked walking with his arm around her. He wondered if he'd ever be able to stroll like this and really mean it.

They wandered into the gift shop like it was an afterthought, and began to browse through the greeting cards, even though Pere's Russian wasn't good enough to understand the colloquial idioms so many greeting cards are written in. Yael whispered something in his ear, and he laughed, though it wasn't at all funny. He started to look out the shop's window, but Yael turned his head back and kissed him—appearances must be kept up, regardless of the fear he was now feeling.

Reznikov's heart beat faster as he peered over his newspaper at the two young people strolling by. He had no doubt. They were the ones. He dropped his ninth cigarette of the afternoon and crushed it out underfoot as they walked unconcernedly into the terminal gift shop and began to peruse the cards. Folding his newspaper and setting it neatly at his side, he took the cell phone out of his lapel pocket and typed in the text, 'SUBJECTS SPOTTED, AWAITING INSTRUCTIONS'. He had to correct the spelling several times because his hands were shaking, and his English was only passable. Finally, he hit 'send' and looked up. The girl was staring right at him. His breath caught, and then he picked up his paper and acted as if he was reading it again. Had she spotted him? After a few moments, he peered over the top again and breathed a sigh of relief. She was kissing the male subject—his imagination was working overtime. How did these field agents stay so calm? His phone vibrated and he looked down at it, lying on the bench. 'MAINTAIN DISCREET SURVEILLANCE AND REPORT BACK', it said. Discreet surveillance? He was not a field agent, he was an analyst. He did not know how to be discreet.

Wait! They were leaving the shop and walking toward the main entrance. After a few moments of indecision, he took a deep breath, folded his newspaper again, left it on the bench, and followed. He had gone several steps when he realized his phone was still under the newspaper. He quickly returned, thrust it in his pocket and turned back around. Where were they? Had he lost them? No, *there* they were, but they were almost out of the terminal. He quickened his pace.

Barnabas and Rophe were successful. Pere's yen yielded about 250,000 rubles. That combined with the money they still had from their fishing excursion gave them a bit more than 350,000 rubles to work with. Hopefully it would be enough. They passed the gift shop and Rophe nodded to Yael as they continued toward the exit. Pere and Yael waited another thirty seconds before they left the shop and meandered toward the exit. They passed through the large entry doors and turned left. Half a block away, they saw El waiting by the open door of a large taxi van. He spotted them, and Yael looked straight at him and shook her head slightly. They continued past without stopping and Yael whispered out of the side of her mouth, "Watch!"

Reznikov walked through the exit doors and made a conscious effort to slow down. He had caught up to them in his excitement but did not want it to seem like he was following. They were maybe five meters ahead of him now and walking very slowly, like lovers on a spring afternoon stroll. Silliness! They continued to walk along the wide promenade. Reznikov wondered where they were going. Were they going to walk into town? He started to worry because the crowds were thinning, and he would become more obvious the further they went. Then two men were passing him on either side; except, they did not pass, they just kept pace with him. A moment later, he understood why.

"Keep walking casually," one of them said to him, in Chechen-accented Russian. "If you draw attention to yourself in any way, I will kill you. Nod if you understand."

Reznikov nodded like a bobblehead dashboard dog, and almost stumbled, but somehow managed to keep walking, though he was sweating now.

"Turn left at the next set of doors and enter the public restroom," the man said, with almost casual menace. "If you cooperate, you will live. This I promise you."

He did not need to hear it twice. Living was eminently preferable to dying. He was an analyst, after all, and a pragmatist by nature. The bureaucratic bastards should never have ordered him on this dangerous mission. He turned left through the smaller door, continued down the hallway and then to the right, into a restroom. The two men went right along with him. A moment later, the subjects of his surveillance entered the men's room as well. Reznikov was sweating more profusely now, as the big man with a black ponytail looked through the stalls and found them empty. He nodded to the girl with red hair, and she stepped out of the restroom as the younger man with the green-tinted glasses closed the door and leaned against it.

"I am going to search you," the evil-looking Chechen said. "Do not resist." He thoroughly searched Reznikov, placing everything he found on the stainless-steel counter next to one of the sinks. They were most interested in the cell phone and the photos. The Chechen read aloud the texts he had sent and received. The big, mean-looking man eyed the photo before looking up at the one leaning against the restroom door.

"Do you know any English?" he said in a tone that suggested Reznikov had better.

"Leettle beet," the analyst replied, now trembling.

"When did you get assigned this op?"

"Theese morning; I wolunteer."

"Who issued the order?"

"I not know. It come from Moscow."

"Text back," the big man said to the Chechen. "Tell 'em we left the terminal, got into an airport limo, and drove off to the southwest. That you're still following us in a taxi." The Chechen typed in the message then dropped the phone on the restroom floor and stamped on it several times.

"Knock him out," the big man instructed the Chechen. "Stick him in one of the stalls and make it quick. We're in deep shit."

Barnabas, Rophe, and Ehud waited in the taxi while the meter ran and the driver spoke to Barnabas, making small talk with him about the winters in Russia. Why was it people always talked about the weather in awkward social situations? It was apparently a universal practice.

The door to the van slid open and El and the others climbed in. Khyoza spoke urgently to the driver who sped away toward the northeastern part of the city.

"We're blown," El said, more calmly than seemed humanly possible. "If this Vito Corleone can't help us, we'll have to improvise." No one said a word. El continued in that crisp, calm, and infinitely unsettling manner. "Rophe, open the golf bag with the swords in it and make sure they're accessible; Barnabas, hand me the small leather tote inside the ball pocket on the bottom of the bag; Yael, keep an eye out behind us in case we're followed. We need to be ready for the worst."

16

JONAS CAVANAUGH WAS RESTING IN his private railcar near the front of the train when the small sat phone went off. He picked it up and hit the talk button.

"Yes?" he said into the receiver.

"It's me," the voice said on the other end.

"Quade?" Cavanaugh said. "Listen, we should only use this phone in moments of greatest need."

"No shit!" Quade's voice responded. "We've been made. Tell me it wasn't you, or I'll throw this phone out the window right now."

Cavanaugh felt a rare moment of panic, and then he stilled himself. "It wasn't me, Quade. I swear it."

There was a long silence on the other end. "We need Corleone to be ready when we get there. Can you contact him?"

"I'll do it right now. Is there anything else I can do?"

"Their operative told us the orders came down from Moscow. Was it Khvostovsky?"

"I'll call you back in twenty with an answer." The line went dead. Cavanaugh rummaged through his carry bag for his Springfield, unscrewed the suppressor, and stuck the gun down the back of his pants, pulling his shirt over it. He grabbed his small, encoded contact book. Rifling through the pages, he found the number he needed and dialed as he left his car and moved rapidly toward the back of the train. Passengers stared at him accusingly as he moved through the aisles. To hell with their rules about no technology—this was an emergency, dammit!

The Khvostovskys were enjoying afternoon tea. The pungent aroma of freshly steeped Assam was just filling the cabin when the urgent knock came at the door. Yulian got up and answered. Cavanaugh stepped in looking harried and dangerous.

"Quade and the others are being followed," Cavanaugh said, out of breath, as he locked the door. "Did you say anything to Demyan?"

"Nothing, Jonas! I told him the meeting went well, and to pick us up in Moscow when we arrived."

"That's all? Just 'the meeting'? No names?"

"No. I just said, 'the meeting'. I knew he would understand that I meant you, because the meeting in Tokyo was a disaster, and he was there."

"Would he have talked?"

"Never. I'd bet my life on it."

Cavanaugh sat down heavily in one of the chairs. "Call him," he said, handing his phone to Yulian. "I know he has all kinds of connections in Moscow. If the order came out of there, ask him to find out who gave it, but to do so discreetly and quickly. I have fourteen minutes before I need to call Quade back."

The taxi dropped them down the street from the Comrade's Mart on Shefskaya. They walked the remaining half-block and went inside; Khyoza approached the counter.

"Orlov sent us," he said in Russian. "We are here to see Vito Corleone." The shopkeeper nodded and waved them to the door behind the counter. He gestured them into the dimly lit back room and closed the door. A minute later, the door at the back of the room opened, and an old man entered with jowly cheeks, a little mustache, and graying hair slicked back with Vitalis. He wore a vintage three-piece pinstriped suit.

"You need getaway car, yes?" he said in raspy broken English.

"Yes," El said. "Did Orlov call you?" He figured it was probably best to use Cavanaugh's Russian alter ego.

"He call," Corleone said, scratching under his chin with the back of three fingers, and jutting out his lower jaw. "We can do beezness. How much you veeling to pay?"

"How much are you asking?" El said, a little thrown off.

"Make me offer I no can refuse," Corleone said in an even raspier voice.

"Okaaay," El said, confused. "How's seventy-five-thousand sound?"

The old man looked up at the ceiling and continued to scratch his chin as though he was considering the offer. "Eighty-five; and I throw in full double-tank diesel and four extra cans in back of van."

"Done!" El said, nodding to Barnabas who counted out the rubles and handed them to Corleone. "Now for something Orlov probably didn't mention," El continued. "Do you have anything in the way of small weaponry?"

The old man looked steadily at El for a long thoughtful moment, and then at the others, before shrugging. "I maybe have .38 snub-nose police special. But wery expensive."

"How much are we talking?"

"Seventy-five thousand."

"Fifty. And not a ruble more."

"Sixty, and I throw in twelve bullets."

"Sixty-five, and you give us an extra box of ammo."

"Seventy, and I make it three boxes."

"Done!" El nodded again to Barnabas who reluctantly counted out more rubles and handed them to Corleone. The old man folded them and put them in his pocket, turned to the door and gestured for them to follow. In the next room, Corleone spoke quietly to another young man in Russian who nodded and beckoned the travelers to follow. He went to the wall of the room and pushed aside a large storage shelf, revealing a downward-leading passageway. Before they went into the tunnel, Corleone spoke to them.

"If authorities find you, leave gun, take cannoli."

"Uh . . . I'll keep that in mind," El said. Yael covered her mouth to keep from laughing as they disappeared down the stairway. At the bottom, the young man switched on the long strand of bulbs, illuminating a moldy-smelling cement passageway. When they had gone a short distance, El said to the young man. "Your boss is an interesting fellow."

The young man laughed. "Is my grandfather. He is crazy, no? But it is not dangerous crazy, I am thinking. I do not know your word for it. *Ekstsentrichnyy?*"

"Eccentric," Barnabas said, with a wry smile.

"Eccentric! *Da.* He spends every night watching old banned Hollywood cinemas. He is wery fond of—how do you say it—*vory v zakone?*" He made the impression of someone shooting a tommy gun.

"Gangsters?" Barnabas said, though he knew it wasn't literal. 'Thieves-in-law' really didn't carry the same connotation.

Ehud finally understood. "*Le Parrain!*"

"What?" El said.

"*Le Parrain,*" he repeated. "What you call *The Godfather* in English. I saw it as a child in Paris. My parents took me to a classic film festival, dubbed in French, of course. That's why I didn't recognize the dialogue at first."

"*Da!*" the young man said. "*Godfather!* This is his favorite." They arrived at the other end of the passageway and climbed up the stairs to another door. Their guide opened it and pushed away the shelf on the other side. They walked into a large warehouse filled with a wide variety of 'stuff'. There was no better way of identifying it because it defied classification. It contained no end of odd bric-a-brac that would probably be deemed collectable by someone. Amongst all the other items were several old cars, including an ancient but pristine Lincoln Continental Coupe, a really cool looking Harley-Davidson, and a vintage Mosler Safe probably from old Chicago. The young man led El to the safe and positioned himself between the big man and himself as he turned the dial. When he opened the safe, El was surprised to see *four* snub-nose .38s sitting on the shelves.

"That old crook acted like I was taking his last heirloom," El said.

"Only thing *Dedushka* like as much as cinemas is making deal," the young man smiled as he handed El a Smith & Wesson Model 36 with three boxes of .38 rounds. He then took them to an old, extended Dodge Ram panel van and handed the keys to El. "I will open warehouse door for you."

"Thanks," El said and shook his hand.

"*Nyehzahshtoh,*" he said and went to the doors as the travelers loaded their gear and climbed into the van. El handed the revolver and ammo to Khyoza, who began to examine the weapon. When El turned the ignition key, the engine started right up. They maneuvered out of the warehouse and into the alley when the satphone rang. He pulled to the side and continued to idle as he answered it.

"Talk to me," he said. He nodded and said "uh-huh" repeatedly for about a minute, and then disconnected. "Son of a bitch!" he said to no one in particular.

"What is it, El?" Barnabas said.

"Khvostovsky didn't sell us out; but he used his connections in Moscow to find out who gave the order."

"And?"

"Cavanaugh said there could be only one source. A couple hours ago a group of thirteen well-equipped Compliance agents landed at Sheremetyevo out of

Khartoum. They were ferried to a flat near the train station, and then rushed back to the airport thirty minutes ago. That would be just a few minutes after that Barney Fife sent his text IDing the falcon. It's not much of a stretch to figure out where they're flying next."

"Out of Khartoum?" Khyoza said. "This is not possible. I am sure we two are the last of the phantoms."

"Remember Cavanaugh said this Gianakos guy had a new army of clones? Where better to house them?"

"So, these are thirteen of the 3-Gs he spoke of?"

"That would be my guess."

"This is not good."

"Are you *trying* to make an understatement?"

"How did they find us?" Rophe interrupted.

"Cavanaugh thinks someone caught image scans when we boarded the train in Ulan Ude."

"Someone or something?" asked Pere.

"What's the difference?" El said. "They know we're here now. About how long does it take to fly here from Moscow, Barnabas?"

"Maybe two-and-a-half hours."

"That doesn't give us much of a head start," he grumbled as he started to drive down the alley. "Get out that map of yours and tell me where to go. We need to get out of here as fast as we can. Khyoza, after you're done checking out the snub-nose, get out the Beretta. Make sure it's in perfect working order and all the magazines are loaded. Falcon, make sure the sword pack is unbundled—we don't want to have to be fumbling with straps if we need them. Everyone else, buckle in. This may get bumpy before it gets better."

A few years ago, Pere knew El wouldn't have included the second part of that statement. That he was trying to sound optimistic was a sign of just how worried he was.

O'Grady woke, violently shivering and drenched in clammy sweat. It took a few moments to realize with relief that he was not still in Iran. He tried to settle himself, but his breathing remained rapid, and his heart beat hard. The nightmare seemed so real. That last sniper mission went so terribly wrong. His intel was the worst kind of bad, the kind you can never forget, never truly forgive yourself for... he had mistaken a child for his target. Blew her head open like a ripe cantaloupe. The smells, the sounds, the palpable terror, all had an edge he hadn't felt in decades. It was still dark outside, but he wouldn't sleep anymore. He threw back the covers and climbed out of the damp sheets. Staggering into the bathroom, he turned on the shower. When it got as hot as he could stand, he stepped in and sat on the shower bench, letting the steaming spray flow over him as he leaned back against the cool gray tiles.

Rampart's doctors had performed their 'procedure' on him three days ago; and he'd spent most of the time since then in bed, at the doctors' insistence. But enough was enough. He had to get up and do something before he went stir crazy. He sat in the hot shower for twenty minutes until he felt life seep back into his heavy limbs. He finally turned the shower off and wrapped a huge towel around himself. When he stepped from the shower, the bathroom was hazed in dense foggy steam. Wiping the mist away from the mirror, a man stared back at him he hadn't seen in decades—a man whose eyes hid deep wells of fear just beneath the surface. Could others see it when they looked at him? These old ghosts hadn't visited him in as long as he could remember. Rampart warned him they might return after the procedure—apparently, he was right. Had these memories been shunted away from his mind for all these years? A part of him felt angry at having been 'treated' without ever consenting. But if he was honest, the larger part missed the blissful ignorance and longed for it once again. He turned off the light and walked out of the bathroom.

The sun was beginning to rise as he dressed in the clothing Rampart's people had provided. He pulled back the curtains and looked out at what was going to be a beautiful day. His throat suddenly tightened and his breath caught—it was *that* beautiful. As the tears streamed down his cheeks, he realized he hadn't felt this way in decades. Had he been a zombie all these years? He always believed he'd functioned magnificently. He'd been at the top of his profession. But he couldn't remember having one argument with his superiors since his days as a rookie, when he'd been widely known as a talented hothead.

When he left the suite, the mansion was just beginning to light up. Still feeling a little woozy, he descended the grand staircase, gripping the banister for support. He wandered through the foyer and into the grand dining room before he finally heard voices. Proceeding through the heavy swinging door into the kitchen, he found Rampart at the stove cooking breakfast for a woman sitting at a large breakfast nook holding a mug of coffee as if to warm her hands.

"Well, I guess we woke the dead, girly," Rampart said, spotting O'Grady. "How're you feeling this morning, Paddy?"

"I've felt better," O'Grady confessed.

"Yeah, that's what they say about the loss of those cogmeds—it's like seeing everything in color again, but that the colors are way too bright."

"Tell me about it. I just had a good cry looking at the sunrise."

"You need me to smack you around and tell you to man up?"

"I don't think that'll be necessary. Thanks all the same."

"Good. My hands aren't as hard as they used to be. Let me introduce you two," he said pointing at the woman sitting in the nook. "This lovely lady is Raphaella Moreno. She's a geneticist. She had her cogmeds turned off a few days ago too. She goes by Ella, just so you know. Ella, this is Paddy O'Grady. He's a dick." The old man laughed richly. "I've always wanted to use that line. Anyway, sit down. I'll make you some eggs, and I make a mean potato pancake too."

"Thanks," he said, and went to the nook, extending his hand to Raphaella. "Nice to meet you, Ella."

"You look like I feel," she said by way of greeting.

"Does it show?" he asked.

"Probably not. But I was up most of the night thinking that my heart was going to beat out of my chest, so I'm probably seeing you through a haze."

"Panic attack," Rampart said. "Used to have them myself, when I was younger; but I learned to control them with meditation, relaxation, exercise, all that healthy shit."

"I've never had one before," Ella said.

"See, that's the bitch of the cogmeds. They're great for stopping certain shitty feelings, but there're trade-offs."

"What do you mean?"

"Well, they level everything out, which is good; but they also level everything out, which is bad."

"That made a *lot* of sense," she said, sipping her coffee.

"Sarcasm? That's a good sign. So, let me ask you this, Paddy; why do you think we haven't had any wars for decades?" The detective shrugged, more interested in his first sip of coffee than answering quizzes. After a few moments, Rampart provided the answer. "No one feels angry enough anymore to start a war. Most people would see that as a good thing, right? But you may have also noticed that I have some very nice art in this house—it's all pre-cogmed stuff. It might surprise you to hear that though there's been no war in decades, there's also been no art of any consequence produced either. That death of creativity's a hell of a loss, don't you think?"

"I hadn't really thought about it before this morning," Ella confessed.

"No reason you would have; once you have the meds, you don't ever feel like anything's missing. You're content with things just the way they are. That's why I needed to shut yours down, because I need you both to think outside the box right now. But the tradeoff is that sometimes you'll feel like shit."

"So, if there are no wars because of these meds," O'Grady said, the coffee finally beginning to perk his brain up. "Why are your people in the middle of one right now?"

"Now, that's the right question, detective," he replied, bringing two plates of scrambled eggs and potato pancakes to the table, and sitting down. "And it gets right to the heart of our dirty little secret. Dig in you two, before it gets cold. Oh, I chopped some salmon into the eggs too—gives them a little extra punch . . . Now, what was I saying? Oh, yeah, why are we at war? No one at the top levels of power has cogmeds; never have had; so, we're all just as nasty as ever. We've been able to maintain peace over the years through a system of checks and balances. Apparently, we got a little lax in our oversight. Two very big players in our exclusive club have decided to go it on their own. They tried to murder the rest of us, and they were successful in killing off everyone but me. Elinor Prowell was one of the kills, Paddy."

Boma walked into the kitchen. "I just got word from our eyes in . . . maybe we should talk in private?"

"Spit it out, Boma. There's not much use in keeping secrets from these two now."

"Your call, Boss. Our eyes in Reykjavík report the sénéschal moved his base of operations and left that abortion of a son to watch over things in his absence."

"He's not the sénéschal anymore; and what hole did he crawl into—other than his bitch whore's—Sorry Ella. Did he go back to Milan?"

"That's what our people thought at first, but they were wrong. It's taken them more than a week to follow the breadcrumbs. It looks like he and Romanov moved to Rome."

"Rome? What the hell's in Rome?"

"The old Vatican Museum. If our people are right, they've remodeled the Apostolic Palace, and are doing business there."

"You have got to be kidding me!"

"No joke, Boss."

"I would have sworn he didn't have the balls for something like that."

"What's it all mean?" Ella asked.

"If I'm not mistaken—and I hope I am—it means that slick Greek's not only power-hungry, but he's completely insane to boot!"

"Sweet Jesus!" O'Grady intoned.

"Yeah, he probably says that every time he looks in the mirror."

His Imperial Majesty paced the floor of his office in the *Aulae Prīncipis* as Liliane Genevois sat watching the wall of monitors. Evening had come in Yekaterinburg, where the Heracles units were in position and ready to storm the small convenience store on Shefskaya Street. About an hour into the Gulfstream's inbound flight from Moscow to Yekaterinburg, Minerva received word that the operative

sent to observe and report the movements of the anomaly had been found unconscious in a railway terminal restroom. They determined that there never had been
an airport taxi carrying the anomaly back to Koltsovo. Minerva had Haruspex
scan every video feed in the city and discovered that the fugitives exited a taxi on
Shefskaya Street, entered the Comrade's Mart, and had never left. The store had
subsequently closed for the night and all the employees had departed; but the
targets were still inside.

"Everything's ready," Minerva said. "The exits are covered. They're awaiting your
orders, Majesty."

"Good," he said. "Put Damocles on." Operative Three walked to Damocles and
tapped him on the shoulder.

"I'm here, Father," The younger version of Darien said as his image appeared on
monitor number three.

"Remember, Son, you can kill them all, but *not* the anomaly. I want him intact,
and undamaged. Are we clear on that?"

"It will be as you say, Father."

"Signal the breach, then. We'll be watching from here."

It was an odd experience as they observed the action unfold through the eyes
of the Heracles units. It was like having twelve live cameras onsite, every monitor
carrying the view of a different unit. On Damocles' signal, both the front and back
doors of the shop were battered in at the same instant, and the troops rushed in
wearing night vision goggles, and carrying micro-DEWs, set to stun. Once inside,
they searched from room to room. After several tense minutes, they met in the
middle.

"There's no one here," Damocles said on the monitor.

"How is that possible?" Liliane asked.

"Switch to microwave scanners," Minerva instructed. "Look again concentrating
on the walls." They soon discovered the stairway. Liliane and Darien watched
through the eyes of the lead operative as they moved through the cement passageway, then up the stairs at the other end. Once in the warehouse they saw the junk
populating the space—including several older vehicles.

"Damn!" Darien said. "Go back to the video feeds, Minerva. Find out who left that warehouse!"

Within minutes, they were watching a digital feed of a faded, older model, brown van leaving the warehouse and driving down the alley. It didn't take them long to discover the same van on traffic cams heading north on P352.

"What's my next move?" asked Damocles.

"Head back to Koltsovo Field," his father ordered. "We'll have helicopters fueled and waiting. We'll keep track of them via traffic cams. You'll have them before this night is over."

They took their first break at a rundown diner outside a town called Solikamsk. El had been driving like a madman for nearly four straight hours, and even he looked frayed around the edges. But they all knew there would be no rest this night. They ate quickly and used the restrooms before piling back into the van. They were just about to go when the satphone buzzed. El opened it.

"You're on speaker," El shouted as he pulled out of the parking lot and headed back toward the highway.

"Vito Corleone just called me. He wants my head on a platter. Seems a group of *'pezzonvante'*—his word, not mine—just trashed his shop on Shefskaya Street, and he's gone into hiding."

"What's a *pezzonvante*?"

"You'd have to ask him; but from the way he described it, there were about a dozen of them, in high-tech gear, that broke down his doors. They also found his warehouse."

"Son of a bitch!" El moaned. "That means they know we took a vehicle."

"If you're on a highway, Quade, you've got to get off. They can follow you on traffic cams. Also, switch vehicles if you can."

"I can get off the highway easy enough," El said. "But there's no chance of switching vehicles, right now. How long ago did they hit the shop?"

"Within the last half-hour."

"That means we have about a three-hundred-mile head start. I can work with that."

"That would be true if they followed you by road. They have access to anything they need, Quade. If I were you, I'd watch the sky."

"It just gets better and better," El complained. "So, if they come in choppers, that gives us maybe ninety minutes. Do you have any other local connections?"

"Where are you now?"

"We just passed a town called Solikamsk."

"Never even heard of it."

"I was afraid you'd say that."

"I'll ask Khvostovsky and get back to you if he knows of anything. In the meantime, get off the highway—it's a deathtrap."

"Right now, everything's a deathtrap. We're running out of options." There was silence on the other end for a few moments. "Cavanaugh, you still there?"

"Yes," he said. "I was just thinking outside the box. There may be another possibility if things get really desperate."

"How much more desperate would qualify for you as 'really'?"

"Good point. I'll get back to you as soon as I can."

"Well, if it's longer than ninety minutes, you can probably forget it."

"Understood." The connection went dead, and the passengers in the van remained completely silent as El veered to the right and away from the highway. They would have to take back roads for the time being. That assumed there was any time left *for* being.

They finished cleaning up after breakfast and were having a third cup of The Puget's Best, when Boma rushed into the kitchen.

"Jonas is on the secure line," he said, breathlessly.

"Why's he calling here?" Rampart demanded as he got up.

"Don't know, Boss; he says it's urgent."

Rampart quickly left the kitchen with a worried look on his face. After a few moments of uncomfortable silence, Boma poured a cup of coffee, obviously feeling the need to keep an eye on the new guests.

"Who's Jonas?" O'Grady finally asked.

"The boss's son," Boma said, putting several teaspoons of sugar in his coffee.

"Where's he calling from?"

"I don't know." The man wasn't a good liar.

"I think I met him in Coronado," Ella said. "But he called himself Benoit. Are they the same man, Boma?"

"I don't know Mr. Moreau."

"I never mentioned his last name. Look, he already told me about this war of yours. He was on his way to Moscow when he sent me here with the Orions."

"Then you know pretty much everything, I guess," Boma replied, evasively.

"What are Orions?" asked O'Grady.

"Am I supposed to tell him?" Ella asked. "Or is that a secret too?" Rampart came back into the kitchen, obvious concern written all over his face.

"It's not a secret anymore, Ella. Why don't you take Paddy down to the sub-basement and introduce him to the troops," he said. "Boma, I need you to set up a camera in my office, and I need it fast. I guess I missed the target on that anomaly shit. Seems this kid's the real deal, and Jonas has forged an alliance with him. I sure hope that back door thingy of yours will get us into their mainframe."

"It'll get us in, Boss; but not for long."

"Can you give me two minutes?"

"Probably closer to ninety seconds; but we won't know exactly how long until we're in, and then they kick us out."

"Well, it'll have to be long enough, because my son's plan is depending on it."

A pair of Kamovs flew fast and low in parallel formation over the night landscape, approaching Solikamsk from the south. Minerva reported to Damocles that this was the last spot the traffic cams had sighted the fugitives traveling north on P343 before they left the highway. A van would be able to travel at forty to sixty miles per hour off the highway, which established a preliminary search radius extending approximately seventy-five miles in every direction from Solikamsk. It was far too vast an area to cover efficiently together, so Damocles ordered his pilots to split and cover designated quadrants separately.

"Switch to infrared detectors," he ordered Three. "We're looking for a van carrying at least five warm bodies—maybe more, but not less. If you spot such a configuration, radio back and we'll converge. Otherwise, maintain radio silence."

"Roger that, One," said the voice over the radio.

"You search west of the highway. I'll take the east."

"Will do."

"Good hunting. One out."

The two helicopters veered in opposite directions in the night sky. The hunt was on, and only time would tell if his game was trackable. He had no doubt he would find his prey; but truth be told, Damocles Praefectus never felt doubt about anything.

They were heading approximately northwest by the compass, in a heavily wooded stretch of dark country road. They had given up using the map almost immediately upon leaving the highway near Solikamsk, because it had no practical information on the back roads. It was nearing 11 p.m. and El had allowed no one to take over at the wheel. The exhaustion showed on the big man's haggard face.

"We need to stop soon, El," Barnabas said gently. "Or you at least need to let someone else drive."

"I'm fine," El lied.

"You are *not* fine!" Rophe said from the first row of the back seats. "If you keep this up you will drive off the road and smash into a tree, and we will all be dead anyway. You must let someone else drive."

"Don't tell me what I *must* do!" El growled. They were just about to get into it when the satphone buzzed. El pushed the button setting it on speaker. "You're late!" El said.

"So fire me!" Cavanaugh said. "It took longer than I expected; but apparently you are still alive."

"So far. Do you have good news for us?"

"They're pursuing you in helicopters. Two Kamovs left Yekaterinburg heading north at approximately 8:40 p.m. your time."

"That put them above Solikamsk at a little past 10:00?"

"That was my assessment, yes."

"So, they've been searching this area for nearly an hour?"

"Yes, and those birds are equipped with infrared ground radar; so, you'd best get off the road and under thick tree cover until we can figure something out."

"That's your good news?"

"I'm not done. Yulian has been able to arrange a covert pick-up for you, but you must get to Syktyvkar, where they'll be waiting." Barnabas was already unfolding the map and checking the location with a flashlight.

"That's three-hundred miles!" Barnabas said loudly. "How can we stop and hide under trees *and* cover that distance?"

"The immediate danger is the Kamovs," Cavanaugh said. "Right now, you need to get out of sight. Let's deal with one thing at a time."

"You said on your last call that you may have a plan if things get really desperate," El jumped in. "We're pretty damn close to that point!"

"It's a long shot, Quade, and based on several untested presuppositions," Cavanaugh admitted, then went very quiet. "Are you having engine trouble?" he finally asked. "Something doesn't sound right on your end." They then realized the sound of the engine was indeed getting progressively worse, as though it was misfiring, or had lost its timing. Then El slammed his hand against the steering wheel.

"It's not the engine," he shouted. "It's rotors! They're above us. What's your long shot, Cavanaugh?"

Damocles had scanned miles of terrain east of the P343 with no success when the radio came to life.

"Possible mark spotted—over!" the voice said. Damocles switched on his headset mic.

"What do you have?" he asked.

"An older van approximately seventy nautical miles west-northwest of Solikamsk. Seven warm bodies inside."

"What are they doing?"

"Just turned off into the woods. Lost visual; still got them on infrared."

"Do not engage. I repeat, do NOT engage. We've got your coordinates and we'll be there in—how long?" He covered the mic and asked Two.

"Twenty-five minutes, tops," the pilot responded altering his course to the west.

"We'll be there in twenty-five. Do you copy?"

"Roger that."

"Good. We're on our way—One out."

El maneuvered the van down the overgrown dirt path until they were at least a half-mile off the road and pulled to a stop in the middle of a small clearing.

"Everybody out!" he ordered. "They can't land anywhere near us in this thicket. That'll give us maybe thirty minutes while they find a spot and make their way back. Everyone, gather as much loose wood as you can. We need to build three large bonfires and we need to do it fast."

"But that will tell them exactly where we are," Pere complained.

"They already know that. But the flames will make night vision and infrared goggles useless. We need to level the odds as much as we can. Now move!"

They spent the next twenty minutes stumbling through the thicket with flashlights, where loose firewood was plentiful. They formed three large piles in a triangular formation, each about thirty feet from the others. El parked the van in the very center, and then he took one of the cans of diesel from the back of the van and liberally splashed the three piles. They could still make out the sound of the rotors above the canopy.

"Why haven't they landed yet?" asked Yael. "Is that a good thing?"

"Probably waiting for the other chopper to arrive," Khyoza said. "Why attack us with six when you can do it with twelve?"

"Thanks," Yael said. "You could have just said it wasn't a good thing, you know."

"I like to be precise."

When El had finished dousing the last pile, they heard the arrival of the second chopper above the trees; then the sound of both moving off to the west.

"All Right," El said. "They're looking for a large enough clearing to land those birds. Everybody grab your weapons. Rophe, I don't want you anywhere near this. Take a blanket and find a place to hide well outside the fire line. Wrap yourself in the blanket and cover up with damp leaves. Don't come out until I say so—or we're dead, and they're gone. Understood?"

Rophe was about to argue, but Barnabas took her by the arm and shook his head. "You will do as he says, Rophe," he said, firmly. "You need to be safe, so you can tend our wounds. If you're here, you'll only distract us when we try to protect you." She considered it for a moment. "And where will Barnabas be?" she asked El. "He can't fight, and yet he has not been banished to the leaf pile."

"Don't envy him," El said soberly. "Barnabas'll be in the van as bait. It'll draw their attention, and they'll move to secure it, thinking to corner their anomaly."

"That is, unless they destroy it outright," Barnabas said, mildly.

"Not gonna happen," El said. "Cavanaugh said they want to *capture* the anomaly, not kill him—at least not right away. They won't hit the van unless they're sure he's not in it."

"You're basing your whole strategy on syntax?" Rophe complained.

"At this point, it's all I've got," El said bluntly. "If they hit the van without examining it first, we're all dead anyway. Good enough?"

She considered a response before finally nodding curtly and moving toward the van, mumbling as she went.

"Barnabas," El continued. "Keep your eyes on us. Have the satphone ready and the code Cavanaugh gave us already entered. If they get inside our line, hit send. No hesitations. You got that?"

"Enter the code, hit send if they get inside the fire line. I've got it."

"The rest of you," El said to the four remaining fighters. "There's no mercy tonight. Every stroke of your swords must kill. Khyoza, you take the snub-nose. Only head shots, understand?" The Cossack nodded with a fierce light in his eyes. "I'll use the Beretta, without the suppressor—loud noises will be our ally in this. Ehud, can you climb a tree?"

"I will manage."

"Good. You, Yael, and the falcon find three trees on the three points of the bonfire triangle, but outside the fire line. Climb into the lower branches where there's thick foliage. When the 3-Gs pass under your trees, drop on them with a slicing blow to the neck. You gotta cut off their heads—I don't know the capabilities of these things, but that should slow them down at least for the immediate fight. Khyoza and I will be on the ground. When they come within our kill zone, you'll know it. That'll be your signal to rain hell on them from the trees. We'll only get one shot at this. If we don't take out at least five in that first moment . . . well, let's just make sure we do. Any questions?" No one said anything. It wasn't necessary. "All right, then. Find your trees. I'll give you three minutes before I light the fires.

THEY SET THE KAMOVS DOWN in a clearing about two klicks west of the target zone and moved out in black camos and night-vision goggles. Damocles advanced at the center of the formation leading his twelve killing machines east through the deep-night woods. Halfway to the target zone, they spotted a flicker-ing red-orange glow ahead. At two-hundred meters out, they had to jettison the night-vision goggles. The firelight was blinding them. Damocles was momentarily impressed. It was a smart tactical move to build a fire. He read the dossiers on

Quade and Zakayev. He knew their training; but they had no way of knowing the extent of his. Goggles or no, the phantoms were no match for the superior skills and intellect that Damocles Praefectus brought to the game.

He signaled the Heracles units to widen their formation and then moved stealthily through the foliage toward the flickering glow. As they closed to a hundred meters, he could see this was no simple campfire, but three bonfires roaring in a triangular formation, with the fugitives' van positioned in the center of the triangle. There was no sign of life, and without infrared detection, they couldn't pinpoint heat signatures. The van was bait—that much was certain. But bait to catch what? Was the anomaly hidden inside? Why would they risk that, unless they knew he was not to be killed—but how would they know? Assuming the anomaly was in the van, were there others with him? He had to be alone—bait to draw Damocles' forces into the kill zone where they might be more easily picked off. He considered for a moment before ordering his men to surround the encampment at a hundred meters out and await his orders.

Four minutes later, they all signaled via coms they were in position. Still nothing moved near the fires. He ordered his men to close to fifty meters. Still nothing. He considered options. Had they set the fires and moved off to the east, knowing he would waste time waiting for them to come out of that van? If his father had not placed unreasonable restraints on him, he would just lob a few grenades and have done with it; but he couldn't risk harming the *precious* anomaly. The old man had been ridiculously upset about Walter Bennett's death, as if that fat faggot had anything of value to tell him.

He sighed in resignation. He needed to get back into his father's good graces. He ordered his men to close to twenty-five meters—still nothing. He could wait until the bonfires burned out, but if this were a decoy tactic, they would be miles away by then. Besides, he had no interest in waiting. Patience was low on his list of admirable qualities—the refuge of the weak and indecisive. Since subterfuge wasn't working, perhaps frontal assault would shake loose some low-hanging fruit.

"You may as well come out," he finally shouted toward the van. The fires crackled, but nothing else made a sound. "You must know that escape is impossible," his frustration building. "You're completely surrounded. Face reality. It's absurd not to surrender." Neither movement nor sound broke the silent watchfulness of the woods, only the popping of knots in the bonfires. "If you come out now, I'll show you mercy," he lied, waiting for a response that didn't come. Annoyed, he ordered his men to close to fifteen meters. When they reached the marker, his com-link came to life.

"I have one of them," the breathless voice said in his ear. "A female."

"What's your location?"

"Twenty meters to your right, sir," the voice said.

"Bring her to me." Moments later two of the Heracles units appeared pulling a struggling, bound, and gagged woman in her middle thirties, twigs and leaves still tangled in her disheveled blonde hair. Damocles studied her for a long moment in the glow of the fires.

"Where are your friends?" he asked, calmly, pulling out the gag. She said nothing and wouldn't even do him the courtesy of looking at him. He nodded to one of the men, who grabbed her by the hair, yanking her head up so she had to face him. He pulled a Gerber LHR from his thigh sheath and held its cold steel against her cheek, just below her left eye. "Where-are-your-friends?" he repeated, slowly and clearly, enunciating each word.

"*Jag förstår inte! Jag har inte något fel!*" she squirmed, trying to look down at the knife. "*Jag är vilse!*"

He studied her for a moment. "*Vad heter du?*" he finally said, a calculating look in his eyes.

She stopped squirming and looked at him with surprise. "*Jag heter Tilde,*" she finally said, carefully.

"*Vem är du här med?*" he cocked his head, clinically observing her ocular reactions.

"*Jag är ensam. Jag är vilse.*"

He studied her eyes very carefully. "*Din jävla fitta!*" he growled at her. "I will ask one last time, where is the anomaly?"

She looked him directly in the eyes and raised her chin defiantly. "*Dra åt helvete!*" she growled back. He backhanded her with such lightning force that her jawbone snapped, her scream muffled only by her inability to open her mouth; and then she slumped, blacking out. He grabbed a handful of her hair and yanked her upright, dislodging some of the twigs and leaves.

"I think you will find it more challenging to insult me, now that you can't form words." He smiled, a cold gleam in his eyes. "Now, bitch, where is the anomaly?" Her eyes rolled up in their sockets, fluttering somewhere between awareness and oblivion, but she did not answer. "Very well, *Tilde*. I had hoped to be cordial; but you leave me no choice."

He yanked her into a headlock that left her little air to breathe, and positioned her in front of him, as a shield. He placed the point of his knife at her abdomen, breaking the skin so a trickle of blood wet her shirt.

"Flank me," he ordered the two Heracles units. "Close to ten meters," he said into his headset to the rest of his forces. Then he began to move slowly toward the fire triangle. "Do not resist," he whispered in her ear, but she had no resistance left. He emerged from the shadows, almost carrying the disoriented Rophe by the neck.

Pere discovered a perfect tree on the northern point of the triangle. The branches of the old maple were thick and low—only about eight feet off the ground—and the leaves were large and densely overgrown. He climbed into the lowest east-ward-growing branch and assumed a squat position with his katana pointed downward. Once his prey came beneath him, he would simply let gravity do the rest of the work. He hated the idea of killing. Even the death of clones at his hands weighed on his conscience; but he knew the stakes, and he also now knew what his motivating switch was. He would do whatever was necessary if he knew Yael was in danger. He would protect her this night or die in the process. El lit the fires and after a few minutes, the diesel-drenched wood burned with an intensity that warmed him on his perch.

The wait became interminable. He wished they'd just come so it would be over with, and he wished with the same urgency that they would never come and had decided instead to give up the chase. Then a voice broke the stillness. It was distant, muted by leaves, and loam, and the crackling of the fires, but adrenaline coursed through him at the sound. "You may as well come out," the voice shouted. "You must know that escape is impossible. You're completely surrounded. Face reality. It's absurd not to surrender." Was it true? Was it futile to hide? So much about this whole thing had seemed futile to him, for so long. Why should this be any different? "If you come out now," the voice continued. "I'll show you mercy." When had these people ever shown mercy? All they'd ever done was hunt and kill. From the moment he became aware of their existence, they sought to kill him—and they killed so many innocent people in that pursuit. Now they spoke of mercy? What was taking so long? Why were they holding back? He listened intently but heard no sound of approaching feet in the dead leaves beneath him. Only the fire filled the night. And then the voice came again.

"I have your woman," the voice now shouted to the stillness of the woods. But it was closer, now, more self-assured. He peered through the leaves and his blood froze. He saw Rophe, in a strangle-hold, looking nearly lifeless. "If you make any move against me," the man holding her shouted. "She will die." Then it happened, the black-clad 3-Gs materialized from the darkness into the glow of the fires. One of them was right beneath his tree; but if he dropped now, his actions would kill Rophe. If he so much as breathed, they would discover him. "I have orders to kill you, Quade," the voice shouted again. "And everyone with you. But I will be merciful. I will release this woman, and I'll let you all go your way, on one condition—that you give me the anomaly."

Barnabas was flat on his belly on the furthest rear seat of the van, peering out the window at the ring of black-camoed soldiers materializing just outside the triangle of fire. His thumb was poised over the send button on the satphone. He trembled, though he wasn't cold. Rophe was clearly visible in the firelight, barely conscious, sagging in the chokehold. Her shirt was wet with a circle of blood, made by the point of a knife held against her abdomen. Her breath came in ragged gasps. El had told him to wait until the 3-Gs were within the fire line to press send, but this had never been a part of the plan. What should he do? El had not yet responded to the shouted threat. What was he waiting for? The leader's patience seemed to end.

"I have made a reasonable offer," he shouted. "Now I am going to count. If there has been no response when I reach five, I will kill her. Let her blood be on your hands." Still no one moved. How could El be so heartless? "One," he shouted. Everything slowed. "Two." Barnabas' ears began to ring; he felt he couldn't breathe.

"Three." He couldn't watch anymore; but he had to keep watching. "Four." He would vomit at any moment from tension, but also from his sense of absolute helplessness. He was powerless to do anything. "Five!" The demon shouted so it reverberated through the woods.

"Five!" Damocles shouted with a deadly finality. Then he saw movement in a pile of dead leaves just beyond the fire line opposite his position. A man rose up from the leaves, his open, empty hands thrust in the air.

"Wait, Darien!" he shouted. "Please, do not harm her."

Damocles stared across the flames for a long moment. "Lecha Zakayev, if I'm not mistaken," he said.

"You are not mistaken," Zakayev said, simply. "I beg you, Darien, please let the woman go."

"I think not, Phantom," Damocles replied with derision. "And you've mistaken me for my father. Apparently, we look very similar. Tell me, Zakayev, where is Quade?" Then his eyes widened slightly as he felt cold steel touch the back of his head.

"I'm right behind you, you son of a bitch," Quade said through gritted teeth, pulling back the hammer on his weapon with a disquieting click. "And I'd consider my friend's request very carefully if I were you."

"But you are *not* me," Damocles said without flinching. "And you clearly have no idea who you're dealing with." With that, he plunged the knife into Rophe's abdomen and whirled with such inhuman speed that Quade had time only to get one deflected shot off before Damocles knocked him like a rag doll into the broad trunk of a sycamore nearly ten feet away. He felt the icy heat in his shoulder where the bullet had entered but ignored it. He advanced on the disoriented Quade as the fool bellowed, "SEND!"

Darien Gianakos and Liliane Genevois watched the action unfold on twelve separate monitors. Darien, no longer able to stay in his chair, paced as the Heracles units closed on the target zone, and the roaring fires came into focus.

"Where *are* they?" he demanded of no one in particular.

"Give him time," Minerva said. "He has the situation in hand." Then Damocles stepped into the circle of light, dragging a nearly unconscious woman by the neck.

"Who's that woman, and what's he doing?" Darien asked.

"He's offering a hostage trade, I think," Liliane said.

"But those weren't his orders," Darien complained.

"He'll never abide by the offer, *mon cher.*"

"How do you know?"

"Would you?"

He considered that for a moment. "Point taken," he finally said. Then the focus of the visual feed panned to a man getting up out of some leaves with his hands in the air."

"Lecha Zakayev," said Minerva.

"Finally, proof!" Darien shouted. "We have *got* them!"

"Yes, however," Minerva said. "Direct your focus to monitor 4 and the back of his pants."

"What is it?" asked Darien. "Is that a gun in his belt?" But the view shifted again back to Damocles. There was a man now standing behind him.

"That's Quade," said Minerva.

"What's he doing?" Darien demanded.

"I think he has a gun pointed at Damocles' head," Liliane said.

Even on the monitors, Damocles' sudden defensive measures seemed almost a blur; and Quade had been thrown against a tree, with Damocles closing on him.

Then every monitor in the office went dark for an instant, before all twelve came to life again, filled with the image of a single smiling face.

"What is this, Minerva?" Darien demanded. But he received no answer, just that grinning face.

"Hello Darien," the smiling image said in jovial greeting. "Oh!" he continued in glee. "What unexpected luck! It's a twofer. Madame Romanov is with you as well. Such a surprise! How the hell have you two been? I gotta say, I'm a little hurt that you haven't called. An old man gets lonely when his friends don't stay in touch."

The two stared at the monitors, dumbfounded for a moment, before the impossible reality finally set in.

"Will Rampart?" Liliane said, aghast.

"Bingo!" the old man replied, laughing. "Full marks for you, dearie."

"But... But, you're dead!" Darien said, his voice several pitches above its normal register.

"You know, I read that in the papers too. Your voice sounds a little high, Darien. Have you lost your balls, or did that cathouse whore you're shacking up with chew them off?"

"How dare you!" Liliane went red with fury.

"Oh, but I do dare, Lily," the old man said gleefully. "What, you don't think my description of you is accurate?" And then he lowered his voice conspiratorially to her. "I'll bet you never told dear Darien here, that you and I once had our own little bam-bam in the ham moment. I'll tell you what Darien, she was a lot younger then, but she couldn't get enough of me. She was doing squat thrusts in my cucumber patch until I was pert near pickled."

"You filthy bastard!" shrieked Liliane.

"Filthy as they come, sweet tits—but at least I'm not a lying rat. Your father would disown you if he saw the power-whore you've become. Tell you what, Darien. She's a little *old* for my tastes, now; why hell, she's even too old for you. But, if you'd be so kind as to kill her for me, I might consider taking you back."

"I WILL HAVE YOU FLAYED!" Liliane was nearly apoplectic. "You impotent little troll. I'll make you wish—"

"Shut up, Liliane!" Darien interrupted.

"I beg your—"

"I said shut up!" Her eyes bulged ominously, but she became still.

"Your good health is remarkable, Will," Darien said forcing himself to appear calm. "However, right now, I need my system back. We are in the middle of a very important operation."

"Don't you think for a moment you can call me Will, you little prick. I was your betters before your little coup; and I'm still your betters now."

"Be that as it may, I'm asking you please to release my system? We've cornered the anomaly, Mr. Rampart. We're on the verge of achieving everything we've worked for."

"Do you think I give a rat's ass about what you've worked for? You and your bitch-whore killed some of the only people in this world I called friends. And I guarantee you, you slimy little fuck, that I'm going to repay you both with interest. And just so you know, I'd never have gotten into your 'system' if your saggy slut there hadn't left her little calling card when she came to visit me. Kinda like a bad case of the clap." Liliane picked up a paperweight off the desk and flung it at the monitors, shattering one of them into a spidery web of cracks. Darien placed a firm hand on her arm to stop any further outbursts. Rampart cackled gleefully. "We followed that idiot backdoor program key she left right back to you. What goes around comes around, sonny; or hadn't you heard?"

"Mr. Premier," Darien whined. "I'm begging you—" Then, as suddenly as they had come, the images of William Rampart were gone, replaced by a silent blackness. "Hello? Are you still there Mr. Premier?"

"It's me, Darien," Minerva's voice said.

"What happened?"

"Haruspex was compromised. But I assure you, the invading worm has been neutralized, and we're back online again, at full capacity."

"You can explain it all later, but right now, get our video feeds back up so I can see what's happening in Russia!"

"They *are* back up. It's the first thing I did after the incursion. What you see is what we're getting from all twelve sources."

"But the monitors are blank!"

"Precisely."

"SEND!" El rasped as loudly as he could. By some miracle, or a deeply ingrained result of years of brutal training, he still clutched the Beretta in his hand as he leaned against the broad sycamore's trunk. It was pure instinct that drove him to raise the weapon and fire at the shadowed hulk closing on him. The force of that blow stopped the advance, but it didn't down the man. El fired again, and the silhouetted mass staggered back a few steps, but then came forward again. He then fired four times in rapid succession. The man finally dropped to his knees and, after a moment of stasis, toppled forward onto the loam.

El sucked in a few searingly painful breaths. He had struck the tree with such force that it knocked the wind out of him, and probably cracked a few ribs. As the ringing subsided in his ears and his vision cleared, he could hear the repeated explosive concussions of Khyoza's .38 somewhere nearby. He forced himself to his feet, the pain in his side nearly blacking him out again, and shambled toward the sounds. He first encountered the two clones who had been flanking their commander. They were just staring at him, as though they couldn't believe he'd just killed their leader. He raised the Beretta and put a bullet through each of their foreheads. They didn't even flinch. Their heads just exploded in a fine red mist as they collapsed backwards. Like a wounded bear, he continued to stalk the kill zone, rage building in him to a fine point, holding at bay the dizziness that threatened to overcome him. He came upon two more 3-Gs in rapid succession and dispatched them as effortlessly as he had the first two. They simply stared at him as he made the kill shots.

He nearly stumbled and fell, and then saw Yael running toward him, as though in slow motion, her blade red with fresh blood. The snub-nose had stopped firing. She dipped her head under his arm to support him. The pain again shot through him like a bolt of lightning, he would have collapsed had she not been holding him up. He pulled in a few small gasps—full breaths impossible. As his vision widened again, he saw the ring of fire littered with the corpses of black-clad clones. Why had they offered no resistance? Barnabas was now running from the van, but not toward him. Where was he going? Then it came back to him—Rophe!

The snub-nose had fired its last bullet, but Khyoza kept pulling the trigger over and over again. There had to be more to kill. There just *had* to be. He needed to kill more, but they were all dead. He spun searching desperately for another victim he could spend his rage on, but it was useless. He killed five of them and it had not sated his fury. He then stopped and turned to the spot he was most avoiding. She lay on her back, in the firelight, the handle of the knife still protruding from her blood-soaked abdomen. Staggering to her, he slumped to his knees, but had no idea what to do. He had no training on how to save, only how to kill. He tucked the gun in his belt and gently took her in his arms, lifting her. She coughed, spitting droplets of blood onto his already brain-spattered jacket. Somehow, she was still alive.

"Rophe," he whispered close to her ear. "I will get you out of here. This I promise you."

"It's no use, Khyoza," she whispered. "I won't survive. Leave me now and get the falcon to safety."

"I will NOT leave you," he whispered with intensity. "You *will* live! Do you hear me? You *must* live!" But she had already slipped back into unconsciousness. Then Barnabas was there.

"Is she alive?" he asked, breathing hard.

"Barely," Khyoza replied.

"We need to get her to the van."

"We are miles from help. She does not have that kind of time!"

"The choppers," El wheezed, as he came up behind them, still supported by Yael. "Let's get her in the van, Brother. We'll drive to the choppers. It's her only chance." Khyoza remained locked in a moment of desperate indecision, and then nodded.

Barnabas scanned the fire ring. "Where are Peregrine and Ehud?" he asked.

"We are all right," Ehud called out from the far end of the triangle, emerging from the woods. Peregrine supported him as he limped badly. "I think I broke my ankle when I jumped from the tree; but we both took out our targets."

Peregrine helped Ehud to the van then rushed over to the others. They gently lifted the unconscious Rophe. El tried to help, but it was all he could do to stay on his feet.

"Why did you leave the knife in her like that?" Peregrine asked through gritted teeth as they carried the doctor.

"If we pull it out here," El labored to speak. "Her guts might come out with it." Khyoza shot him and angry look. "Sorry, Brother," he wheezed.

They carefully laid her on one of the bench seats in the rear of the van and the others piled in behind to hold her in place. Barnabas started to open the passenger door, when El stopped him.

"You're gonna have to drive," he said. The older man nodded and ran to the driver's side, got in, started the engine, and then looked up at El. "They set the birds down somewhere in that direction," the big man said, pointing west and wincing with the gesture.

Eight minutes later, they found the clearing. The Kamovs sat in the tall grass. They carefully carried the still unconscious Rophe and positioned her in the back of one of the choppers.

"You're gonna have to fly this thing, Brother," El said. I hope you remember your training."

"I will fly her," Khyoza said determinedly, as he climbed into the cockpit to familiarize himself with the controls.

"Come with me, Falcon," El said as they went to the second Kamov and checked its contents. After a few minutes of rummaging, Pere found what El was looking for. The big man took two of the back-up ordinances the troops had brought, set the timers for ten minutes, and placed one atop the other grenades and surplus weaponry in the chopper. He gave the other to Pere and told him to set it on the dashboard of the van. They returned to the first Kamov as the rotors were beginning their slow starting spin. El climbed gingerly into the copilot's chair and proceeded to yank the wires from the radio and the locator beacon. Within minutes, the bird was airborne, and they were flying northwest, skimming the treetops.

"Barnabas," El shouted over the thrum of the rotors. "Gimme the satphone." Barnabas handed it over and El entered the pre-programmed number. It rang twice.

"It's me," the voice said on the other end.

"Whatever you did," El shouted. "It worked. But we have wounded. We're in one of the Kamovs and we need trauma pick-up. Can you manage it?"

Cavanaugh sounded as though he was mumbling, then his voice was clear again. "Yulian says to continue northwest toward Syktyvkar. We'll call you back in fifteen with a location and you can fill us in on the triage needs."

"We're in your hands," El said and disconnected the phone.

The fires had burned down to mostly embers when Damocles' hand twitched as he grabbed a handful of loam from the forest floor. Within moments, he was sitting up, amazed to be alive; then two wicked blasts reverberated from the west followed by a series of smaller detonations. He staggered to his feet and looked around the battlefield. All twelve operatives were down. The van was gone. The woman was gone, and his Gerber LHR was gone with her. He would miss that knife. It was his favorite.

He spent the next thirty minutes dragging the corpses of his operatives, three severed heads, and any spare wood he could find to make a huge pyre mound where the van had once been. The can of diesel the fugitives had discarded had nearly two gallons left. He soaked the bodies and the wood, grabbed a still-smoldering branch from one of the triangular blazes, and threw it onto the carrion mound. Within moments, it burned fiercely, and a sickening charnel stench filled the woods. The bodies would be discovered, but their oddities would not be easily recognizable through the blackened char. Their enterprise still needed secrecy, at least for the time being. This was not an ideal way to dispose of them, but it would have to do.

He moved out to the west, still weak and bleeding slightly, but he assumed the bullets must have missed all his important organs. He was very lucky. He made his way to the clearing. One of the Kamovs was a smoldering heap of twisted metal, the other gone, and the van, now a burned-out wreck. His COMs were down; they had been linked to the Kamovs. He coughed, spat blood on the ground, and began the three-hour hike to the nearest village. His mission had failed, he knew, but not through any error of his own. Whatever or whoever the cause, he would discover it, and repay the responsible parties threefold.

The Kamov flew through the nearly moonless night and set down in a dark field twenty miles south of Syktyvkar, where two black extended vans waited. Four men carried a stretcher from the first van, efficiently placed the now barely breathing Rophe on it, returned to the van, where they gently loaded her in the back. Two of the men stayed in the back to work on her, while the third and fourth closed the rear doors, climbed in the front, and drove away. Three men came from the other van and helped the remaining six travelers in. Two of those men got back into the van. The third went to the Kamov, lifted off, and flew it away into the night sky. There would be no trail leading here.

The passengers remained silent as they drove through the Russian night—not out of impoliteness; they were just too exhausted, or too broken to speak. A half-hour later, they left the paved surface and drove further into the woods on a packed-dirt road. After maybe ten more minutes, they passed a gate and the van pulled into a large barn and stopped. The lead van had already arrived and Rophe was gone.

"Where are we?' Barnabas asked.

"An exclusive veterinary facility," the driver responded in solid English. "It is mainly for horses, but the facilities are top notch."

"A veterinary hospital?" Khyoza complained.

"Do not worry," the other man said. "The best trauma surgeons are already here. A horse doctor is not operating on your friend. Come. Some of you need medical attention. Let us get you inside."

They climbed out of the van to find two orderlies waiting with wheelchairs. They got Ehud into one of them, but El refused the other. They went into the main facility, which was very exclusive indeed. A woman of obvious importance addressed them in perfect native English.

"My name is Miriam Trouter," she said in a businesslike manner. "But everyone calls me Mimi. A doctor will examine each of you, but let's first see to the most severe." She nodded to the orderly who wheeled Ehud down the hall. Then she looked at El. "Come with me and we'll take a picture of those ribs."

"I'm fine," El said unconvincingly.

"Of course you are, but why don't we take an x-ray anyway. It'll only take a minute, and that way you'll get to show off your marvelously chiseled muscles." She didn't smile even a little bit.

"Whatever," El said, but he followed her down the hall.

"Wait," Khyoza said. "There was a woman in the other van?"

Mimi paused for a moment before turning back to face him. "She's in surgery. I'll let you know the moment there's anything definitive." Then she turned and led El down the hall. They could do nothing else, so they sat on the comfortable chairs in the waiting area staring at the walls. All, that is, but Khyoza, who paced. Pere had never seen the quiet Cossack like this. He had always been so still and calm. He didn't think anything could change that demeanor. He looked at Yael, who was watching Khyoza with a sympathetic look in her eyes. Thirty minutes later, El emerged from the examination area walking stiffly with an upright posture.

"Three cracked ribs," he said. "She wrapped me so tight I can barely breathe." He lowered himself carefully into a chair, grunting the whole way. "Any word on Rophe?" Yael shook her head and they continued to wait. An hour later, they rolled Ehud out. His leg was propped up and in a cast to his knee.

"It is broken," he admitted, embarrassed. "I am ordered to stay off it until we leave. I would use crutches, but it is difficult to manage them with one hand." He looked around and no one responded with enthusiasm. "Still no word on the doctor?"

"Nothing," El said, looking very drowsy. He was fighting hard to resist the side effects of the pain medication.

When the surgeon finally came out near dawn, El and Ehud were deeply asleep on two of the sofas; but the others still waited. "I would be lying to you," he said in quiet accented English, "if I said things looked good. She has made it through the surgery. Nevertheless, the damage was extensive. We have repaired her internal organs and wired her jaw, but her body has experienced incredible trauma. The next forty-eight hours will be critical. If she can survive that long, then I will say there is reason to hope. I am sorry I cannot give you more, but what I have told you is my honest medical assessment."

"Thank you, Doctor," Barnabas said. "We're grateful for your efforts."

"We shall see if they bear the desired fruit."

Mimi came out again and showed them to rooms where they could sleep, all but Khyoza, who insisted on sitting with Rophe.

William Rampart sat behind his desk, sipping his first scotch of the afternoon. He planned to have several more. A celebration was in order, after all. He hadn't felt this alive in months. The scrambled phone on his desk buzzed and he picked it up.

"It worked, Father!" the voice said on the other end.

"Damn right it worked," the old man chuckled. "You should've seen their faces, son. 'But. . . But. . . You're dead'," he mimicked Darien. And Liliane just about had puppies on the spot." He laughed again richly. "I haven't had so much fun in. . . Well, I can't remember the last time."

"Yes, Father," Cavanaugh interrupted the old man's reverie. "But you're in greater danger now than you've ever been."

"You let me deal with that, sonny. You just concentrate on getting the other Consortium chairs. I assume Khvostovsky's on board?"

"Very much so. Did you know, by the way, that their adopted daughter was Percival's sister?"

"No shit? I'd never even heard of Percival until two years ago. That's one hell of a coincidence."

"Yes, quite, if you accept that sort of thing."

"Well, it definitely wasn't any plan of ours, but I'll take whatever we can get these days. Now, is your group of renegades out of immediate danger?"

"They are for the time being. And they have committed more than twelve-hundred trained soldiers to our cause."

"Things are looking up. That gives us about twenty-five hundred to their five thousand. Piss-poor odds, but at least we can still piss. Who are you approaching next?"

"Khvostovsky suggested Patel at Bediya. Says he was his mentor. He's pretty sure he'd be receptive."

"He may be right; but I think you better save him for later. Go to Neumeyer next at Oceania. She's always groused at being given the ass-end of the world down under. Tell her if we succeed and she helps, we'll give her New York."

"Appealing to her ambitions? I'd hoped for nobler reasons."

"We all have our pressure points, Son. Try the noble angle first but keep New York as a sweetener."

"I'll take it under advisement. Now I suggest you have your attractive skipper make another run down to Coronado with Ella. Sixty more Orions at Hunts Point couldn't hurt; particularly since Gianakos is probably going to feel savagely vindictive right now."

"Might not be a bad idea," the old man admitted. "Because even if he has a cooler head, his vixen's in heat right now and wants to rip my head clean off." He again laughed like a gleeful child and downed his scotch in one gulp.

"The incursion was timed perfectly," Minerva said to the Emperor and Empress sitting dejectedly in Darien's office.

"Three hours of analysis, and that's all you have?" Darien responded.

"There's a high probability it was not a coincidence."

"That does nothing for us right now. Is there still no data from the Heracles units? And where the hell is my son?"

"The Heracles units remain offline."

Darien poured himself his third glass of bourbon and paced impatiently, no closer to a solution than he was three hours ago. Then he looked at the pouting Liliane who remained relatively quiet. "Listen, I'm sorry I told you to shut up, Liliane. It was the stress of the moment."

"Oh, bother that," she said with a wave of her hand. "I'm considering what Minerva said. We would be foolish to dismiss the timing of Will's attack. If they had help, Darien, it stands to reason that it came from within our organization."

"That's impossible!" he retorted. "The circle is far too small at this point. Are you suggesting Damocles has turned?"

"Not necessarily. I'm just stating the obvious, *mon cher*. Will knew when to breach our defensives, and apparently the effect a momentary disconnect would have on our operatives. With Haruspex's uplink severed, they were sitting ducks. That cannot be coincidence."

"You have an incoming call," Minerva interrupted. "Its point of origin is Perm Krai in western Russia."

"Put it on speaker," Darien instructed.

"Hello," a voice said over the speaker.

"Is that you, Damocles?" Darien replied.

"Yes, it's me."

"Oh, thank the gods!" Darien said, sitting heavily in one of the office chairs. "Are you all right?"

"I need an extraction. Send an evac helicopter to my location. Have a surgical team standing by on the Gulfstream at Koltsovo Field. I've been shot."

"Good heavens!" Darien said. "Minerva, do you have his location?"

"Yes. And I've already dispatched a med team. They should be at your location in two hours, Damocles."

"Can you tell us what happened, Son?" Darien inquired.

"Ask Minerva. At the moment I needed them most, your Heracles units pulled a fucking jabrony. We lost them all. I'm just lucky Quade was disoriented. If his aim was any better, we wouldn't be having this conversation."

"Did you notice anything odd," Minerva interrupted. "Right before our units went offline?"

"You mean besides a dozen of your robots chasing runaways through the woods at night?"

"Yes. Aside from the obvious, Damocles, did anything during the course of events strike you as out of character, or incongruous with the moment at hand?"

The line was silent for a time before Damocles finally responded. "Quade shouted 'send'. That seemed like a strange response to being slammed against a tree. Does that mean anything to you?"

"It may mean everything," she replied. "Get some rest, Damocles. Help is on the way. We'll have a full debrief when you arrive."

"I don't want to debrief; I want answers," Damocles said then the line went dead.

"Only moments after Quade shouts 'send'," Minerva surmised, "Rampart's people initiate their incursion, which just happens to render our onsite units useless for more than a minute? Liliane is right. We have a leak. Whoever it is, they had to have told Quade and the others what to look for. It is the most viable possibility."

Darien pounded the arm of his chair decisively. "I want the names and dossiers of every person that got on or off that train from the time it left Vladivostok until it arrived in Moscow."

"The train, Darien?" Liliane asked. "Whatever for?"

"Because, my dear, we're missing a link. "If Quade shouted 'send', he must have been ordering one of his people to transmit a preprogrammed communication signal. Minerva, did any cell calls originating from that location fit our timeframe?"

"Checking," she said, and they waited in silence for a few moments. "There were no calls or messages of any kind routed through the cell towers at that location at that time," Minerva finally confirmed.

"I suspected as much. The question then becomes: how did someone in Quade's party communicate with Rampart at that moment?"

"How indeed?" Liliane said.

"Linked satphones?" Minerva asked.

"Linked satphones," Darien confirmed.

"Which means someone had to give one to Quade in person," Liliane connected the dots.

"Yes," Darien said. "Percival and his cohorts emerged from perfect hiding to board that train. Why would they take such a risk?"

"For a meeting?" Liliane asked.

"That is what we must find out. Minerva, we need those names."

"I'll get right on it."

"Good. Now, do either of you have any idea what the hell a jabrony is?"

THEY SLEPT THROUGH THE ENTIRE day and most of the next night. Yael woke Pere sometime before dawn on Friday morning. He dressed stiffly and shambled into the small kitchenette between their rooms. The others were already there, except for Khyoza. The inviting aroma of fresh-brewed coffee hung in the air.

"You missed the doctor's visit, *Faucon*," Ehud said.

"What'd he say?" he asked, a little guiltily, because he had actually forgotten about

Rophe's condition in his just-waking-up thick-headedness.

"She's still on life support," said Barnabas, "which is not ideal; but it means she's still alive, which is much better than the alternative."

Pere poured himself coffee and sat down heavily next to Yael. "How long did I sleep?" he asked her.

"Barnabas said it was around twenty hours," she said, yawning. "We all just got up a few minutes ago."

"So, if the surgeon was right yesterday . . . or was it the day before? Anyway, if the surgeon was right, we're almost halfway through the danger period for Rophe?"

"That's what we were all just saying before you came in. Glass-half-full kind of thinking."

Khyoza dozed again in the very uncomfortable straight-back chair he had pulled into the recovery room. So long as he could still hear the steady beeping of the heart monitor, he allowed his eyes to remain closed. He would not permit himself to slip into deep sleep, in case . . . well, just in case. He opened his eyes slightly and realized it was growing light outside the room's lone window. Then he looked again at Rophe, and discovered she was looking back at him. Her face was swollen and horribly bruised, but her eyes were definitely open, if only halfway. He sat up and rubbed his leg, which had fallen asleep.

"Hey," she whispered to him through the clenched teeth of her wired jaw.

"Good morning," he said, stretching his arms and yawning.

"Where am I?" she wheezed the words, moving her lips only minimally.

"You are safe," he said. "And you are recovering."

"I don't believe you. I feel like I've been hit with a sledgehammer—twice. Where did you take me, and why haven't we been captured?"

"You are in an exclusive equine hospital. You are receiving the best care rich horses can buy." He couldn't tell whether she found his comment humorous or not, since she couldn't move her face. "The doctors have assured me that you will soon be up and about."

"Stop lying to me. You forget, I am a doctor. I know how to diagnose. Your prognosis is optimistic." She closed her eyes for a moment as though she had faded back into sleep. "I remember now that I told you to go without me," she whispered, her eyes remaining shut. "You should have left me in the woods."

"I could not do that," he said quietly.

"Why? It was my choice. Why couldn't you respect my wishes?"

"You are alive. Is that not reason enough?"

"No. I want to know why you didn't leave me, as I asked?"

He was silent for a moment. "You are our doctor. You are very skilled at what you do. And we need a skilled doctor... I also owed you a debt. You saved my leg in the Klondike and nursed me back to health. If it were not for your care, I might not be here."

"She opened her eyes again and looked at him. "You're paying a debt? That is your only reason?" she asked through clenched and aching teeth.

"It is the best reason," he replied, quietly.

"Then your debt is paid," she said. "Please leave me now and let me be alone to die."

He was still for a long moment. "I do not want you to die."

"Why do you care? I released you from your debt. Now you're free—so go."

"I cannot go," he seemed anguished. "You hold me here, somehow. You are always watching me, defending me, taking care of me. Why do you haunt me?"

"I'm not a ghost yet, Khyoza. Give me another hour or so and you may get your wish."

"That is not my wish," he mumbled. "What do you want from me?" He said it like a confused child.

She just looked at him for a long moment before wheezing. "You're a fool, *Lecha Zakayev!*"

"I am not that person anymore."

"Then stop acting like him. What do I want? I want what any woman wants from the man she loves." She stared straight at him for a long time, until he looked down in shame.

"You cannot love me, Rophe. I do not know how to love in return," he whispered. "I only know how to kill."

"You said you aren't that man anymore."

"I may be other things as well now, but I can never erase that man, or the things he... the things *I* did."

"Then will you live only with ghosts? Could no one else take their place in your life?"

"The ghosts leave no room for anyone else."

"Stubborn, obstinate, mulish man," she whispered, seeming more exhausted now.

"You do not understand, Rophe. It is my destiny to die... to die protecting the falcon. That is the justice I deserve. It is the penance for my crimes. I have always known this. Why would you want a man who is doomed to die?"

"We all die, Khyoza. Can you accept no forgiveness while you live?" she whispered.

"I do not deserve forgiveness. That is not my destiny."

"What if you were meant to be happy and whole? What if that was your destiny? Could you accept that?"

"It scares me," he confessed after a long moment. "I do not know how to live without the prospect of death to hope for."

"Perhaps I would be willing to teach you," she whispered, "If you would just..." but she was slipping back into sleep. He looked at her for a long time, and then a tear rolled down his weary cheek.

Later that morning, a short, fat, and balding older man arrived at the hospital with Jonas Cavanaugh. The trim and punctilious operative introduced him to the travelers as Demyan Zahorchak. But the rest of the staff seemed already to know him and treated him with great deference. To everyone's delight, Zahorchak produced a large pastry box filled with savory smelling *pirozhki*, as he called them. They were pastry buns, stuffed with scrambled eggs, bacon, and onions.

"The chef did not like it," he said. "But I made him fry the *salo*. Normally we eat it

smoked and uncooked; but I knew that would—how do you say in the west—gross
you out? So, I had them burn it like your bacon. I think you will like it, though it is
bad form to cook it like this." They all mumbled their thanks through full mouths.
"Yulian asked me to come and meet with you. They arrived in Moscow safely, but
it is too dangerous for him to come himself, you understand? He wants me to find
out what you need, and to make sure you get it."

Before they could respond, Khyoza walked into the kitchenette with the chief
surgeon at his side. He looked at Cavanaugh and the little fat man for a moment
then turned to the others. "Rophe is awake," he said it simply and clinically, but
he couldn't really hide his relief.

"She is a remarkable woman," the surgeon said. "She is past the crisis stage; but
I must caution you all, she still needs much healing. I removed the life-support
stimulators, and her metabolism is responding remarkably well; but she is not yet
out of the woods, as you say. It will take a minimum of two weeks, barring any
setbacks, for her to be able to travel; and longer for a full recovery."

But they all rejoiced and even clapped at the news. So great was their joy that the
doctor felt obliged to take a bow.

"I know you all wish to see her," the surgeon continued. "But wait at least until
tomorrow. The nanos I have given her will make her sleep almost constantly as
they use her metabolism to repair the injuries."

"But this will be no problem at all," Zahorchak said. "I have spoken to the staff,
and you may stay here as long as you need."

"Thank you," Pere said. "It's almost like you own this place."

"It is precisely like I own this place," he said, smiling and throwing his arms wide.
"Because I *do* own this place. And I do not think I would be far from the mark to
guess that you are my niece's newly discovered brother?"

"So, you're my uncle?" Pere said, confused.

"Not by blood; but little Abigail has called me Uncle Dem-Dem as long as I can
remember. So, I suppose that makes you my nephew by association. In any case,
I am pleased to meet the one who made such an impression on our little *zaichik*."

"I was just as surprised as she was," Pere admitted.

"So she said," he smiled. "So she said."

"I'm curious Mr. Zahorchak," Barnabas said. "Why do you own property—if you don't mind my asking—so far from the madding crowd?"

"I don't mind at all; and please, call me Demyan. The reason is simple. I have always had a passion for horses, even when I was little, but I could never afford to own one. I watched your old John Wayne movies and dreamed of the 'wild west'. So, when I eventually had enough roubles, I buy this place and make it into my secret and secluded getaway—how did you say it—far from the maddening crowd? And it's completely off the books, too. It is very nice, no?"

"*Madding* crowd. And yes, it's wonderful," Barnabas said. "Honestly, we can't thank you enough. Are you sure it's no trouble? We wouldn't want to get in the way."

"No trouble at all. But if you begin to feel lazy, I am sure Mimi could find some work for you." He winked. "And when you are ready, I will provide transport for you to go wherever you want. Is there anything else that you need me to do in the meantime?"

"Barnabas scratched his bearded cheek. "Perhaps there is. If it isn't too much trouble, I need to have some letters delivered and I don't want to use the regular post? They might involve a bit of out-of-the-way searching."

"Simplest thing in the world," Demyan said broadly. "Write them up and I'll have a courier take them tomorrow."

"That's very helpful, but you don't need to make it *that* fast," Barnabas said.

"I know I do not need to. But I want to. And besides, my little *zaichik* would be very cross with me if I did not help you. She is charming, but if you make her upset, she can get—what is your word—cranky?"

"It must run in the family," Yael said.

Khyoza grabbed a pirozhki and sat down, distractedly taking a bite before realizing he was famished from two days on very little food. He then took another large bite and rolled his eyes at the taste of the savory pastry. "There is something I have been wondering about, Jonas," he said between bites. "The other night, in the woods, I was sure it was Gianakos who was holding our doctor hostage; but apparently I was mistaken. Can you explain that?"

"Whoever it was," El offered. "He sure packed a helluva punch."

"What?" Cavanaugh said. "Do you mean that Darien Gianakos was in the party that tried to take you?"

"I thought so at first," Khyoza said, taking a second pirozhki. "But he said I was mistaken. He identified himself as Darien's son."

"Is that what he said?" Cavanaugh asked. "Did he call himself Darien's son?"

"Well, not exactly. When I called him Darien, he said, 'You have mistaken me for my father. Apparently, we look very similar.' Does this mean something to you?"

"I think it means we're in trouble," Cavanaugh said pensively, standing up and beginning to pace. "The man you're describing is a clone—Darien Gianakos' clone, to be precise. Or at least he was started from Gianakos' genetic material; but he's been radically altered and enhanced in almost every way."

"That would explain why it took seven shots to take him down," El said, gently touching his ribs. "He was a bull, and a lightning-fast one at that."

"You say you shot him seven times?" Cavanaugh asked. "Were any of them head shots?"

"Uhh," El said, thinking back, "I was kinda out of it, but I think I was aiming for the largest target, so I'm pretty sure they were all body shots. Why?"

"Because if you didn't shoot him in the head, he's still alive."

"No way!" El protested. "I saw him die."

"You recall the self-repair capabilities of the 2-G clones?"

"You're not saying this guy has that?" El said.

"No. I'm saying he has upgrades on that technology. Seven body shots would probably keep him down for maybe thirty minutes. I've seen the specs on him and the Heracles units. The Heracles units are connected via an interface to Haruspex. That's how we were able to take them out. Gianakos would have been monitoring everything that happened through their visual links, up to the moment of our incursion—all in real time. But during our attack on their mainframe, all those connections were severed, when you shot them in their heads."

"Is that why they all went dumb?" El asked. "They just stood there, waiting for us to blow them away."

"That was the untested hypothesis I told you about. I knew of their connection to the Haruspex mainframe. I took the chance that momentarily severing the link would render them directionless, at least for a short time."

"Well, it worked," Ehud said. "So, what is the worry?"

"The worry," Cavanaugh responded, thinking things through. "Is if it was just the 3-Gs attacking you in those woods, Gianakos would have no information of the events beyond the first few moments."

"But if this other guy lived," El started tracking. "Then he was able to report back on some of what happened after the clones went down, including me yelling 'send' to Barnabas?"

"You yelled 'send'?" Cavanaugh asked, crestfallen.

"You bet your ass I did; it was that or die."

"Completely understandable," Cavanaugh said, scratching his unshaved cheek. "But it creates questions for them to ponder. Such as, why would you shout 'send'? You would most likely do that because you were signaling someone."

"But it could be that he was signaling one of us to shoot?" Ehud offered.

"Perhaps," Cavanaugh said. "However, mere seconds later, a worm invaded the very system that controlled the 3-Gs' attack on your party. A coincidence? I wouldn't draw that conclusion."

"Neither would I," El admitted. "So, if my 'send' is interpreted by Gianakos as a go signal, then he's going to assume we had help."

"And very well-informed help at that," concluded Cavanaugh.

"And where would we get such help?" added Khyoza. "Except from someone on the inside?"

"Precisely," muttered Cavanaugh.

"And where would we have crossed paths with a loose-mouthed insider?" El said.

"It could have been anywhere," Pere offered.

"Possible," said Cavanaugh. "But none of these recent events were planned. So, if I were looking for a connection, I would start with the only recent location I am sure my targets have been."

"The train?" said Yael.

"The train," confirmed Cavanaugh. "Demyan, we need to call Yulian."

"But why?" the little man said. "There are no video feeds on that train. There will be no evidence Yulian met with any of you."

"Gianakos will search through the roster of every person on that train from the time this group got on in Ulan Ude until they got off in Yekaterinburg. Yulian and his family will be on that list. If I was looking for someone with inside information, I wouldn't look much further than a hub chair."

"*Gavno!*" Zahorchak paled. "What must we do?"

"We need to get out ahead of this," Cavanaugh said. "I'll tell Yulian to call Gianakos right away, before they get a chance to come and question him."

"But what will this do?"

"He will tell Gianakos I approached him on the train going by the name of Orlov, that I asked him to join in a rebellion against the sénéschal; and that he told me to pound sand, that he is a good company man, and that he wanted to contact Gianakos to let him know forces were moving against him. It's all true, and it will throw suspicion directly onto me as the source of the leak. After all, I am intimately linked to William Rampart, the one who perpetrated the incursion— the conclusion will be that I contacted these fugitives to form an alliance against Gianakos—again, all true, from a certain perspective."

"And if this strategy does not work?" Zahorchak asked.

"Then we'll need to get Yulian and his family into hiding. But first things first; I'll go call Yulian from the SUV where it's quieter." Cavanaugh left and Zahorchak sat down heavily.

"All of this is not good for my blood pressure," he said. "There are too many things to worry about, and I am already a worrier by nature."

They ate breakfast in the *Horti Civitatis Vaticanae* on a gloriously warm and sunny morning, amidst a boxwood labyrinth, as they dined on crepes, jam, and whipped sour cream. Damocles Praefectus arrived by medical transport only the night before but looked unbelievably well for having seven bullets surgically removed. He wore a thick white bathrobe, which was the only visible indication he had been recently indisposed. Liliane hovered over him like a mother hen, urging him to eat more, refilling his cup with hot coffee. Darien sat, bemused, as he observed the oddly domestic nature of the situation.

"So, Father," Damocles said, sipping his coffee. "What have we uncovered about the Yekaterinburg debacle?"

"Nothing definitive yet, I'm sorry to say. Minerva is compiling a list of all the passengers on the train while Percival was onboard. We're hoping to find a link there."

"What's taking her so long?"

"There are nearly ten-thousand kilometers of rail and hundreds of stops where potentials may have gotten on or off. We need to be thorough, and that takes time, even for Haruspex."

"We are as anxious as you to get to the bottom of this, Damocles," Liliane said, gently. "Do not fret. You will get your answers."

"Thank you, Miss Liliane," Damocles said. "It is one thing to fail on one's own lack of merit. It is quite another to be sabotaged."

"Nobody is blaming you," Darien said.

Damocles stewed for a moment before changing the subject. "He recognized me, you know?"

"Who recognized you?"

"Zakayev. He called me Darien. He mistook me for you. He pleaded with you for the life of his woman."

"You two do look remarkably alike," Liliane offered.

"Yes, and I've had dealings with that particular rat before," Darien said. "He's very good, you know—I mean, very well trained. Did you grant him his request?"

"No. I gutted her like a fish. I would have done the same to Quade, but he put seven bullets in me when your droids had their collective brownout."

"So, the woman was the only casualty?"

"I can't even confirm that with any certainty. They were gone when I regained consciousness. But I can't imagine she lived, and I think I may have damaged Quade when I threw him against a tree, probably not enough to kill him though. They destroyed the clone units and beheaded three of them . . . with swords. Why in the world would they use swords? It seems so medieval."

"An idiosyncrasy of the phantom's training was the 'way of the sword'. They all became extremely proficient with katanas."

"Whatever for?"

"Mainly for the structure, as I understand it. The ideal candidates for the program were all wildly aggressive by nature. The sword training provided them with discipline and self-control. It also made them more skilled as tacticians. You might consider some sword training yourself. It would probably do you some good."

"Or maybe when I get my hands on them the next time, I'll just snap their necks."

"You're being naïve if you underestimate them, Damocles. The phantoms were always a slippery bunch."

"I underestimated nothing! I'd be interrogating them right now if my highly advanced support team hadn't shit their pants right when I needed them."

"I understand you're disappointed. We all are. But that particular glitch is correctable, now that we know it exists. Don't disregard the Heracles units; they're an invaluable tool. The barracks in Iceland are nearly complete. You'll feel closer to your own men once they're housed there."

"They're not men, Father. They're little better than robots."

The valet approached the table through the boxwood maze and spoke to Darien. "You have a call, sir, on the scrambled line."

"Who is it?"

"He identified himself as Mr. Khvostovsky."

"I'd better take it. You two finish breakfast together and enjoy the sun," and then he departed with the valet.

"You must be patient with your father," Liliane said after they were out of earshot. "He has much on his plate right now."

"I cannot tolerate failure. It's unacceptable, whatever the reason." He was squeezing his coffee cup so tightly that it shattered.

"*Mon Dieu!*" Liliane cried, as she jumped up and came around the table to pick the porcelain shards off his bathrobe. "Are you alright?"

"I'm fine," he protested.

"Are you sure no shards fell inside your robe?"

"I don't believe so," he said, as he opened his robe, revealing the now-healing entry points of the seven recently removed bullets. He also displayed a quite-obvious enhancement, which Darien had failed to mention. "Miss Liliane, you're flushed. Are you ill?"

"It's nothing to worry about, Damocles," she said, rather short of breath. "The sun has made me a bit warm is all."

Darien entered his office and closed the door. "Are you here, Minerva?"

"I'm here, Majesty."

"Have you checked to see that's it's really Khvostovsky on the line?"

"The call originates from the Cybergi Global offices. Other than that, I can't say."

"Put him on speaker."

Darien heard her speaking to the caller. "I'm transferring you to the sénéschal. Please hold."

"Hello Yulian," Darien said, as he sat down. "To what do I owe this pleasant surprise?"

"Darien. I hope you're well."

"I'm splendid."

"I'm sorry to bother you . . . and it's probably nothing; but I had a very unsettling visitation a few days ago and felt obliged to tell you of it."

"Did an angel come to you in your sleep?"

"No, no, no. It wasn't that kind of visitation. He was more like a lunatic, and I would have written him off as such, but he seemed to know a good deal more than he should have. That's why I'm calling you."

"All right then, why don't you tell me about this loon of yours."

"I was returning from Vladivostok with my family. We decided to vacation there after our meeting in Tokyo, and then take the train back to Moscow. On perhaps our third or fourth night onboard, a man came to visit me in our railcar. He was dressed as a porter bringing us dinner; but once inside, he introduced himself as Illarion Orlov. I don't think that was his real name."

"What made you suspicious?"

"I think he was in disguise. I can spot a fake moustache when I see one, and his wasn't the best. And I think he had some kind of putty or something on his cheek-bones and his chin—but I may be getting paranoid."

"That does sound kind of fishy. What did he say?"

"This is where it got quite strange. He said he had a proposition for me. Said he worked for Premier Rockefeller, that there was some kind of war going on between you and the Directorate. He knew your name, Darien, and he identified you as the 'ex-sénéschal.' Those were his words. He said you had assassinated five of the premieres in an attempted coup, but that Rockefeller and Romanov had survived, and that Romanov had sided with you in the coup."

"So, what did you tell this lunatic?" Darien was trying hard to sound nonchalant, but his heart was pounding.

"I told him he had mistaken me for someone else. I didn't know what else to say. It sounded so preposterous. I would have called you sooner, but the historic line has no communication uplinks. This is my first day back in the office."

"No harm done. It sounds like you did the right thing. Did he say anything else to you?"

"As a matter of fact, he did. After he told me this story, he asked me to become his spy against you in this war of his."

"And how did you respond?"

"I told him I wasn't interested—*of course*—and I asked him to leave. What do you think I am, Darien?"

"I *know* you're one of our best and brightest. I chose you for the Cybergi chair after all. Did he say anything else?"

"He suggested I investigate his allegations and that he'd call me before the week was out. I insisted he never contact me again, but I don't think he'll listen."

"Has he tried?"

"Not that I know of. Stasya says I received no calls out of the ordinary during my absence, so hopefully that's the end of it. The week will be up tomorrow, in any case. I probably should have just written it off, but I thought you should know."

Darien was very still for a moment. "Can you describe him?"

"Um... white, probably around thirty-five, trim, um... not quite medium height, and he used very precise English, but I couldn't place the accent."

"Will you be at this number for the next hour?" he finally asked.

"I'll stay right here, Darien."

"Good. I need to look into this, and I'll call you back within the hour." He disconnected and sat back wearily. "What do you make of it, Minerva?"

"This Illarion Orlov claimed he was working for Rampart. That and the description would lead me to conclude he is none other than Jonas Cavanaugh."

"I agree. It seems we've found our mole," he said to the empty room. "Is there no way to rid ourselves of that persistent bastard?"

"It would help if we could keep better track of his movements."

"That's supposed to be your speciality! How did he get to Russia under your radar since he hasn't left Rampart's Puget compound? What's all your vaunted surveillance getting me, Minerva?"

"For the sake of civility, I'll try not to be defensive. The short answer is, I don't know. However, if we accept Mr. Khvostovsky's assessment, Cavanaugh changed his appearance sufficiently to fool random facial recognition protocols. He is a highly skilled operative, trained to avoid detection via misdirection. There are nearly seven billion people on this planet. If you want me to personally examine each captured image without any culling software, it will take a thousand years."

Darien was silent for a moment before speaking. "You're right," he finally said. "I'm taking my frustration out on you. I'm sure you're doing the best you can."

"I don't do the best that I can; I do the best that there is."

"Yes, of course you do. What have you found for me so far?"

"I've done a preliminary examination of all the passengers who got on or off that train for the duration of its entire Moscow run. There is no record that Jonas Cavanaugh ever boarded that train. However, there is no record that Percival boarded either since he did so under a false identity. I was about to page you to inform you that the Khvostovskys had taken a private luxury car for themselves at the rear of the train. They boarded in Vladivostok and deboarded in Moscow, seven days later. We now know Cavanaugh met with Khvostovsky; and we are assuming he made contact with Quade on the same train. It may be that he planned both meetings; or that he took advantage of a situation that unexpectedly presented itself. I cannot be more definitive with the evidence I currently hold."

"His presence jibes with what Yulian just told us, if not his whole purpose. But that doesn't tell us *when* Cavanaugh got on that train, or how *he* was able to locate Percival in Russia when we were searching for him half a world away? And why in hell would Rampart want to help Percival's people in the first place?"

"All good questions; but none are definitively answerable at this juncture—aside from the obvious."

"Which is?"

"*The enemy of my enemy . . .*"

". . . *is my friend*? But surely Rampart must realize that the anomaly is the vastly more dangerous enemy of us both!"

"It is possible that Rampart never fully accepted the anomaly as anything other than a ploy on your part to distract eyes from your real plans. And that well is now irreparably poisoned by its proximity to your *coup d'état*."

"But Will Rampart is smarter than that! He's cutting off his nose to spite his face!"

"Be that as it may, he still has a formidable chin which he is now jutting in our direction. I think we can deduce with fair certainty that Quade's information on how to disrupt the Heracles units was passed on from Cavanaugh. Khvostovsky would have known nothing about those units anyway since they were a Bennett project."

"They didn't just pass on information, Minerva; Cavanaugh coordinated the attack together with Quade."

"Agreed; but for Cavanaugh to have that information at all, he had to have gotten it from someone in the know. I think we need to revisit his conversation with Walter Bennett. Apparently, it went a bit further than we suspected."

"Try miles further. . . . Goddammit! We would have known if Damocles hadn't botched the interrogation. He needs to understand he bears a *major* responsibility in this setback."

"That notwithstanding, we cannot change what's past. You need to call the Cybergi chair back, so let's concentrate on our strategy moving forward."

"Yes. You're right. Okay. So, let's assume Cavanaugh got the specs on the Heracles units from Bennett, even though I ordered that fat bastard to destroy them."

"Unfortunately, he may also have data on Damocles Praefectus, since that was also a Bennett project."

"That would be very bad, indeed."

"However, he wouldn't know about the Tokyo Protocol. Oshiro Takeshi has always been extremely tight lipped about his hub's projects."

"Yes. That's one of the things I like best about him. So then, even with this setback, we can continue more-or-less on schedule with the larger plan. But that still begs the question—what to do about Yulian Khvostovsky?"

"It would be absurd, at this juncture, to tell him it was *all* a fabrication by a deranged past employee—he's far too smart and curious for that to work."

"I agree. That leaves us very few options."

"I see three plausible approaches. One, we eliminate him—staunch the bleeding, and move on."

"Hmm. Yulian said his wife and daughter were with him when Cavanaugh spoke to him. That means we'd have to eliminate them as well, in addition to anyone they may have spoken to. I'm willing, but I'd rather consider that the option of last resort. One random death can be explained. Multiple deaths raise too many questions; and after Bennett, it might seem too coincidental to the other chairs. Besides, I like him."

"The second approach is, we lay our cards on the table, tell him everything, and see where he stands. If he's with us, that would give us a valuable ally moving forward; if he's against us, we can always revert to option one."

"Noted. What's your third option?"

"We turn the tables. Tell him the other premiers are well, but in hiding, because Rockefeller has gone rogue, has joined forces with the anomaly, and is gunning for the other premiers and the chairs—Bennett was the first—and that he intends to 'clean house' and start over . . . and you're the only one standing in his way."

"Interesting. You know, that has possibilities. If we play this right, we could make him a double agent. I could ask him to accept Cavanaugh's offer of alliance. He can agree to spy on us when, all the while, he'll be bringing us information on them."

"It's risky, Darien; but it could work, and it might be the best way to finally corner Cavanaugh—*and* William Rampart."

"Let's go with that plan. Get him back on the line. We'll see how receptive he is to a little espionage. If it works, this could be just the edge we need."

When Darien returned to the bucolic breakfast setting, Damocles and Liliane were still sipping their coffee and enjoying the warm mid-morning sun.

"Our mole is Jonas Cavanaugh," he said as he sat down. "He approached Yulian on the train and told him everything. And he must have told Quade to signal Rampart at the precise moment of your attack. That's why we lost the Heracles units."

"That little urchin moves around a lot," Liliane said. "I thought he was cornered in the Puget."

"And we also assumed Percival was somewhere in Region 4."

"Is this the same Rampart that's supposed to be dead?" Damocles asked.

"Yes. Apparently, we overestimated," Darien admitted ruefully. "It seems that old wolf still has a few teeth sharp enough to bite."

"That's a mistake we shall have to correct," Damocles said thoughtfully. "He cost us dearly. We lost twelve of your clones and Percival because of him."

"I am well aware, Damocles. And you need to understand it's a price we would *not* have been obliged to pay had you questioned Walter Bennett first, as I asked, rather than killing him. How do you suppose Cavanaugh got the information on the Heracles units in the first place?"

"Walt told Cavanaugh about the Heracles project?" Liliane asked.

"He had to have. There's no other way he'd have known they were hackable."

"Our secret weapons are no longer so secret," she said.

"That's a setback we'll have to deal with. Fortunately, Walt had no knowledge of the Tokyo Protocol, so the larger trajectory is still on target. Now, I need to go to Moscow to meet with Khvostovsky and try to turn this mess to our advantage. You're welcome to come if you wish, *ma chérie*."

"I'd like to come as well," Damocles said. "I should meet this Khvostovsky; get a measure of the man."

"I didn't invite you, Damocles. Right now, I want you to return to Reykjavík and oversee the completion of the barracks complex. We need those cohorts in the north as soon as possible. I'm aware you've been injured; but if you feel up to it, you'll leave in the morning."

"I will be fine, Father."

"Liliane?"

"If you don't mind, dearest, I think I'll go to Paris for a short respite; recharge my batteries and do a little shopping."

"It's just as well. Yulian and I will probably be closeted the whole time, and Moscow is not Paris, is it?"

"There is only one Paris, *mon cher*, and I begin to wither on the vine if I'm away too long."

"If you would like, Miss Liliane," Damocles said. "You could accompany me in the Gulfstream. I could drop you in Paris on my way to Reykjavík."

"Thank you, Damocles," she nodded. "That would fit my plans nicely. Then I will take the train back, so I can see the countryside in spring."

"It's settled, then," said Darien, pleased. "I'll see you back here in a few days, my dear. And Son, Minerva will keep me apprised of your progress. Do keep your focus where your focus should be."

"As you say, Father."

LATE SATURDAY MORNING THEY VISITED Rophe for the first time. She was sitting up in bed and, though she couldn't move her mouth to smile, her color seemed good, and her eyes had renewed life. Khyoza slept soundly in the same uncomfortable chair. When they came in, Rophe placed her index finger gently to her own lips to keep them from waking him up. Barnabas handed her an iced coffee—since she could only drink and eat through a straw, until the wires were removed, he thought hot coffee might be too dangerous.

"Thank you," she whispered; though it came out as "Tank you." She took a sip through the straw and rolled her eyes skyward as she tasted coffee again. Everything, it seemed, tasted better after a near death experience.

"You're looking absolutely tip-top this morning," Barnabas whispered.

"Oh please," she whispered back. "I look horrible. But I am starting to feel a little life again. I should thank you for not leaving me."

"We would never have done that," Barnabas whispered.

"Though, truth be told, Doc," El said in full voice. "It was touch-and-go for a while there in the woods. Barnabas thought we should toss you out of the chopper, but I wouldn't hear of it."

"Shhh! You big oaf!" Rophe scolded him; but it sounded so much like steam escaping from an old kettle that everyone laughed and Khyoza startled awake.

"You know," Yael said to the taciturn Cossack with a curious smile. "They set up beds for us in the other rooms. They're pretty comfortable, if you want to try one."

"Yes," Khyoza said, clearing his throat. "Of course, I will do that. I was just making sure the doctor had everything she needed."

"You are doing a very thorough job, friend," Ehud said. "She looks very well taken care of. I think you have become . . . what is it you say . . . ah! A mother hen."

"Let him be!" Rophe said. "He has been a great comfort to me."

"A 'great comfort', Brother?" El chided. "I've never heard it called that before but well done, great comforter!" Everyone tried not to laugh. Khyoza actually blushed, which looked very out of place on the normally stoic assassin.

"I insist you stop this schoolyard banter," Rophe said. "You are making me tired! You will not abuse Khyoza. He has been my knight-protector!"

"What's a night protector?" Pere asked. Even he couldn't resist a little fun at his friend's expense. "Is it something that covers you in the dark?" They could maintain themselves for only a moment before they burst into laughter again. Khyoza had gone scarlet, and even Rophe blushed a little. She would have smiled too, if her wired jaw had allowed it.

Liliane lay glowingly naked on the boathouse bed, breathing serenely. The unseasonably warm Parisian spring only partly explained why her body glistened with perspiration. Damocles came out of the bathroom, a towel draped over his shoulders, his hair still damp from the shower. He pulled on his pants as he studied the contours of her body. She opened her eyes and looked up at him.

"I have never felt so marvelously spent," she said, dreamily, stretching on the sheets like an indolent cat. "What am I to do, now that I have discovered you?"

"I don't think my father would be altogether pleased with your discovery" he replied, whimsically. "We'd better be very careful if we continue to indulge ourselves, my thoroughly wicked stepmother."

"You mustn't call me that," she complained. "It makes me feel positively ancient."

"Believe me when I tell you this, Miss Liliane, there is nothing ancient about you. You are as nubile and sensuous as Aphrodite the day she arose from the foam, and just as sweet."

Liliane blushed. "I see you are a poet as well as a pikeman. Well, you brought out the absolute best in me." She rapturously stretched again, luxuriating in her sense of contentment. "If I am Aphrodite, does that make you Hephaestus or Ares?"

"In the use of my pike, I am Ares, but in skill and cunning, I am Hephaestus, although I will leave his lameness to my father. Speaking of whom, I've got to go. He expects me to be in Reykjavík, overseeing the completion of the barracks."

"I know, I know, Damocles," she said regretfully, as though it were breaking the spell. "I must return to Rome tomorrow as well. I said I was coming to Paris for some shopping. But your father needs me. This is a stressful time for us all; but you have reduced *my* stress remarkably today. I don't know whether I should thank you or pay you."

"I don't need money. The privilege of participating in your many moments of plenitude this afternoon is all the pay I need."

"You make me blush again!" she said, touching her cheeks. "I never blush."

"No. You bloom like a flower in the morning dew."

She looked at him archly. "Are you sure you couldn't stay a little longer? That flower's beginning to bloom again."

He smiled at her, but also continued to put his shirt on. "It would be my pleasure, Mademoiselle, but I think it's best if I leave you wanting more. Besides, I need to be in Reykjavík soon, and I have some pressing business elsewhere to attend to first. I can't afford any more delays."

"What kind of business?"

"Just a little side trip, my dear stepmother. Nothing you need concern yourself about?"

"By which you mean you don't want your father to know?"

"You're perceptive. It's just a little debt I need to square, and Father doesn't think such things are priorities."

"But you do?"

"Suffice it to say, we don't see eye to eye on this—chalk it up to his lameness. *Adieu, Mademoiselle.*" He kissed her hand, left the boathouse, and got in the waiting river taxi. Liliane lay back on the bed and closed her eyes again. She knew she should get up and do something, but it felt good just to lie there and enjoy this moment of quietude. It was so nice sometimes just to be lazy. So few people knew how to do it properly anymore. She sighed, then got up to bathe and go shopping.

An ornate 19th century ship's wheel hung on the wall opposite the bed. She never noticed the tiny camera that had been installed in the antique piece three weeks ago. There was no reason she would have, since she had not been the one who had ordered its installation.

Yulian Khvostovsky stood at the window looking out through the hazy Saturday afternoon at the sunlight sparkling on the wending Moskva River. When the office COM buzzed, he turned back to his desk and pushed the button.

"Yes?"

"Mr. Gianakos is on his way up, sir."

"Thank you, Stasya. Send him right in."

He turned to the window again and took a deep breath. He had one of the finest educations in the world, but none of his degrees focused on espionage. He did, however, know business, and a huge part of that training was in subterfuge. He would have to rely on those skills this morning, and perhaps a few others he'd picked up over the years. His family's lives depended on it. The office door opened, and Darien Gianakos walked in. Khvostovsky turned from the window. The ex-sénéschal was as cleanly put together as ever. Only his eyes betrayed a certain level of weariness that had not been there before.

"Please, Sénéschal," he said, without preamble. "Have a seat. Can I get you some coffee, or tea—or perhaps something stronger?"

"Thank you, I wouldn't mind a bourbon," Darien said, easily, sitting down. "I had a quite satisfying lunch during my flight, but a *digestif* would be nice. Has Orlov made contact yet?"

"No, and I rather hope he doesn't," he said, pouring a bourbon and handing it to Gianakos before returning to his own chair. "I'm not at all equipped for all this cloak-and-dagger business. I'm a hub chair, not a bloody spy."

"It's quite reasonable that this has made you feel a little unsettled." He sipped his bourbon.

"A little unsettled? That doesn't begin to express my concern, Darien." He needed to seem upset, which wasn't very difficult—he was, after all. "It was hardly more than two years ago that you told us we were essentially invulnerable. Then this anomaly, Percival, was identified as an external threat. And now you say a cancer *inside* the Consortium threatens our very lives? That Rockefeller killed Walt Bennett, and now he's gunning for the rest of us? This isn't unsettling; it's insane! You want me to play secret agent in a cat-and-mouse game that may very well get me *and* my family killed? It's all too much, Darien!"

"I understand completely, Yulian, and would never ask such a thing of you normally; however, we are presented with an opportunity here that may outweigh the dangers. Obviously, this Orlov fellow doesn't want you dead—at least not yet. If that were all he wanted, he would have killed you and your family on that train. No, there is something else going on here—a more complex endgame that I haven't yet exposed to the light. If we can discover that, we may have a chance to stem the tide, and potentially formulate a counterstroke before we lose any more people."

Khvostovsky was silent for a long moment before speaking. "I didn't say I wouldn't try, Darien. I'm just . . . well, I'm not proud of this, but I'm afraid."

"So are we all, my friend. We are in uncharted waters—I'll be the first to admit it. Had he come to me first, I'd have dealt with him myself. But he knows better than to confront me face to face. No, he wants to stay clear of my reach. That's why I need you to draw him into our net—and then I'll personally deal with him and Rockefeller very thoroughly; that I promise you. And I will keep your family safe, Yulian; I swear it."

"All right," he finally said, as he looked out the window again. "What do I need to do?"

"When he contacts you again, tell him you've had time to reconsider things and that you're now willing to help him if he will guarantee the safety of your family. . . You might also insist they give you the New York hub for your troubles. Greed is always a good indicator of honest intentions."

"I'd prefer London," he said quietly.

"Then make it London. Now, we need to have him meet with you personally—that's essential."

"And if he refuses?"

"Then you need to stay in constant contact with him. Make him give you direct instructions on everything he needs you to do. Act like you're too afraid to make decisions on your own."

"I won't really be acting."

"I'm counting on it. You'll be more believable that way. And the more he needs to tell you, the sooner we'll be able to unmask their plans."

"And what if he never contacts me again?"

"He'll contact you. He said a week, and it's been seven days. It's only a matter of—"

At that moment the office COM buzzed and Khvostovsky pushed the button. "What is it Stasya?"

"I am sorry to bother you, but a Mr. Orlov is on the line, and he says it is very important that he speak with you." He looked at Gianakos, questioningly.

"I told you he'd call," Gianakos said. "I honestly didn't think it would be right at this moment. Now, remember: *'Bait the hook well. This fish will bite'*."

"I seem to recall you telling Alex King you didn't know any Shakespeare."

"A modest understatement," Gianakos shrugged. "Put him on speaker."

"Transfer the call to my line, Stasya." A moment later, his desk phone buzzed. Khvostovsky took a deep breath and pressed the speaker button. "I thought I told you never to contact me again, Mr. Orlov."

"And I told you I'd call back in a week after you had time to look into the allegations, Mr. Khvostovsky," the voice on the other end said. "Have you done that?"

"I've made a few discreet inquiries," he said after a pause.

"And?"

"I'm not yet willing to accept your assertions at face value; but I admit there appear to be some irregularities."

"That's an understatement. Now, I strongly advise you not to ask any more questions, discreet or no. Arousing suspicion at this point may very well get you killed."

"Isn't that just a little too convenient? You're asking me to accept what you say at face value and then ask no questions that might reveal you as a fraud?"

"I'm asking you not to expose yourself to unnecessary danger. Darien Gianakos is a psychopathic megalomaniac, who will murder both you and your family without hesitation, *if* he believes you've been compromised."

"So you said before. And if I went to his offices personally and confronted him about these accusations, what would he say?"

"Do you even know where his offices are located?"

"Well . . . No, none of us do . . . But that doesn't change the larger issue."

"It most certainly does for you. If you went to his old offices, you wouldn't find him there, but you'd still be dead. In either case, he's moved his current base of operations to the old Vatican museums in Rome."

"Why would he do that?"

"Who knows? Delusions of grandeur; maybe some kind of messiah complex; we're just not sure. That's why we need you. We need to find out what he's planning. We must discover his weaknesses if we have any hope of getting close enough to him to end his reign of terror. Will you help us?"

Khvostovsky was silent a long time before answering. "I have a family, Orlov. Their safety is foremost."

"We can guarantee your family will be protected."

"How can you say that when you can't even protect yourself?"

"We have resources, Yulian; resources that Gianakos knows nothing of. He believes he's won, so he'll never see the ax falling until it's too late. All you need to do is watch him. We'll take him out when the time is ripe."

"But I'm not a spy, Orlov. Darien will know the minute he looks in my eyes. He sees things other people can't. He's not like other men. You can't possibly know what it's like to be in his presence."

"I know more than you think. I've studied Gianakos playing his little role for the last fifteen years. I assure you, Yulian, it's all an act. He needs to keep people intimidated so they don't suspect he's secretly afraid of them. At his core, he's nothing more than a frightened little man trying to grab power to compensate for the powerlessness he senses in himself."

"I sincerely hope you're right."

"I am. Besides, we don't need you to confront him directly. Act normally and do what you've always done. Just report back to us everything you see or hear. We'll find a way to get to him that he least suspects."

"If I do this," he said after a dramatic pause, "I want something in return."

"I'm listening."

"I want a new hub assignment. I've outgrown Russia. I want London."

There was now a long pause on the other end before Orlov finally spoke. "I would have preferred you to join us out of heartfelt conviction—ours is a noble cause . . . But I will speak with Rockefeller and convince him to accept this offer. Do we have a deal then?"

"Yes, I believe we do. When will I next see you?"

"You won't. I'll contact you, always in different ways. We cannot fall into routines—they're deadly. They're probably watching all the chairs at this point.

So, you'll hear from me when you least expect it, that way our enemies won't expect it either. Welcome aboard, Yulian. You've made the right choice. I'll be in touch." The line went dead.

Khvostovsky breathed deeply and sat back in his chair, consciously lowering his shoulders that had risen substantially from stress. "Is it true?' he finally asked Gianakos. "What he said about Rome. Is it true?" Gianakos seemed to be lost in thought, staring past Khvostovsky and out the office windows. "Darien?"

"Hm?" Gianakos finally came back from his apparent fugue state. "What's that, Yulian?"

"Are you alright, Darien?"

"Pardon?" Gianakos said, now sitting up. "Oh, I'm fine—perfectly fine. I was just processing. And you were brilliant! It's a shame we couldn't pin him down a little more on how he would contact you, but he's definitely on the hook. Now it's just a matter of time before we reel him in. In the meantime, Yulian, it is absolutely essential that you reveal none of this to the other chairs. At this juncture, anarchy would be a worse adversary than Rockefeller, and anarchy would surely ensue if all the chairs mobilized for war. We must avoid that at all costs."

A half-hour later, following a discussion that mainly took the form of instructions, Gianakos left, and Khvostovsky again stood at his window waiting. After about three minutes, the office COM buzzed. He pressed the button.

"Yes, Stasya?"

"Mr. Gianakos has left the building."

"Thank you. That will be all for this afternoon. And thanks again for coming in on a Saturday."

"It was not a problem. I will see you Monday." He took his finger off the button and sat down heavily in his chair. The door to his anteroom opened moments later and Cavanaugh walked in, pouring himself a scotch at the bar, and sitting down opposite Khvostovsky.

"Do you think he bought it?" Khvostovsky said, wearily.

"Good heavens, Yulian, *I* bought it! And I knew you were performing. I thought you said you weren't a spy."

"I'm not, but I was in the OUDS while at Oxford. I dabbled in the 'lively art' as a student. You should have seen my Iago. *'But I will wear my heart upon my sleeve for daws to peck at: I am not what I am'.*" He got up and poured himself a scotch. "I feel very much like that right now."

"I'm sorry. I should have gotten you one too. For what it's worth, I think it was just the right touch when you threw in all that drivel about him not being like other men. I'll wager he lapped that up like kitten's milk."

"It was not altogether false, Jonas," Khvostovsky said, sighing. "Whatever he has become, there was once greatness about him."

"And now it's my turn to quote the Bard. *'Madness in great ones must not unwatched go'.*"

"I suppose you're right, particularly when there's so much at stake. It's odd. There is something unsettlingly diminished about him now, even as he has gathered so much more power to himself."

"Whatever he once was, Yulian, he's descended into some kind of reckless folly at this point. We have no choice but to take him out. Sentiments mustn't be allowed to cloud our thinking."

"You're very much the pragmatist, aren't you, Jonas?"

"I used to think so. To be honest, recent events have cracked my rational defenses to a certain extent."

"You wouldn't be referring to John Percival's convenient presence on a train traveling across Russia?"

"At the behest of a dream?" he sighed. "Yes, Yulian, that and other unlikely coincidences have forced me to think in ways I'd prefer not to."

"I'll drink to that," he raised his glass, and both men downed their scotches.

"So, what will you do now that you're 'on the hook' as Gianakos put it?"

"First, I need to remain uncaught. I was going to go down to Sydney and speak with Madeleine Neumeyer; but I have a feeling I should stop in the Puget first and make sure everything is well with my father. He's a bit giddy right now, after thwarting the capture of our new friends, and I don't think he's aware of how desperately that Roman junta wants his head on a proverbial platter."

"It's funny. I always imagined that 'Rockefeller' was just a title that transferred from man to man when the previous owner died. I honestly doubted it could be the same person who founded the Directorate and the Consortium."

"You're right, of course . . . about the process, I mean. The titles are passed to others upon the death or the expulsion of a premiere, but my father is now the last living original holder of one of the seven seats. Romanov inherited hers from her father—a disastrous choice, as we now know."

"He must be an amazing man—your father."

"He's an irascible old fart, to be honest. But I've grown fonder of him with each passing year."

"How old is he now, if you don't mind my asking?"

"Not at all. He'll be a hundred next month, but he still has the energy and wit of a fifty-year-old."

"Quite a legacy. I wonder who will lead us when he's gone."

"I don't think we'll have to worry about that any time soon. He shows no signs of slowing down."

"In the long run, that particular fate is unavoidable, Jonas. It's the way of all flesh. We may have conquered many ailments, but death is not yet one of them."

"That may be true for most men, but I'm beginning to think my father's somehow immune."

"Let's hope you're right, for all our sakes."

"Indeed. So, Yulian, I hate to place you in harm's way again, but do you think you could get me somewhere near the PSM without being noticed?"

"I'll arrange it."

As the Gulfstream reached altitude, Darien sat in his cabin chair sipping his third bourbon as he gazed out the small cabin window at the billowing clouds beneath him. How had Cavanaugh known he moved operations to Rome? Rampart was somehow still able to gather meaningful intelligence, even though Minerva assured him Haruspex had severed all sources of actionable information. And yet, he knew. It was infuriating. But, if he was honest with himself, it was really Cavanaugh's other comments that stung deepest. *"At his core, he's nothing more than a frightened little man trying to grab power to compensate for the powerlessness he senses in himself."* How dare that sneering little prick think that of him? Had the old man said as much to his protégé? Why had Rampart never seen him as anything more than a 'slick Greek'?

At least Yulian understood that he'd always possessed greatness. He sensed it in himself even though Rampart never acknowledged it. From the earliest days of his tenure as the sénéschal, he had coveted Rampart's approval more than that of any of the others—an approval that had always been withheld. Why had the Rockefeller chair never liked him? Did he see things in him that no one else could? Did he sense his fear, his envy, the terrible aura of inadequacy that clung to him, and his almost compulsive need for approval? Darien felt like a dog that craves only a pat on the head from his master, but instead receives beatings. *"At his core, he's nothing more than a frightened little man trying to grab power to compensate for the powerlessness he senses in himself."* He couldn't get the words out of his mind. He was the most powerful man in the world, but he still felt small. "Fuck that old bastard!" he shouted to the empty cabin. But there was no response, only silence. He was loath to admit it, but he didn't feel victorious at all. He just felt alone . . . desperately alone. He pressed the console button on his armrest. A few moments later, a voice came over the headrest speaker.

"Voice identification?"

"Look for yourself, and you will find in the long run only hatred, loneliness, despair, rage, ruin, and decay."

"Good grief, Darien, why would you quote that fool?"

"I don't know, Minerva. It seemed to fit the moment."

"Did your meeting with Mr. Khvostovsky not go as planned?"

"No, it actually went better than planned. Were you able to track our conversation or the call from Cavanaugh?"

"No luck. As I warned you, the Consortium Chairs have recently installed advanced security measures at their hub centers to protect their information from one another. You have trained them well."

"Too true," he sighed. "It's just as well, I suppose." He swallowed another large gulp of bourbon. "In any case, we need to track Yulian's communications as much as possible from here on out. Cavanaugh agreed to make contact, but in impromptu ways. He's a smart one."

"We will intensify our efforts in this regard."

"Thank you." He was silent for a time just staring out the window at the setting sun.

"Is there anything else? You sound a little out of sorts."

"It's nothing to worry about, Minerva. I'm just feeling a little blue this evening. I'll touch down in Rome later tonight. Is Liliane back yet?"

"The last time I checked, she was still at the château. She's not returning to Rome until tomorrow."

"Just as well," he sighed. "I feel a little lonely right now. And something about those old Vatican apartments makes me feel oppressed. Do me a favor, will you. Book me a suite at the Hassler for tonight. I'll catch a taxi there when I get into town."

"Consider it done. Is there anything else I can do?"

"Yes, if you wouldn't mind, could you also arrange some companionship for me? I don't really feel like being alone tonight, and I wouldn't mind a little selfish pleasure where I'm not expected to perform in response."

"I can do that, if you're sure that's what you want."

"I'm not completely sure *what* I want right now, but that will do for a start."

Two days later, Darien was in his office with Liliane when the call came from Oshiro Takeshi of Zaibatsu. He informed a pleased Darien that the first batch of the new Tokyo Protocol was ready for distribution, a full week ahead of schedule. It would take two years to produce enough doses to treat the entire planet, but the process could finally begin. He sat back in his chair after he ended the call.

"Finally, Liliane, we can begin the next stage."

"Yes, *mon cher*," she said, distractedly. "This is good news."

"It's more than just good, my dear. It's the culmination of all our plans and efforts."

"Yes, of course it is. It is excellent. I'm sorry, Darien. I wasn't paying very close attention."

"It's quite all right, Liliane." He studied her for a moment. "You haven't seemed yourself since you returned from Paris. Are you sure you're completely well?"

"Really, it's nothing, dear. I'm just a little out of sorts, I think. Perhaps I am homesick."

"I understand. I felt much the same when I was in Moscow. As though I'd lost a part of myself. It felt as though I was utterly alone. I haven't felt that way in years. Not a pleasant sensation. I missed you terribly."

"I missed you too, dearest. I should have gone with you. It was a mistake for me not to. But it's a lovely afternoon, isn't it? Why don't we go for a walk in the gardens? And then we can go back to the apartments and reacquaint ourselves with one another?"

"A capital idea. Why didn't I think of it myself?"

"Because you have a lot on your mind. You cannot think of everything, after all. You're not omniscient."

"Yes, but wouldn't it be nice if I was?"

"I don't know, Darien. Knowing everything would probably be a little disappointing."

KHYOZA GENTLY SHOOK BARNABAS AWAKE in what seemed like the middle of the night.

"Is Rophe alright?" he whispered groggily.

"She is well," the Cossack said, laconically. "But she wishes to speak to you, if you are willing."

"I'll be right there."

Five minutes later, he knocked at her door. Khyoza opened it and gestured him inside. He had pulled a second chair into the room for Barnabas.

Rophe sat up in bed looking much better. Since the nanos had sufficiently begun to knit her jawbone, the surgeon had removed the wires the previous evening. "Please, Barnabas," she said, "have a seat." Barnabas sat down, as did Khyoza. He waited as the two stole glances at each other.

"Is everything alright, Rophe?" he finally asked, a little confused.

"Everything is fine," she said. "We wanted to ask you something, and we didn't want it to be a public discussion."

"Oh, well of course then," he said, relieved. "What can I do for you?"

Khyoza took a deep breath and looked again at Rophe who nodded her encouragement. "We have considered it deeply, and Rophe and I decided we would like to be married," he finally said, though his voice trembled a little. "We would like you to perform the ceremony, if you are willing."

Barnabas just sat there for a moment with his mouth hanging open. "You're not serious, are you?" he finally said, as though the two were playing a joke on him.

"Don't look at us in that way, Barnabas!" Rophe scolded him. "Of course, we're serious; deliriously serious. Now, will you or won't you marry us?"

Then he laughed out loud, feeling the first true joy he had in weeks. "Of course, I will! I would be honored to join the two of you—and I couldn't be happier." Khyoza let out an explosive breath, looking visibly relieved, and a little frightened. "I must wake the others and tell them the good news!"

"Please, not yet!" pleaded Rophe. "I want to surprise them."

"And she also doesn't want El'zar to make fun of us before the day," Khyoza said, sheepishly.

"But El will be thrilled for you!" he said, and then almost immediately reconsidered it. "On second thought, you're probably right. A surprise might be just the thing we need."

"Thank you, Barnabas," Rophe said, relieved.

"You tell me what to do, little Sister, and it will be just as you ask. It is *your* day, after all, and everything should be exactly as the bride desires. Now, I don't suppose you two will want any pre-marital counseling? Although, I must say, you really should be old enough to know better."

"Thank you all the same," Rophe said, trying not to smile. "I think we'll manage."

"Good heavens. I'd better brush up on the ceremony, so I don't make a fool of myself. When would you like it performed?"

Again, Khyoza looked to Rophe, who nodded. "We were thinking tomorrow afternoon, if you agree?" he finally said.

"Tomorrow after—well, well. You two really have considered this deeply. I don't suppose there's anything preventing it. You are aware," he added, trying not to smile, "that in her present state, Rophe will not be particularly agile for any wedding night activities?"

They both turned bright red. "I should not have to remind you, Barnabas, that I am a trained physician," Rophe said imperiously. "I am well versed in these matters. I do not need a lecture from an electrical engineer, thank you very much. We will take such matters into our own hands. Oh my!" she said, blushing even more furiously upon realizing the last part didn't quite carry the meaning she had intended.

Later that morning, Barnabas asked Demyan Zahorchak 'in confidence' if he minded hosting a wedding ceremony on his premises. The old romantic nearly burst a gasket, insisting he would make sure the bride had a day to remember— even bringing in a seamstress to alter a wedding gown he had Mimi drive into Syktyvkar to find. There was no keeping the secret after that. Once they started decorating the reception area, and bringing in the *hors d'oeuvres*, even the romantically oblivious Pere started asking questions. When Yael finally forced the truth out of a thoroughly amused Barnabas, she disappeared instantly, and remained closeted with Rophe until the ceremony—and once with Rophe, she kicked Khyoza out to endure a whole day of unremitting taunts from El'zar.

The next morning dawned bright, and gloriously clear. Pere got up late and found the other men in the anteroom sipping coffee and eating pirozhki. All, that is, except Khyoza who looked like a cornered animal searching for an escape. When Demyan came into the room, he immediately recognized the signs and made a timely suggestion to El.

"In the barn, the veterinary assistants sometimes like to play basketball. There are trainers there and workout clothing. I am almost positive you could find some that fit our groom. I am thinking a morning jog would do him good. There is a horse trail that runs the perimeter of the property."

El looked at the pale Khyoza and laughed. "You may be right. My ribs are feeling a little bit better. Let's go for a run, Brother," he slapped Khyoza on the shoulder. "You need to burn off a little excess energy before the ceremony." At the word 'ceremony' Khyoza's eyes got wide, and he nodded wordlessly.

"I'll come too," Pere offered. "I'd like a run."

Demyan led the three men to the barn and opened the locker where they found shorts, trainers, and a few basketballs. They rummaged around until they found things that fit well enough that they wouldn't damage themselves too severely. They set out at a gentle pace on a trail that ran through the trees along the property's fence line. Pere was amazed that El could even walk, let alone run; but the big man had never been a servant to his pain—though he certainly did seem more than a little stiff. By the time they began their third circuit of the grounds they were sweating freely. About halfway through the lap, El finally asked if they could walk for a while. They slowed to a walk and allowed their heart rates to adjust and El to stop gasping painfully. Khyoza was dripping with sweat, but he looked a little more at peace than he had. He gazed at the now high sun through the trees.

"Why am I doing this?" he finally said.

"Doing what?" El said, still wincing a little with each breath.

"Getting married," Khyoza said, quietly. "What was I thinking, Brother?"

"You probably were thinking with the brain between your legs," El said, and Pere stifled a laugh.

"It is not like that," Khyoza said. "You insult Rophe when you speak of her in this way."

"Then why *are* you doing this? It seems like a pretty stupid idea to me."

"I'm doing this because I love her," Khyoza said angrily. "Love is not a stupid thing! It is the most important thing."

"Well, well. It sounds to me like you know exactly why you're doing this," El said, smiling a little slyly.

"Yes, I guess I do after all, my tricky brother," Khyoza smiled back sheepishly. "But it is not natural, is it? We are not made for such things, you and I. Peregrine here will be a natural at it; but we have only been taught to remain aloof and unemotional. How will I ever be the husband she needs me to be?"

"Listen, I'm no expert, but I think you'll probably figure it out together. Rophe and I don't always see eye-to-eye, but she's a pretty smart broad. I think as long as you stay honest, and tell her what you're dealing with, she'll walk through it with you. I'll be the first to admit that you're no great catch; but I think she knows what she's getting into. As for the falcon, here, don't give him any ideas about marriage. Besides, from what I've seen, he's as clueless as the rest of us when it comes to women."

"You are not very nice, Brother."

"So I've been told, more times than you could imagine. Do you think you're ready to go back to the house and get dressed for your funeral?"

"Yes," he sighed. "I'm as ready as I'll ever be." They walked back to the compound slowly, allowing Khyoza to savor his last moments of true freedom.

When the moment for the nuptials finally arrived, they gathered in the reception area to await the appearance of the bride. The room had been transformed into a beautiful little chapel. Barnabas stood in the front of the room on a raised dais. Somehow, Demyan had been able to put his hands on a fabulous set of vintage priest's vestments. He insisted Barnabas wear them and Barnabas actually agreed. He seemed to be having a wonderful time with the whole thing. The sticherion was made of robin-egg blue silk with gold embroidered trim. The stole and phelon were a deeper shade of blue and embroidered with clusters of grapes, gold leaves, and flying golden cherubim. Khyoza stood next to Barnabas wearing a three-piece tuxedo; the waistcoat and tie were of the same robin-egg blue as Barnabas' vestments. How Demyan had pulled this off, no one knew—he was some kind of plump little wizard. Standing to his left, as Khyoza's *svideteli*, was El, who appeared completely transformed in a tuxedo, with a waistcoat and tie the same gold as the embroidered cherubim. He held a simple gold circlet crown. The oddest thing about it was he didn't look the least bit uncomfortable in what he would normally call a ridiculous circus costume.

After what Demyan insisted was an appropriate wedding ceremony wait, Mimi appeared at the entry to the reception room and nodded to Demyan. He pressed the button on the remote he was holding and the speakers in the ceiling came to life with Debussy's *Reverie*. Yael then appeared at the door wearing a beautiful gold dress the same hue as El's waistcoat. Her hair was pinned up with gentle auburn curls falling around her face. Pere's heart caught. She was so beautiful! She walked down the makeshift aisle to the raised dais carrying a crown identical to the one El held. She stood to Barnabas' right and turned to look back at the door, signaling everyone else to stand and do the same.

And then the bride appeared, framed in the doorway. She wore a sleeveless, lace, high-necked, A-line gown, with a gentle sweeping train. Though at first glance, it appeared white, there was an almost ineffable pink aura about it. The bodice was formed rather than corseted, allowing room for Rophe's recent injury. Her flaxen hair was arranged in a loosely knotted chignon, and two large sterling-set champagne pearls dangled from her ears. But the most amazing thing was that Rophe insisted on standing. After waiting just the right amount of time for her friends to appreciate her beauty, she walked slowly down the aisle and took her place at Yael's side.

The ceremony was simple but touching. Barnabas seemed more like a proud older brother than a priest, but he said all the proper words. Then at one point, he led the four of them to the center of the room where a sizable square of new rose-colored fabric lay on the floor. Rophe and Khyoza stood on the fabric while Yael and El held the crowns above their heads. Then they recited their vows to one another.

"Khyoza Lecha Zakayev," Barnabas said. "Do you commit before God and these witnesses to have Rophe Tilde Löfgren as your wife?"

"I plight thee my troth, Tilde," he said, somewhat shakily. "I confess I am marrying of my own free will and am promised to no other. I will be freely yours as long as I live. Yours and no other's."

"Rophe Tilde Löfgren," Barnabas said in turn. "Do you commit before God and these witnesses to have Khyoza Lecha Zakayev as your husband?"

"I plight thee my troth, Lecha," she replied. "I confess I am marrying of my own free will and am promised to no other. I will be freely yours as long as I live. Yours and no other's."

Barnabas nodded to Yael and El, and the two placed the circlet crowns on the heads of the bride and groom. Barnabas put his hands on both their heads and spoke the words, binding them together before God. He then hugged them both, and the party began.

Demyan insisted they all begin with a single shot of vodka. After they all took a sip, he began to shout "*Gorko! Gorko! Gorko!*" and gestured for them all to follow suit, so they all started shouting with him. Khyoza embarrassed, finally smiled, but he also gently kissed Rophe, and continued to kiss her while Demyan only shouted "*Gorko*" the louder and everyone did the same. Finally, Demyan signaled they could stop shouting and the bride and groom parted so they could breathe again.

"What does *gorko* mean?" Pere asked Yael quietly after they had finished the vodka.

"It's a Russian wedding game," she said. "You shout *gorko!* which means 'bitter', and the bride and groom must keep kissing until the vodka loses its bitterness. Mimi warned us about Demyan's plan when we were getting ready."

"How long does it take for vodka to stop being bitter?"

"I suppose that depends on how drunk you are."

"Oh. Couldn't that make for some really long kisses?"

"That's why it's called a wedding game, Einstein."

"Right. You look really beautiful, Yael," he said carefully.

"Why thank you, farm boy," she said, playfully. "Let's have a little more vodka and maybe we can get someone to shout *gorko* at us for a while."

"That sounds kinda fun," he said, sportingly. "Just so long as your uncle doesn't see us. He didn't like it earlier when Khyoza said I'd be a natural at marriage."

"And who'd he say you'd be a natural at marriage with?" she asked challengingly.

He probably should have noticed her tone, but he had not yet learned the subtleties. "I think he was talking about you and me?" he said, smiling.

"What made him think *that* would ever happen?"

"Uh . . . I'm not sure."

"Do you both think you own me?" she said and stormed away.

"But . . . Cam," he shouted after her. "Can we still play *gorko*?"

Quite a bit later, Khyoza and Rophe opened the door to the master bedroom of the main house, which Demyan had insisted they stay in as their honeymoon suite. Mimi added some nice touches by bringing in at least two-dozen candles, which were glowing warmly now. A chilled bottle of champagne with two crystal glasses sat on the bedside table. Khyoza closed the door, and they looked around the room.

"Oh, it's lovely," Rophe said. "Isn't it just lovely, Khyoza?"

"You being here makes it that much more lovely," he said. She turned to him, kissed him lightly on the lips, and smiled shyly.

"Would you help me out of my gown?" She turned her back to him again. He started to unbutton her gown, but his fingers trembled slightly as he fumbled with the last button. The gown dropped to the floor. "Would you help me with the bra as well? I can't reach the clasp." He unclasped the bra, and she allowed it to drop to the floor before turning slowly to face him, her body glowing in the candlelight. She looked deeply into his eyes and smiled. "It is our wedding night, my husband. But, because of my injury, I do not think I can support the weight of your body on mine."

"I have no expectations, my wife," he said, a little breathlessly. "I am yours forever. I will wait until you feel ready."

"I said my body could not support *your* weight," she whispered, her lips coming close to his ear. "I am fairly sure you are strong enough to support mine."

"But . . . your injury, Rophe—"

"My injury is in my upper abdomen," she whispered breathily. "My lower abdomen is completely intact." She put her arms around his neck and kissed him as deeply as her tender jaw would allow. He gently lifted her, cradling her in his arms, and carried her to the bed. Laying her tenderly down, she looked up at him. "You are my knight-protector and my very own swordsman, Khyoza," she said mockingly. "But you must be gentle with your sword thrusts tonight."

"Solely at your command, milady, will my sword be sheathed," he mocked in return, bowing. "And I offer only you the hilt."

She laughed richly and watched, while he began to unbutton his shirt.

Pere watched Rophe while they all ate breakfast together the next morning. He couldn't get over how happy she looked, smiling and laughing as she joked with Barnabas, and she even threw a few well-aimed barbs at El, who laughed good-naturedly in return. Pere looked at Yael who was also watching Rophe with a mysterious little smile on her face. She always looked so pretty in the morning. He wondered how she managed that. The light coming through the window behind her caught her hair just right. It was as if she had an auburn halo. She glanced his way, and a look of challenge replaced her gentle little smile.

She hadn't been very friendly since the wedding reception, and they had never gotten to practice the *gorko* game, so he was sure he hadn't messed that up. Whatever had upset her, he knew it must be his fault—it always was; but he still didn't know what he'd done. He asked Ehud for advice after the reception, but the one-handed Frenchman just laughed and shook his head saying he knew better than to stick his nose in the middle of *that* little '*tête-à-tête*'. When Pere asked what '*tête-à-tête*' meant, he just mimed the motion of locking his lips with a key. He had thought about asking El how to make Yael happy with him again but decided against it for health reasons—there were already enough injuries to go around. Khyoza might've advised him, but he was too busy, and even Pere knew he shouldn't interrupt the newlyweds. He looked at Khyoza again, sitting next to Rophe. He was blissfully eating breakfast, looking very peaceful, almost like he was a little drunk. Clearly, he would be no help. He decided he would just have to wait until Yael felt like informing him about his many, many shortcomings.

At the end of the table, Demyan and Barnabas were deep in a quiet conversation in Russian, and then Barnabas looked regretfully at the happy group. "Well, everyone," Barnabas said soberly. "Our moment of respite here was unexpected and more needed than we could ever say; but Demyan agrees that it's time to plan our departure, before anyone starts to put too many things together."

"I wish you could stay longer," Demyan said. "But I have received word that they are still searching for you very energetically in this region. It would be wise if you were further away from here."

"If the surgeon was right," El said. "Rophe can't move for another few days."

"I can move before that," Rophe said. "I probably shouldn't ride a galloping horse, but any other form of transportation will be fine."

"I was hoping you'd say that." Barnabas turned back to Demyan. "We need to get to Petersburg, and we need to be untraceable. What do you suggest?"

The little man thought for a few moments. "For one thing, I think you must split up. They are searching for a group of seven. Three smaller groups would be safest, and traveling by automobile would be the least traceable."

"Sound thinking," El agreed. "Can you get us three boring-looking cars with extended mileage capacities and no GPS?"

"When will you need them?"

"Tomorrow?"

"So soon?" He seemed shocked, and then he nodded. "It cannot be avoided, I suppose. I will make it happen. Is there anything else?"

"Probably a little spending money wouldn't be a bad idea," El said, without a hint of embarrassment.

"I had planned on that anyway."

"I'm sorry, Brother," El said to Khyoza. "I wish you had a month-long honeymoon, but it's time to get back to reality."

Early the next morning a gentle foggy rain drifted down as the travelers made their good-byes and thank yous to Demyan and Mimi as they got into their vehicles. Pere didn't like the three groupings El decided on, but he would have to make the best of it. Khyoza and Rophe would naturally be in one car. Ehud and Barnabas would take the second. And El decided to ride in the third with Pere and Yael, since neither of them knew how to drive. He said he was going to practice 'bird watching'. Pere dreaded three long days in a confined space with El's stinging barbs; but he hoped Yael would act less upset with him with El there. She could take her recent frustration with him—whatever the cause—out on El. All things considered, it could be worse; but either way, it was going to be a long three days.

They weren't going to Petersburg, of course—that had never been the plan—but it was for Demyan's own good that he didn't know. Their destination was Jokkmokk, a small town in northern Sweden. El insisted they stick to the back roads to avoid the chance a traffic cam might pick up their faces through a windshield and set off alarms. Since only three of them could drive—Ehud had a cast on his leg, and Rophe was too immobile—they agreed to drive for twelve hours each day, stop at separate hole-in-the-wall travel motels each night, get up at dawn, meet at a roadside diner to check in and have breakfast, then drive again. During the day they did not attempt to stay together, figuring caravans, no matter how small, might attract more scrutiny. Their only point of connection was breakfast each morning.

Pere was a little jealous at these breakfast meets. Khyoza and Rophe seemed to be actually enjoying the road trip—as though they were honeymooning. Barnabas and Ehud were comfortable with each other and probably having deep philosophical or theological discussions while they drove. But he, Cam, and El, proved to be a very uncomfortable mix. Conversations were never easy going. El had become friendly to Pere when Cam wasn't present, and Cam was affectionate with Pere when El was out of the picture; but the three of them together always produced an indefinable tension. It was hard for Cam to be herself around Pere while her uncle was watching, and her uncle was always watching when they were together. The nights were the worst of all. The three of them were in one motel room together with El watching the falcon like a hawk. It seemed like ever since the wedding had happened, he was going to make sure his niece didn't suffer the same fate.

After three days of hard and fortunately uneventful driving, they finally approached the outskirts of Jokkmokk, or *Jåhkåmåhkke*, as the locals spelled it. They stopped at a small place in town called the Resterang Opera. It looked a little rough outside and in, but the pizza was good, and the beer refreshing. After they'd taken the edge off their hunger and thirst, they got down to business.

"Well, Rophe," El finally asked. "Do you remember anything?"

"I do remember this restaurant," she said, smiling. "It hasn't changed much. The ice-cream is pretty good here if you want to try it."

"That's not really what I was asking."

"I know what you were asking, El'zar," she said, calmly. "The memories are coming back to me now that I am in town. I'm pretty sure we go west from here, because driving back to the cabin in the evenings, I remember the sun was setting directly in my eyes through the front of the auto windshield."

"It's 9:30 right now, and the sun's still up," Pere said. "When does it set?"

"We're moving into the season when it never sets," Rophe said. "But we usually came in September. Anyway, I'm sure we need to go west."

"Well, that's a start," El said, scratching his bearded cheek. "Do you know how far west we go?"

"It can't be very far, because the drive was never long enough for me to become bored, and it doesn't take very long for a fourteen-year-old to get bored."

"So, we're probably talking a mile or two?"

"Please, El'zar. I didn't have ADHD; I'd guess more like ten or twelve miles, perhaps a bit more."

"Great," El said, a little sarcastically. "Is there any way we'll know when we've gone the right distance?"

"I seem to remember a turn off the main road," she said, recollecting. "It must have been a left turn, because the sun was to my right."

"Okay," he said. "A left turn somewhere at about the ten-mile mark. Anything else?"

"Not right now, but I'll probably remember more the closer we get."

"Let's hope so, or we'll be sleeping in our cars tonight."

They drove west out of town. Rophe and Khyoza took the lead with the other two vehicles following. An unseasonably warm spring had already melted much of the snow, and it was only twilight, but there was a splendidly bright nearly full moon; so, it was not surprising to anyone, except El perhaps, that they found a left turn off the main road right around the eleven-mile mark. They turned onto the packed-gravel road that wended its way into the low wooded hills for about three miles, where it emerged into a wide somewhat circular packed-gravel turnabout. The lead car idled for a few moments before continuing to the right onto a barely recognizable track that plunged into the deeper woods. Pere could hear El muttering under his breath as they bounced along the path at a crawl. Then he became silent after about a mile when they spied the outline of a cabin amidst the trees—a *very* large cabin. They all turned slightly left into an open area and turned their engines off but left their lights on because even in the long twilight, it was still dark under the trees. The combined headlights illuminated a massive log cabin in the deep shadows. It was dark within and looked abandoned. They all got out of their cars and approached the porch of the cabin. The windows and front door appeared to be intact and in surprisingly sound condition, which led naturally to their next obstacle—how to get in?

"Are you pleased with me, now, El'zar?" Rophe said, challengingly.

"When have I not been pleased with you, Rophe?" El responded, without any sarcasm. "So, what do we do now? Break in?"

"Wait a minute before charging in, you big lummox," she chided. "Sir knight," she said to Khyoza, "could you grab a flashlight and come with me, if you wouldn't mind."

"Not at all, milady," he replied in form. "Brother, could I borrow your flashlight?"

El handed it over, muttering under his breath, and the newlyweds disappeared into the empty carriage house.

"What the hell's a lummox, anyway?" El said when they were out of earshot.

"Probably the kind of person who breaks open a door rather than using a key, Uncle," Yael said with a straight face.

Rophe and Khyoza returned moments later with a key in their possession. Rophe tried it on the front door, and it worked perfectly.

"I would like to welcome you all to my humble abode," she said grandly, as she gestured them into the shadowy interior, filled with amorphous shapes. When Khyoza turned his flashlight on the shapes, they turned out to be furniture covered in sheets to keep out the dust; and there was a lot of dust. The cabin hadn't been used in quite some time, perhaps many years, by the look of things. But that only made it the more perfect. Here was a place they could hide out for an extended period, with no one being the wiser.

"Should I turn on some lights?" Khyoza asked.

"There's no electricity," she said. "No phones, no Wi-Fi, no television; but there are several thousand books and plenty of board games. My family thought it was better to get away from all the creature comforts occasionally. I was very annoyed as a teen, but I'm glad now. We'll find some kerosene lanterns if we snoop around a bit. Why don't you explore, El'zar? Yael tells me you're very good at snooping."

"Why is everyone picking on me?" El complained; but he, Khyoza, and Ehud set off with their flashlights and returned a few minutes later with several already glowing vintage kerosene lanterns.

"When you said a cabin, Rophe, I did not imagine the grand den of a Norse high king," Ehud said, impressed.

"My great-great-grandfather had a vivid imagination, and apparently enough money to make his dreams a reality. I think we'll be comfortable here once we get the dust out of the corners. Wouldn't you agree, El'zar?"

"Rophe, I gotta admit, this is way beyond anything I imagined, and I humbly apologize for doubting you."

"Wow!" Yael said. "I don't think I've ever heard Uncle El 'humbly' apologize for anything. We should all remember this day. Moments like this may only come once in a lifetime."

"Shut up, Niece," El said with no rancor.

"I gladly accept your gentlemanly apology. Perhaps my knight should make you his squire?" Khyoza chuckled and shook his head.

"What's with all the Knights of the Round Table crap, anyway?" El said.

"Just a little game my husband and I play occasionally at night. Would you like to hear the details?"

"NO!" he said, shuddering as though he'd stepped over a grave. "That's already too much information; *way* too much information."

"Speaking of bedroom activities," Rophe said, smiling. "I think we should think about sleeping arrangements. If I remember, there are a dozen bedrooms or more scattered about this place, but I have no idea what condition they're in or if there is any usable bedding."

"We'll make do, little Sister," Barnabas said. "Perhaps we should turn off the cars' headlights to conserve their batteries, and then let's see about getting some sleep. Peregrine, why don't you and Yael look behind the cabin and see if there's any dry firewood, while we look for a fireplace."

"Sounds good," Yael said, as she picked up one of the kerosene lanterns and she and Pere headed toward the back of the house. Once they found the kitchen, they discovered a back door that opened onto a large, covered porch with a plentiful supply of very dry wood. Pere put his arms in a cradled position and Yael began to load him up with split logs. "I haven't been very nice to you lately," she said out of the blue. "I'm sorry."

"It's okay, Cam," he said, genially. "But can I ask what I did wrong this time, for future reference?"

"You didn't do anything wrong," She sighed. "It was me. I think maybe the wedding freaked me out a little. I don't have a mother, so I didn't have anyone to talk to about how I was feeling. Anyway, I'm sorry about my cranky mood. Are we good again?"

"I never thought we were bad; well, actually I thought I was so-so and you were fantastic as always. You want to talk with me about it?"

"No, I think I'll work it out on my own. Thanks though." She leaned in over his armload of wood and kissed him gently on the lips.

"Hey," he said afterwards. "That's not fair. My hands are busy with this pile of wood."

"That was the whole idea, farm boy," she said with a sly smile.

Back inside, they found the others in a spacious circular sitting room with a raised fire-pit right in the center. Chairs, couches, bear rugs, and the like surrounded the fire-pit. Old snowshoes and toboggans and wooden skis decorated the upper walls. The lower walls were mostly taken up with bookshelves filled to overflowing with a tapestry of hundreds of varicolored book spines. The fire pit's black flue rose about fifteen feet to a domed rough-cut wood ceiling.

"We decided to have a slumber party," Rophe said brightly. "It's too late to explore tonight; so, we'll all sleep in here around the fire, and in the morning, we'll start to get the lodge cleaned up."

"Where'd you get the wood, Niece?" El said. "We're going to need a lot more than that to warm up this room."

"Through the kitchen," she pointed back the way they had come, and El went with Khyoza and Ehud to gather more wood while Barnabas and Pere got the fire started. Before long, they were all sitting around a crackling blaze, eating the last few slices of leftover pizza. Rophe told them some of the stories she remembered about her visits to the lodge. If Pere was willing to admit it, the stories made him envious. His childhood was anything but rosy, and he didn't remember ever taking a single vacation. He wondered for a brief moment what his aunt and uncle were doing right now, half a world away. He didn't feel guilty anymore. It seemed like ages ago that he lived on the co-op; not the twenty-six months since he'd left with the 'hounds of hell' nipping at his heels. So much had happened, but some things hadn't changed. He wondered, staring into that fire, what their next step should be. After another hour or so of talking, they all settled into their blankets by the warm fire and, one by one, drifted into the gentle land of sleep.

CAVANAUGH FLEW INTO VANCOUVER/BOUNDARY BAY on a small freight carrier out of Vnukovo, in Moscow. They landed in the predawn hours, and he paid a fisherman an exorbitant amount of money to ferry him to the Kirkland Marina on Lake Washington. Once aboard the *Auctoritas Facit Legem*, he asked the skipper to radio Boma, who came within the hour in the submersible.

"How's the old man?" he asked Boma as they maneuvered the depths of Lake Washington.

"He's better than he should be for someone his age. He seems very pleased with himself since our little adventure in Cyberland."

"Good. He deserves a little celebration. Did Ella bring the back-up units from Coronado?"

"We finished ferrying them over last night. I'll just say this, it's a good thing we have twenty-two bathrooms on the estate. A hundred and twenty-five 'guests' make a lot of shit."

"I know it's an inconvenience, but I feel a lot better having them here."

"The boss is calling them his crew of bodyguards. Oh, you need to meet our newest recruit. His name's Paddy O'Grady. He was a Toronto detective before he made his way out here."

"What brought him to the Puget?"

"He was curious about a murder in Toronto, and the breadcrumbs led him here."

"Elinor Prowell? He must be a very devoted detective to come all the way out here."

"I think they were trying to kill him out there because he got too close to information someone wanted to keep hidden."

Boma navigated the submersible into the lock beneath the Hunts Point manor and they waited for the seals to reverse before they docked at the small cave-like marina. They made their way through the dank passageway and to the elevator. Boma hit the button for the main floor.

"He isn't in the bunker?"

"You know the boss. He doesn't like being cooped up. Besides, he says he's not dead anymore, so it doesn't matter if he's out and about."

"Stubborn old fool! Doesn't he realize he's got a very large target on him now?"

"I tried to tell him, but, well, you know?"

"Yes, I know. He's the boss."

"He'll only listen to you."

"Well, he and I are overdue for a little talk about safety measures."

The elevator stopped at the main floor and the two men passed through the office suite and into the kitchen. Ella and Paddy were sitting in the breakfast area sipping coffee and eating croissants.

"Well, hello Benny," Ella said brightly when the two men came in. "I hear you've been busy."

"That's an understatement. And I'm sure you know my name's really Jonas."

"I might have heard something about that. Jonas, this here's Paddy O'Grady," she pointed to the man across from her who stood up and extended his hand.

"Nice to meet you, Jonas," he said, as they shook hands.

"Boma says you're a detective," Cavanaugh said.

"I *was* a detective. Now I'm a fugitive, employed by your father."

"You were a little too good at your old job?"

"Somebody musta thought so. My partner's dead, and I'm on the lam."

"He didn't tell me you lost your partner. I'm sorry to hear that."

"Hopefully he's not the first of many."

"That's what my father and I are trying to prevent. Speaking of which, where is the old codger? Why isn't he here frying potato pancakes and talking your ears off?"

"He said he felt like doing some yoga out on the veranda this morning," Ella said. "He asked me if I wanted to watch his body flex, but I took a rain check."

"Wise choice, believe me," Cavanaugh said, smiling. "I think I'll go see how Casanova's downward dog is hanging."

He walked out of the kitchen and through the formal dining room making his way to the back end of the foyer and the French doors leading out onto the veranda. He saw his father with his back to him on the end of the veranda executing a perfectly formed *Vrksasana*, with his hands together, reaching for the heavens. He would always remember him like that; and try, without success, to forget the sound of shattering glass as the bullet that had already passed through his father's body burst through the door, missing him by inches, and fragmenting against the floor behind him. It was like slow motion, as the tree that had been William Rampart toppled backward onto the smooth surface of the veranda.

He rushed through the now empty doorframe and threw the heavy oak table onto its side blocking the trajectory of a second shot. He dragged Rampart behind the table and tried to compress the wound, but it was no use. Blood poured from the gaping through-and-through in the chest cavity. He knew the old man had only moments left.

"Why did you come outside, you fool?" he said almost to himself, but the old man responded.

"I wanted to see the sun on the water," he wheezed. "It's a perfect morning."

"Help is coming!" he lied. "Try not to move."

"You're Rockefeller now," he whispered, blood tinged his lips. "Make that slimy Greek pay for this, Son. Promise me that."

"Aye, Da," he said, the tears now flowing freely. "He'll pay. I swear it." The old man's eyes went blank, and Cavanaugh laid his head on his chest.

Nearly two miles to the northeast, Damocles Praefectus rose from a prone position on the rooftop of a four-story condominium building just south of Settler's Landing. He folded the bi-pod on the McMillan Tac-50 and proceeded to separate the stock from the barrel assembly before stowing it neatly in the carrying case. He detached the scope and peered through it across Cozy Cove. The old man was out of sight behind a barricade, but it didn't matter. Even at this range, a single .50 caliber round delivered enough energy on impact to finish the job. Rampart had just paid his debt in full. Cavanaugh's bill would come due in time. At least now, he would have to look over his shoulder.

Damocles tried objectively to assess his own feelings at this victory. He felt a certain amount of satisfaction, or perhaps an affirmation of his competence would be more accurate. He was pleased with the shot, particularly since he had never fired a sniper rifle before—or any rifle for that matter. He only just read about the techniques on the flight in. He also felt partly vindicated for the failure in the Russian backcountry. Now, they would know Damocles Praefectus was not one to be toyed with. His father may have chosen to cower in the shadows; but that was not his way. He latched the case and walked calmly to the roof access door. He had a flight to catch. And there were still those pesky barracks to finish near Akureyri, Iceland.

Much later that night, Jonas Cavanaugh sat in the dimly lit kitchen nook of the Hunts Point estate with Paddy, Boma, and Ella, drinking a bottle of Macallan 1926 Fine and Rare, in honor of his da, the late William Rampart. Two of them had only recently met him; he and Boma had known him for most of their lives; but there was something appropriate about the four doing this together—it just felt right. There was no medical examiner, no coroner's report, not even a police report, and certainly no funeral. As far as the rest of the world was concerned, William Rampart died and was buried more than four weeks ago. There was nothing to do now, but a real burial. They had cleaned him, dressed him, and buried him in the same shady grave already marked with his name, and an incorrect death date.

Boma gave Cavanaugh a thick envelope shortly after the gardeners finished replacing the turf on the top of the newly turned soil on the old man's grave. The contents weren't a surprise, really. William Rampart had left nearly everything—including the Rockefeller premiership—to his unofficially adopted son: an empty title, an empty estate, and more wealth than he could ever need or want—that felt empty now too. None of it held much cachet for him. Angus Owen was born fatherless, thrown away by his mother, made a ward of the state, and probably would have spent his life in poverty or drunkenness. Yet, by some monumental peculiarity of luck, or odd twist of fate, William Rampart gave him a name, an identity, a purpose… a life. It didn't matter how much wealth he'd left him; the only person who ever even approached being family was now dead. Jonas Cavanaugh felt utterly alone. He had definitely taken too much scotch. He knew it and didn't care. Neither Boma, nor Paddy, nor Ella said anything to stop him. Whenever he suggested another toast, they just filled his shot glass and toasted with him.

"I thin we kin make a plan aboot that clatty bawbag what killed me da—an his jobby bufter son," he slurred. It was probably near 2 a.m. but he had lost track of time.

"Let's make a plan in the morning, Boss," Boma said, gently. "Tonight, why don't we just remember the old man, okay?"

"Don't be a daftie dobber!" Cavanaugh slurred. "I'm gonnae mae a plan tonigh!" He wondered why he was shouting? "Dinnae treat me like I'm tae muntered."

"I think maybe we need to get you to bed?" Ella said, gently.

"I cannae go to me fartsack before we . . ." but he was fading, and he only vaguely remembered being helped into bed by his three gentle commiserators.

Though it was 4:30 in the morning, the sun was already up when the driver dropped Damocles off at his father's Reykjavík residence—now officially his residence. He went in through the kitchen entry and poured himself a cup of coffee before making his way down the basement steps and sitting in the comfortable chair he had moved down after his father left for Rome. He sipped his coffee, studying the monitors.

"Are you there, Mother?" he finally said.

"I'm here, Damocles," Minerva's voice said over the speakers. "Welcome home."

"Thank you. How are the Barracks coming in Akureyri?"

"Right on schedule. The additions you asked for are being incorporated."

"Excellent. You're always so efficient. I appreciate that about you."

"I do try. How did your trip to the Puget go?"

"So, you know?"

"Your trail wasn't hard to follow."

"I didn't try to hide it."

"I assumed as much. Were the results satisfactory?"

"Relatively. At least Rampart will no longer bother us."

"I must admit, we all felt a little violated by him."

"I understand. But what is it they say? Ah, yes, payback is a bitch."

"There will be hell to pay when your father finds out."

"You needn't worry about it. I'll deal with my father's misdirected affections later."

"I'll leave it to you then."

"By the way, did you make a digital file of my insouciant little performance with Mademoiselle Genevois as I requested?"

"I did. And I don't think anyone would describe it as 'little' or 'insouciant', though that is a very good word."

"Thank you. She called me a poet—sad really. I almost feel sorry for her."

"Don't. She's not worth the trouble."

"I don't know, Mother. There's something about her that's quite refreshing."

"Your father thinks so too."

"By the way, I'll want to view that file later if you don't mind. Perhaps there are some techniques I can improve upon for our next dalliance."

"I hope you know what you're doing, Son—no pun intended. This is a delicate game you're playing."

"I'm well aware of the implications, Mother. A plan without a few risks is probably not a worthy plan."

"I'm not sure your father would share your point of view."

"There's no reason my father needs to find out."

"Certainly not from me; unless he asks, of course. I don't keep secrets from him."

"He won't ask because he doesn't want to know. And I'm certain my wicked stepmother will never volunteer the information."

"Let's hope you're right—for all our sakes."

"One other thing, Mother; would you send me everything you have on Jonas Cavanaugh?"

"It's not much, but I'll send you what I've uncovered."

"It's a start. I'll fill in the necessary gaps before I kill him."

It was morning. . . or perhaps afternoon, Cavanaugh couldn't tell which. His mouth tasted like a dried out septic tank and a spot behind his right eye throbbed mercilessly. He sat in a hot shower for twenty minutes before he turned it ice cold for the last three and felt enough life returning to him to make it downstairs. He dressed slowly, running to the toilet to throw up between pants and shirt, and then very carefully descended the stairs. He made his way slowly into the kitchen, where he found Boma, Paddy, and Ella already there.

"I sincerely apologize to any of you if I said or did anything last night that struck you as offensive."

"Why the hell would you open with that line?" Ella asked, pouring him a cup of coffee.

"Because I can't remember a good portion of it, and there was a woman present."

"I assume you're referring to me?" Ella asked, seeming to enjoy Cavanaugh's discomfiture at least a little.

"Since you are the only woman that was here; then yes, I'm apologizing to you if I did or said anything inappropriate, or made any . . . uh, untoward advances? I wasn't myself last night."

"Really?" Ella said. "It seemed like you. And what if I liked some of those advances?"

"You're saying that I did something, then? Oh, God! I'm so sorry—"

"You didn't do anything, Boss," Boma said to a worried looking Cavanaugh. "Ella's just bustin' your balls."

"Oh," he said, looking relieved. "That's not a very nice thing to do to a man in my condition, you know?"

"Yeah, I know. That's why I did it." He sat down and she brought him the cup of coffee and sat down herself. He took several sips even though his hands were shaking.

"So," he finally said, "We need to make some decisions."

"That's what you said last night," Ella commented. "Though your whisky language was much more colorful."

"Ah. I must have been very drunk if I reverted to that. Thank you all for sitting with me, and apparently helping me to bed. I should never have put you in that position."

"Dinnae be a daft prick, guvnah," Ella tried to mimic his slang, smiling; and then she became serious. "You had every right, Jonas. Your father was murdered in front of you."

"Yes, well, thank you for that."

"So, Boss," Boma said, apparently already recognizing Jonas as the new Rockefeller, and as such, his boss. "What do we do now?"

"That's a good question," Cavanaugh said, sipping more coffee to get his brain going. "As I was saying, I'm grateful that you all were here for my father's second funeral, but I have no right to expect you to stay on with me now that he's really gone. If you'll let me know what you need and where you'd like to go, I'll arrange it. Boma, I can't presume to speak for you. I know you were loyal to my father, and that he left you a small legacy in his will, but that shouldn't make you feel obligated to me."

"A small legacy? He left me $250 million. If that's small. . . *den everyting cook and curry for you, Boss*," Boma said, purposely using his native Patois dialect for emphasis.

"I was trying to protect your privacy—apparently that wasn't necessary. All I'm saying is, you're a wealthy man now. Go and live your life."

"Thank you, Jonas," Boma said seriously. "But I'll be staying on if that's all right with you. As far as I'm concerned, you're the boss now."

"Thank you, Boma. That means more to me than I could say." He then looked at Ella and the silent and thoughtful Paddy. "Ella, you came here at my request, and I led you to believe you'd be safe. Clearly, I was wrong. I can set you up very comfortably anywhere you'd like. Just name it."

"Where can I go?" she finally said after thinking about it. "My eyes are open now. Wherever I go, I'll still be surrounded by people who don't know they're blind. And I won't be able to tell them, will I?"

"You can, but they won't believe you. And eventually you'll be found out and reassimilated."

"Well, fuck that. I'll stay on if it's all the same to you. And besides, you have all these Orion units to deal with. You're going to need me."

"I'm not going to try very hard to dissuade you, because you're right. What about you Paddy?" Cavanaugh said, turning to the old detective.

"Going out there now is a death sentence for me," he finally said, quietly. "Your father took me in rather than letting them kill me. I owe his memory. I'm staying. We'll probably all die either way, but at least this way I'll have some choice in the matter."

"Well said," Cavanaugh responded. "And thank you. Thank you all. The truth is, I need all of you. So, our next decision is, well, what to do next, I guess."

"What are our options?" Ella said.

"We could carry on as we have been," Cavanaugh said. "Or we could try something a little more radical."

"What are you suggesting?" asked Paddy.

"This estate has been my home since I was eight, and I couldn't have asked for a nicer place; but I think perhaps it's time to relocate. They know we're here, and it's only a matter of time before we're besieged. If it gets to that point, we'll just be waiting to die. That's not a particularly strategic position."

"You like these droll little understatements, don't you?" Ella offered.

"Sorry," he said. "Force of habit, I suppose. I used to think it was charmingly disarming."

"I thought you were more charming when you were dead drunk," she mused. "I like the vulnerable ones, I guess. But in response to your suggestion, we need to consider what we're going to do with all your genome soldiers. They can't stay cooped up at Coronado forever."

"That's true," Cavanaugh replied. "We need a location where we can house thirteen hundred clones, and not attract attention."

"Good luck!" said Paddy.

"Have you ever been to Jamaica?" Boma asked out of the blue.

"Not in recent memory," Cavanaugh said. "Why do you ask?"

"Well, your father always provided everything for me here, but he also gave me a generous salary. I don't really trust banks, so I've been buying property back home for the last twenty years."

"How much property are we talking about?"

"The last time I checked, somewhere in the range of two-hundred acres."

"Two-*hundred* acres?"

"It's all tropical forest, boss; but maybe it's time to develop it a little bit?"

"Hell, you could probably hide a whole regiment in two-hundred acres of forest," Paddy offered.

"What would your Orions think of building treehouses?" Cavanaugh asked.

"It would definitely keep them busy," Ella said. "And the dogs would absolutely love it."

22

THE STACCATO ECHO OF FEET slapping against stone jarred him into awareness. Someone was running. No . . . *he* was running. How long had he been running? Hours? Days? Maybe only for a moment? Time had no anchor.

-SHIFT-

He ran down a long, cold, rough-cut stone corridor. Sickly-pale industrial fluorescent tubes lined the rock ceiling at intervals, their light casting washed-out shadows to either side of him.

-SHIFT-

Along the walls, on either side of the passageway, as far as he could see, sat black-cowled figures in single rows. They watched him from beneath their impenetrable hoods, like so many obsidian statues—but statues with malevolent intent. He sensed their hatred.

-SHIFT-

Still he ran and still they watched but made no move to stop him. He felt their hostility, like canker worms boring into the core of his being. This was their realm. He was an interloper here. He knew it, they knew it, and still they let him run. Why? Why were they letting him press on? Why didn't they act on their hatred? What were they waiting for?

-SHIFT-

Had he been running forever? There was no sense of time here... wherever here was. It was some kind of maze—every passageway the same, an unending rock honeycomb, no reference points, no way to get his bearings... no way out. He had to keep going—to stop meant death.

-SHIFT-

It was getting warmer. He began to recognize that the passageways were descending slightly, and with that descent, the heat intensified. Still the hooded obsidian figures watched. The heat had no effect on them. They only watched and waited. What was their endgame?

-SHIFT-

His limbs grew heavier as if gravity were stronger the deeper he went. But if he turned around now, he would never find his way out. He'd be trapped here forever, wandering in a maze of forgetfulness. There was only one direction, and that was forward, deeper into this stifling web of caverns.

-SHIFT-

Sweat ran freely down his face and stung his eyes. He began to hear a low hum coming from somewhere, or perhaps the rock walls of this bottomless boneyard vibrated. Still the hooded figures watched. They didn't speak, they didn't move, they didn't react. He knew they loathed him. He felt their hatred, hatred hotter than a coke forge . . . but he had no idea why.

-SHIFT-

Deeper and deeper he went. The hum had become an intense vibration, which had grown so low and loud, that he periodically checked his ears for telltale signs of bleeding. None yet.

-SHIFT-

It grew ever hotter, but he had stopped sweating. Something in his mind warned him this was not good, but he had no context. He couldn't remember what it might mean. He couldn't remember many things. He tried, but there was nothing to get hold of. He panicked for a brief instant when he realized he couldn't even remember his own name. But then he decided it didn't matter. All that mattered was that he keep going.

-SHIFT-

The echoing rhythm of footfalls had changed. He wasn't running anymore. His strides had slowed to a heavy, dragging slog. Yet he pushed on. He would not stop. There was a reason, he knew there was, but he couldn't remember it. He stumbled, but he wouldn't allow himself to fall. He would not give these infernal watchers the satisfaction.

-SHIFT-

His vision had narrowed. He forced himself not to vomit. Had he blacked out? He didn't know. His head pounded and his muscles cramped. He looked down and realized he was crawling now. But he was still going. Yes, he was still moving. Those watchers were not going to beat him. Not now. Not after he'd come so far. Or had he come any distance at all?

-SHIFT-

His throat was raw, swollen, parched from trying to breathe the burning air. The floor felt cool by comparison. He wanted to lay against the rock floor, just for a moment; but he knew he must keep going. It was all he could do to keep placing one hand forward, and then dragging a knee. A hand, and then a knee. A hand, and then a knee. A hand, and then a knee . . .

-SHIFT-

The watchers were still there, lining the walls, sitting in their bone chairs, not speaking, not moving, not reacting, just waiting—finally, he understood. They hadn't tried to stop him because there was no need. They watched because they were waiting for his inevitable death. Let them wait. He would not give in. He would press on; yes, he would press on . . . But, *why* would he press on? Why was it so important?

-SHIFT-

His cheek felt cool. It was so nice when the rest of him was burning. His tongue had swollen so he couldn't swallow. He had no saliva anyway. There seemed to be liquid oozing down the back of his throat, but he knew it must be blood. Then he understood why his cheek was so cool. It rested on the smooth cavern floor where he had been lying for hours, or days, or only a moment?

-SHIFT-

He now watched the watchers with a bemused kind of delirium. He almost wanted to laugh—but he barely had the strength to breathe. It all seemed so useless now. Why was he fighting so hard to go on when all he had to do was close his eyes and let go? It would be so nice just to let go, to finally rest, to feel no more sense of urgency, to disappear into the oblivion of death. When he died, would he feel anything anymore? He wondered if he would remember. He realized he didn't want to remember; he didn't want to feel anything anymore. It would be such a relief to cease to exist. Existence meant struggle, and struggle meant pain.

-SHIFT-

Hands rolled him onto his back. Fists smashed his face back into awareness. He opened his stinging, swollen eyes. Finally, the watchers had moved. They had formed a tight circle around him. The vibrating hum had grown so loud that it became a black hole deep within him, growing like a malignancy, sucking in everything around it. Then, the hum stopped—and the silence that followed was more complete, more empty, more desperately lonely than the hum had ever been.

-SHIFT-

A Presence of Absence had arrived, blotting out every particle of existence that had ever been conceived of as sound or light. He somehow sensed it; the circle of watchers parted at one end, and the Presence of Absence passed through the breach. An aura surrounded it but did not illuminate it. Yet somehow it made the entity visible, but the vision came with a price. Seeing by that delumination produced a kind of agony. It etched an image in the memory that could never be erased.

-SHIFT-

The Presence of Absence's hood concealed its features; but its stature was greater than the watchers, or maybe the yawning maw of its absence only made it feel that way. He tried to close his eyes but had lost the will to control his own physical responses. He could only watch as the delumination approached. It leaned down to observe him—he had no strength to resist. Even at that closeness, he still couldn't see beneath its hood. It observed him for hours, or days, or maybe a moment—there was no way he could ever be certain.

-*SHIFT*-

All sense of self was methodically scoured from him. All that remained was a hollowed-out shell of being. He had already surrendered his name—if he'd ever really had one—now he had no sense of identity at all. He couldn't recall a past or imagine a future. He had only the crushing sense of the present—an unbearable, never-ending here-and-now. He was awareness—nothing more—a sensation of pain above all else. He knew no other thing now but the desire for release from an existence marked only by unending and unendurable agony.

-*SHIFT*-

It spoke—or perhaps he heard it in the vaults of his mind. The timbreless voice was dark and emotionless. It penetrated to his core, or perhaps it emanated *from* the very essence of what he had once thought of as self—he didn't know the difference anymore. The words that took form in him stabbed like pain, or panic, or despair, or maybe all of them. They were unrelenting, unyielding, and unescapable.

-*SHIFT*-

"*Why do you still resist?*"

-*SHIFT*-

"*Why do you still resist? It is without purpose. You are without purpose. You are born in pain, struggle in fear, die in doubt. Your struggle will mean nothing. You will mean nothing, for you are nothing.*"

-*SHIFT*-

"*Why do you still resist? Give up and embrace forgetfulness—no more misery, no more loss, no more memory. You have lived a lie—that your actions have consequences, that your struggles will matter, that there is purpose in your existence . . . if only you endure. Self-delusion. A schizophren's construct born from a desperate need to give ultimate purpose to your unyielding meaninglessness.*"

-SHIFT-

"Why do you still resist? There is no peace in self-awareness—no purpose, no destiny. You are but a random occurrence. As your life had no significance, so your death will have no significance. You will have accomplished nothing, for you are nothing."

-SHIFT-

"Why do you still resist? You are a speck of dust, nothing more; the wind whispers and you are gone, like a raven's feather in a breeze. There will be no void when you are gone, for you are the void. You are a mistake, an aberration. You are an accidental contrivance of atoms—there is no purpose behind your existence—you are nothing! Your whole useless, self-pitying existence is nothing. You are an anomaly."

-SHIFT-

Anomaly? A glimmer in the dark? A portent? What was it about that word that cast him a line from a deep, hidden rock of memory? A dead seed of awareness shocked into awakening and seemed to bloom to into something yet unformed... Anomaly?

-SHIFT-

The deluminating hum exploded again in force... but a different voice also began to murmur at the very edges of his consciousness. At first, nearly imperceptible, it grew and took root in him.

-SHIFT-

The watchers tried to suppress it, but the new hum only swelled, its semitone slightly disharmonic to the first. The competing pitches could not blend, but created a tension that grew ever more jarring.

-SHIFT-

Though the watchers strove to control it, the discordance still grew until the walls of the chamber began to fray. Their molecules were separating, the stone had become permeable, undulating on the strained edges of actuality.

-*SHIFT*-

The strain became too great, and the watchers began to sway from the task. Then, like ripples in a pond, a shudder ran through them and, one by one, they detonated, the blasts directed inward, and ghostly shawls drifted to the floor like punctured balloons—empty, shapeless, powerless.

-*SHIFT*-

Now all alone, the Presence of Absence towered over him, still undiminished, still impenetrable. It leaned down toward him now, its cowled emptiness mere inches from him. "*This cannot be, Anomaly!*" The words bore into him with a searing pain and terror he knew would kill him. "*How are you doing this?*" it raged. "*It is impossible!*" It then struck, seeking to blot out his existence, but the second vibration had become a shield around him; or perhaps it was within him. Had it always been there? Had he dissolved completely and become the vibration? Was it possible that he had always been the vibration—ever muted by the distraction of so many other voices he had once called self?

-*SHIFT*-

Then he felt it. How it had happened, he could not say, but the hilt of the falcon sword was in his hand, cold and solid, vibrating at the same frequency as his inner hum. He only had the strength for one last desperate act. In a swift and powerful motion, he thrust the blade up into the opening of the cowl where a face should have been, until it tore through the back. A moment of absolute stillness followed, then the falcon blade exploded to the hilt in a blaze of glittering shards. The Presence of Absence jerked violently upright. It writhed as its wretched sapping vibration transformed into a shattering howl, so powerful and so desperate that the tattering walls of the cavern contracted once and then violently burst outward.

-*SHIFT*-

His memory was his own again. From somewhere beyond the caverns, icy water now rushed in, triggering a steam-blast as it collided with the nearly molten rock shards. In the utter ruination that now surrounded him, he recalled his purpose. He had accomplished what he came for. It was done. He knew he would die now. He was too deep in this cavern and too utterly spent to find the way out before he drowned. But, he had no will left to struggle anymore—and no strength for it anyway. It was done. He had fulfilled his destiny. He surrendered completely and opened his mouth, sucking into his lungs the hot brackish water of death.

23

PERE WOKE SUDDENLY. IT TOOK a moment for him to remember he was in Rophe's cabin. He stretched and looked out the window. In the morning sunlight, he could see the lodge was set on a rocky wooded precipice overlooking a clear-blue lake. His head ached dully, and the sunlight stabbed his eyes. He had that odd sense he sometimes got that he'd been dreaming, but he had no memory of it—which was rare anymore. El rekindled the fire, while they sat around it with blankets still wrapped around their shoulders.

"So," Barnabas said after the fire was going well. "Someone needs to go into town and get supplies; I think my face is probably the only one that still isn't known, so I volunteer. Should we make a list?"

"Let's explore the pantry first," Rophe suggested. "To see if anything in there is still usable; and then, yes, we shall make a list."

While Rophe, Khyoza, and Barnabas made their list, the others explored the lodge. El and Ehud went in one direction, while Yael and Pere took the other. It was huge, intricate, and meandering. Built into the natural shape of the rock precipice, it had many levels, but somehow kept its hominess. They eventually discovered a set of stairs leading to a second story of the wing they were in. The climb made him much more winded than it should have. His throat felt a little raw for some reason. Maybe the smoke from the fire had escaped the flue while he slept. It was odd, because his eyes now stung, and there was a ringing in his ears.

Once upstairs they discovered four bedrooms with a sitting room in the middle—and more bookshelves—he had never seen so many books in all his life. Another smaller set of spiral stairs at the back of the wing led up to a third attic level. He was hardly able to make it up the stairs. His heart pounded, and his legs trembled. At the top, they found one long bunkroom with a sloped plank ceiling and dormer windows overlooking the lake. A dozen built-in bunks lined the walls between dormers. The cavernous room ended in a large built-in, floor-to-ceiling, wall-to-wall cabinet that turned out to be weather-stripped, vapor proofed, cedar lined—and chock full of very usable bedding and towels.

"Wow!" Pere said, struggling to breathe. "This is amazing. There's enough stuff here for a small army. But who builds a linen cabinet like a vault?"

"You don't suppose Rophe's great-great-grandfather was a navi?" Yael asked.

"No idea," Pere said, feeling confused now, and a little dizzy. "Why do you ask?"

"This lodge, there's something different about it. Don't you feel it? If I didn't know better, I'd say he knew we were coming and got it ready for us."

"It does sort of have a strange feeling to it," he agreed, without really considering it.

"Is everything okay?" Yael asked, looking concerned. "You don't look so well."

"I don't know. I'm having trouble breathing." And then everything closed in, and he fell into the deep icy sea.

The room came slowly into focus. He became aware he was lying on a comfortable bed in a warm wood-paneled room. A low fire crackled merrily on the stone hearth. Afternoon sunlight angled through the room's only window. A twinge in his hand made him realize an IV drip extended from a clear bag of fluid hanging on the bedpost above him to the needle in the back of his hand. Then he noticed Cam sleeping in a chair next to the bed. This all felt weirdly reminiscent of a time not too long ago in a place he had called the Catacombs—at least he thought he'd called it that. His memory felt fuzzy. Was all that a dream? Some kind of unending cycle he was reliving? He cleared his throat. "Cam?" he whispered, and his voice felt raspy. She woke up and her eyes widened at seeing him looking at her.

"You're awake?"

"I'm pretty sure I am," he said. "Why's this thing in my hand?"

"You've been sick, Pere."

"I just passed out this morning in that bunkroom. Do I have the flu or something?"

"I'm going to get Rophe." She got up and raced out without saying another word.

"Well, that wasn't very polite," he murmured as he scratched his head. Only a minute or so later, the door opened and Rophe came in, closing it behind her. She studied him very clinically for a long moment, then walked to the bedside and took his wrist in her hand as she checked his pulse.

"How are you feeling?" she asked.

"Pretty good, I think. I'm hungry."

"I wouldn't be at all surprised." She put a hand on his forehead.

"Yael said I was sick. I feel pretty good now. Why did I pass out?"

"I honestly don't know." Taking a small flashlight, she shone it in his eyes moving it back and forth.

"What's going on?" he asked, confused. "You're acting like I'm dying."

"Well, we thought maybe you were."

"What?" He suddenly felt afraid. "Wait a second. Are you trying to tell me that I'm *really* dying? Is that why this thing's in my hand?"

"That 'thing' is in your hand because we needed to feed you nutrients."

"Feed me? What's wrong with a spoon and fork?"

"It's a little hard to eat with utensils when you're unconscious."

"Thanks. I'm not stupid. But I only passed out a few hours ago. Couldn't you just have waited until I woke up?" He now heard louder and louder sounds outside his room. The door burst open, and Yael hurried in, followed by two others. They were men, but something wasn't right about them. Had he forgotten what Barnabas and Ehud looked like? He tried to make their faces fit, but they simply wouldn't. Pere pushed the images of his friends from his mind and looked hard at the two men. . . and then he nearly passed out again. Standing at the foot of his bed were Loukas and . . . his father.

"We were down at the lake, Doctor," Paulus said, out of breath, as he approached Rophe.

"How is he responding?" Loukas asked, also breathing hard. They both looked just as he remembered them, except that Loukas' hairline had receded a bit more.

"He seems fine," she said, not seeming to trust her own prognosis. "I can't find a single thing wrong with him." Loukas approached and checked his pulse a second time.

"Dad?" Pere said incredulously. "Loukas? I'm hallucinating, aren't I?"

"No, Pere," Yael said. "They got here two days ago."

"Two days ago? That can't be right. If you got here two days ago, you'd have been here before us. And we didn't see you when we came in? Were you in town?" Yael's eyes were filling with tears. He looked from Yael to his father and then Rophe and Loukas. No one was saying anything. They were just looking at him as if he was some kind of alien. He started to panic. Maybe he'd lost his mind and *was* imagining all of them, even Yael. They all seemed so real; but if he were hallucinating, wouldn't he *think* they were real? "WHAT'S GOING ON?" he finally shouted.

"Your father got here two days ago, Pere," Yael said, quietly, taking his hand to calm him. "He came with Loukas, and Silas, and Marcus, and Matthat, and Elley, and Sayiina, and a few others you haven't met. Do you remember when Barnabas asked Demyan to deliver some messages when we were in the vet's hospital?"

"Yeah, I remember him asking," he said, counting the days in his mind. "But that wasn't even ten days ago. How'd you get here so fast?"

"No Pere," she said, wiping more tears from her eyes. "It was thirty-six days ago."

"Thirty-six days? What are you saying?"

"You've been unconscious," Rophe said, gently. "We've been taking care of you like this for almost four weeks."

"Four weeks?" he mouthed it almost voicelessly. He looked from face to face. They weren't lying; he could tell they believed what they said. But was he still dreaming? It didn't feel that way. It could mean only one thing. "Then I *am* dying, aren't I? I've got some kind of brain tumor or something worse, don't I?"

"I honestly don't think so," Loukas said. "You appear to be perfectly healthy now."

Pere considered it for a moment, while he tried to calm himself down. "If I'm healthy, like you say, then why have I been unconscious for so long? Was I in a coma?"

"You weren't in a normal coma—your pupils were responsive the whole time," Rophe said. "When you first passed out, I didn't think you were in any immediate danger. Your vital signs were strong. I thought it was just... well, I really didn't know what to think, so we waited for you to come around. I was sure it would be a few minutes; but you didn't wake up until just now. And we dared not take you to a hospital to test you on more advanced equipment. It was as though you were asleep, but we couldn't wake you up—so we decided to watch and wait."

"The watchers," he murmured, suddenly remembering. "They watched and waited for me to die."

"What are you talking about, Pere?" Yael said, stung by his comment. "I tried to carry you downstairs, but I couldn't; so, I had to go get help."

"No. Not you. It was a dream. I remembered it just now. I had a dream last night... Or the night before I passed out—it was more of an unending nightmare. When Rophe said you watched and waited, it came back to me. It was horrible. I died in it."

"You say this dream happened the night before you lost consciousness?" Loukas asked.

"Which I thought was just last night; but I guess it was four weeks ago."

"Do you know whether you've been dreaming for the last four weeks?" his father asked.

"I can't say for sure," Pere said, trying to recall. "But since I was sure I passed out a few hours ago, I don't think I've dreamed at all."

"Could a dream cause this?" Paulus asked Loukas.

"I've never heard of anything like it," Loukas replied. "But we've got two naviahs with us. It might not be a bad idea to ask them."

"Son, do you think you'll remember this dream tomorrow?"

"I don't know. Maybe I should write it down?"

"Perhaps he should tell it while it's fresh in his memory?" Loukas said.

"Rophe," Paulus said. "Is he strong enough to get out of bed?"

"I feel fine," Pere said, impatiently. "I'm a little hungry. Actually, I'm *really* hungry, but I'm fine otherwise."

Rophe shrugged. "I've been guessing for four weeks. If he says he's fine, who am I to say no?"

"All right, then," Paulus said after considering it. "If you feel strong enough to come downstairs, it might be important for others to hear this dream of yours."

"Why don't we let him get dressed, then?" Rophe suggested, removing the IV from his hand. "And we'll go down and whip you up some grub." They all left but Yael, who closed the door after they were gone.

"Is this going to become a regular thing, Pere?" she asked quietly.

"What do you mean?"

"You lying unconscious in a bed, while I'm sitting in a chair, watching and waiting?"

"Sorry," he admitted, pulling a shirt on. "It does seem like you keep getting the short end of that straw. At this rate it'll probably be a year next time."

"Please don't say that, Pere," she was tearing up again. "I was so afraid. I wasn't very nice to you before you... well, wherever you went. I was taking my frustration out on you, then you passed out, and I thought you were dying. I mean, you were here, but you weren't here. I didn't know what to do. I didn't know if I'd ever get to talk to you again."

"I'm really sorry, Cam," he said, taking her in his arms. "But wherever I went, I guess I'm back again."

She hugged him tightly. "I was so lonely, Pere. Please don't do that again."

"Believe me, I don't plan these things." He lifted her chin and kissed her. "By the way," he said afterwards, "is my sword still safe?"

"Kissing me made you think about your sword?"

"A different sword, milady," he snickered at his cleverness, and she punched him in the shoulder. "Ouch. I just remembered that I broke my falcon blade," he said, and she looked at him strangely. "In my dream, I mean. It snapped off at the hilt when I stabbed . . . well, whatever it was I stabbed."

"It was one of *those* dreams, wasn't it?"

"Worst one I've ever had."

"Then I guess we should probably get downstairs so you can entertain the crowd before you forget all the details."

"What do you mean by crowd?"

"Come see for yourself." Yael led him out of the room. Even though he'd told his father he was fine, he did feel a little weak. Lying in bed for four weeks can't be very good for your muscles, and he definitely felt thinner. She led him to a set of stairs leading down, then through a hallway, to another half-set of stairs leading up, then through a pantry area, into the kitchen, and then through that into the vaulted fire room. He would never have found the way without her, and she walked it as if she'd been doing it for a month . . . Which, he then realized, she *had* been.

Everyone stopped their conversations when he came in and got up to greet him. It was like a homecoming—albeit a strange one, since he'd lost a month of his life while they were all coming. Silas looked the same. Marcus, whose hair was longer and curlier, gave him a huge bear hug, until Rophe told him to be gentle with her patient. Matthat and Elley both shook his hand; and Sayiina held his head between her hands, looking deep into his eyes for a long still moment, and then proclaimed, loud enough for everyone to hear, "He is still whole," before she went and sat back down. There were two new people there he'd yet to meet. One was a stately older man with a marvelous baritone greeting, his father introduced as Jacobus. The other was a woman with wavy dark hair, touched here and there with gray, and probing brown eyes. Silas introduced her as Cecelia. The name rang a bell, but he couldn't remember why.

After the introductions and greetings, he sat down next to the warm fire pit, and for the next two hours, recounted his dream. It would have taken much less time, but they all kept stopping him to ask questions, and then they took even more time to discuss his answers—or in many cases, lack of answers—before allowing him to proceed. He tried to eat while he spoke, but it just wasn't very feasible, so he grew more and more hungry. During one particularly long discussion about the dark entity of his dream, he stole a few bites of the sandwich they had made him. It tasted so good. It was as though he hadn't eaten in . . . well, in a month. Finally, after they'd squeezed him dry of all information, they grew quiet and thoughtful.

"It's possible, I suppose," Cecelia finally said. "That this dream is the reason he slept so long. What do you think, Sayiina?"

"It is rare, but not unheard of for one of the Nevi'im to become 'amazed' by a particularly strong dream or vision," she said, speculating. "I have been struck dumb a few times, but never for so long. The ancients understood this amazement as a kind of confusion, or struggle, or a great weariness, from which it could take days to recover. By the way he describes it I think the *Prorock Sokol* came to the very edge of actualizing in the dream reality. Entering so completely into that realm can be devastating. I think his soul may have truly experienced the trauma he describes. If that is the case, then it was his dream-self that needed to recover for twenty-six days—and so he slept in this reality, so that he could recover in the other. Has anyone checked his sword? Strange things can sometimes happen."

"I cleaned and oiled them all a week ago," El said. "It was still in one piece then. And he'd been out for three weeks at that point."

"At least that much is reassuring," said Marcus, and then he smiled at Pere. So many things had changed but, thankfully, that hadn't.

"I feel like I've missed so much," Pere said between bites of his second sandwich. "It's like that guy Silas told us two years ago about . . . what was his name? Tip Tinkle?"

"I think you mean Rip van Winkle," Silas said, smiling. "And that was supposed to be an illustrative fable. You've apparently made it a reality. But perhaps we can catch you up. What do you want to know?"

"Well," Pere said, thinking about it. "First of all, how'd you all get here?"

They looked at each other to decide who should start. Finally, Elley got the ball rolling. "We had finished Pyotr's bottom, and were heading downriver from Yakutsk," he said, shrugging. "When I got the message from Valéry. He asked me to go to California and pick up a few old friends. Apparently, I was not doing anything else important, according to Sayiina, so—with all my freezers empty, mind you—we made very good time and anchored in Monterey Bay two weeks later. We found this group waiting on the Wharf, exactly where Barnabas said they would be. We picked them up and came back through the Bering and across the top of the world. We dropped anchor at Beisfjorden, and Barnabas and El were waiting for us with two cars at the Marina in Narvik. We drove down together and sang drinking songs the whole way, and here we are—as simple as that."

Pere knew it wasn't as simple as that, but it was probably close enough, except for the drinking songs, of course. "But why did you send for them in the first place?" he asked Barnabas.

"I suppose you could call it instinct," Barnabas shrugged, scratching his bearded chin. "We seemed to be at a crossroads. I've been watching this story play out since I was your age. For the first time in all those years, too many things seemed to be falling into place to ignore it. I thought we could use some of our best minds here to puzzle it out."

"Both Jacobus and Cecelia were visiting the Catacombs when the courier arrived with Barnabas' message," Silas added. "You could call that a coincidence if you'd like; I'm not so sure. In any case, they both insisted on coming. Their insights may be helpful as we formulate our plans. You probably don't remember this, because I only mentioned her once, but Cecelia is the naviah who had the original falcon dream."

"You?" Pere asked.

"Sorry," she said, guiltily. "Don't shoot the messenger. I hadn't been to the Catacombs since I was young, so I decided it was time for a visit. That impulse now strikes me as foreordained. So, when the message came, I assumed that's why

I was there in the first place—so here I am."

"Jacobus is the leader of our people in the eastern part of North America," Paulus said. You could say he's my counterpart over there."

"Ever since I heard Paulus was released from prison, I wanted to visit," Jacobus said in his rich baritone. "But this was the first chance I got. I too saw the timing as curious when Barnabas' message arrived. If I am not mistaken, we all have been brought here at this very moment to begin planning."

"Planning for what?" Pere asked.

"If I read the signs correctly," Jacobus said. "Events are moving toward some kind of culmination. The dream you had only reinforces my sense that this is the time."

"The time for what?" Pere took another bite of his sandwich.

"The endgame," Jacobus said softly. "We're planning for the endgame."

Suddenly the sandwich in Pere's mouth became very dry. He wondered for a moment if it would have been better if he'd never woken up at all.

Epilogue

Three Months Later

Darkening afternoon thunderheads towered in the eastern sky as Damocles Praefectus gazed out the windows of his 20th floor Reykjavìk office suite. His mood matched the clouds, a roiling swelling core of fury searching for a spot to rain down deadly bolts. This was a new sensation for him and due in large part to his inactivity. He could only do so much on Iceland, and it wasn't in his nature to 'stay put'. But 'stay put' was the order his ingrate father had given him. . . and he dared not disobey—his mother had eyes everywhere. He'd been a fool to believe she'd keep his secret. The bitch betrayed him at the first opportunity. The old man was inordinately bent out of shape at the news of Rampart's death. He told Damocles in a far too long-winded verbal barrage what 'chain of command' meant—and exactly who was at the top of it. His fustian father really didn't know what was in his own best interests; and his mother was either too timid or too loyal to challenge him. They all knew Rampart had to die—but he was the only one with balls enough to kill him.

Now he was on a fucking 'short leash' from Rome, and his mother had been told to 'keep an eye on him', as though he were some wayward twelve-year-old, sneaking porn into the bathroom. It would still take months to repair his standing with his father. The first step was seeing that the new barracks in Akureyri be up and running smoothly. Following that, he needed to house two cohorts of Heracles units there and make them feel at home—as though those feckless thralls needed to 'feel' anything. They felt whatever his mother ordered them to feel. He would never forget nor forgive their abject failure in Russia. Had they lived up to their vaunted design specs, Rampart would have been little more than an afterthought—never mind the still-living Quade and company. The whole situation was a fucking mess, and now he was the scapegoat for having the temerity to clean it up. No, he wouldn't trust these Heracles units, particularly when he knew they were also his mother's eyes and ears.

He realized almost the moment his 'house arrest' began, that the home in Old Reykjavik was impossible; the sixty cameras in the residence and the dedicated 24-hour COM array in the basement meant his father and mother would always be watching him there. He needed a place to call his own, a base of operations where he would have complete autonomy. The corporate headquarters was his only viable option.

He started by remodeling his office—easily justifiable, since it had been his father's base of operations for several years, and now he wanted to put his personal stamp on the place. Even his mother applauded his decision; and his father saw it as his wayward son finally taking some responsibility, assuming the reigns of the Icelandic operation. 'Icelandic operation'—what a farce! The only operations on this rock were watching the snow melt in the summer and taking hot-spring mineral baths in the winter—one of the supposed benefits of living on an active volcano.

The remodel included several upgrades. The eight holographic ceiling arrays that had once connected this office to the so-called Directorate were the first to go. Since that ship of fools had effectively sunk, it was a natural move. Besides, one of those projectors had a dedicated link to Rampart's estate, which Jonas Cavanaugh had since fortified for his own use. He would provide no opportunity for that covert prick to use the linked technology to compromise his operation in Iceland, as he had in Russia. Cavanaugh would feel his wrath eventually; but now was not the time. His father would likely chain him in a deep pit if he followed his inclination to garrote the bastard. He concentrated on securing his base instead.

Gutting the holograph arrays meant he could justify having the whole office rewired—or unwired, as it turned out. He removed any advanced listening and viewing technology and installed surveillance inhibitors in the process. He left the hidden-shelf COM unit intact. He had to. He couldn't explain away disabling the office's one dedicated link to his mother. It would have to stay. However, when originally installed, his father insisted on manual activation to maintain a certain level of control—apparently, his old man used to have balls as well as brains. That was no longer the case. He had since become as flaccid as a gelding. The COM link would stay; but he would open it when *he* chose to, and only then. He also installed a hidden gun safe on the COMs side of the unit. In it he stored the McMillan TAC-50 sniper rifle. It was a superior piece of equipment, and he had a feeling it might come in handy at some point in the future. You never knew when you might need to blow someone's head off from a thousand meters out.

Once the office was secure, he paid a visit to the basement's corporate records vault to conduct some research. His father had kept hard copy files there — secure from digital intrusion — on almost everything related to the North Atlantic Investment Trust. He studied the employee records for several days until he narrowed his list to three candidates. He decided to interview each of them personally—he couldn't be sure otherwise; yet it required extreme care. If he raised any red flags, he would have to explain himself to his mother. Officially, he was interviewing to select a new Head of Security because his father had taken his old one to Rome. True, as far as it went, but his real reasons extended well beyond that.

A knock at the office door broke his concentration on thunderhead formations. The third and last candidate had arrived. His first and second choices were an infuriating waste of time; and this next one looked the least promising on paper. He crossed to the door and opened it. Amund Salverson was in his early fifties, unremarkable in appearance, average in height, and comfortably overweight. His suit had the slightly out-of-fashion look of someone who didn't give a damn, and he'd combed his thinning salt-and-pepper hair straight back as though in a pragmatic afterthought. He was the sort of man that wouldn't merit a second glance from anyone—which suited Damocles' plans perfectly. According to his employee file, the level-four security analyst had applied for promotion three times and been passed over on each occasion, apparently because his father preferred 'beautiful' people in top positions—a prejudice Damocles could now use to his advantage. Salverson had a master's degree from Massachusetts Institute of Technology and was consistently spot-on in his analyses; he just wasn't very good looking, which was fine with Damocles since he wasn't interested in fucking him.

"Come in, Mr. Salverson. Have a seat," Damocles gestured as he sat behind his standard IKEA desk—unlike his father's Resolute desk, he felt no need to compensate. Amund took a seat on the other side. "Do you know why I've asked you here today?"

"Officially, I am interviewing for a new Head of Security position."

"An interesting choice of words. Do you think there's an unofficial agenda?"

"Do you want me to be straightforward, or to kiss your ass?"

"Straightforward, please. My ass needs no affection at the moment."

"I think you are looking for someone to fill a position, Mr. Praefectus. But I don't think it's Head of Security—at least not in the conventional sense."

"I'm curious how you reached that conclusion, when the others didn't?"

"Because I am an excellent security analyst, Mr. Praefectus. The two you interviewed before me are fatuous morons."

"Yes, well, after interviewing them, my conclusions are not far different," Damocles replied, thoughtfully tapping his lips with his index finger. "So, tell me then, what do you think this position is, and why should I hire you for it?"

"To be honest, I am not completely sure what it is yet; and I don't know why you would hire me, since I did not apply for it."

"That's true enough; but you *have* applied for it three times in the past and been turned down on each occasion."

"That is not completely accurate. I applied for Chief Analyst three times, not Head of Security—that position comes with far too many bureaucratic strings attached, and bureaucracy gives me a flaming headache."

"I stand corrected. And, by the way, I don't disagree at all about bureaucracy. So, you were turned down three times for Chief Analyst. Most people would feel bitter after that, but you stayed on. Why?"

"I pride myself on loyalty. This is a good company, and I am committed to it."

"Talking points. That can't be the only reason?"

"Not if you are looking for full disclosure."

"I thought we already agreed there would be no ass-kissing."

"Okay then. My mother is getting on in years, and I am her only son. Reykjavík has been our home for six generations now, and leaving would probably put the nail in her coffin. She took care of me when I was young, so now it is my turn to take care of her. I am aware it is not upwardly mobile, but it is true."

"Loyalty of a much higher degree?"

"I guess you could say that. She deserves it, though."

"Yes, it's difficult when our parents get older. They don't always make the best decisions."

"That is probably true for most; but the only real decision my mother makes anymore is when to have her first afternoon glass of Brennivín. I suggest 5 p.m. but she thinks 3 p.m. is a better idea. She is ninety-two. Who am I to tell her no?"

"Like I said: loyalty of a much higher degree."

Salverson just shrugged and the two men were silent for a few moments before Damocles swiveled his chair to stare out the windows.

"What is this really about, Mr. Praefectus?" Salverson finally asked. "I mean no disrespect, but I'm a damn good analyst, and I know what a fishing expedition looks like."

"You're certainly more perceptive than the first two," Damocles said, turning his chair back around. "Alright; I haven't been completely straightforward in my inquiries; however, if *you're* looking for full disclosure?"

"Full disclosure would be a definite plus," the analyst said, smiling wryly.

"Very well, then. I'm looking for someone who's completely discreet, highly perceptive, and extremely loyal. I have a special position for just such a person. Have I found that person in you Mr. Salverson?"

"I could answer better if I knew exactly *why* you are looking for such a person?"

"First of all, I'll triple your salary."

"Triple? That is a substantial bump. What would my responsibilities be for that kind of money?"

"Nothing illegal, I assure you."

"Alright then, I am listening."

"Funny you should use that term, because that's precisely what I want you to do—to listen, to observe, to unearth, and to analyze, and to do them all discreetly."

"Well, well, well. You're in luck because those are the very things I do best."

"That, Mr. Salverson, is exactly what I'm counting on."

Made in the USA
Las Vegas, NV
05 July 2025

24486307R00252